A TEXT BOOK OF

DISTRIBUTED SYSTEM

FOR
SEMESTER – II

FINAL YEAR (B.E.) DEGREE COURSE IN
INFORMATION TECHNOLOGY

**As Per the New Revised Syllabus of
Savitribai Phule Pune University, Pune.**
(2012 Pattern)

Mrs. Rama Gaikwad (Londhe-Patil)
M. E. (Computer Networks),
Asst. Professor,
Computer Engg. Deptt.,
Anantrao Pawar College of Engg. & Research,
Parvati, Pune.

Sachin V. Todkari
M.E (IT)
Asst. Prof. & Head
Info. Tech. Deptt.
Jayawantrao Sawant College of Engg.
Hadapsar, Pune.

NIRALI PRAKASHAN
ADVANCEMENT OF KNOWLEDGE

N3741

DISTRIBUTED SYSTEMS (BE IT SEM. II)　ISBN 978-93-5164-900-7

First Edition	:	January 2016
New Edition	:	January 2017
©	:	Authors

Published By :
NIRALI PRAKASHAN
Abhyudaya Pragati, 1312, Shivaji Nagar,
Off J.M. Road, PUNE – 411005
Tel - (020) 25512336/37/39, Fax - (020) 25511379
Email: niralipune@pragationline.com

☞ **DISTRIBUTION BRANCHES**

PUNE
Nirali Prakashan : 119, Budhwar Peth, Jogeshwari Mandir Lane, Pune 411002, Maharashtra
Tel: (020) 2445 2044, 66022708, Fax: (020) 2445 1538
Email: bookorder@pragationline.com, niralilocal@pragationline.com
Nirali Prakashan : S. No. 28/27, Dhyari, Near Pari Company, Pune 411041
Tel: (020) 24690204 Fax: (020) 24690316
Email: dhyari@pragationline.com, bookorder@pragationline.com
MUMBAI
Nirali Prakashan : 385, S.V.P. Road, Rasdhara Co-op. Hsg. Society Ltd.,
Girgaum, Mumbai 400004, Maharashtra
Tel: (022) 2385 6339 / 2386 9976, Fax: (022) 2386 9976
Email: niralimumbai@pragationline.com

☞ **DISTRIBUTION BRANCHES**

JALGAON
Nirali Prakashan : 34, V. V. Golani Market, Navi Peth, Jalgaon 425001,
Maharashtra, Tel: (0257) 222 0395, Mob: 94234 91860
KOLHAPUR
Nirali Prakashan : New Mahadvar Road, Kedar Plaza, 1st Floor Opp. IDBI Bank
Kolhapur 416 012, Maharashtra. Mob: 9850046155
NAGPUR
Pratibha Book Distributors : Above Maratha Mandir, Shop No. 3, First Floor,
Rani Jhanshi Square, Sitabuldi, Nagpur 440012, Maharashtra
Tel: (0712) 254 7129
DELHI
Nirali Prakashan : 4593/21, Basement, Aggarwal Lane 15, Ansari Road, Daryaganj
Near Times of India Building, New Delhi 110002
Mob: 08505972553
BENGALURU
Pragati Book House : House No. 1, Sanjeevappa Lane, Avenue Road Cross,
Opp. Rice Church, Bengaluru – 560002.
Tel: (080) 64513344, 64513355,Mob: 9880582331, 9845021552
Email:bharatsavla@yahoo.com
CHENNAI
Pragati Books : 9/1, Montieth Road, Behind Taas Mahal, Egmore,
Chennai 600008 Tamil Nadu, Tel: (044) 6518 3535,
Mob: 94440 01782 / 98450 21552 / 98805 82331,
Email: bharatsavla@yahoo.com

niralipune@pragationline.com | www.pragationline.com

Also find us on f www.facebook.com/niralibooks

Dedicated to...

Our Family Members & Friends

...Authors

PREFACE TO THE NEW EDITION

We are glad and excited to announce that the First Edition of this book received an overwhelming response from the engineering student community, compelling us to release its New Edition within a very short period of time.

This New Edition has been updated with including all University Question Papers In Sem. February 2016, End Sem. May 2016 and November 2016.

Special care has been taken to maintain high degree of accuracy in the theory and numericals throughout the book.

We take this opportunity to express our sincere thanks to Dineshbhai Furia of Nirali Prakashan, a reputed pioneer in the publication field. Our special thanks to Jignesh Furia for their effective cooperation and great care in bringing out this revised edition. We also appreciate the efforts of M. P. Munde and the entire staff of Engineering Books Deptt. of Nirali Prakashan namely Mrs. Deepali Lachake (Co-ordinator) for bringing this book to the students in a timely manner.

We sincerely hope that this "New Edition" will also be warmly received by all concerned as in the past.

Valuable suggestions from our esteemed readers to improve the book are most welcome and highly appreciated.

Pune

Authors

PREFACE TO THE FIRST EDITION

It gives us great pleasure to bring out the book on **"Distributed System"**. This book is strictly written as per New Revised Syllabus of Savitribai Phule Pune University, Pune (2012 Pattern) for the students of Final Year Degree Course in Information Technology.

The book is as per New Revised Examination Scheme which has been implemented from this academic year. According to this, In-Semester Examination carries 30 Marks over first three units and End-Semester Examination carries 70 Marks over entire syllabus of which the first three units will carry 20 Marks and units 4, 5 and 6 will carry 50 Marks.

We have given **Sample Question Papers of In-Semester University Exam (30 Marks) and End-Semester University Exam. (70 Marks) in this book for practice and also Past University Year Wise Questions at the end of Each unit.**

This book covers a set of basic and advance topics in distributed system. The focus is on principles, architectures, and communication used in modern distributed system, such as IPC, RPC, RMI etc.

We have tried to provide the best possible material in simple and lucid language to the students preparing for degree course. The subject is divided in to Six Units and each unit is explained thoroughly with diagrams and examples (Wherever necessary). So, we are sure that, this book will fulfill all needs of the subject. Sufficient number of questions are also included at the end of each unit for the revision of the subject.

We would like to express our gratitude to the many people who saw us through this book; to all those who provided support for this book.

We are very thankful to the management of our institutes for their continuous support and encouragement.

Above all, we want to thank our family members and friends, who supported and encouraged us in spite of all the time it took us away from them. It was a long and difficult journey for them.

We gratefully acknowledge co-operation from **Shri. Dineshbhai Furia, Shri. Jignesh Furia, Mrs. Nirali Verma, Shri. M.P. Munde** and **Mrs. Deepali Lachake** (Co-ordinator) of **Nirali Prakashan.**

Despite the best efforts taken by authors, it is possible that some unintentional errors might have taken place. Authors would gratefully acknowledge if any of these is pointed out. Suggestions and comments for further improvement of this book will be gratefully received and acknowledged from the students, teachers and others.

Pune   **Authors**
January 2016

SYLLABUS

Unit I : Introduction   **5 Hours**

Introduction, Examples of distributed systems, Trends in distributed systems, Focus on Resource Sharing, Challenges.

System Models: Physical models, Architectural Models, Fundamental Models.

Case Study: The World Wide Web

Unit II : Communication   **6 Hours**

Inter-process Communication: Introduction, The API for the Internet Protocols, External Data Representation and Marshalling, Multicast Communication.

Network Virtualization: Overlay Networks.

Case Study: MPI

Remote Invocation: Request-reply Protocols, Remote Procedure Call, Remote Method Invocation,

Case Study: Java RMI

Indirect Communication: Group Communication, Publish-subscribe Systems, Message Queues, Shared Memory approaches.

Unit III : Middleware   **6 Hours**

Distributed Objects and Components: Introduction, Distributed Objects, Case Study: CORBA. From Objects to Components,

Case Studies: Enterprise JavaBeans and Fractal.

Web Services: Introduction, Web Services, SERVICE Descriptions and IDL for Web Services, A directory service for use with web services, XML security, Coordination of web services, Applications of Web Services.

Peer-To-Peer Systems: Introduction, Peer-to-peer middleware, Routing overlays Application.

Case Study: Squirrel.

Unit IV : Distributed Algorithms   **6 Hours**

Time and Global States: Introduction, Clocks, Events and Process States, Synchronizing Physical Clocks, Logical Time and Logical Clocks, Global States.

Coordination and Agreement: Introduction, Distributed mutual exclusion, Elections, Coordination and Agreement in Group Communication, Consensus. Replication: Introduction, System Model and the role of Group Communication, Fault-tolerant Services.

Case Study: Coda.

Unit V : Distributed Storage and Multimedia Systems   **6 Hours**

Distributed File Systems: Introduction, File Service Architecture, Sun Network File System, and HDFS.

Name Services: Introduction, Name Services and the Domain Name System, Directory Services.

Case Study: 1. The Global Name Service, 2. The X.500 Directory Service.

Distributed Multimedia Systems: Characteristics of Multimedia Data, Quality of Service Management, Resource management, Stream Adaptation.

Case Study: BitTorrent and End System Multicast.

Unit VI : Security In Distributed Systems   **7 Hours**

Introduction to Security: Security Threats, Policies, and Mechanisms, Design Issues, Cryptography.

Secure Channels: Authentication, Message Integrity and Confidentiality, Secure Group Communication.

Case Study: Kerberos.

Access Control: General Issues in Access Control, Firewalls, Secure Mobile Code, Denial of Service. Security Management: Key Management, Secure Group Management, Authorization Management. Emerging Trends In Distributed Systems: GRID COMPUTING, SOA, Cloud Computing.

CONTENTS

✠ ✠ ✠

INTRODUCTION TO DISTRIBUTED SYSTEM

1.1 INTRODUCTION

A distributed system is a software system in which components located on networked computers communicate and coordinate their processing by passing messages to each other. The components interact with each other in order to achieve a common objective. Three significant characteristics of distributed systems are: concurrency of components, lack of a global clock, and independent failure of components.

The word distributed in terms such as "distributed system", "distributed programming", and "distributed algorithm" originally referred to computer networks where individual computers were physically distributed within some geographical area. The terms are nowadays used in a much wider sense, even referring to autonomous processes that run on the same physical computer and interact with each other by message passing.

In this unit we will be looking at every basic concept in DS, what are recent trends and fundamental models.

This section gives the introduction to the distributed system where we have to study some basic concept, different architectures that support distributed system, advantages and disadvantages of distributed system so we will start with definition.

By considering the interconnection of processors we can divide system into two types:

    (1) Tightly coupled system

    (2) Loosely coupled system.

(1) Tightly Coupled System:

In the tightly coupled system, there is a single system wide primary memory (address space) that is shared by all the processors. If one of the processor writes, e.g. the value 30 to the memory location x, any other processor subsequently reading from location x will get the value 30. So, in these systems, any communication between the processors usually takes place through the shared memory.

(2) Loosely Coupled System:

In the loosely coupled system, the processors do not share memory, and each processor has its own local memory, if any processor writes the value 30 to the memory location x, this write operation will only change the contents of its local memory and will not affect the contents of the memory of any other processor. So, if another processor reads the memory location x, it will get whatever value was there before in that location of its own local memory.

Definition: **[Dec. 2011, 12, 13, May 2014]**

- "A distributed system is a collection of processors that do not share memory or a clock. Instead, each processor has its own local memory. The processors communicate with one another through various communication networks, such as high-speed buses or telephone lines etc."

- A 'distributed system' is a collection of loosely coupled processors interconnected by a communication network. From the point of view of a specific processor in a distributed system, the rest of the processors and their respective resources are remote. Whereas its own resources are local.

- The processors in a distributed system may vary in size and function. They may include small microprocessors, workstations, mini-computers and large general-purpose computer system.

- The processor is having different names, such as, sites, nodes, computers, machines, and hosts.

1.2 REASONS FOR BUILDING DISTRIBUTED SYSTEMS

There are four major reasons for building distributed systems,

  (1) Resource sharing,

  (2) Computation speedup,

  (3) Reliability and

  (4) Communication.

(1) Resource Sharing:

In resource sharing if a number of different sites are connected to one another, then a user at one site may be able to use the resources available at another.

Example: one user at site A may be using a large printer located at side B. or one user at B may access file that is at side A.

(2) Computation Speedup:

In computation speedup if particular computation can be partitioned into sub computations that can run concurrently, then a distributed system allows us to distribute the sub-computations among the various sties, the sub computations can be run concurrently and thus provide computation speedup.

If one of the site is currently overloaded with Jobs, then some of jobs may be move to other, lightly loaded site; this movement of Jobs is called 'load sharing'.

(3) Reliability:

If one the site fails in a distributed system, then remaining sites can continue operating, giving the system better reliability.

If system is composed of small machines, each of which is responsible for some system function then a single failure may half the operation of the whole system.

The failure of a site must be detected by the system, and appropriate action may be needed to recover from the failure.

(4) Communication:

When we think about communication the distributed system in which different sites are connected to one another by a communication network, the users at different sites have the opportunity to exchange information. At low level messages are passed between systems, much as messages.

1.3 ADVANTAGES OF DISTRIBUTED SYSTEM OVER CENTRALIZED SYSTEM

In last few years we use centralized systems i.e. single-processor systems which are having single CPU, its memory, peripherals and some terminals but its having some disadvantages to overcome that we use distributed system.

- The main advantages of distributed system over centralized system is 'economics'. Basically 'The computing power of a CPU is proportional to its cost'. If we pay twice as much, you could get four times the performance. This observation correct in case of mainframe technology but with microprocessor technology this observation is fail for a few hundred dollars you get the chip CPU that can execute more instruction per second, as a result we can use number of cheap CPU together in a system. i.e. Distributed system is having a much better price/performance ratio than the centralized system.

- Distributed system also gives absolute performance that no centralized system achieve at any price.

- Some applications are inherently distributed so, we required distributed system. Example: If there is group of people, located far from each other, and they are working together to produce a Joint-Report then, we required distributed system, such system are also called **"computer supported cooperative work"**.

- Another advantage of distributed system is "higher reliability". If we divide the workload over many machines a single chip failure will bring down at most one machine, rest of the machines are not damaged. i.e. if 5 present of the machines are down at any moment, the system should be able to continue to work with a 5 present loss in performance. In critical application, such as control of aircraft or nuclear reactors, using a distributed system we achieve high Reliability.

- The incremental growth is easy in distributed system.

Example:

If company will buy a mainframe with the intention that, it can do it all work on it. If the company prospers and the workload grows, at a certain point the mainframe will not be adequate. The only solution is either to replace the mainframe with a large one or to add second mainframe; both solutions can have number of problems. In contrast, with a distributed system, it may be possible simply to add more processors to the system.

Those advantages are summarized in Table 1.1.

Table 1.1: Advantages of Distributed System over Centralized System

Item	Description
Economics	Microprocessors gives a better price/performance than mainframes
Speed	A distributed system may have more computing power as compare to mainframe
Inherent distribution	Some application require separated machines
Reliability	If one machine fail, the system as a whole can still survive
Incremental growth	Computing power can be added in small increments

1.4 ADVANTAGES OF DISTRIBUTED SYSTEM OVER INDEPENDENT PC'S

The distributed system having number of advantages over independent PC's these are discuss in this section we start with data sharing

- **Data Sharing:** It is possible using Distributed system.

  Example:

  Airline reservation clerks need access to the master database of flights and existing reservations. Providing the own private copy of the entire data base for each clerk would not work, since nobody would know which seats the other clerks had already sold shared data are essential to this and to many other applications, so the machines must be interconnected i.e. the use of distributed system.

- **Device Sharing:** It is possible using distributed system. e.g. we can share expensive peripherals like color laser printer, scanner, phototypesetter, etc.

- **Communication:** We can achieve enhanced person-to-person communication. electronic-mail (e-mail) is more beneficial, it is faster than paper mail, does not require both parties to be available at the same time as does the telephone and unlike fax, produces documents that can be edited, rearranged, stored in the computer.

- A distributed system is potentially **"more flexible"** than giving each user an isolated personal computer. In distributed system total workload can be spread over the computers, and the loss of a few machines may not affect if we consider system.

Table 1.2: Advantages of DS over Independent PC

Items	Description
Data sharing	Allow many users access to a common database
Device sharing	Allow many user to share peripherals
Communication	Make person-to-person communication easier, e. g. e-mail
Flexibility	Divide the workload over the machines in the most cost effective way.

1.5 DISADVANTAGES OF DISTRIBUTED SYSTEM

Even if distributed system provide us solution for different problems but still it having some problems these are discuss in this section.

- First problem with distributed system is "Software" with the current state-of-the-art, we do not have much experience in designing, implementing and using distributed software. What kind of OS, programming languages, and application are appropriate for these systems? How much should the users know about distribution? How much should the system do and how much should the users do. As more research is done, this problem will diminish, but for the moment it should not be underestimated.

- Second problem is due to the "Communication network". It can lose messages, which requires special software to be able to recover, and it can become overloaded. When the network saturates, it must either be replaced or added. In both cases, some portion of one or more buildings may have to be required at great expense, or network interface boards may have to be replaced
(e.g. fiber optics). Once the system comes to depend on the network its loss or saturation can negate most of the advantages of Distributed system.

- The third problem is "Security problem" because of easy data sharing people can easily access data all over the system, so some secret data are also access by all people.

Table 1.3: Disadvantages of DS

Item	Description
Software	little software exists at present for distributed system
Networking	The network can saturate or cause other problem
Security	Easy access also applies to secret data

1.6 EXAMPLES OF DISTRIBUTED SYSTEMS

1.6.1 Internet

The best example is internet which is vast interconnected collection of computer networks of different types. It basically provides following types of services.

    (a) Global access to everybody,

    (b) Enormous size (open ended),

    (c) No single authority,

    (d) Communication types.

The internet itself is a very large distributed system. It enables users, wherever they are, to make use of services such as the World Wide Web, email and file transfer.

The set of services is open-ended-it can be extended by the addition of server computers and new types of service. Fig. 1.1 shows collection of internets. i.e. Sub-networks operated by companies and other organization. Internet Service Providers (ISP's) are companies that provide modem links and other types of connection to individual users and small organizations enabling them to access services anywhere in the internet as well as providing local service such as email and web-hosting.

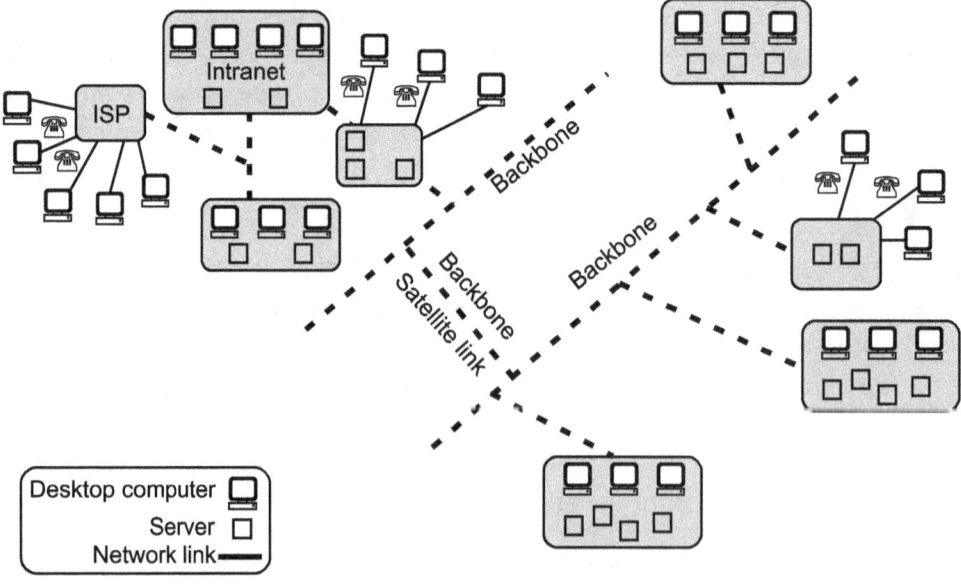

Fig. 1.1: Internet

The internet is interconnected together by backbones. A backbone is a network link with high transmission capacity, employing satellite connections, fibre-optic cables and other high-bandwidth circuits. Internet provide multimedia services also, user can access audio and video data including music, radio and TV-channels and to hold phone and video conference.

1.6.2 Intranets

An intranet is a subpart of the Internet that is separately administered and has a boundary that can be configured to enforce local security policies. Fig. 1.2 the basic concept of Intranet. It is combination of several Local Area Networks (LAN's) connected by backbone connections.

An intranet is connected to internet through a router, which allows the user which are placed inside the intranet to make use of services elsewhere like web or email etc. It also allows the user in other intranets to access the services which are provides.

All organizations which use intranet they required to protect their own services from unauthorized use.

Example: A company will not want secure information to be accessible to other company, companies also want to protect themselves from harmful programs such as viruses entering and attacking the computers in the intranet and destroy some important data. The 'Firewall' is used to protect the intranet from unauthorized used messages. Firewall is implemented by filtering incoming and outgoing messages. Example: According to source and destination.

Some organizations do not want to connect their internal networks to the internet.
Example: crime-branches or other security agencies are having their internal networks that are isolated from the outside world. Some Army organizations do not want to connect their internal networks from the internet at the time of war but even those organizations wants benefit from internet which can be done using internet communication protocols. The solution for such type of organizations PS to operate the internet as described above, but without the connection to the intranet. Such as intranet can deal out with the firewall or we can say that it has the most effective firewall possible in absence of any physical connections to the internet.

Some important issues that to be consider in the design of components for use in internets that are,

- File services are needed to enable users to share data.
- Firewalls provide the access to services according to rules only. When resource sharing between internal and external users is required, firewalls must be complemented by the use of fine-grained security mechanisms.
- The cost of software installation and support is an important issue. These costs can be reduced by the use of system architectures such as Network computers and thin clients etc.

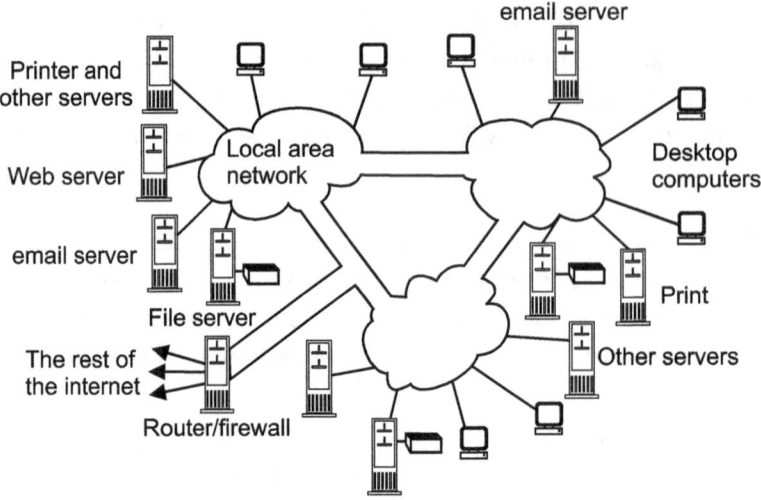

Fig. 1.2: Intranet

1.6.3 Mobile and Ubiquitous Computing

Mobile Computing:

- Mobile computing describes the use of small and portable computing devices in wireless enabled networks that provide wireless connections to a central main server. These devices include laptops, notebook PCs, tablet PCs, palmtops, personal digital assistant (PDAs) and other hand held devices.

- A radio-signaling device is installed inside these devices for receiving and transmitting electronic data.

- In mobile computing the use of distributed system technology to enable users also are not fixed in a single physical position to communication with computers which form part of a network, more often than non these computers act as some of server.

- This is one of the major development areas in distributed computing with many manufactures attempting to embed the same function found in normal computers into hand-held devices such as mobile phone.

- Now a days mobile computing uses the distributed system as a core port so that many mobile user access various application such as internet, value added services all these application are based on distributed system.

- In these applications information related to that particular application is stored on server side as distributed object and all client that are access this information by using their mobile device.

- In wireless networks such as Wi-Fi users with different devices can access the distributed application properly.

Ubiquitous Computing:

In ubiquitous computing the word 'ubiquitous' can be defined as "existing", "Constantly encountered" when we applying this concept to technology, the term ubiquitous implies that technology is everywhere and we use it all the time.

Ubiquitous technology is always wireless, mobile, and networked, making its users more connected to the world around them and the people in it. The presence of computers everywhere only becomes useful when they can communicate with one another. e.g. it is convenient for user to control their TV or any Wi-Fi systems from a 'universal remote control' device in a home.

Fig. 1.3 below shows user's home intranet and the host intranet at the site that the user is visiting. Both intranets are connected to the rest of the Internet.

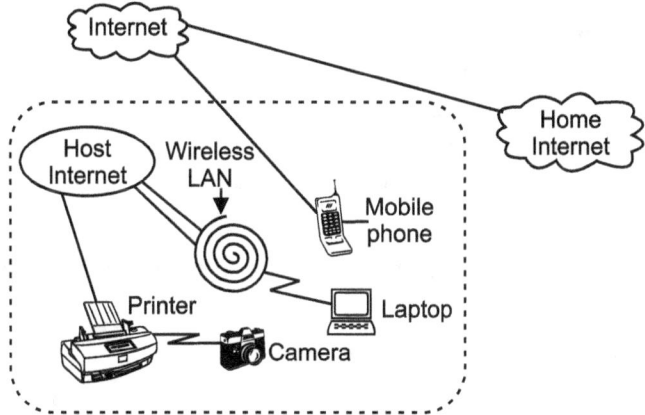

Fig. 1.3: Portable and hand held devices in a distributed system

As shown in Fig. 1.3, the user can access to three types of wireless connection

    (1) Laptop

    (2) Mobile phone and

    (3) Digital camera,

    (4) Printer.

- The Laptop is having connection to host in wireless LAN. This Network provides coverage of a few hundreds of metres; it connects to the rest of the host intranet via a gateway.

- The mobile phone is connected to internet, this phone gives access to the pages of simple information, which it can presents on its small display and finally user caries a digital camera, which is communicate over a personal area wireless network with a device such as printer etc.

- With this type of system, user can perform simple tasks at host site using the various devices which they carry.

- Users can take a print of photos which are present in there camera through wireless link and Laptop also take a print through wireless link but required that camera and Laptop is within the specific area.

1.7 DISTRIBUTED SYSTEM CHALLENGES

While designing the distributed system designer face many challenges. In this section we discuss them all.

Designing a distributed system is more difficult than designing a centralized operating system for several reasons. In the design of a centralized operating system, it is assumed that the operating system has access to complete and accurate information about the environment in which it is functioning. However, a distributed system must be designed with the assumption that complete information about the system environment will never be available. In a distributed system, the resources are physically separated, there is not common clock among the multiple processors, delivery of messages is delayed, and messages could even be lost due to all these reasons, a distributed system does not have up-to-date, consistent knowledge about the state of the various components of the underlying distributed system.

The design of distributed system is having lot of scope to develop more ambitious services and applications.

There are various challenges in the distributed system design.

    (1) Heterogeneity

    (2) Openness

    (3) Security

    (4) Scalability

    (5) Failure handling

    (6) Concurrency

    (7) Transparency

1.7.1 Heterogeneity

- Heterogeneous distributed system consists of interconnected sets of dissimilar hardware or software because of diversity, designing heterogeneous distributed systems is far difficult than designing homogeneous distributed system in which each system is based on the same, or closely related hardware and software.

- Heterogeneity is preferred by many users because heterogeneous distributed systems provide the flexibility to their users of different computer platforms for different applications.

- Example: a user may have to flexibility of a super-computer for simulations, a Macintosh for document processing, and a UNIX workstation for program development.
- Heterogeneity can be applied on networks, computer hardware, operating systems, programming languages and implementation of different developers. Internet is having many types of network like intranet, ISP etc. and the all computers connected through this network types use the internet protocol to communicate with each other.
- Example: a computer attached to an Ethernet has an implementation of the internet protocols over the Ethernet.
- Similarly a computer on a different sort of network will-require an implementation of internet protocols for that network. Data type such as integers or float may be represented in different ways on different type of hardware. If we want to transfer Example: messages from one Hardware to another and representation of that Hardware is different then problem may occur.
- Operating system of all computers on the internet required to include an implementation of the internet protocols, it is not necessary that all OS provides same application programming interface to the protocols.
- Application program for exchanging messages in UNIX are different from the calls in windows.
- Different programming languages use different representation of Data-structures such as Array and records, characters.
- This difference come forward if programs written in one language want to communicates with programs written in other languages.

We required common standards for communication between different programs written by different developers. Internet protocols provide the common standards for network communication and the representation of primitive data items and data structures.

1.7.1.1 Introduction to Middleware

Definition of Middleware:

Middleware is defined as it is computer software that connects software components or applications. The software consists of a set of services that allows multiple processes running on one or more machines to interact with each other.

OR

The software layer that lies between the operating system and applications on each side of a distributed computing system in a network

OR

- Software that provides a link between separate software applications. Middleware is sometimes called plumbing because it connects two applications and passes data between them. Middleware allows data contained in one database to be accessed through another.

- The middleware technology evolved to provide for interoperability in support of the move to coherent distributed architectures, which are used most often to support and simplify complex, distributed applications.

- It includes web servers, application servers, and similar tools that support application development and delivery.

- Basically Middleware is integration to modern information technology based on XML, SOAP, Web services, and service-oriented architecture.

- Middleware sits "in the middle" between application software that may be working on different operating systems. It is similar to the middle layer of three-tier single system architecture, except that it is stretched across multiple systems or applications.

- Examples include EAI software, telecommunications software, transaction monitors, and messaging-and-queuing software.

- The difference between operating system and middleware functionality is, to some extent, arbitrary. While core kernel functionality can only be provided by the operating system itself, some functionality previously provided by separately sold middleware is now integrated in operating systems.

- A typical example is the TCP/IP stack for telecommunications, nowadays included in virtually every operating system.

- Middleware services provide a more functional set of application programming interfaces to allow an application to:

  - Locate transparently across the network, thus providing interaction with another service or application.

  - Be independent from network services.

  - Be reliable and always available when compared to the operating system and network services.

- Middleware provides some unique technological advantages for business and industry. For example, database systems are usually deployed in closed environments where users access the system only via a restricted network or intranet (Example: an enterprise's internal network).

- With the phenomenal growth of the World Wide Web, users can access virtually any database for which they have proper access rights from anywhere in the world.

1.7.1.2 Types of Middleware

The classification of middleware is based on scalability and recoverability:

- **Remote Procedure Call:** Client makes calls to procedures running on remote systems. Can be asynchronous or synchronous.

- **Message Oriented Middleware:** Messages sent to the client are collected and stored until they are acted upon, while the client continues with other processing.

- **Object Request Broker:** This type of middleware makes it possible for applications to send objects and request services in an object-oriented system.

- **SQL-Oriented Data Access:** middleware between applications and database servers.

- **Embedded Middleware:** communication services and integration interface software/firmware that operates between embedded applications and the real time operating system.

- To solve the problems of heterogeneity middleware provides a uniform computational model for use by the programmers of servers and distributed applications.

- These models are like remote object invocation, remote event notification, Remote SQL access and Distributed transaction processing.

- Example: CORBA provides remote object invocation, which allows an object in a program running on one computer to invoke a method of an object in a program running on another computer.

- Its implementation hides the fact that messages are passed over a network in order to send the invocation request and its reply.

Middle Code:

- The middle code is nothing but the code that can be sent from one computer to another computer and run at the destination side.

- Example: A Java applet is one example.

- Code suitable for running on one computer is not necessarily suitable for running on another because executable programs are normally specific both to the instruction set and to the host OS.

- Example: if we send executable file through mail from windows/X86 users then it is not running on X86 computer running Linux or Macintosh computer running Mac OSX.

- The concept of 'virtual machine' is used for making code executable on any hardware. The compiler for a specific language generates code for a virtual machine instead of generating code for particular hardware.

- Example: Java compiler produce a code for the Java virtual machine and on each hardware we have to implement that code once to enable Java programs to run however, the Java solution is not applicable to programs written in other languages.

1.7.1.3 Concept of Middleware According to Distributed Systems

(1) Trends and Challenges:

- When we consider about trends and challenges there are two fundamental trends influence the way we conceive and construct new computing information systems.

- The first is that information technology of all forms is becoming highly commoditized *i.e.,* hardware and software artifacts are getting faster, cheaper, and better at a relatively predictable rate.
- The second is the growing acceptance of a network-centric paradigm, where distributed applications with a range of Quality of Service (QoS) needs are constructed by integrating separate components connected by various forms of communication services.
- The nature of this interconnection can range from.
  - (a) The very small and tightly coupled, such as avionics mission computing systems to
  - (b) The very large and loosely coupled, such as global telecommunications systems.
- The interconnection of these two trends has gives new architectural concepts and services into the layers of *middleware.*
- These layers are interposed between applications and commonly available hardware and software infrastructure to make it feasible, easier, and more cost effective to develop and evolve systems using reusable software.
- Middleware stems from recognizing the need for more advanced and capable support–beyond simple connectivity–to construct effective distributed systems.
- A significant portion of middleware-oriented R&D activities have focused on:
  1. The identification, evolution, and expansion of our understanding of current middleware services in providing this style of development and
  2. The need for defining additional middleware layers and capabilities to meet the challenges associated with constructing future network-centric systems.
- These activities are expected to continue forward well into this decade to address the needs of next-generation distributed applications.
- Middleware perform their role in the following Challenges of distributed system:
- Growing focus on integration rather than on programming.
- Demand for end-to-end QoS support, not just component QoS.
- The increased viability of open systems.
- Increased leverage for disruptive technologies leading to increased global competition.
- Potential complexity cap for next-generation systems.

1.7.1.4 Middleware Solve Distributed Application Challenges

- Middleware addresses the challenges in distributed application like Requirements for faster development cycles, decreased effort, and greater software reuse motivate the creation and use of *middleware* and *middleware-based architectures.*

- Middleware is systems software that resides between the applications and the underlying operating systems, network protocol stacks, and hardware.

Middleware role in Distributed Application:

- Functionally bridge the gap between application programs and the lower-level hardware and software infrastructure in order to coordinate how parts of applications are connected and how they interoperate and

- Enable and simplify the integration of components developed by multiple technology suppliers.

- When we implement this concept properly, middleware can help to:

- Shield software developers from low-level, tedious, and error-prone platform details, such as socket-level network programming.

- Amortize software lifecycle costs by leveraging previous development expertise and capturing implementations of key patterns in reusable frameworks, rather than rebuilding them manually for each use.

- Provide a consistent set of higher-level network-oriented abstractions that are much closer to application requirements in order to simplify the development of distributed and embedded systems.

- Provide a wide array of developer-oriented services, such as logging and security that have proven necessary to operate effectively in a networked environment.

1.7.2 Openness

- In distributed system Openness determines whether the system can be extended and re-implemented in various ways.

- The openness of distributed systems is determined primarily by the degree to which new resource-sharing services can be added.

- If we want to achieve openness then, the specification and documentation of the key software interfaces of the components of a system are made variable to software developers, i.e. you have to publish key interfaces.

- The publication of interfaces is only the starting point for adding services in a distributed system.

- The challenge to designers is to take the complexity of distributed systems consisting of many components engineered by different people.

- Open distributed systems can be constructed from heterogeneous hardware and software, possibly from different vendors.

1.7.3 Security

- In distributed system security is very important area that is to be considered. If the resources of a computer system are protected from distribution and unauthorized access then users can trust on the system.

- Applying security in distributed system is more difficult than centralized system because of the lack of a single point of control and use of insecure networks for data communication.

- But when we think about centralized system, all users are authenticated by the system at login time, and the system can easily check whether a user is authorized to perform the required operation or not, but in distributed system, the client server model is often used for requesting and providing services, when a client sends a request message to a server, the server must have some way of knowing who is the client.

- This is not so simple because any client identification field in the message cannot be trusted.

- This is because an intruder (a person or program trying to obtain unauthorized access to system resources) may pretend to be authorized client or may change the message contents during transmission.

- So, to apply security in distributed system required some addition requirement, these are as follows:

  - It should be possible for the sender of a message to know that the massage was received by the intended receiver.

  - It should be possible for the receiver of a message to know that the message was sent by the genuine sender.

  - It should be possible for both the sender and receiver of a message to be guaranteed that the contents of the message were not changed while it was in transfer.

- Cryptography is the best method for dealing with these security aspects of a distributed system. In this method, comprehension of private information is prevented by encrypting the information, which can be then decrypted by authorized users.

- The system whose security depends on the integrity of the fewest possible entities is more likely to remain secure as it grows.

- Example: It is simple to ensure security based on the integrity of the much smaller number of servers rather than trusting thousands of clients.

- In this case, it is sufficient to only ensure the physical security of these servers and the software that run.

Some of the security challenges have not yet been fully met:

(1) Denial of Service Attacks:

If user wants to disrupt a service for some reason, this can be done by bombarding the service with such a large number of pointless requests that serious users are unable to use it. This is called Denial of service attacks. From time to time, there have been several recent denial of service attacks on well-known web services. Currently such attacks are countered by attempting to catch and punish the perpetrators after the event, but that is not a general solution to the problem. Counter-measures based on improvements in the management of networks are under development.

(2) Security of Mobile Code:

You have to handled mobile code very carefully Example: consider that someone is receives an executable program as e-mail, the possible effects of running the program are unpredictable Example: it may seem to display an interesting picture but in reality it may access local resources, or perhaps be part of a denial of service attack.

1.7.4 Scalability

- In distributed system scalability refers to the capability of a system to increased service load.

- Distributed system will grow with time since it is very common to add new node or an entire sub-network to the system to take care of increased workload or organizational changes in a company.

- Therefore distributed system should be designed to easily cope with the growth of nodes and users in the system.

- Example: Some of the important principals for designing scalable distributed systems are as follows:

1. Avoid Centralized Entities:

- The use of centralized entities such as single central file server or a single database for the entire system makes the distributed system non-salable due to following reasons.

- The failure of the centralized entity often brings the entire system down. Hence, the system cannot tolerate faults in a graceful manner.

- The performance of the centralized entity often becomes a system bottleneck when contention for it increases with the growing number of users.

- Even if the centralized entity has enough processing and storage capacity, the capacity of the network that connects the centralized entity with other nodes of the system often gets saturated when the contention for the entity increases beyond a certain level.

- In a wide-area network consisting of several interconnected local area networks. It is obviously inefficient to always get a particular type of request serviced at a server node that is several gateways away. This also increases network traffic.

2. Centralized Algorithms must be Avoided:

- In centralized system centralized algorithm operates by collecting information from all nodes, processing this information on a single node and then distributed the result to other node.

- The use of such algorithm in the design of a distributed system is also not acceptable from a scalability point of view.

- Example: A scheduling algorithm that makes scheduling decision by first inquiring from all the nodes and then selecting the most lightly loaded node as a candidate for receiving Jobs has poor scalability factor.

- Such algorithm work fine per small networks but it get crippled when it applied to large networks because, the inquirer receives a very large number of replies almost simultaneously and the time required to process the reply messages for making a host selection is normally too long, the complexity of the algorithm is $O(n^2)$ and it creates heavy network traffic and quickly consumes network bandwidth.

- So only decentralized algorithm is used in the design of distributed system, in the algorithm, global state information of the system is not collected or used, decision at a node is usually based on locally available information and it assumed that a system wide global clock does not exist.

3. Most of Operations Perform on Client Workstations:

- To scale the system if possible then the operation should be performed on the clients own workstation instead of server machine. A server is a common resource for several clients, and hence server cycles are more precious than the cycles of client workstations.

1.7.4.1 Scalable System

- As a property of systems, scalability is generally difficult to define and in any particular case it is necessary to define the specific requirements for scalability on those dimensions that are deemed important.

- It is a highly significant issue in electronics systems, databases, routers, and networking. A system, whose performance improves after adding hardware, proportionally to the capacity added, is said to be a scalable system.

- An algorithm, design, networking protocol, program, or other system is said to scale, if it is suitably efficient and practical when applied to large situations (Example: a large input data set or a large number of participating nodes In the case of a distributed system). If the design fails when the quantity increases, it does not scale.

- The concept of scalability is desirable in technology as well as business settings. The base concept is consistent - the ability for a business or technology to accept increased volume without impacting the contribution margin (= revenue - variable costs).

- Example: a given piece of equipment may have capacity from 1-1000 users, and beyond 1000 users, additional equipment is needed or performance will decline (variable costs will increase and reduce contribution margin).

Measures

Scalability can be measured in different dimensions, such as:

- **Administrative Scalability:** The ability for an increasing number of organizations or users to easily share a single distributed system.

- **Functional Scalability:** The ability to enhance the system by adding new functionality at minimal effort.

- **Geographic Scalability:** The ability to maintain performance, usefulness, or usability regardless of expansion from concentration in a local area to a more distributed geographic pattern.

- **Load Scalability:** The ability for a distributed system to easily expand and contract its resource pool to accommodate heavier or lighter loads or number of inputs. Alternatively, the ease with which a system or component can be modified, added, or removed, to accommodate changing load.

Examples:

- A routing protocol is considered scalable with respect to network size, if the size of the necessary routing table on each node grows as O(log N), where N is the number of nodes in the network.

- A scalable online transaction processing system or database management system is one that can be upgraded to process more transactions by adding new processors, devices and storage, and which can be upgraded easily and transparently without shutting it down.

- Some early Peer-to-Peer (P2P) implementations of Gnutella had scaling issues. Each node query flooded its requests to all peers. The demand on each peer would increase in proportion to the total number of peers, quickly overrunning the peers' limited capacity. Other P2P systems like Bit Torrent scale well because the demand on each peer is independent of the total number of peers. There is no centralized bottleneck, so the system may expand indefinitely without the addition of supporting resources (other than the peers themselves).

- The distributed nature of the Domain Name System allows it to work efficiently even when all hosts on the worldwide Internet are served, so it is said to "scale well".

Scale Horizontally vs. Vertically:

- When we consider scaling system we have to consider methods of adding more resources for a particular application fall into two broad categories that is horizontally and vertically.

Scale Horizontally (Scale Out)

- To scale horizontally (or scale out) means to add more nodes to a system, such as adding a new computer to a distributed software application.

- An example might be scaling out from one Web server system to three.

- As computer prices drop and performance continues to increase, low cost "commodity" systems can be used for high performance computing applications such as seismic analysis and biotechnology workloads that could in the past only be handled by supercomputers.

- Hundreds of small computers may be configured in a cluster to obtain aggregate computing power that often exceeds that of single traditional RISC processor based scientific computers.

- This model has further been improved by the availability of high performance interconnects such as Myrinet and InfiniB and technologies.

- It has also led to demand for features such as remote maintenance and batch processing management previously not available for "commodity" systems.

- The scale-out model has created an increased demand for shared data storage with very high I/O performance, especially where processing of large amounts of data is required, such as in seismic analysis.

- This has fuelled the development of new storage technologies such as object storage devices.

Scale Vertically (Scale Up)

- To scale vertically (or scale up) means to add resources to a single node in a system, typically involving the addition of CPUs or memory to a single computer.

- Such vertical scaling of existing systems also enables them to use virtualization technology more effectively, as it provides more resources for the hosted set of operating system and application modules to share.

- Taking advantage of such resources can also be called "scaling up", such as expanding the number of Apache daemon processes currently running.

Tradeoffs

- There are tradeoffs between the two models. Larger numbers of computers means increased management complexity, as well as a more complex programming model and issues such as throughput and latency between nodes; also, some applications do not lend themselves to a distributed computing model.

- In the past, the price difference between the two models has favoured "scale out" computing for those applications that fit its paradigm, but recent advances in virtualization technology have blurred that advantage, since deploying a new virtual over a hyper visor (where possible) is almost always less expensive than actually buying and installing a real one.

- Configuring an existing idle system has always been less expensive than buying, installing, and configuring a new one, regardless of the model.

Database Scalability

- There are number of different techniques that enable databases to grow to very large size while supporting an ever-increasing rate of transactions per second. Not to be discounted, of course, is the rapid pace of hardware advances in both the speed and capacity of mass storage devices, as well as similar advances in CPU and networking speed.

- Beyond that, a variety of architectures are employed in the implementation of very large-scale databases.

- One technique supported by most of the major Database Management System (DBMS) products is the partitioning of large tables, based on ranges of values in a key field.

- In this manner, the database can be scaled out across a cluster of separate database servers. Also, with the advent of 64-bit microprocessors, multi-core CPUs, and large SMP multiprocessors, DBMS vendors have been at the forefront of supporting multi-threaded implementations that substantially scale up transaction processing capacity.

- Network-Attached Storage (NAS) and Storage Area Networks (SANs) coupled with fast local area networks and Fibre Channel technology enable still larger, more loosely coupled configurations of databases and distributed computing power.

- The widely supported X/Open XA standard employs a global transaction monitor to coordinate distributed transactions among semi-autonomous XA-compliant database resources.

- Oracle RAC uses a different model to achieve scalability, based on a "shared-everything" architecture that relies upon high-speed connections between servers.

- While DBMS vendors debate the relative merits of their favoured designs, some companies and researchers question the inherent limitations of relational database management systems.

- Giga Spaces, for example, contends that an entirely different model of distributed data access and transaction processing, named Space based architecture, is required to achieve the highest performance and scalability.

- On the other hand, Base One makes the case for extreme scalability without departing from mainstream database technology. In either case, there appears to be no limit in sight to database scalability

1.7.4.2 Techniques and Technologies for Scalability

- There are various ways to define what scalability is. A scalable system should have a system architecture that will be capable of offering its users similar response times in varying circumstances.

- One definition of scalability is "Scalability is the ability to support the required quality of service as the system load increases without changing the system".

- This definition therefore means that if a system has to be altered in order to accommodate an increase in users, then it was not scalable to start with and so it will need to be made scalable with suitable architectural extensions.

- Such a redesign would involve temporarily taking the system out of operation or attempting to provide users with the service whilst restructuring.

- Every system, when designed will have in its functional requirements, a time period that relates to an acceptable amount of time that users are willing to wait before they become dissatisfied e.g.: users must receive results from their query within 8 seconds.

- The aim of designing a scalable system is to satisfy this requirement regardless of the number of users using the distributed system.

- Scalable system can also be a system that allows added capacity to be handled by altering the system slightly but without having to take it out of action for a detrimental period of time i.e.; this could be done dynamically.

- Other definitions of scalability include with the simplest being "scalability is an application's ability to support a growing number of users". Scalability can be measured by a number of metrics. These include the number of users that can be supported and still be offered adequate response times and the time to process request in seconds or milliseconds.

1.7.4.3 The Importance of Scalability

- Scalability is very important factor in distributed system basically Scalability is required to maintain a satisfactory level of service for users.

- Maintaining a high quality response time in an application such as a search engine is important, as offering poorer response times when the system is used under a heavier load is likely to drive users away from using the system.

- This situation would not be that problematic with applications such as search engines (especially if they were good search engines) as on occasions, we simply accept that systems are being heavily used, as we would accept that a road network was being heavily used.

- However, when using applications such as on-line share purchasing schemes, users will not return to systems that offer them poorer response times just because the system is being heavily used.

- If this is the case, they will simply switch to another service that is scalable and is therefore able to provide them with their desired level of service.

- Also, by not designing a system that offers scalability, a really good idea cannot be exploited to its full potential and many users who would have used the system may be denied service and then never return.

- A good example of this is the 1891 National UK census that was made available on-line in 2002 only to be accessed by hundreds of thousands of interested users, who overloaded the system and made it inaccessible to many.

- This system was inaccessible for many weeks, by which time, a large proportion of users will have forgotten about it and not returned.

- If scalability had been taken into account from the offset i.e.; the designers realizing the potential popularity of the service, this venture would have been a lot more successful.

- Therefore, scalability is a very important issue that needs addressing in order to capture and keep customers as "business's customers dictate it's ultimate success".

- E-commerce companies highlight this factor, as their entire income will come from Internet users (if the system is not available to users, they cannot spend their money).

- The ability to provide the users with a service, and maintain this service (retaining customers), is fundamental to their survival "an organisation with inadequate site performance will frustrate users and drive customers away".

- The term fundamental does not imply that the company will not make a profit if their system is not scalable but making a system scalable and therefore keeping response times to a minimum enhances the users experience and potentially profits.

1.7.4.4 Way to Achieve Scalability in Distributed System?

- The increase in the number of COTS servers means that scalability can take place from a software point of view i.e.; using these servers or scalability can be achieved from a hardware point of view i.e.; by designing very application specific servers or enhancing the network infrastructure to increase bandwidths and reduce latency.

- The following discussion will discuss both approaches.

Techniques and Locations for Scalability

- There are various techniques to adding/improving scalability in systems and these can take place at different places within the system architecture. Fig. 1.4 (a) below shows very general system architecture analogous to the three-tier architecture, of a distributed system.

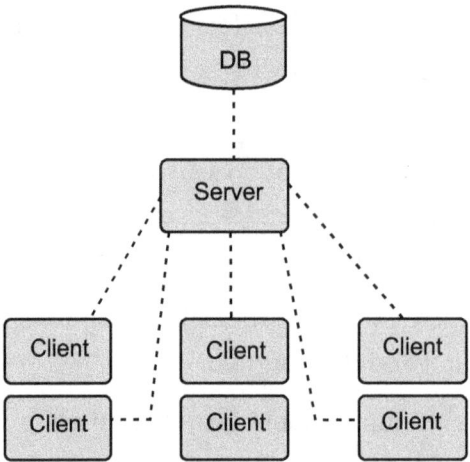

Fig. 1.4 (a) : Three tier architecture shows location of scalability

- Systems can be made more scalable by adopting strategies and using technologies in various parts of the architecture above.

- Using such approaches, scalability can be implemented in the "back-end" i.e.; replicating the database that is used so that multiple copies are available for user access.

- Improved scalability can also be achieved in the middle-tier i.e.; adding more servers such as web servers to create a collection of servers or it can be used at the "front-end" i.e.; by improving the functional capabilities of the client-side applications.

- These three scalability techniques will now be addressed using references to specific technology where appropriate

1.7.4.5 Scalability at the Back-End

- To scale the system we have to consider at backend so scalability at the back-end can be achieved by replicating databases or file servers.

- Several copies of a database may be available in a system and system clients can access multiple versions.

- These databases may be held at different locations, which would actually aid fault-tolerance and availability for larger systems.

Fig. 1.4 (b) shows a general architecture for data and management of replicated data. Clients communicate with front-ends i.e.; web servers, which in turn communicate with databases. Replica managers enforce data integrity/consistency constraints

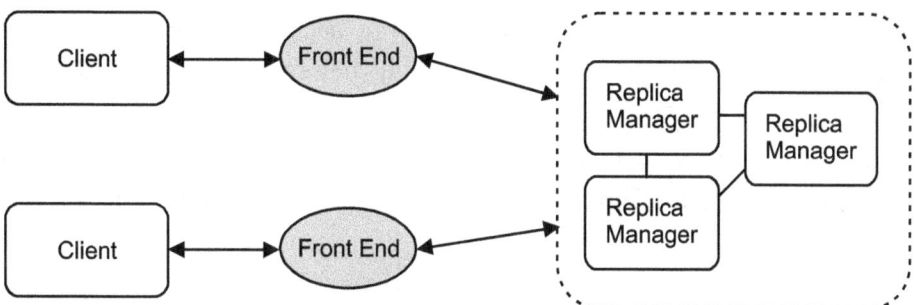

Fig. 1.4 (b) : Scalability at backend using replica manager

- When we consider one database/file server that offers the benefit of data consistency but when more than one database is used then problems then arises in terms of keeping these databases or file servers consistent with one another.

- This issue is obviously affected by the data that is held by the databases i.e.; is it date-sensitive such as share price information, in which case any modifications to data will have to be issued to all databases i.e.; using an "eager scheme", which may mean that users are temporarily prevented from querying systems as all data sites are updated using a multicast protocol.

- In this environment client will use the "write-once, update everywhere policy". The alternative being to use a "lazy" approach and propagate database changes not immediately and so consistency is not totally achieved but database access times to clients is not as poor.

- This problem of data inconsistency is especially problematic when systems allow caching of files to take place at clients.

- The Coda File System specifies that all clients have to update servers if they modify a file that they have in their cache (using what is referred to as a Venus process that resides on the client).

- Problems can then arise whereby servers are not actually available i.e.; they are disconnected and so they do not receive updates.

- The Andrew File system also offers a restricted replication strategy, whereby file servers are replicated but only contain read-only files so scalability is enhanced but the added problems of data inconsistencies are not present.

- The Coda file system accepts that replicating data at servers and in cache and allowing such data to be written to, can be problematic "it is a principle of the design of Coda that copies of files residing on servers are more reliable that those residing in caches on workstations".

- Coda file system attempts to solve this problem by allowing potential inconsistencies to exist for a short period of time before checking that cached copies and centrally held copies of files are consistent.

- Due to Coda operating such an optimistic replication strategy, eventually there are problems with system files and human intervention will be required to resolve these problems.

- Coda demonstrates that trade-offs are always present with such systems. Example: clients using Coda to modify files will send such changes to all Coda servers (using a multicast protocol), this takes this task away from servers which should basically be handling client requests.

- However, this enables the problem described above whereby not all system entities are informed of updates and so inconsistencies will arise.

- In terms of providing increased system scalability by replicating databases and file servers, there seems to be some disagreement.

- Some applications stress that consistency is of utmost importance but this is not easily implemented in large scale distributed systems as updates need to be made available to all databases and due to the atomicity of transactions, extensive locking strategies and techniques will need to be deployed to maintain consistency.

1.7.4.6 Scalability in the Middle-Tier

- One technique that can be used is using only one server in a system. This technique at first looks illogical due to availability and fault-tolerance reasons but is actually an option especially with the availability of extremely powerful servers running multiple processors.

- Example: Intel servers using Xeon MP processor that are designed for multiprocessor servers. These servers offer extreme benefits using technologies such as "on-chip" cache and hyper-threading (one processor behaving like two processors, whilst using one cache).

- Major companies in the server market such as IBM, HP and UniSys are fast adopting this type of technology.

- Intel are investing heavily in this type of technology as they believe that many companies prefer to use one high-end server using multiple processors than have to manage a group of separate servers using appropriate software.

- Although, as this technology is in its infancy, it is not evident how large a system it could adequately support but it seems that it will be for more medium-sized systems i.e.; Google are unlikely to switch over to a few high-end servers.

- Scalability is enhanced as when the load of a system increases, additional processors are simply added i.e.; upgrading from 8 to 12 processors, therefore enabling the handling of more requests.

- This approach is generally not used for the reason that the single server is also a single point of failure and the inability to provide a service to users could be disastrous for certain companies.

- Also, if a single server is used then a service would not be operational during an upgrade process.

- Another major criticism of the single server approach is that it is inflexible.

- Example: the load that a system experience can often fluctuate e.g.; an on-line florist would receive a lot more client requests around Valentine's Day or the BBC would receive a lot more client requests during and leading up to a major sporting festival.

- Therefore, it would be a costly exercise to upgrade servers only to discover that these upgrades were only required for a short time period.

Basically, purchasing a server to cover the worst case is a static approach to a dynamic environment. The example just described is often referred to as "scaling up".

1.7.4.7 Scalability at the Front-End

- When we think about the scalability of a large distributed system it can be also enhanced to some extent by placing functionality that could reside in servers (application logic or actual data) into actual applications or clients themselves.

- There are two approaches that improve the scalability are rich and thick clients.

Rich Clients: This approach basically involves client application interfaces being able to contain extra functionality and possess more data that they can use effectively i.e.; a good example of this would be Napster, the mp3 downloading utility also works on this principle as the user interface that was used to access files actually resides on client machines and so each time the service is accessed, there is no requirement to download multiple interface components each time just to perform a simple file query. The obvious problem here being that it is up to the client to keep the interface up to date by having appropriate versions. This idea decreases latency for the user but its influence is limited in its effect at enhancing scalability. The .NET framework uses win Forms and web Forms to achieve the above. "Win Forms allow Windows-based applications to take full advantage of the rich user interface features available in the Microsoft Windows operating system".

Thick Clients: It is stated that "thin clients require more clicks than thick clients. This means that "thinner" clients are interacting more with servers than with application logic residing on their own machine. Thicker clients are often preferred and an example of a thick client would be a java applet. A user would download an applet and then be able to perform calculations within this applet i.e.; they have downloaded code that allows them to perform tasks that would previously have been a requirement of the server side/middle-tier. This enables faster calculation of results due to the client possessing application logic, reduced load on servers and allows disconnected operation to take place. Again, the problem arises whereby servers would have to inform clients of updates to the application logic in order to update their software.

By placing added functionality within the client in terms of interfaces, the quality of the user experience is improved but scalability is not aided greatly. Also, the thicker client approach is more ideally suited to applications whose database and business logic are fairly persistent, therefore allowing the thicker client approach can be more fully exploited.

1.7.4.8 Caching

- Another way to achieve scalability in a large-scale distributed system at the client-side, middle-tier and server-side through the use of caching.

- Caching is basically a strategy that is based around storage space, whether it be at the client itself or in a proxy server slightly "nearer" to the client than say a web server.

- Objects such as web pages or files that are frequently accessed are held within cache, as it is likely that they will be accessed again soon.

- Example: popular web pages that are accessed by a client machine can be cached locally on that machine or files that are accessed frequently in a large file system such as Coda will be cached to prevent that file from being frequently accessed from disk, which is a more lengthy process.

- The use of caching is especially important for large-scale systems that operate over "poorer" networks that offer users poor bandwidth and latency.

Caching at the Server: Files that are frequently accessed using a server to access a database should not remain simply on the database. They should be stored within memory on that server to improve access speeds. This is called a "disk-block cache" and studies have shown that there are "substantial performance gains as result of the use of a disk block cache}". Therefore, each time a client requires a file, it will check the cache first and then if the file is present in cache it will use this copy and if not (a cache miss) then it will access the file from a database.

This highlights the fact that increasing the size of the cache would improve access speeds to files in such a system. However, the problem with caching is that caches must be kept accurate and up-to-date i.e.; the object in the database must be the same as the object in the cache. This means that when a client writes to a database i.e.; they have altered a file, purchased a car etc, all caches must be updated to prevent clients from accessing inaccurate cache data. This would require database/server-cache communication and this results in a communications overhead (usually multicast messages to all caches) as cache consistency is maintained.

Caching at the Client: One of the major problems with caching at the server side is often summarised by "the bottleneck is simply being moved around" and the problem of enhancing scalability is not actually being addressed.

By using caching at the server, the bottleneck (a large build-up of requests) is no longer located in queues waiting to access databases and so file/web servers are capable of offering greater performance. However, what if the situation exists whereby the server simply becomes the new bottleneck as many clients are left queuing for access to the cache? Also, a network may offer poor latency due to bandwidth limitations or network load and so the solution of server side caching only seems to serve the purpose of moving the bottleneck away from back-end databases.

With the research and development of in-memory databases, server-side caching seems like its influence will be reduced as databases will effectively be able to be stored in memory and so the disk access problem is now on its way to being solved. Another solution is client side caching i.e.; client machines caching frequently accessed web pages. This solves the problem described above and introduces slight problems such as web pages being out-of date in cache.

The larger problem is that other client caches have to be informed that their cached file portion is now dated. Systems such as NFS do not solve this problem well as each time a client attempts to access an item such as a directory, it has to check with the server if its cached copy of the directory is dated or not which defeats the point of caching. NFS attempts to solve this by stating that all cached directories are valid for 30 seconds, after which, contact the server to validate if it is still valid. For these reasons, cache consistency is often the responsibility of severs and is achieved using server call-backs.

Coda adopts a different approach in that it enforces that clients take the responsibility off servers and it is their task to inform of cache updates. Using pre-fetching in addition to caching can also enhance scalability. Pre-fetching is often used when caches are being underutilized or some future knowledge is already known about future system access on behalf of clients.

For example, there may be a lot of activity with a particular file in a distributed file system. System administrators could realise in advance that this file has suddenly gained in performance and enforce that all clients cache it immediately.

1.7.4.9 Publish-Subscribe

- In large scale distributed system Publish-subscribe is an approach used to aid for scalability. The basic reason behind the development of publish subscribe system architectures (also referred to as "pull software" or "smart-push" software) is illustrated by the following statement.

- "Applications that need a consistent and up-to-date view on continuously changing information published on the web spend an inordinate amount of time polling known sites for updates.

- This approach leads to chained inaccuracies and seriously limits scalability". By constantly polling servers for updates, network bandwidth is wasted and prevents applications that require bandwidth more urgently, from using the network effectively as possible.

- Latency times therefore extend for all interested clients.

- The publish-subscribe paradigm means that applications that are interested in updates to data (these are called consumers) do not poll anymore.

- They simply register an interest in a particular type of event and are informed of data changes by brokers that work on behalf of producers of data "firing" events.

- It should be noted that clients can also be informed of events on a regular basis i.e.; they receive data based a on a pre-agreed frequency.

- An example of this scenario would be a client could receive information about a rising/falling share price (content-based) that they are interested in when a change occurs or they could simply ask to be informed about the current price of that share at 5pm everyday (subject based).

- The publish-subscribe architecture also aids scalability, as "subscribers do not necessarily require the location of the publisher".

Issues in Publish-Subscribe Systems are as Follows:

- Deploying a protocol that distributes data to all interested parties reliably i.e.; a scalable reliable multicast protocol needs to be used.

- The approach taken to distribute data to subscribers is especially important in large-scale distributed systems, as certain approaches that operate fine in smaller systems do not scale to larger systems i.e.; protocols that frequently send data to uninterested clients are basically wasting resources.

- Matches have to be made accurately to interests and events to prevent excessive filtering of unnecessary information being required by the client.

- The matching process is not discussed in detail here but it has a major influence the efficiency and success of publish subscribe systems.

- Tibco's TIB/Rendezvous is an example of publish-subscribe and this piece of middleware uses a bus architecture for publishers and subscribers to communicate in a peer-to-peer manner.

- All system members use a Rendezvous daemon that is used to communicate with this bus. These daemons are basically brokers that communicate with the system bus to aid the communication between publishers and subscribers.

- The idea of publish-subscribe may seem like the savoir to improving scalability but there are some problems.

- These include clients who are no longer interested in particular events simply forget to unsubscribe to that event and so they do not use the data they receive yet they still waste resources receiving it.
- A solution to this is that subscriptions could time out after a set period and then subscribers have to re-subscribe to events.
- Other issues include publishers wanting to end publishing particular events and not being able to as clients still have "bound contracts" with them.
- In a traditional RPC environment, this would not happen as a request would be made and no valid data would be returned.
- Also, events in publish-subscribe systems cannot be too rigid/really specific as not many clients will wish to subscribe to them whereas if too much data is encompassed in events to basically make sure there is "an event for everyone" then the matching process of subscriptions to events is made a more difficult task.

1.7.5 Failure Handling in Distributed System

- Failure handling is very important concept in distributed system in this part we discuss how distributed system handle failure.
- Sometime computer system fails. When fault occurs in hardware or software then programs may produce incorrect results or they may stop before they have completed. In a distributed system failure are partial.
- Some components fail while others continue to function, so, the handling of failure is particularly difficult.

There are some important techniques which deal with failure that are as follows,

(a) Detecting Failures:

- Some failure can be detected but there are some failure which we cannot detect Example: Remote crashed server in the internet. We have to manage presence of failure that cannot be detected but may be suspected.

(b) Masking Failures:

- Some failures that have been detected can be hidden or made less severe.
  Example:
  - Messages can be transmitted when they fail to arrive.
  - File data can be written to a pair of disks so that if one is corrupted, the other may still be correct. Just dropping a message that is corrupted is an example of making a fault less severe.

(c) Tolerating Failure:

  - Most of the services in the internet do exhibit failures, it would not be practical for them to attempt to detect and hide all of the failure that might occur in such a large network with so many components.

- These clients can be designed to tolerate failures, which generally involve the users tolerating them as well.
- Example: when a web browser cannot contact a web server, it does not make the user wait for ever while it keep on trying it informs the user about the problem, leaving them free to try again later.

(d) Recovery from Failures:

- Recovery involves the design of software so that the sate of permanent data can be recovered or 'rolled back' after a server has crashed.

(e) Redundancy:

- Service can be made to tolerate failures by the use of redundant components.
  Example:
  - There should always be at least two different routes between any two routers in the internet.
  - In the Domain name system, every name table is replicated in at least two different servers.
  - A database may be replicated in several servers to ensure that the data remains accessible after the failure of any single server; the servers can be designed to detect faults in their peers. When a fault is detected in one server, clients are redirected to the remaining servers.

1.7.6 Concurrency

- The term Concurrency we use when there are more than one node share a common resource. Both services and applications provide resources that can be shared by clients in a distributed system.
- Therefore there is possibility that several clients will attempt to access a shared resources at the same time.
- Example: Data structure that records bids for an auction may be accessed very frequently when it gets close to the deadline time.
- The process that manages a shared resource take one client request at a time, but this is having limits. Therefore services and application generally allow multiple client requests to be processed concurrently.
- Any object that represents a shared resource in a distributed system must be responsible for ensuring that it operates correctly in a concurrent environment, this applies not only to servers but also to objects in applications.
- For an object to be safe in a concurrent environment, its operations must be synchronized in such a way that its data remains consistent.
- This can be achieved by standard techniques such as semaphores, which are used in most operating system.

1.7.7 Transparency

- Transparency is one of the main goals of a distributed system in which the basic idea is to make the existence of multiple computers invisible and provide a single system image to its users. i.e. distributed operating system must be designed in such a way that a collection of distinct machines connected by a communication subsystem appears to its users as a virtual uni-processor.

- To achieve the complete transparency is a difficult task.

- There are basically eight forms of transparency provided by the international standards organizations. Reference model for open distributed processing:

    (1) Access transparency

    (2) Location transparency

    (3) Replication transparency

    (4) Failure transparency

    (5) Migration transparency

    (6) Concurrency transparency

    (7) Performance transparency

    (8) Scaling transparency

(1) Access Transparency:

- In distributed system access transparency means that users should not need or be able to recognize whether a resource (either hardware or software) is remote or local, this means that the distributed system should allow users to access remote resources in the same way as local resources.

- That is, the user interface, which takes the form of a set of system calls, should not distinguish between local and remote resources, and it should be the responsibility of the distributed system to locate the resource and to arrange for servicing user requests in a user transparent manner.

- It is not possible to design system calls that provide complete access transparency. However, the area of designing a global resource naming facility has been well researched.

(2) Location Transparency:

There are two main aspects of location transparency.

    (a) Name transparency

    (b) User transparency

(a) Name Transparency:

- The name of resource it may be either hardware or software that should not reveal only hint as to the physical location of the resource.

- That is the name of a resource should be independent of the physical connectivity or topology of the system or the current location of the resource.

- Resources which are capable of being moved from one node to another in a distributed system (like file) must be allowed to move without having their names changed. Therefore, resource names must be unique system wide.

(b) User Transparency:

- The refers to the fact that no matter which machine a user is logged onto, he or she should be able to access a resource with the same name. That is, the user should not be required to use different name to access the same resource from two different nodes of the system.

- In a distributed system that supports user mobility, user can freely log on to any machine in the system and access any resource without making any extra effort. Both name and user transparency requirements call for a system wide, global resource naming facility.

(3) Replication Transparency:

- In distributed system for achieving better performance and reliability all distributed operating systems have to create replicas (addition, copies) of file and other resources on different nodes of the distributed system.

- In this type of systems, both the existence of multiple copies of a replicated resource and the replication activity should be transparent to the users.

- The important thing related to replication transparency are, naming of Replicas and replication control, it is the responsibility of the system to name the various copies of a resource and to map a user-supplied name of the resource to an appropriate replica of the resource.

- Replication control decision such as, how many copies of the resource should be created, where should each copy is placed, and when should a copy be created/deleted should be made entirely automatically by the system in a user-transparent manner.

(4) Failure Transparency:

- In distributed system failure transparency play very important role basically it deals with masking from the user's partial failures in the system, such as a communication link failure, a machine failure, or a storage device crash.

- If file service of a distributed system is to be made failure transparent. This can be done by implementing it as a group of file servers that closely cooperate with each other to manage the files of the system and that function in such a manner that the users can utilize the file service even if only one of the file servers is up and working. In this case, the users cannot notice the failure of one or more file servers, except for slower performance of file access operations.

- Any type of service can be implemented in this way for failure transparency. However in this type of design, care should be taken to ensure that the cooperation among multiple servers does not add too much overhead to the system.

- Complete failure transparency is not possible with the current state of the art in distributed system because all types of failures cannot be handled in a user transparent manner.

(5) Migration Transparency:

- Migration transparency is used for better performance, reliability and security of an object that is capable of being moved (such as process or a file) is often migrated from one node to another in a distributed system.

- The aim of this transparency is to ensure that the movement of the object is handled automatically by the system in a user transparent manner.

- Three are three important issues to achieve this goal:

  (a) Migration decisions such as which object is to be moved from where to where should be made automatically by the system.

  (b) Migration of an object from one node to another node should not require any change in its name.

  (c) When the migrating object is a process, the inter process communication mechanism should ensure that a message sent to the migrating process reaches it without the need for the sender process to resend it if the receiver process moves to another node before the message is received.

(6) Concurrency Transparency:

- In a distributed system, multiple users who are separately use the system concurrently. In such a situation, it is economical to share the system resources (either hardware or software) among the concurrently executing user processes.

- However, the number of available resources in a computing system is restricted, one user process must necessarily influence the action of other concurrently executing user processes, as it competes for resources.

- Example: concurrent update to the same file by two different processes should be prevented. Concurrency transparency means that each user has a feeling that he or she is the sole user of the system and other users do not exist in the system.

- For providing concurrency transparency, the resource sharing mechanisms of the distributed operating system must have the following four properties.

  (a) An event-ordering property ensures that all access requests to various system resources are properly ordered to provide a consistent view to all users of the system.

(b) A mutual-exclusion property ensures that at any time at most one process accesses a shared resource, which must not be used simultaneously by multiple processes of program operation PS to be correct.

(c) A non-starvation property ensures that if every process that is granted a resource, which must not be used simultaneously by multiple processes, eventually releases it, every request for that resource is eventually granted.

(d) A non-deadlock property ensures that a situation will never occur in which competing processes prevent their mutual progress even though no single one requests more resources than available in the system.

(7) Performance Transparency:

- In distributed system the aim of performance transparency is to allow the system to be automatically reconfigured to improve performance, as load of the system vary dynamically. A situation in which one processor of the system is overloaded with Jobs while another processor is idle should not be allowed to occur. i.e. Processing capability of the system should be uniformly distributed among the currently available Jobs in the system.

(8) Scaling Transparency:

- The aim of this transparency is to allow the system to expand in scale without disrupting the activities of the users.

- This requirement calls for open-system architecture and the use of scalable algorithms for designing the distributed system components.

1.8 SYSTEM MODELS

- System models are basically of two types:
    (1) Architectural models
    (2) Fundamentals models

- The Architectures models are concerned with the placement of its ports and the relationships between them.

- Example: (1) Client-server model.
            (2) Peer-to-peer model.

- Fundamental models are concerned with a more formal description of the properties that are common in all of the architectural models.

- There is no global clock in a distributed system, so the clocks on different computers do not give the same time to one another.

- All communication between processes is achieved by using messages.

- Message communication on computer network can have various problems such as it affected by delays; it can suffer from a variety of failures and is vulnerable to security attacks.

- Then these problems/issues are discussed through three models.

  - **The Interaction Model:** It deals with performance and with the difficulty of setting time limits in a distributed system. Example: message delivery.

  - **The Failure Model:** It gives a precise specification of the faults that can be exhibited by processes and communication channels. It defines reliable communication and correct processes.

  - **The Security Model:** In this we discuss the possible threats to processes and communication channels.

1.8.1 Architectural Models

- In this section we discuss the distributed system architectural models basically the architectural model defines the way in which the components of system interact with one another and the way in which they are mapped onto an underlying network of computer.

- We can classify processes as,

  (1) Server processes

  (2) Client processes

  (3) Peer-processes.

- This classification of processes shows responsibility of each and so helps to assess their workloads and to determine the impact of failures in each of them.

- To understand Architectural model we first understand the architecture of software i.e. "Software architecture".

- Software architecture referred to the structuring using of software as layers or modules in a single computer, we can also offers services located in the different computers.

Fig. 1.5 below shows service layers in distributed system.

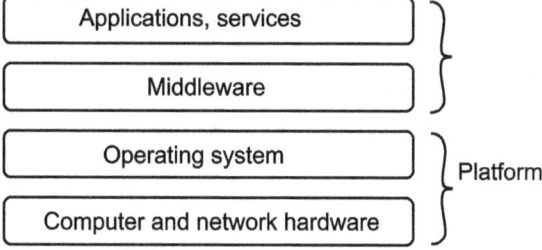

Fig. 1.5: Service-layers in distributed system

Application and Services:

- A server is a process that accepts requests from other processes and gives replay back.

- A distributed service can be provided by one or more server processes, interacting with each other and with client processes in order to maintain a consistent system wide view of the services resources as shown in Fig. 1.5 above there are two important terms present platform and middleware.

Platform:

- The lowest level hardware and software layers are called platform for distributed system. These low-level layers provide service to the layers which are above them. e.g. X86/windows, Linux X86/index etc are some examples.

Middleware:

- **Middleware** is one type of software that connects software components or applications. The software consists of a set of services that allows multiple processes running on one or more machines to interact with each other.

- The software layer that lies between the operating system and applications on each side of a distributed computing system in a network

- Middleware is sometimes called plumbing because it connects two applications and passes data between them.

- Middleware allows data contained in one database to be accessed through another.

- This technology basically used to provide for interoperability in support to coherent distributed architectures, which are used most often to support and simplify complex, distributed applications.

- It includes web servers, application servers, and similar tools that support application development and delivery.

1.8.1.1 System Architecture

In distributed system the system architecture is a model which is responsible for distribution of work in the system as needed. There are basically two main types of Architectural models these are as follows.

    (1) Peer-to-Peer Architecture

    (2) Client-Server Architecture

(1) Peer-to-Peer Architecture

Peer-to-peer architecture is one the system architecture which used by distributed system we start our discussion with definition

Basic Concept of Peer-To-Peer Architecture

- "P2P architecture is a class of applications that takes advantage of resources storage, cycles, content, human presence available at the edges of the Internet.

- Because accessing these decentralized resources means operating in an environment of unstable connectivity and unpredictable IP addresses, P2P nodes must operate outside the DNS system and have significant or total autonomy from central servers."
- "Distributed network architecture may be called a Peer-to-Peer network, if the participants share a part of their own hardware resources (processing power, storage capacity, network link capacity, printers...).
- These shared resources are necessary to provide the Service and content offered by the network (e.g. file sharing or shared workspaces for collaboration).
- They are accessible by other peers directly, without passing intermediary entities. The participants of such a network are thus resource (Service and content) providers as well as resource (Service and content) requestors.
- "Peer-to-Peer computing is the sharing of computer resources and services by direct exchange between systems.
- These resources and services include the exchange of information, processing cycles, cache storage, and disk storage for files.
- Peer-to-Peer computing takes advantage of existing desktop computing power and networking connectivity, allowing economical clients to leverage their collective power to benefit the entire enterprise.
- In a Peer-to-Peer architecture, computers that have traditionally been used solely as clients communicate directly among themselves and can act as both clients and servers, assuming whatever role are most efficient for the network.
- This reduces the load on servers and allows them to perform specialized services (such as mail-list generation, billing, etc.) more effectively.
- At the same time, Peer-to-Peer computing can reduce the need for IT organizations to grow parts of its infrastructure in order to support certain services, such as backup storage."

Peer:
- "A peer is a network node that can act as a client or a server, with or without centralized control, and with or without continuous connectivity.
- The term "peer" can apply to a wide range of device types, including small handheld and powerful server-class machines that are closely managed."

Node:
- A node is a computing device residing on a network. Nodes may be general-purpose computers, or they may be specialized to provide particular services or capabilities (e.g. a storage node or control node).
- Note the term computing device is used in the most generic sense in that a node can range from a multi-processor server to embedded systems."
- As it is stated above, there are two different approaches for Peer-to-Peer architecture: pure and hybrid. Both architectures will be described in more detail below.

(A) Pure Peer-to-Peer Architecture:

- "A distributed network architecture has to be classified as a "Pure" Peer-to-Peer network, if it is firstly a Peer-to-Peer network according to definition which we discussed above and secondly, if any single, arbitrary chosen terminal entity can be removed from the network without having the network suffering any loss of network service."

- In this architecture each peer is an equal participant. There is no peer with special or administrative roles.

- According to the definition, no central server is needed to control and coordinate the connections between the peers, see Fig. 1.6 (a).

- Therefore nodes have to self-organize themselves, based on whatever local information is available and interacting with locally reachable nodes (neighbors). Normally the data within such systems is distributed across multiple peers.

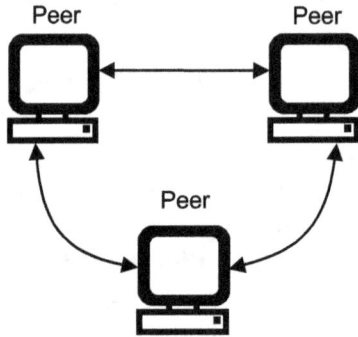

Fig. 1.6 (a): Pure peer-to-peer architecture

(B) Structured Peer-to-Peer Systems

- Structured P2P network provides a globally consistent protocol to ensure that any node can efficiently route a search to some peer that has the desired file, even if the file is extremely rare.

- Such a guarantee necessitates a more structured pattern of overlay links.

- By far the most common type of structured P2P network is the distributed hash table (DHT), in which a variant of consistent hashing is used to assign ownership of each file to a particular peer, in a way analogous to a traditional hash table's assignment of each key to a particular array slot.

Distributed Hash Tables:

- Distributed Hash Tables (DHTs) are a class of decentralized distributed systems that provide a lookup service similar to a hash table: (*key*, *value*) pairs are stored in the DHT, and any participating node can efficiently retrieve the value associated with a given key.

- Responsibility for maintaining the mapping from keys to values is distributed among the nodes, in such a way that a change in the set of participants causes a minimal amount of disruption.

- This allows DHTs to scale to extremely large numbers of nodes and to handle continual node arrivals, departures, and failures.

- DHTs form an infrastructure that can be used to build peer-to-peer networks. Notable distributed networks that use DHTs include BitTorrent's distributed tracker, the Kad network, the Storm botnet, YaCy, and the Coral Content Distribution Network.

- DHT-based networks have been widely utilized for accomplishing efficient resource discovery for grid computing systems, as it aids in resource management and scheduling of applications.

- Resource discovery activity involves searching for the appropriate resource types that match the user's application requirements.

- Recent advances in the domain of decentralized resource discovery have been based on extending the existing DHTs with the capability of multi-dimensional data organization and query routing.

- Majority of the efforts have looked at embedding spatial database indices such as the Space Filling Curves (SFCs) including the Hilbert curves, Z-curves, k-d tree, MX-CIF Quad tree and R*-tree for managing, routing, and indexing of complex Grid resource query objects over DHT networks.

- Spatial indices are well suited for handling the complexity of Grid resource queries. Although some spatial indices can have issues as regards to routing load-balance in case of a skewed data set, all the spatial indices are more scalable in terms of the number of hops traversed and messages generated while searching and routing Grid resource queries.

(C) Unstructured Peer-to-Peer Systems:

- In distributed system the Unstructured P2P network is used when the overlay links are established arbitrarily.

- Such networks can be easily constructed as a new peer that wants to join the network can copy existing links of another node and then form its own links over time.

- In an unstructured P2P network, if a peer wants to find a desired piece of data in the network, the query has to be flooded through the network to find as many peers as possible that share the data.

- The main disadvantage with such networks is that the queries may not always be resolved. Popular content is likely to be available at several peers and any peer searching for it is likely to find the same thing.

- But if a peer is looking for rare data shared by only a few other peers, then it is highly unlikely that search will be successful. Since there is no correlation between a peer and the content managed by it, there is no guarantee that flooding will find a peer that has the desired data.

- Flooding also causes a high amount of signaling traffic in the network and hence such networks typically have very poor search efficiency. Most of the popular P2P networks are unstructured.

- In *pure* P2P networks: Peers act as equals, merging the roles of clients and server.

- In such networks, there is no central server managing the network, neither is there a central router. Some examples of pure P2P Application Layer networks designed for file sharing are Gnutella and Free net.

- There also exist *hybrid* P2P systems, which distribute their clients into two groups: client nodes and overlay nodes.

- Typically, each client is able to act according to the momentary need of the network and can become part of the respective overlay network used to coordinate the P2P structure.

- This division between normal and 'better' nodes is done in order to address the scaling problems on early pure P2P networks. Example: for such networks are for example Gnutella.

- Another type of hybrid P2P network are networks using on the one hand central server(s) or bootstrapping mechanisms, on the other hand P2P for their data transfers.

- These networks are in general called 'centralized networks' because of their lack of ability to work without their central server(s). An example for such a network is the eDonkey network (eD2k).

(D) Hybrid Peer-to-Peer Architecture:

- Hybrid Peer-to-Peer model is basically used to incorporate some traces of the Client-Server relationship. Hybrid in the case of Peer-to- Peer means, that there is a central server in the system, but it takes only an intermediary role in the system.

- Central servers within the network fulfil two primary functions. First, they act as central directories where either connected users or indexed content can be mapped to the current IP address. Second, the servers direct traffic among the peers.

- Normally the initial communication of a peer is done with a server(1) , e.g., to obtain the location/identity of a peer, followed by(2) direct communication with that peer, See Fig. 1.6 (b).

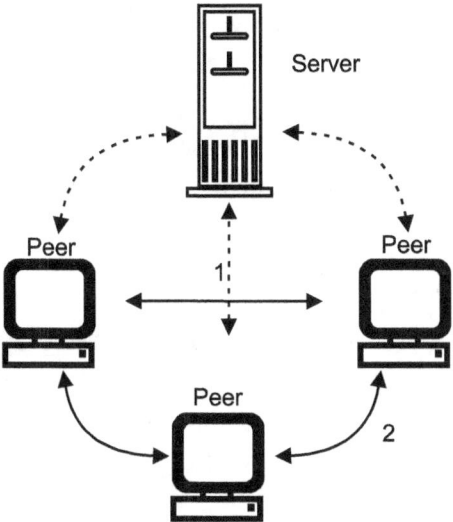

Fig. 1.6 (b): Hybrid peer-to-peer architecture

Advantages and Disadvantages of Hybrid Peer-to-Peer Architecture

Here we discuss the advantage and disadvantage of hybrid peer-to-peer architecture we start with advantages

Advantages:

- In a pure Peer-to-Peer architecture there is no single point of failure that means, if one peer breaks down, the rest of the peers are still able to communicate. Peer-to-Peer provides the opportunity to take advantage of unused resources such as processing power for computations and storage capacity. In Client-Server architectures, the centralized system bears the majority of the cost of the system. In Peer-to-Peer, all peers help spread the cost, Example: Napster used the file storage space of participating peers to store all the files.

- Peer-to-Peer allows preventing bottleneck such as traffic overload using central server architecture, because Peer-to-Peer can distribute data and balance request across the net without using a central server.

- There is better scalability due to a lack of centralized control and because most peers interact with each other.

Disadvantages:

- Today many applications need a high security standard, which is not satisfied by current Peer-to-Peer solutions.

- The connections between the peers are normally not designed for high throughput rates, even if the coverage of ADSL and Cable modem connections is increasing.

- A centralized system or a Client-Server system will work as long as the service provider keeps it up and running. If peers start to abandon a Peer-to-Peer system, services will not be available to anyone.
- Most search engines work best when they can search a central database rather than launch a Meta search of peers. This problem is circumvented by the hybrid Peer-to- Peer architecture.

(2) Client-Server Architecture:

Client server architecture is basic architecture of distributed system we define the client-server architecture as follows

Definitions

- "A Client-Server network is a basic distributed network which consists of one higher performance system that is nothing but server, and several mostly lower performance systems, that are clients. The server is the central registering unit as well as the only provider of content and service. A client only requests content or the execution of services, without sharing any of its own resources."

- "Client-Server architecture is network architecture in which each computer or process on the network is either a client or a server. Servers are powerful computers or processes dedicated to managing disk drives (file servers), printers (print servers), or network traffic (network servers). Clients are PCs or workstations on which users run applications. Clients rely on servers for resources, such as files, devices, and even processing power."

Architecture:

- The most commonly used architecture in constructing distributed systems is the Client-Server model.

- In this scheme clients request services or content from a server.

- The client and server require a known set of conventions before the can communicate. This set of conventions contains a protocol, which must be implemented at both ends of a connection.

- Examples of protocols are the TELNET protocol used in the Internet for remote terminal emulation, the Internet file transfer protocol, FTP and the most widely used hypertext transfer protocol, http.

Server:

- Basically servers accept the request from client and return them the result with an appropriate protocol.

- A server as a provider of services can be running on the same device as the client is running on, or on a different device, which is reachable over the network. The decision to outsource a service from an application in form of a server can have different reasons.

- **Performance:** In certain circumstances the clients are inefficient devices, which have interfaces to high performance demanding applications. In this case the computation is done on a high-performance server. Today this approach is less used, but has still its area of application, Example: virtual reality computations for film scenes.

- **Central Data Management:** This aspect of the Client-Server model does have the most impact today. Data is stored on a server, which can be used or manipulated from different clients.

   Typical examples of services provided by a server are:
   - **File Server:** One server provides multiple clients with a file system. Tasks of this server include access control and transaction control (only one client may access a file with write permissions at a time).
   - **Web Server:** The Web server provides multiple clients (Web browser on different devices) with information. The information can be static on a Web server or dynamic, generated by different service applications.

Client:

- A client is typically a device or a process which uses the service of one or more servers. Since clients are often the interface between server-information and people, clients are designed for information input and visualization of information. Although clients had only few resources and functionality in the past, today most clients are PCs with more performance regarding resources and functionality.

- Early clients had only the task to display the application that was running on the server and to forward inputs of the user to the server. All computations are done on the server. In this case one speaks of a thin client. A thin client has limited local resources in terms of hardware and software.

- It functionally requires processing time, applications and services to be provided from a centralized server. Network computers are examples of the development of thin clients.

- A thick client is functionally rich in terms of hardware and software. Thick clients are capable of storing and executing their own applications as well as network centric ones.

- Thick client typically refers to a personal computer. Client-Server architectures can be classified into **flat** and **hierarchical**. If the Client-Server model is flat, all clients communicate only with a single server; see Fig. 1.7 (a).

- If the Client-Server model is hierarchical the servers of one level are acting as clients to higher level servers.

- A pretty good example is a request of a certain web page. The user enters a URL into the web browser (client).

- The client establishes a connection to his nearest name server to ask for the address. If that server does not know the name, it delegates the query to the authority for that namespace.

- That query, in turn, may be delegated to a higher authority, all the way up to the root name servers for the Internet as a whole. Name servers operate both as clients and as servers, see Fig. 1.7 (b).

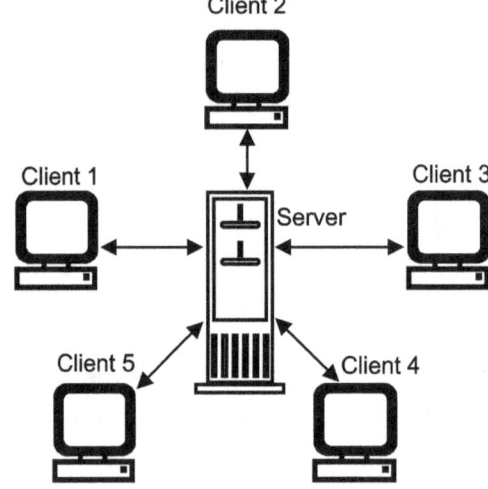

Fig. 1.7 (a) : Flat architecture

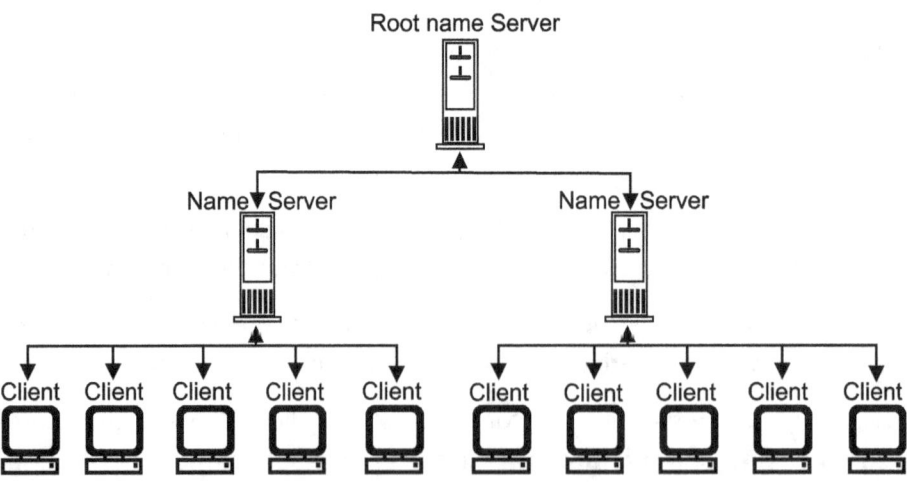

Fig 1.7 (b) : Hierarchical architecture

Advantages and Disadvantages of Client-Server Architecture

Here we discuss the advantage and disadvantage of client server architecture

Advantages

- Data management is much easier because the files are in one location. This allows fast backups and efficient error management. There are multiple levels of permissions, which can prevent users from doing damage to files.
- The server hardware is designed to serve requests from clients quickly. All the data are processed on the server, and only the results are returned to the client. This reduces the amount of network traffic between the server and the client machine, improving network performance.
- Thin client architectures allow a quick replacement of defect clients, because all data and applications are on the server.

Disadvantages

- Client-Server-Systems are very expensive and need a lot of maintenance.
- The server constitutes a single point of failure. If failures on the server occur, it is possible that the system suffers heavy delay or completely breaks down, which can potentially block hundreds of clients from working with their data or their applications. Within companies high costs could accumulate due to server downtime.
- Several variations is there in Peer-to-Peer and Client-Server Architecture, with considering factors such as:
  - Multiple servers and caches
  - Mobile code and mobile agents
  - Low-cost computers at the users' side - mobile devices

1.8.2 Fundamental Models

- In this section, we discuss models based on the fundamental properties that allow us to be more specific about their characteristics and the failure and security risks of the distributed system.
- Basically there are three types of fundamental models
  - Interaction model
  - Failure model
  - Security model.

(1) Interaction Model:

- Incremental model deals with performance and with the difficulty of setting time limits in a distributed system, e.g. message delivery. The distributed systems are composed of many processes, interacting in complex-way.

- Example: Multiple server processes may cooperate with one another to provide a service. The Domain Name Service (DNS) partitions and replicates its data at servers throughout the Internet. A set of Peer processes may cooperate with one another to achieve a common goal.

Performance of Communication Channels:

- If we want to communicate over a network then you have to consider the following performance characteristics:

    (a) Latency,

    (b) Bandwidth and

    (c) Jilter.

(a) Latency:

- Latency is nothing but the delay between the start of a message's transmission from one process of the beginning of its receipt by another is referred to as 'Latency'.

- It includes the time taken for the first of a string of bits transmitted through a network to reach its destination. e.g. The latency for the transmission of a message through a satellite link is the time for a radio signal to travel to the satellite and back.

- The delay in accessing the network, which increase significantly when the network is heavily loaded.

- The time taken by the OS communication services at both the sending and receiving processes, which varies according to the current load on the operating systems.

(b) Bandwidth:

- Bandwidth is nothing but it is the total amount of information that can be transmitted over it in a given time. When a larger number of communication channels are using the same network, they have to share the available bandwidth.

(c) Jilter:

- Jilter is the variation in the time taken to deliver a series of messages. Example: if consecutive samples of audio data are played with differing time intervals then the sound will be badly dlstorted.

Clock Timing Events:

- In distributed system every computer has its own internal clock, which can be used by local processes to obtain the value of the current time. So, two processes running on different computers can associate timestamps with their event.

- However, even if two processes read their clocks at the same time, their local clocks may supply different time values.

- This is because computer clocks drift from perfect time and more importantly, there drift rates differ from one another.

- The clock drift rate means relative amount that a computer clock differs from a perfect reference clock.

- Computer may use radio receivers to get time readings from the global positioning system with an accuracy of about 1 μ-second. But GPS receivers do not operate inside buildings, nor can the cost be justified for every computer.

- Instead a computer that has an accurate time source such as GPS can send timing messages to other computers in the network.

- It is difficult to set time limits on the time taken for process execution, message delivery or clock drift, so we use two models (systems).

   (1) Synchronous distributed system.

   (2) Asynchronous distributed system.

- First system provides strong assumption of time and in second system there are no assumptions about time.

Synchronous Distributed System:

- Synchronous distributed system is system in which following restriction are defined:

   (1) The time to execute each step of a process has known lower and upper bounds.

   (2) Each process has local clock whose drift rate from real time has known bound.

   (3) Each message transmitted over a channel is received within a known bounded time.

- It is not possible to get real values of upper and lower bounds for process execution time, message delay and clock drift rate in distributed system and if we are not get real-value then any design based on these values are not reliable, but we get idea of design will be have in real distributed system.

- In synchronous system it is possible to use timeouts.

Asynchronous Distributed System:

- There are many distributed systems that are very useful without being able to qualify as synchronous systems. e.g. Internet, such system is called Asynchronous Distributed system.

In this system there are no restrictions on

(a) Process Execution Speeds:

- There is no restriction on process execution speed, one process may require less time and other may require more time.

(b) Message Transmission Delays:

- There is no restriction on message transmission delay e.g. any message from process A to process B may be delivered within a few time or may require several time.

(c) Clock-Drift Rates:

- There is no restriction on drift rate of clock.

- In Asynchronous model we can assume the time intervals for any execution. e.g. Internet, in this there is no bound on server or Network load. So, it is not conform how long it takes i.e. if we want to transfer a file, then sometime it require time and sometime is transfer within a short time.

  Actual distributed system is Asynchronous because of the need for processes to share the processors and for communication channels to share the network.

(d) Ordering of Events:

- Some time, you don't know whether an event (sending or receiving message) at one process occurred before, after or concurrently with another event at another process. The execution of system is described in terms of events and ordering of events is important.

(2) Failure Model:

- Here we discuss the failure model of distributed system. In a distributed system both processes and communication channels may fail. The failure model finds the ways in which failure may occur in order to provide an understanding of the effects of failures in distributed system.

- Failures are of following types

  (a) Omission failure

  (b) Arbitrary failure

  (c) Timing failure

(a) Omission Failure:

- In omission failure when a process or communication channels fails to perform actions that it is supposed to do then such fault/failure is under omission failure. When we say process is crashed it means it is halted and it is not executed further.

- The processes either function correctly or else stop other processes may be able to detect such type of crash in the processes.

- The process crash is called 'fail-stop' if other processes can detect certainly that the process has crashed. This 'fail-stop' behaviour can be produced in a synchronous system if the processes use timeouts to detect when other processes fail to respond and messages are guaranteed to be delivered.

- Here we take example if processes 'A' and 'B' are programmed for 'B' to reply to a message from 'A', and if process 'A' has received no-reply from process 'B' in a maximum time measured on 'A's local clock, then process 'A' may conclude that process 'B' has fail.

- There may be failures in communication also, Example:

- Consider there are two processes 'A' and 'B' and 'A' want to send message to the process 'B' and message which 'A' want to send is stored in 'outgoing message buffer' of 'A', and process 'B' receives the message from 'A' and it is present in 'incoming message buffer' of B.

- This message transfer operation is done through communication channel. Fig. 1.8 below shoes the above description.

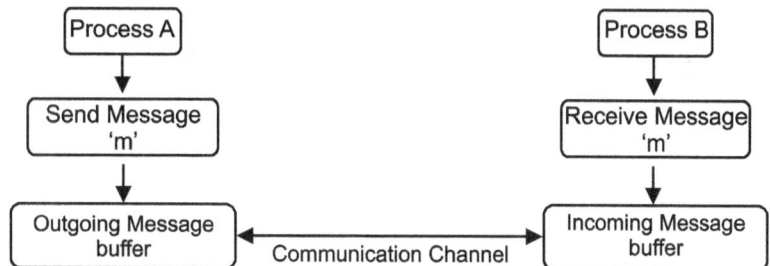

Fig. 1.8 : Communication between processes

- Communication channel produce omition-failure if it does not transfer a message from 'A' to 'B'. This failure is called as 'dropping messages'.

- The reason of such type of failure is the lack of buffer space at the receiver side or at the interviewing gateway, or Network transmission error.

- The loss of messages between the sending process and the outgoing message buffer is called a 'send-omission failures'.

- The loss of massages between the incoming message buffer and the receiving process is called 'receive omission failures' and the loss of message between outgoing message buffer and incoming message buffer is called 'channel omission failure'.

(b) Arbitrary Failure:

- Arbitrary failure means any worst possible failure, in this any type of error may occur. Example: Process may send or receive wrong value in it data items. Arbitrary failure cannot detect easily.

- In communication channel arbitrary failure may occur. Example: Message contents may be corrupted or message may be delivered more than one time or wrong message/non-existent message may be delivered.

- The communication software is used to avoid such type of arbitrary failure in communication channels, this software recognize the failure and reject the faulty messages.

(c) Timing Failure:

- Timing failures occurs in synchronous distributed system because in this there is time limit on process execution time, message delivery time and clock drift rate.

- In Asynchronous distributed system, an overloaded server may respond very slowly, but we cannot say that it has a timing-failure. If we want to transfer video-information or any video then we require a very large amount of data to be transferred and to deliver such information without timing failure can make very special demands on both the operating system and the communication system.

(3) Security Model:

- Now we move towards the security related issues of distributed system where we can achieve the security in distributed system by securing the processes and the channels used for their interactions. We can also give protection to the objects so it cannot be access by unauthorized access.

- The object can be used to hold the data of different users.

- Take an example that some object may hold users private data such as mailbox or policy details or some object may hold shared data such as web pages, community etc you have to provide access-rights to different users i.e. some users may access this object but some are not or some users may read data but cannot modify etc.

- Users in this model is having their own authority, it is called 'principal'. Fig. 1.9 (a) below shows object and principals. In this Fig. 1.9 (a) invocation come from user/client and server gives the result back to user/client.

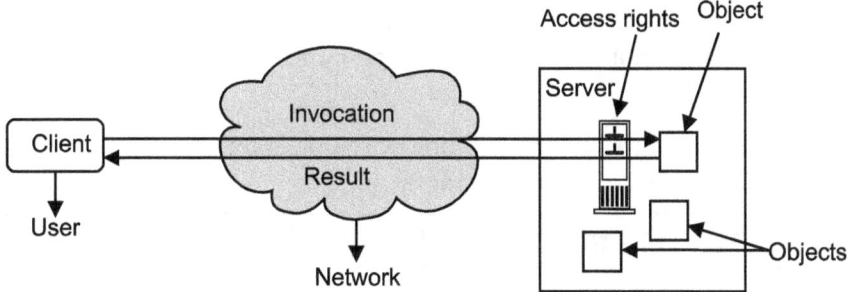

Fig. 1.9 (a) : Object and principals

- The server is responsible for verifying the authority or principal of each user or each invocation.

- If two process want to communicate with each other then they send message, this message is transfer through network and communication services, but these are the open so there must be possibility of attacks on the sending message but if the message is important and they want security e.g. messages related to financial transaction, online banking, online shopping etc then there may be problem.

- Such attacks are called 'enemy', these enemy is capable of sending any message to any process and reading or copying any message between a pair of processes.

Fig. 1.9 (b) below shows such enemy.

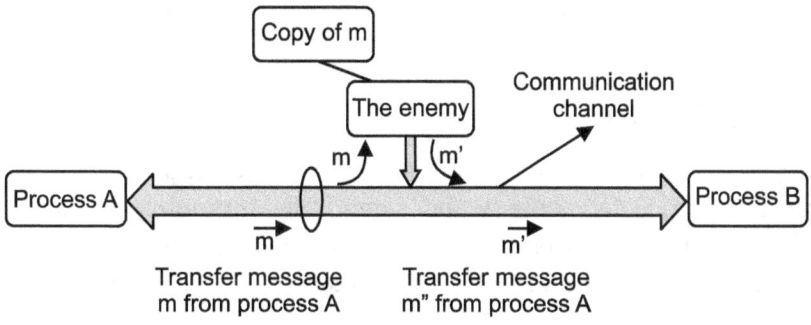

Fig. 1.9 (b) : Attack of enemy

- As shown in Fig. 1.9 (b), the attack of enemy is possible by using computer connected to a network to run a program that reads network messages addressed to other computer on the network.

- The attacks come from computers which are connected to network in unauthorized manner.

- When any process receives a message from any other process then it cannot necessarily determine the identity of the sender.

- Communication protocol such as 'IP' includes the address of the source computer in each message, but it is not difficult for any enemy to generate a message with a frode source address.

- There may be different attacks possible on communication channel; you can avoid these attacks by using the concept of cryptography.

1.9 CASE STUDY: THE WORLD WIDE WEB

- WWW stands for World Wide Web, and it is an advanced information retrieval system. Currently it is in an experimental stage, but it is being developed fastly. WWW supports information like pictures, graphs, colors, and fonts, if the user's device supports them. Voice can also be delivered, if the user's device has a sound generator.

- The important and basic part of the WWW is hypertext, which means, among other things, that when the user is navigating on the information he can pick up an interesting word or expression within a text and request for more information about it.

- Web applications become the one of the largest growth areas in software. Web applications not only offer us new types of applications, but also provide an entirely new way to set up software applications to the users.

- Web applications use a number of languages, technologies, and programming models to implement highly interactive applications. As the modern Web applications are complicated, interactive programs with complex GUIs and numerous back-end software components, the analyzing, modeling and testing these applications present a number of new challenges to software developers and researchers. Web applications are much complex than simple HTML Web pages, and consist of more than just the front-end graphical user interfaces that users see.

- A Web site is a collection of Web pages and linked software components which are associated semantically by content and syntatically through links and other control systems. Web sites may be dynamic and interactive. A Web application is a program that runs in whole or in part on one or more Web servers which is run by users through a Web site.

- Many people use the terms Internet and World Wide Web (the Web) interchangeably, but in fact the two terms are not synonymous. The Internet and the Web are two separate but related things.

- The Internet is a massive network of networks, a networking infrastructure. It connects millions of computers together globally, forming a network in which any computer can communicate with any other computer as long as they are both connected to the Internet.

- Information that travels over the Internet does so via a variety of languages known as protocols.

- The World Wide Web, or simply Web, is a way of accessing information over the medium of the Internet. It is an information-sharing model that is built on top of the Internet.

- The Web uses the HTTP protocol, only one of the languages spoken over the Internet, to transmit data. Web services, which use HTTP to allow applications to communicate in order to exchange business logic, use the Web to share information.

- The Web also utilizes browsers, such as Internet Explorer or Firefox, to access Web documents called Web pages that are linked to each other via hyperlinks. Web documents also contain graphics, sounds, text and video.

- The Web is just one of the ways that information can be disseminated over the Internet. The Internet, not the Web, is also used for e-mail, which relies on SMTP, Usenet news groups, instant messaging and FTP. So the Web is just a portion of the Internet, but the two terms are not synonymous and should not be confused.

HTML:

- HTML is a language for describing web pages. HTML stands for Hyper Text Markup Language HTML is not a programming language, it is a markup language. A markup language is a set of markup tags ,HTML uses markup tags to describe web pages.

- HTML markup tags are usually called HTML tags ,it is keywords surrounded by angle brackets like <html> ,it normally come in pairs like <b> and </b>.The first tag in a pair is the start tag, the second tag is the end tag. Start and end tags are also called opening tags and closing tags.

- HTML documents describe web pages, it contain HTML tags and plain text It is also called web pages.

- The purpose of a web browser (like Internet Explorer or Firefox) is to read HTML documents and display them as web pages. The browser does not display the HTML tags, but uses the tags to interpret the content of the page.

- The text between <html> and </html> describes the web page. The text between <body> and </body> is the visible page content. The text between <h1> and </h1> is displayed as a heading, The text between <p> and </p> is displayed as a paragraph.

HTML Elements:

An HTML element is everything from the start tag to the end tag:

Start Tag	Element Content	End Tag
<p>	This is a paragraph	</p>
<a href="default.htm" >	This is a link	</a>

- The start tag is often called the opening tag. The end tag is often called the closing tag. An HTML element starts with a start tag / opening tag and ends with an end tag / closing tag.

The element content is everything between the start and the end tag. Some HTML elements have empty content. Empty elements are closed in the start tag. Most HTML elements can have attributes. Most HTML elements can be nested

Example:

```
<html>
<body>
<p>This is my first paragraph.</p>
</body>
</html>
```

The example contains 3 HTML elements.

(1) The <p> element:

```
<p>This is my first paragraph.</p>
```

The <p> element defines a paragraph in the HTML document. It has start tag <p> and an end tag </p>. The element content is: This is my first paragraph.

(2) The <body> element:

```
<body>
<p>This is my first paragraph.</p>
</body>
```

The <body> element defines the body of the HTML document. It has a start tag <body> and an end tag </body>.The element content is another HTML element(<p> and </p>).

(3) The <html> element:

```
<html>
<body>
<p>This is my first paragraph.</p>
</body>
</html>
```

The <html> element defines the whole HTML document. It has a start tag <html> and an end tag </html>.The element content is another HTML element (the body element).

1.9.1 Hypertext Transfer Protocol

- **Hypertext Transfer Protocol (HTTP)** is an application-level protocol for distributed, collaborative, hypermedia information systems. Its use for retrieving inter-linked resources, called hypertext documents

- There are two major versions, HTTP/1.0 that uses a separate connection for every document and HTTP/1.1 that can reuse the same connection to download, for instance, images for the just served page. Hence HTTP/1.1 may be faster as it takes time to set up the connections.

- The standards development of HTTP has been coordinated by the World Wide Web consortium and the Internet Engineering Task Force (IETF), culminating in the publication of a series of Requests for Comments (RFCs. HTTP is a request/response standard as is typical in client-server computing.

- A client is the application (web browser, spider) or computer used by an end-user, the server is the computer hosting a web site.

- The client submitting HTTP requests is referred to as the *user agent*. The responding server which stores or creates *resources* such as HTML files and images is called the *origin server*. In between the user agent and origin server may be several intermediaries, such as proxies, gateways, and tunnels.

- HTTP is not constrained in principle to using TCP/IP, although this is its most popular application via the Internet.

- Indeed HTTP can be "implemented on top of any other protocol on the Internet, or on other networks." HTTP only presumes a reliable transport; any protocol that provides such guarantees can be used."

- Resources to be accessed by HTTP are identified using Uniform Resource Identifiers (URIs) or, more specifically, Uniform Resource Locators (URLs).

Getting the Web Page

- When you open up a browser and request a web page (either by setting a default page or by entering a Uniform Resource Locater or URL), the first thing that happens is that the browser relies upon the operating system to resolve the host name in the URL to an IP address.

- Normally this is done via a DNS (Domain Name System) query over UDP (User Datagram Protocol) on port 53. However, if the host is listed in the local hosts file, the operating system will not make a DNS query.

- When the IP address is obtained, the browser will attempt to open a TCP (Transmission Control Protocol) connection to the web server, usually on port 80. Once the TCP connection is made, the browser will issue an HTTP request to the server using the connection.

- The request comprises a header section, and possibly a body section (this is where things like POST data go).

- Once the request is sent, the browser will wait for the response. When the web server has assembled the response, it is sent back to the browser for rendering.

Overall Operation

- In this section we discuss the basic operation of HTTP. The HTTP protocol is based on a request/response paradigm.

- A client make a connection with a server and sends a request to the server in the form of a request method, URI, and protocol version, followed by a MIME-like message containing request modifiers, client information, and possible body content.

- The server responds with a status line, including the message's protocol version and a success or error code, followed by a MIME-like message containing server information, entity met information, and possible body content.

- Most HTTP communication is invoked by a user agent and consists of a request to be applied to a resource on some origin server. In the simplest case, this may be accomplished via a single connection (v) between the User Agent (UA) and the Origin Server (O).

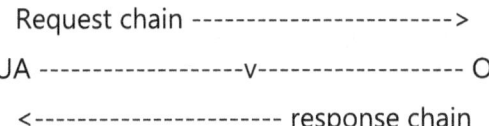

```
Request chain ----------------------->
UA ------------------v------------------ O
      <---------------------- response chain
```

- A more complicated situation occurs when one or more intermediaries are present in the request/response chain.

- There are three common forms of intermediary: proxy, gateway, and tunnel. A proxy is a forwarding agent, receiving requests for a URI in its absolute form, rewriting all or parts of the message, and forwarding the reformatted request toward the server identified by the URI.

- A gateway is a receiving agent, acting as a layer above some other server(s) and, if necessary, translating the requests to the underlying server's protocol.

- A tunnel acts as a relay point between two connections without changing the messages; tunnels are used when the communication needs to pass through an intermediary (such as a firewall) even when the intermediary cannot understand the contents of the messages.

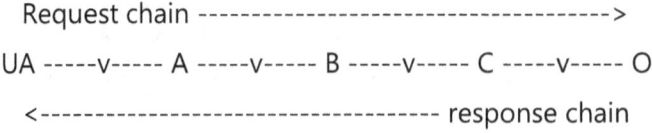

```
Request chain --------------------------------------->
UA -----v----- A -----v----- B -----v----- C -----v----- O
     <------------------------------------- response chain
```

- The example above shows three intermediaries (A, B, and C) between the user agent and origin server. A request or response message that travels the whole chain must pass through four separate connections.

- This distinction is important because some HTTP communication options may apply only to the connection with the nearest, non-tunnel neighbor, only to the end-points of the chain, or to all connections along the chain.

- Although the diagram is linear, each participant may be engaged in multiple, simultaneous communications. For example, B may be receiving requests from many clients other than A, and/or forwarding requests to servers other than C, at the same time that it is handling A's request.

- Any party to the communication which is not acting as a tunnel may employ an internal cache for handling requests.

- The effect of a cache is that the request/response chain is shortened if one of the participants along the chain has a cached response applicable to that request.

- The following illustrates the resulting chain if B has a cached copy of an earlier response from O (via C) for a request which has not been cached by UA or A.

Request chain ---------->

UA -----v----- A -----v----- B - - - - - - C - - - - - - O

<--------- response chain

- Not all responses are cachable, and some requests may contain modifiers which place special requirements on cache behavior. Some HTTP/1.0 applications use heuristics to describe what is or is not a "cachable" response, but these rules are not standardized.

Method Definitions

The set of common methods for HTTP is defined below:

1. **GET**

- The GET method means retrieves whatever information is identified by the Request-URI. If the Request URI refers to a data-producing process, it is the produced data which shall be returned as the entity in the response and not the source text of the process, unless that text happens to be the output of the process.

- The GET method changes to a "conditional GET" if the request message includes an If-Modified-Since header field. A conditional GET method requests that the identified resource be transferred only if it has been modified since the date given by the If-Modified-Since header.

- The conditional GET method is intended to reduce network usage by allowing cached entities to be refreshed without requiring multiple requests or transferring unnecessary data.

2. HEAD

- The HEAD method is same as a GET except that the server must not return any Entity-Body in the response. The meta information contained in the HTTP headers in response to a HEAD request should be identical to the information sent in response to a GET request.

- This method can be used for obtaining meta information about the resource identified by the Request-URI without transferring the Entity-Body itself.

- This method is often used for testing hypertext links for validity, accessibility, and recent modification.

- There is no "conditional HEAD" request analogous to the conditional GET. If an If-Modified-Since header field is included with a HEAD request, it should be ignored.

3. POST

- The POST method is used to request that the destination server accept the entity enclosed in the request as a new subordinate of the resource identified by the Request-URI in the Request-Line.

- POST is designed to allow a uniform method to cover the following functions:

Release the Existing Resources:

- Posting a message to a bulletin board, newsgroup, mailing list, or similar group of articles; Providing a block of data, such as the result of submitting a form, to a data-handling process;

Extending a Database through an Append Operation.

- The actual function performed by the POST method is determined by the server and is usually dependent on the Request-URI.

- The posted entity is subordinate to that URI in the same way that a file is subordinate to a directory containing it, a news article is subordinate to a newsgroup to which it is posted, or a record is subordinate to a database.

- A successful POST does not require that the entity be created as a resource on the origin server or made accessible for future reference.

- That is, the action performed by the POST method might not result in a resource that can be identified by a URI.

- In this case, either 200 (ok) or 204 (no content) is the appropriate response status, depending on whether or not the response includes an entity that describes the result.

Uniform Resource Locator (URL)

- URL stands for Uniform Resource Locator, which means it is a uniform way to locate a resource (file or document) on the Internet.

- The URL specifies the address of a file and every file on the Internet has a unique address. Web software, such as your browser, uses the URL to retrieve a file from the computer on which it resides.

- The actual URL is a set of four numbers separated by periods. An example of this would be 202.147.23.8 but as these are difficult for humans to use, addresses are represented in alphanumeric form that is more descriptive and easy to remember.

- Thus, the URL of my site which is URL 209.164.80.192 can also be written as www.simplygraphix.com.

- The Internet Domain Name System translates the alphanumerical address to numeric.

Format of a URL:

Protocol://site address/path/filename

For example, the URL of my company site is:

http://www.abc.com/

And a typical page on this site would be:

http://www.abc.com/xyc/4.html

The above URL consists of:

- Protocol: **http**
- Host computer name: **www**
- Domain name: **abc**
- Domain type: **com**
- Path: **/xyc**
- File name **4.html**

Protocols

In addition to the http protocol (mentioned above), there are a few other protocols on the Internet.

- **File:** Enables a hyperlink to access a file on a local system.
- **FTP:** Used to download files from remote machines.
- **Gopher:** Helps in accessing a gopher server.
- **mailto:** Calls SMTP (the Simple Mail Transport Protocol) and enables a hyperlink to send an addressed email message.
- **News:** helps in accessing a USENET newsgroup.
- **Telnet:** Provides the means for a hyperlink to open a telnet session on a remote computer.

Site Address

The site address consists of the host computer name, the domain name and the domain type. The domain name should be descriptive for easy comprehension and is usually the name of the organization or company. There are various domain types. Some of them are listed below:

com: Specifies commercial entities.

net: Highlights networks or network providers.

org: Organizations (usually non-profit).

edu: Colleges and universities (education providers).

gov: Government agencies.

mil: Military entities of the United States of America.

The general format of such URLs is:

Machine Name.Domain Name.Domain Type. Country code.

This represents a more localized domain name. The country code is a two-letter extension standardized by the International Standards Organization as ISO 3166. Some country codes are given below:

in: India

de: Germany

ca: Canada

jp: Japan

uk: United Kingdom

Domain types can also be different for different countries. For example, an educational site can have the domain name www.school.ac.uk in the United Kingdom. Thus **ac** (academic) is used instead of **edu**. Similarly **com** is represented as **co** for Indian domain names.

Path Name

Path name specifies the hierarchic location of the said file on the computer. For instance, in http://www.simplygraphix.com/portfolio/4.html the file **4.html** is located in **portfolio** subdirectory under the server root directory.

Port

Browsers communicate with the server using entry points called ports. Associated with each protocol is a default port number, such as HTTP defaults to port 80.

The server administrator can configure the server to handle http requests at a different port. In such cases, the port number has to be supplied as a part of the URL. The port number is placed at the end of the URL after a colon.

Example: : www.some-address.com:50

HTML Anchors

HTML anchor is basically used to specify anchors within files. These anchors are end points to hyperlinks placed either in the same file or some other files. Anchors are placed to link to specific locations in a file. They can be a part of the URL and are represented with a hash symbol (#) followed by the link name.

www.some-address.com/some-file.html#some-location

Web Services: Purpose of the Web Service Architecture

The basic purpose of the Web services is to provide a standard means of interoperating between different software applications, running on a variety of platforms and/or frameworks. The (WSA) is intended to provide a common definition of a Web service, and define its place within a larger Web services framework to guide the community. The WSA provides a conceptual model and a context for understanding Web services and the relationships between the components of this model.

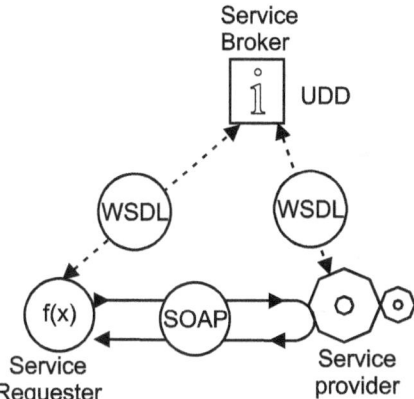

Fig. 1.10: Web services architecture.

The Web services architecture is interoperability architecture: it identifies those global elements of the global Web services network that are required in order to ensure interoperability between Web services.

What is a Web Service?

Definition: A Web service is a software system designed to support interoperable machine-to-machine interaction over a network. It has an interface described in a machine-processable format (specifically WSDL). Other systems interact with the Web service in a manner prescribed by its description using SOAP messages, typically conveyed using HTTP with an XML serialization in conjunction with other Web-related standards.

Agents and Services

A Web service that must be implemented by a concrete agent. The agent is the concrete piece of software or hardware that sends and receives messages, while the service is the resource characterized by the abstract set of functionality that is provided. To illustrate this distinction, you might implement a particular Web service using one agent one day (perhaps written in one programming language), and a different agent the next day (perhaps written in a different programming language) with the same functionality. Although the agent may have changed, the Web service remains the same.

Requesters and Providers

The purpose of a Web service is to provide some functionality on behalf of its owner a person or organization, such as a business or an individual. The *provider entity* is the person or organization that provides an appropriate agent to implement a particular service.

A *requester entity* is a person or organization that wishes to make use of a provider entity's Web service. It will use a *requester agent* to exchange messages with the provider entity's *provider agent*. In most cases, the requester agent is the one to initiate this message exchange, though not always. Nonetheless, for consistency we still use the term "requester agent" for the agent that interacts with the provider agent, even in cases when the provider agent actually initiates the exchange.

Web Service Process

In this section we study the basic web service process basically there are many ways that a requester entity might engage and use a Web service. In general, the followingbroad steps are required, as illustrated in Fig. 1.11.

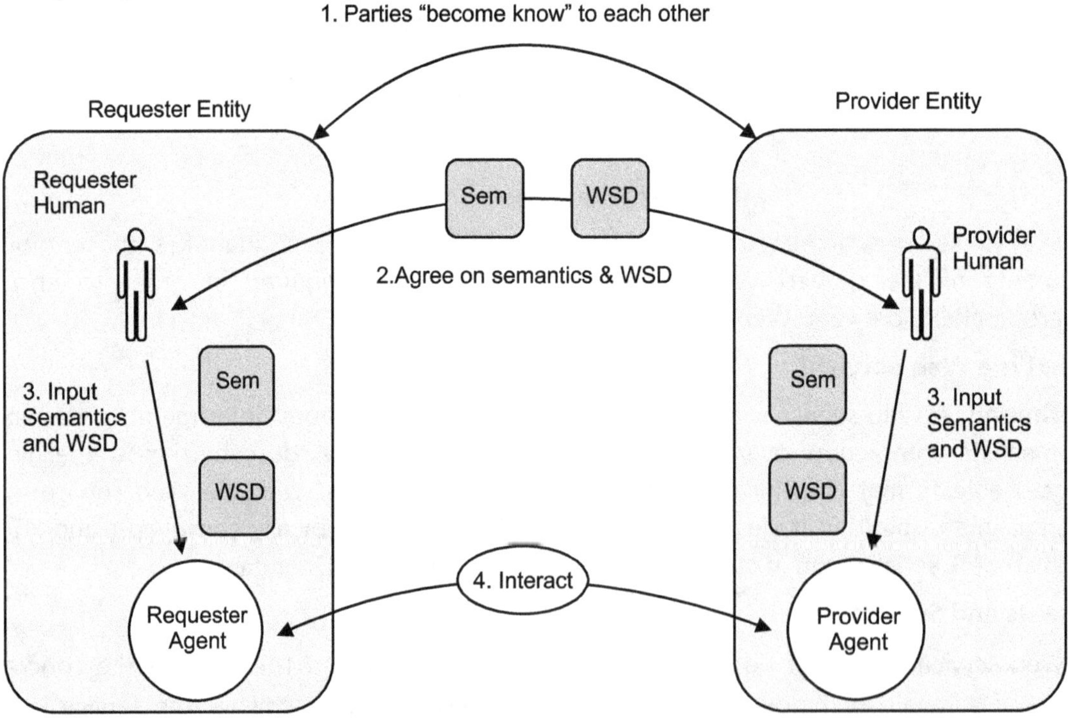

Fig. 1.11: The general process of a web service

- The requester and provider entities become known to each other (or at least one becomes known to the other);

- The requester and provider entities somehow agree on the service description and semantics that will govern the interaction between the requester and provider agents;

- The service description and semantics are realized by the requester and provider agents; and

- The requester and provider agents exchange messages, thus performing some task on behalf of the requester and provider entities.

REVIEW QUESTIONS

1. Give an example implementation of an object reference such as Java code that allows a client to bind to a transient remote object.

   Ans:

   - Using Java, we can express such an implementation as the following class:

```
public class Object3reference {

InetAddress server3address; // network address of object's server

int server3endpoint; // endpoint to which server is listening

int object3identifier; // identifier for this object

URL client3code; // (remote) file containing client side stub

byte[] init3data; // possible additional initialization data

}
```

   - The object reference should at least contain the transport level address of the server where the object resides. We also need an object identifier as the server may contain several objects.

   - For implementation, we use either a URL to refer to a (remote) file containing all the necessary client-side code. A generic array of bytes is used to contain further initialization data for that code. Or directly put the client code into the reference instead of a URL.

2. How would you incorporate persistent asynchronous communication into a model of communication based on RMIs to remote objects?

Ans. An RMI should be asynchronous, that is, no immediate results are expected at invocation time. Moreover, an RMI should be stored at a special server that will forward it to the object as soon as the latter is up and running in an object server.

3. Would it make sense to limit the number of threads in a server process?

Ans. Yes, for two reasons.

(a) First, threads require memory for setting up their own private stack. Consequently, having many threads may consume too much memory for the server to work properly.

(b) Another, more serious reason, is that, to an operating system, independent threads tend to operate in a chaotic manner. In a virtual memory system it may be difficult to build a relatively stable working set, resulting in many page faults and thus I/O. Having many threads may thus lead to a performance degradation resulting from page thrashing.

4. Distinguish between the client server and peer - to - peer models of distributed systems.

5. Highlights desirable features of good distributed file system. List the functions of distributed file system.

6. What is the difference between distributed operating system and network operating system?

7. Explain different types of system models in a Distributed System.

8. Explain different transparencies in distributed system with suitable examples.

9. Enlist and discuss different failure models.

10. Explain different scalability techniques in distributed system.

11. Explain what transparency in a Distributed System, and give examples of different forms of transparency.

12. Use the World Wide Web as an example to illustrate the concept of resource sharing, client and server.

13. What is the role of middleware in a distributed system?

14. What is an open distributed system and what benefits does openness provide?

15. Explain in brief different challenges in designing distributed systems.

16. Explain different scalability techniques in distributed system.

UNIVERSITY QUESTIONS

May 2012

1. Following are the classical set of assumptions made by developers   in distributed systems. **[8]**

   (i)   The network is reliable.   (ii) Latency is zero.

   (iii) Bandwidth is infinite.   (iv) The network is secure.

   Discuss why these assumptions maybe wrong. Justify these assumptions may not always true while designing the real distributed systems.

2. List the main software components that may fail when a client process invokes a method in a server object. Suggest how the components can be made to tolerate one another's failures? **[8]**

Oct. 2012

3. Show an example of transparency that may not be desirable in distributed systems. **[8]**

4. Why is a process pool an attractive model from the view point of distributed computation and transparency? **[8]**

5. What are the advantages and disadvantages of using diskless work stations in a distributed system? **[8]**

6. What is distributed system? Explain different examples of distributed system. **[8]**

May 2013

7. Describe architecture model of the Distributed System design. How these models play important roles in the design of a Distributed System. **[8]**

8. When a Distributed System can be considered as an Open Distributed System?

   Mention benefits provided by an Open System. **[8]**

Dec. 2013

9. What is distributed system? Explain three fundamental models that help to reveal key problems for the designers of distributed systems. **[8]**

10. Compare distributed operating system, network operating system and middleware systems. **[8]**

11. Write a short note on scalability and transparency of a distributed system.   **[8]**

12. Describe Internet as a Distributed system. Explain working of World Wide Web in detail.   **[8]**

May 2014

13. Compare migration transparency and relocation transparency.   **[4]**

14. Explain challenge of heterogeneity in Distributed System and how it is overcome?   **[8]**

15. Write a short note on various failure models.   **[6]**

16. Explain Peer-to-Peer Architecture and its advantages.   **[4]**

17. Give different types of hardware resources and data or software resources that can be shared. Give examples of their sharing as it occurs in Distributed System.   **[8]**

18. Define Distributed System. List advantages and disadvantages of the same.   **[6]**

Dec. 2014

19. Describe the working of Distributed system based upon middleware software system. Also clearly describe the role played by middleware in Distributed system.   **[9]**

20. Describe various architectural models and their variations with suitable examples.   **[9]**

21. Compare Distributed System versus Centralized Systems.   **[9]**

22. What are types of failures? Classify the following failures based on types of failures with justification.   **[9]**

    (i)   Sudden shutdown of a system

    (ii) Network crash

    (iii) System reset while working

    (iv) Unnoticed event handler closing a word document

23. Define and explain following along with one application of it. Synchronous Distributed Systems.   **[8]**

May 2015

24. Describe architecture model of Distributed System design. How these models play important role in the design of a distributed system.   **[9]**

25. Discuss different challenges in designing distributed system.   **[9]**

26. What is failure model ? Explain different failures in detail.   **[9]**

✠ ✠ ✠

COMMUNICATION

2.1 INTRODUCTION

- This unit is concerned with the distinctiveness of protocols for communication between processes in a distributed system i.e., interprocess communication.

- Interprocess communication in the Internet provides both datagram and stream communication.

- The Java APIs for these are presented, together with a argument of their failure models.

- They provide substitute building blocks for communication protocols.

- This is complemented by a learning of protocols for the representation of collections of data objects in messages and of references to remote objects.

- Together, these services offer support for the construction of higher-level communication services.

2.2 THE API FOR THE INTERNET PROTOCOLS

2.2.1 The Characteristics of Interprocess Communication

- Message passing between a pair of processes can be supported by two message communication operations, *send* and *receive*, defined in terms of destinations and messages.

- To communicate, one process sends a message to a destination and another process at the destination receives the message.

- This activity may involve the synchronization of the two processes.

1. **Synchronous and Asynchronous Communication**

- **Synchronous Communication:** It is the form of communication, the sending and receiving processes synchronize at every message. In this case, both send and receive are blocking operations. Whenever as end is issued the sending process (or thread) is blocked until the corresponding receive is issued. Whenever a receive is issued by a process (or thread), it blocks until a message arrives.

- **Asynchronous Communication:** The use of the send operation is non blocking in that the sending process is allowed to proceed as soon as the message has been copied to a local buffer, and the transmission of the message proceeds in parallel with the sending process. The receive operation can have blocking and non-blocking variants. In the non-blocking variant, the receiving process proceeds with its program after issuing a receive operation, which provides a buffer to be filled in the background, but it must separately receive notification that its buffer has been filled, by polling or interrupt.

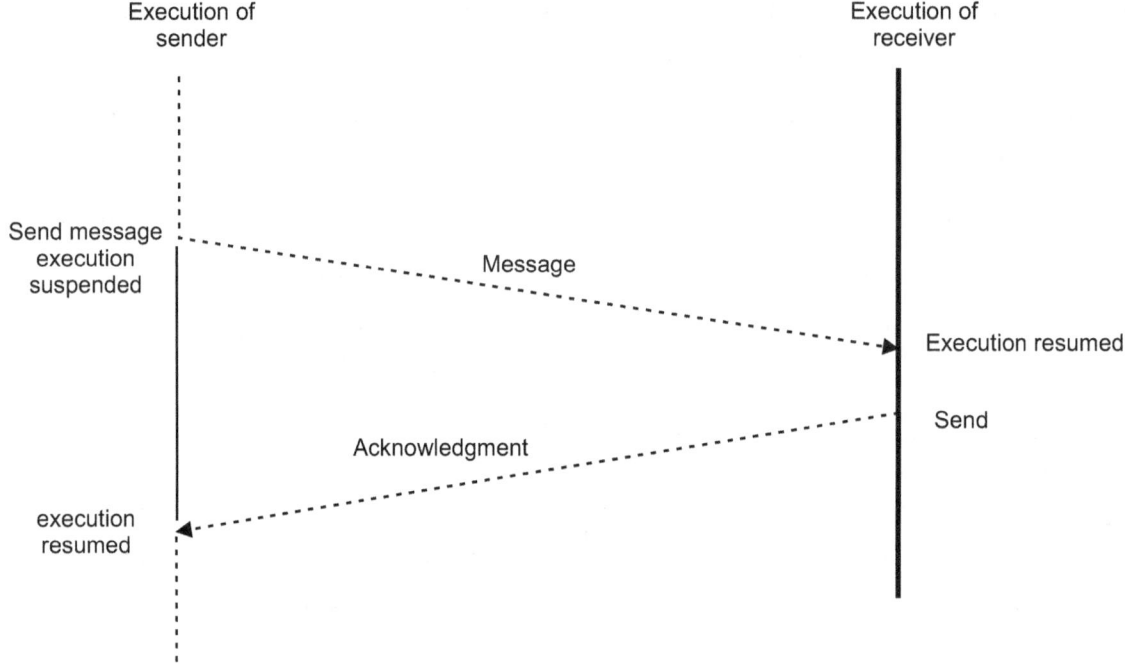

Fig. 2.1: Synchronization mode

2. Message Destinations

A local port is a message destination within a computer, specified as an integer. A port has exactly one receiver but can have many senders. Processes may use multiple ports to receive messages. Any process that knows the number of a port can send a message to it. Servers generally publicize their port numbers for use by clients.

3. Reliability

A point-to-point message service can be described as reliable if messages are certain to be delivered in spite of a 'reasonable' number of packets being dropped or lost. In compare, a point-to-point message service can be described as unreliable if messages are not assured to be delivered in the face of even a single packet dropped or lost. For integrity, messages must arrive uncorrupted and without duplication.

4. Ordering

Some applications require that messages be delivered in sender order – that is, the order in which they were transmitted by the sender. The delivery of messages out of sender order is regarded as a failure by such applications.

2.2.2 Sockets   [May 2010, 14]

Both forms of communication (UDP and TCP) use the socket abstraction, which provides an endpoint for communication between processes. Interprocess communication consists of transmitting a message between a socket in one process and a socket in another process. For a process to receive messages, its socket must be bound to a local port and one of the Internet addresses of the computer on which it runs. Messages sent to a particular Internet address and port number can be received only by a process whose socket is associated with that Internet address and port number. Processes may use the same socket for sending and receiving messages

2.2.3 Java API for Internet Addresses

- As the IP packets underlying UDP and TCP are sent to Internet addresses, Java provides a class, Inet Address that represents Internet addresses. Users of this class refer to computers by Domain Name System (DNS) hostnames.

- For example, to get an object representing the Internet address of the host whose DNS name is *flipkart.com*, use:

  ### *Inet Address a Computer = Inet Address. get By Name ("flipkart.com");*

- This method can throw an *Unknown Host Exception*. Note that the user of the class does not need to state the explicit value of an Internet address. In fact, the class encapsulates the details of the representation of Internet addresses.

- Thus the interface for this class is not dependent on the number of bytes needed to represent Internet addresses – 4 bytes in IPv4 and 16 bytes in IPv6.

UDP Datagram Communication

- A datagram sent by UDP is transmitted from a sending process to a receiving process without acknowledgement or retries.

- If a failure occurs, the message may not arrive. A datagram is transmitted between processes when one process sends it and another receives it. To send or receive messages a process must first create a socket bound to an Internet address of the local host and a local port.

- A server will bind its socket to a server port – one that it makes known to clients so that they can send messages to it.

- A client binds its socket to any free local port. The receive method returns the Internet address and port of the sender, in addition to the message, allowing the recipient to send a reply.

- The following are some issues relating to datagram communication

Message Size

- The receiving process needs to specify an array of bytes of a particular size in which to receive a message

Blocking

- Sockets normally provide non-blocking sends and blocking receives for datagram communication (a non-blocking receive is an option in some implementations).

Timeouts

- The receive that blocks forever is suitable for use by a server that is waiting to receive requests from its clients. But in some programs, it is not appropriate that a process that has invoked a receive operation should wait indefinitely in situations where the sending process may have crashed or the expected message may have been lost. To allow for such requirements, timeouts can be set on sockets.

Receive from Any

- The receive method does not specify an origin for messages. Instead, an invocation of receive gets a message addressed to its socket from any origin.

- The receive method returns the Internet address and local port of the sender, allowing the recipient to check where the message came from.

- It is possible to connect a datagram socket to a particular remote port and Internet address, in which case the socket is only able to send messages to and receive messages from that address.

Java API for UDP Datagrams

- The Java API provides datagram communication by means of two classes: Datagram Packet and Datagram Socket.

- **Datagram Packet:** This class provides a constructor that makes an instance out of an array of bytes comprising a message, the length of the message and the Internet address and local port number of the destination socket, as follows:

Datagram Packet

Array of bytes containing message	Length of message	Internet address	Port number

- An instance of Datagram Packet may be transmitted between processes when one process sends it and another receives it.

- This class provides another constructor for use when receiving a message. Its arguments specify an array of bytes in which to receive the message and the length of the array.

- A received message is put in the Datagram Packet together with its length and the Internet address and port of the sending socket.

- The message can be retrieved from the Datagram Packet by means of the method get Data. The methods get Port and get Address access the port and Internet address.

TCP Stream Communication

- The API for stream communication assumes that when a pair of processes are establishing a connection, one of them plays the client role and the other plays the server role, but after that they could be peers.

- The client role engages creating a stream socket bound to any port and then making a connect request asking for a connection to a server at its server port. The server role engrosses creating a listening socket bound to a server port and waiting for clients to request connections.

- The listening socket maintains a queue of incoming connection requests.

- In the socket model, when the server acknowledge a connection, a new stream socket is created for the server to communicate with a client, meanwhile retaining its socket at the server port for listening for connect requests from other clients.

Java API for TCP Streams

- The Java interface to TCP streams is provided in the classes Server Socket and Socket: Server **Socket:** This class is intended for use by a server to create a socket at a server port for listening for connect requests from clients. Its accept method gets a connect request from the queue or, if the queue is empty, blocks until one arrives. The result of executing accept is an instance of Socket: a socket to use for communicating with the client.

2.3 EXTERNAL DATA REPRESENTATION AND MARSHALLING

[MAY 2012, 13]

One of the following methods can be used to enable any two computers to exchange binary data values:

- The values are converted to an agreed external format before transmission and converted to the local form on receipt; if the two computers are known to be the same type, the conversion to external format can be omitted.

- The values are transmitted in the sender's format, together with an indication of the format used, and the recipient converts the values if necessary.

Note, however, that bytes themselves are never altered during transmission. To support RMI or RPC, any data type that can be passed as an argument or returned as a result must be able to be flattened and the individual primitive data values represented in an agreed format. *An agreed standard for the representation of data structures and primitive values is called an external data representation.*

Marshalling is the method of taking a group of data items and assembling them into a form appropriate for transmission in a message. Un marshalling is the process of disassembling them on arrival to make an equivalent collection of data items at the target. Thus marshalling consists of the conversion of structured data items and primitive values into an external data representation. Similarly, un marshalling consists of the creation of primitive values from their external data representation and the restoration of the data structures

Three alternative approaches to external data representation and marshalling are discussed here

- CORBA's common data representation, which is concerned with an external representation for the structured and primitive types that can be passed as the arguments and results of remote method invocations in CORBA. It can be used by a variety of programming languages.

- Java's object serialization, which is concerned with the flattening and external data representation of any single object or tree of objects that may need to be transmitted in a message or stored on a disk. It is for use only by Java.

- XML (Extensible Markup Language), which defines a textual form at for representing structured data. It was originally intended for documents containing textual self-describing structured data.

In the first two cases, the marshalling and un marshalling activities are intended to be carried out by a middleware layer without any involvement on the part of the application programmer. Even in the case of XML, which is textual and therefore more accessible to hand-encoding, software for marshalling and un marshalling is available for all commonly used platforms and programming environments.

2.4 MULTICAST COMMUNICATION

A multicast operation is that sends a single message from one process to each of the members of a group of processes, usually in such a way that the membership of the group is transparent to the sender

Multicast messages provide a useful infrastructure for constructing distributed systems with the following characteristics:

- **Fault Tolerance Based on Replicated Services:** A replicated service consists of a group of servers. Client requests are multicast to all the members of the group, each of which performs an identical operation. Even when some of the member fail, clients can still be served.

- **Better Performance through Replicated Data:** Data are replicated to increase the performance of a service in some cases replicas of the data are placed in users' computers. Each time the data changes, the new value is multicast to the processes managing the replicas.

- **Propagation of Event Notifications:** Multicast to a group may be used to notify processes when something happens. For example, in Facebook, when someone changes their status, all their friends receive notifications. Similarly, publish subscribe protocols may make use of group multicast to disseminate events to subscribers

2.4.1 IP Multicast an Implementation of Multicast Communication

- IP multicast is built over the Internet Protocol (IP). IP multicast permit the sender to transmit a single IP packet to a set of computers that forma multicast group.

- The sender is uninformed of the identities of the individual recipients and of the size of the group. Being a member of a multicast group allows a computer to receive IP packets sent to the group.

- The membership of multicast groups is dynamic, allowing computers to join or leave at any instance and to join an random number of groups. It is possible to send datagrams to a multicast group exclusive of being a member.

- At the application programming level, IP multicast is offered only via UDP. An application program performs multicasts by sending UDP datagrams with multicast addresses and ordinary port numbers.

- It can connect a multicast group by making its socket join the group, enabling it to receive messages to the group.

- At the IP level, a computer belongs to a multicast group when one or more of its processes has sockets that fit into that group. When a multicast message arrives at a computer, copies are forwarded to all of the local sockets that have joined the particular multicast address and are bound to the specified port number. The following details are specific to IPv4:

Multicast Routers: IP packets can be multicast both on a local network and on the wider Internet.

Multicast Address Allocation: Class D addresses (that is, addresses in the range 224.0.0.0 to 239.255.255.255) are reserved for multicast traffic and administer worldwide by the Internet Assigned Numbers Authority (IANA). The management of this address space is reassess yearly. This document defines a partitioning of this address space into a number of blocks, including:

- Local Network Control Block (224.0.0.0 to 224.0.0.225), for multicast traffic within a given local network.

- Internet Control Block (224.0.1.0 to 224.0.1.225).

- Ad Hoc Control Block (224.0.2.0 to 224.0.255.0), for traffic that does not fit any other block.

- Administratively Scoped Block (239.0.0.0 to 239.255.255.255), which is used to implement a scoping mechanism for multicast traffic (to constrain propagation).

2.5 NETWORK VIRTUALIZATION: OVERLAY NETWORKS

- Network virtualization is apprehensive with the construction of many diverse virtual networks over an existing network such as the Internet. Each virtual network can be planned to support a particular distributed application.

- For example, one virtual network might support multimedia streaming, as in BBC iPlayer, BoxeeTV [boxee.tv] or Hulu [hulu.com], and coexist with another that supports a multiplayer online game, both running over the same underlying network.

Overlay Networks

An *overlay network* is a virtual network consisting of nodes and virtual links, which sit on top of an underlying network (such as an IP network) and propose something that is not otherwise provided:

- A service that is customized towards the needs of a class of application or a particular higher-level service for example, multimedia content distribution;

- More efficient operation, in a given networked environment, for example routing in an ad hoc network;

- An additional feature for example, multicast or secure communication.

Overlay Networks have the Following Advantages:

- They facilitate new network services to be defined without requiring changes to the underlying network, a vital point given the level of consistency in this area and the difficulties of modifying underlying router functionality.

- They support testing with network services and the customization of services to particular classes of application.

- Multiple overlays can be defined and can coexist, with the end result being a more open and extensible network architecture.

Disadvantages of Overlay Networks:

- The disadvantages are that overlays introduce an extra level of indirection (and hence may incur a performance penalty) and they add to the complexity of network services when compared, for example, to the relatively simple architecture of TCP/IP networks.

2.6 CASE STUDY: MPI

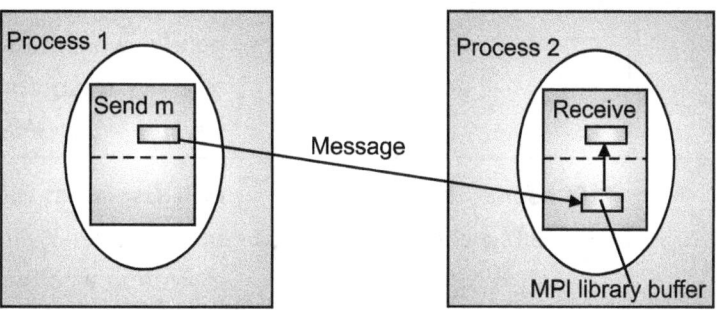

Fig. 2.2: MPI

- In this section, we present a case study of the Message Passing Interface, developed by the high performance computing community.

- MPI was first introduced in 1994 by the MPI Forum [www.mpi-forum.org] as a reaction against the wide variety of proprietary approaches that were in use for message passing in this field.

- The standard has also been strongly influential in Grid computing

- The goal of the MPI Forum was to keep the intrinsic straight forwardness, practicality and efficiency of the message passing approach but improve this with portability in the course of presenting a standardized interface independent of the operating system or programming language-specific socket interface.

- MPI was also designed to be flexible, and the result is a complete specification of message passing in all its variants

- The underlying architectural model for MPI is relatively simple and captured in Fig. 2.2.

- MPI library buffers in both the sender and the receiver, managed by the MPI library and used to hold data in transit. Note that this Fig. 2.2 shows one pathway from the sender to the receiver via the receiver's MPI library buffer (other options, for example using the sender's MPI library buffer, will become apparent below).

- To provide a flavour of this complexity, let us examine a number of the variants of send summarized in table 2.1.

Table 2.1: Selected Send Operations in MPI

Send Operations	Blocking	Non-Blocking
Generic	**MPI_Send**: the sender blocks until it is safe to return	**MPI_Isend**: the call returns immediately and the programmer is given a communication request handle, which can then be used to check the progress of the call via *MPI_Wait*or *MPI_Test*
Synchronous	**MPI_Ssend**: the sender and receiver synchronize and the call only returns when the message has been delivered at the receiving end.	**MPI_Issend**: as with *MPI_Isend*, but with *MPI_Wait*and *MPI_Test* indicating whether the message has been delivered at the receive end
Buffered	**MPI_Bsend**: the sender explicitly allocates an MPI buffer library (using a separate *MPI_Buffer_attach*call) and the call returns when the data is successfully copied into this buffer.	**MPI_Ibsend**: as with *MPI_Isend* but with *MPI_Wait*and *MPI_Test* indicating whether the message has been copied into the sender's MPI buffer and hence is in transit
Ready	**MPI_Rsend**: the call returns when the sender's application buffer can be reused (as with *MPI_Send*), but the programmer is also indicating to the library that the receiver is ready to receive the message, resulting in potential optimization of the underlying implementation.	**MPI_Irsend**: the effect is as with *MPI_Isend*, but as with *MPI_Rsend*, the programmer is indicating to the underlying implementation that the receiver is guaranteed to be ready to receive (resulting in the same optimizations),

2.7 REMOTE INVOCATION   [Dec. 2009, 10, May 2011, 12]

Let us inspect the two most prominent remote invocation techniques for communication in distributed systems:

- **The Remote Procedure Call (RPC):** Approach extends the common programming abstraction of the procedure call to distributed environments, allowing a calling process to call a procedure in a remote node as if it is local.

- **Remote Method Invocation (RMI):** It is similar to RPC but for distributed objects, with added benefits in terms of using object-oriented programming concepts in distributed systems and also extending the concept of an object reference to the global distributed environments, and allowing the use of object references as parameters in remote invocations.

2.7.1 Request-Reply Protocols

- In the normal case, request-reply communication is synchronous because the client process blocks until the reply arrives from the server.

- It can also be reliable because the reply from the server is effectively an acknowledgement to the client.

- Asynchronous request-reply communication is an alternative that may be useful in situations where clients can afford to retrieve replies later.

- The protocol we describe here is based on a trio of communication primitives, *do Operation, get Request* and *send Reply*.

- The *do Operation* method is used by clients to invoke remote operations. Its arguments specify the remote server and which operation to invoke, together with additional information (arguments) required by the operation. Its result is a byte array containing the reply.

- It is assumed that the client calling *do Operation* marshals the arguments into an array of bytes and un marshals the results from the array of bytes that is returned.

- The first argument of *do Operation* is an instance of the class *Remote Ref*, which represents references for remote servers.

- This class provides methods for getting the Internet address and port of the associated server.

- The *do Operation* method sends are quest message to the server whose Internet address and port are specified in the remote reference given as an argument.

- After sending the request message, *do Operation* invokes *receive* to get a reply message, from which it extracts the result and returns it to the caller.

- The caller of *do Operation* is blocked until the server performs the requested operation and transmits a reply message to the client process.

HTTP: An Example of a Request-Reply Protocol

- The Hyper Text Transfer Protocol (HTTP) used by web browser clients to make requests to web servers and to receive replies from them. To recap, web servers manage resources implemented in different ways:

- As data: For example the text of an HTML page, an image or the class of an applet;

- As a Program: For example, servlets [java.sun.com III], or PHP or Python programs that run on the web server.

Client requests specify a URL that includes the DNS hostname of a web server and an optional port number on the web server as well as the identifier of a resource on that server.

HTTP is a protocol that specifies the messages involved in a request-reply exchange, the methods, arguments and results, and the rules for representing(marshalling) them in the messages. It supports a fixed set of methods (*GET, PUT, POST,* etc) that are applicable to all of the server's resources. It is unlike the previously described protocols, where each service has its own set of operations. In addition to invoking methods on web resources, the protocol allows for content negotiation and password-style authentication:

2.8 REMOTE PROCEDURE CALL   [Dec. 2010, 12, May 2012]

2.8.1 Basic Operation

- Here we describe the basic function of RPC; basically there is no architectural support for making remote procedure calls.

- A local procedure call generally involves placing the calling parameters on the stack and executing some form of a *call* instruction to the address of the procedure.

- The procedure can read the parameters from the stack, do its work, place the return value in a register and then return to the address on top of the stack. None of this exists for calling remote procedures.

- We'll have to simulate it all with the tools that we do have, namely local procedure calls and sockets for network communication.

- This simulation makes remote procedure calls a *language level* construct as opposed to sockets, which are an *operating system level construct.*

- This means that our compiler will have to know that remote procedure call invocations need the presence of special code.

- The entire trick in making remote procedure calls work is in the creation of *stub functions* that make it appear to the user that the call is really local.

- A stub function looks like the function that the user intends to call but really contains code for sending and receiving messages over a network.

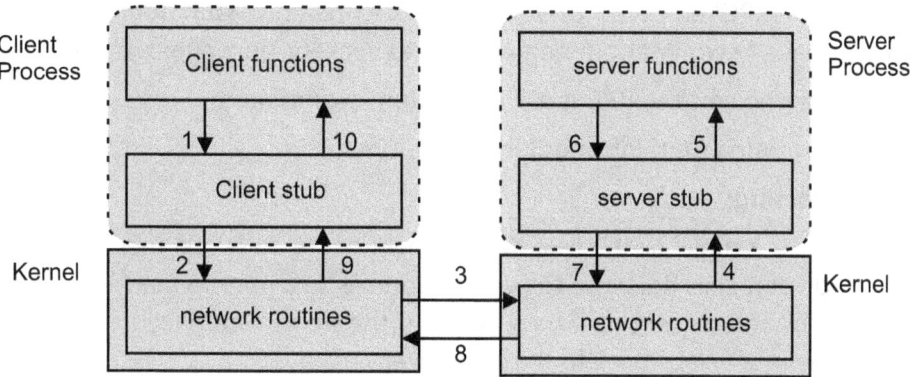

Fig. 2.3 (a): Functional steps in a remote procedure call

Functional Steps in a Remote Procedure Call is as Fallow

- The client calls a local procedure, called the *client stub*. To the client process, it appears that this is the actual procedure. The client stub packages the arguments to the remote procedure (this may involve converting them to a standard format) and builds one or more network messages. The packaging of arguments into a network message is called *marshaling*.

- Network messages are sent by the client stub to the remote system (via a system call to the local kernel).

- Network messages are transferred by the kernel to the remote system via some protocol (either connectionless or connection-oriented).

- A *server stub* procedure on the server receives the messages. It *un marshals* the arguments from the messages and possibly converts them from a standard form into a machine-specific form.

- The server stub executes a local procedure call to the actual server function, passing it the arguments that it received from the client.

- When the server is finished, it returns to the server stub with its return values.

- The server stub converts the return values (if necessary) and marshals them into one or more network messages to send to the client stub.

- Messages get sent back across the network to the client stub.

- The client stub reads the messages from the local kernel.

- It then returns the results to the client function (possibly converting them first).

The client code then continues its execution. The major benefits of RPC are twofold: the programmer can now use procedure call semantics and writing distributed applications is simplified because RPC hides all of the network code into stub functions. Application programs don't have to worry about details (such as sockets, port numbers, byte ordering).

Using the OSI reference model, RPC is a presentation layer service.

Several issues arise when we think about implementing:

1. Parameter Passing:

Passing by value is simple (just copy the value into the network message). Passing by reference is hard – it makes no sense to pass an address to a remote machine. If you want to support passing by reference, you'll have to copy the items referenced to ship them over and then copy the new values back to the reference.

If remote procedure calls are to support more complex structures, such as trees and linked lists, they will have to copy the structure into a pointer less representation (e.g., a flattened tree), transmit it, and reconstruct the data structure on the remote side.

2. Representation of Data

- On a local system there are no data incompatibility problems the data format is always the same.

- With RPC, a remote machine may have different byte ordering, different sizes of integers, and a different floating point representation.

- The problem was solved in the IP protocol suite by forcing everyone to use big endian1 byte ordering for all 16 and 32 bit fields in headers (hence the *htons* and *htonl* functions).

- For RPC, we need to select a "standard" encoding for all data types that can be passed as parameters if we are to communicate with heterogeneous systems. Sun's RPC, for example, uses XDR (eXternal Data Representation) for this process.

- Most data representation implementations use *implicit typing* (only the value is transmitted, not the type of the variable). The ISO data representation (ASN.1 Abstract Syntax Notation) uses *explicit typing*, where the type of each field is transmitted along with the value.

3. Binding:

- We need to locate a remote host and the proper process (port or transport address) on that host. Two solutions can be used.

- One solution is to maintain a centralized database that can locate a host that provides a type of service.

- A server sends a message to a central authority stating its willingness to accept certain remote procedure calls.

- Clients then contact this central authority when they need to locate a service. Another solution, less elegant but easier to administer, is to require the client to know which host it needs to contact.

- A server on that host maintains a database of locally provided services.

4. Use of Transport Protocol

- Some implementations allow only one to be used (e.g. TCP). Most RPC implementations support several and allow the user to choose.

5. Error Handling

- There are more opportunities for errors now. A server can generate an error, there might be problems in the network, the server can crash, or the client can disappear while the server is running code for it.

- The transparency of remote procedure calls breaks here since local procedure calls have no concept of the failure of the procedure call.

- Because of this, programs using remote procedure calls have to be prepared to either test for the failure of a remote procedure call or catch an exception.

6. Semantics of Calling Remote Procedures

The semantics of calling a regular procedure are simple: a procedure is executed exactly once when we call it. With a remote procedure, the "exactly once" aspect is quite difficult to achieve. A remote procedure may be executed:

- 0 times if the server crashed or process died before running the server code.

- Once if everything works fine.

- Once or more if the server crashed after returning to the server stub but before sending the response. The client won't get the return response and may decide to try again, thus executing the function more than once. If it doesn't try again, the function is executed once.

- More than once if the client times out and retransmits. It's possible that the original request may have been delayed. Both may get executed (or not).

If a function may be run any number of times without harm, it is *idempotent* (e.g., time of day, math functions, read static data). Otherwise, it is a *non idempotent* function (e.g., append or modify a file).

7. Performance

- Just calling the client stub function and getting a return from it incurs the overhead of a procedure call.

- On top of that, we need to execute the code to marshal parameters, call the network routines in the OS (incurring a context switch), deal with network latency, have the server receive the message and switch to the server process, un marshal parameters, call the server function, and do it all over again on the return trip.

- Without a doubt a remote procedure call will be much slower.

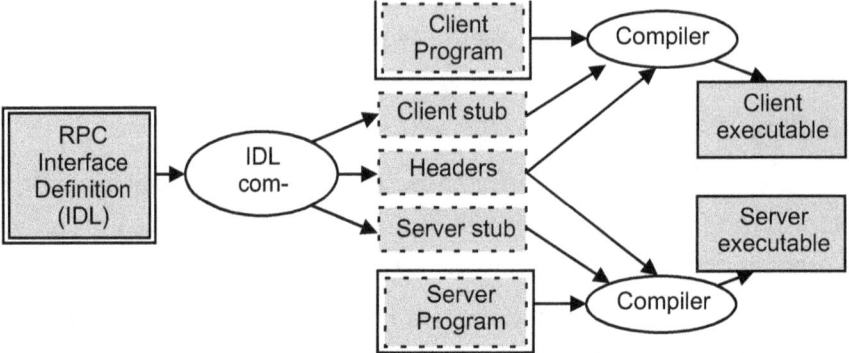

Fig. 2.3 (b): Compilation steps for remote procedure calls

2.8.2 Programming with Remote Procedure Calls

- Most popular languages today (C, C++, Java, Scheme, *et alia*) have no concept of remote procedures and are therefore not capable of generating the necessary stub functions.

- To enable the use of remote procedure calls with these languages, the commonly adopted solution is to provide a separate compiler that generates the client and server stub functions.

- This compiler takes its input from a programmer specified definition of the remote procedure call interface. Such a definition is written in an *interface definition language*.

- The interface definition generally looks similar to function prototype declarations: it enumerates the set of functions along with input and return parameters.

- After the RPC compiler is run, the client and server programs can be compiled and linked with the appropriate stub functions (Fig. 2.3(b)).

- The client procedure has to be modified to initialize the RPC mechanism (e.g. locate the server and possibly establish a connection) and to handle the failure of remote procedure calls.

2.8.3 Advantages of RPC

- Here we discuss some advantage of RPC; when we use RPC you don't have to worry about getting a unique transport address (a socket on a machine).

- The server can bind to any port and register the port with its RPC name server. The client will contact this name server and request the port number that corresponds to the program it needs.

- The system is transport independent. This makes code more portable to environments that may have different transport providers in use. It also allows processes on a server to make themselves available over every transport provider on a system.

- Applications on the client only need to know one transport address that of the *rpcbind* (or *portmap*) process.

- The function-call model can be used instead of the send/receive (read/write) interface provided by sockets.

2.8.4 Generation of Remote Procedure Calls

1. The First Generation

- Sun Microsystems's was one of the first systems to provide RPC libraries and a compiler, developing it as part of their Open Network Computing (ONC) architecture in the early 1980's.

- Sun provides a compiler that takes the definition of a remote procedure interface and generates the client and server stub functions.

- This compiler is called *rpcgen*. Before running this compiler, the programmer has to provide the interface definition.

- The interface definition contains the function declarations, grouped by version numbers (to support older clients connecting to a newer server) and a unique program number. The program number enables clients to identify the interface that they need.

- Other components provided by Sun are XDR, the format for encoding data across heterogeneous machines and a run-time library that implements the necessary protocols and socket routines to support RPC.

- All the programmer has to write is a client procedure, the server functions, and the RPC specification. When the RPC specification (a file suffixed with .x, for example a file named date.x) is compiler with *rpcgen*, three or four files are created.

- These are (for date.x):

  - **date.h:** Contains definitions of the program, version, and declarations of the functions. Both the client and server functions should include this file.

  - **date_svc.c :** C code to implement the server stub.

  - **date_clnt.c:** C code to implement the client stub.

  - **date_xdr.c:** Contains the XDR routines to convert data to XDR format. If this file is generated, it should be compiled and linked in with both the client and server functions.

- The client and server functions do not have to be modified much from a local implementation. The client must initialize the RPC interface with the function *clnt_create*, which creates an RPC handle to the specified program and version on a given host. It must be called before any remote procedure calls are issued.

- The parameters that we give it are the name of a server, the name of the program, the version of the program, and the transport protocol to use. Both the name and version of the program are obtained from the header file that was generated by *rpcgen*.

- In older versions of, the transport protocol would be either the string "tcp" or the string "udp" to specify the respective IP service RPC (this is still supported and must be used with the Linux implementation of RPC).

- To make the interface more flexible, UNIX System V release 4 (SunOS ≥ 5) network selection routines allow a more general specification. They search a file (/etc/netconfig) for the first provider that meets your requirements.

- This last argument can be:

    - **"netpath":** Search a NETPATH environment variable for a sequence of preferred transport providers)

    - **"circuit_n":** Find the first virtual circuit provider in the NETPATH list), "datagram_n" (find the first datagram provider in the NETPATH list) "visible" find the first visible transport provider in /etc/netconfig)

    - **"circuit_v":** Find the first visible virtual circuit transport provider in /etc/netconfig)

    - **"datagram_v":** Find the first visible datagram transport provider in /etc/netconfig).

- Each remote procedure call is restricted to accepting a single input parameter along with the RPC handle2. It returns a *pointer* to the result. The server functions have to be modified to accept a pointer to the value declared in the RPC definition (.x file) as an input and return a pointer to the result value.

- This pointer must be a pointer to static data (otherwise the area that is pointed to will be undefined when the procedure returns and the procedure's frame is freed).

- The names of the RPC procedures are the names in the RPC definition file converted to lower case and suffixed by an underscore followed by a version number.

- **For example**, BIN_DATE becomes a reference to the function *bin_date_1*. Your server must implement *bin_date_1* and the client code should issue calls to *bin_date_1*.

Running the Program:

The Server:

- When we start the server, the server stub runs and puts the process in the background (don't forget to run *ps* to find it and kill it when you no longer need it).

- It creates a socket and binds any local port to the socket. It then calls a function in the RPC library, *svc_register*, to register the program number and version. This contacts the *port mapper*.

- The port mapper is a separate process that is usually started at system boot time. It keeps track of the port number, version number, and program number.

- On UNIX System V release 4, this process is *rpc bind*. On earlier systems, it was known as *port map*. The server then waits for a client request (i.e., it does a *listen*).

The Client:

- When we start the client program, it first calls *clnt_create* with the name of the remote system, program number, version number, and protocol.

- It contacts the port mapper on the remote system to find the appropriate port on that system.

- The client then calls the RPC stub function (*bin_date_1* in this example). This function sends a message (e.g., a datagram) to the server (using the port number found earlier) and waits for a response. For datagram service, it will retransmit the request a fixed number of times if the response is not received.

- The message is then received by the remote system, which calls the server function *bin_date_1*) and returns the return value back to the client stub.

- The client stub then returns to the client code that issued the call.

RPC in the Distributed Computing Environment (DCE RPC)

- The Distributed Computing Environment (DCE) is a set of components designed by the Open Software Foundation (OFS) for providing support for distributed applications and a distributed environment.

- After merging with X/Open, this group is currently called The Open Group. The components include a distributed file service, a time service, a directory, service, and several others. Of interest to us here is the DCE remote procedure call. It is very similar to Sun's RPC.

- Interfaces are written in an interface definition language called *Interface Definition Notation (IDN)*. Like Sun's RPC, the interface definitions look like function prototypes.

- One deficiency in Sun's RPC is the identification of a server with a "unique" 32-bit number. While this is a far larger space than the 16-bit number space available under sockets, it's still not comforting to come up with a number and hope that it's unique.

- DCE's RPC addresses this deficiency by not having the programmer think up a number.

- The first step in writing an application is getting a unique ID with the *uuidgen* program. This program generates a prototype IDN file containing an interface ID that is guaranteed never to be used again.

- It is a 128-bit value that contains a location code and time of creation encoded in it. The user then edits the prototype file, filling in the remote procedure declarations. After this step, an IDN compiler, similar to *rpcgen*, generates a header, client stub, and server stub.

- Another deficiency in Sun's RPC is that the client must know the machine on which the server resides. It then can ask the RPC name server on that machine for the port number corresponding to the program number that it wishes to access.

- DCE supports the organization of several machines into administrative entities called *cells*. Every machine knows how to communicate with a machine responsible for maintaining information on cell services – the *cell directory server*.

- With Sun's RPC a server only registers its {program number → port mapping} with a local name server (*rpcbind*).

- Under DCE, a server registers its endpoint (port) on the local machine with the RPC daemon (name server) as well as registering its {program name → machine} mapping with its cell directory server.

- When a client wishes to establish communication with an RPC server, it first asks its cell directory server to locate the machine on which the server resides.

- The client then talks to the RPC demon on that machine to get the port number of the server process. DCE also supports more complicated searches that span cells.

2. Second Generation RPCs: Object Support

- As object oriented languages began to gain popularity in the late 1980's, it was evident that both the Sun (ONC) and DCE RPC systems did not provide any support for instantiating remote objects from remote classes, keeping track of instances of objects, or providing support for polymorphism.

- RPC mechanism still functioned but they did not support object oriented programming techniques in an automated, transparent manner.

Microsoft DCOM

- In April 1992, Microsoft released Windows 3.1 which included a mechanism called OLE (object linking and embedding).

- This allowed a program to dynamically link other libraries to allow facilities such as embedding a spreadsheet into a Word document OLE evolved into something called COM (Component Object Model).

- A COM object is a binary file. Programs that use COM services have access to a standardized interface for the COM object (but not its internal structures).

- COM objects are named with globally unique identifiers (GUIDs) and classes of objects are identified with class IDs.

- DCOM (Distributed COM) was introduced with Windows NT 4.0 in 1996 and is an extension of the Component Object Model to allow objects to communicate between machines.

CORBA

- Even with DCE fixing some of the shortcomings in Sun's RPC, certain deficiencies still remain. For example, if a server is not running, a client cannot connect to it to call a remote procedure.

- It is an administrator's responsibility to ensure that the needed servers are started before any clients attempt to connect to them.

- If a new service or interface is added to the system, there is no means by which a client can discover this.

- In some environments, it might helpful for a client to be able to find out about services and their interfaces at run-time. Finally, object oriented languages expect polymorphism in function calls (the function may behave differently for different types of data).

- Traditional RPC has no support for this.

- CORBA (Common Object Request Broker Architecture) was created to address these, and other, issues. It is an architecture created by an industry consortium of over 500 companies called the Object Management Group (OMG).

- The specification for this architecture has been evolving since 1989. The goal is to provide support for distributed heterogeneous object-oriented applications.

- Objects may be hosted across a network of computers (a single object is not distributed).

- The specification is independent of any programming language, operating system, or network to enable interoperability across these platforms.

Java RMI

- CORBA aims at providing a comprehensive set of services for managing objects in a heterogeneous environment (different languages, operating systems, networks). Java, in its initial inception, supported the downloading of code from a remote site but its only support for distributed communication was via sockets. In 1995, Sun (the creator of Java) began creating an extension to Java called Java RMI (Remote Method Invocation).

- Java RMI enables a programmer to create distributed applications where methods of remote objects can be invoked from other Java virtual machines.

- A remote call can be made once the application (client) has a reference to the remote object. This is done by looking up the remote object in the naming service (the *RMI registry*) provided by RMI and receiving a reference as a return value.

- Java RMI is conceptually similar to RPC butt supports the semantics of object invocation in different address spaces.

- One area in which the design of Java differs from CORBA and most RPC systems is that RMI is built for Java only. Sun RPC, DCE RPC, Microsoft's DCOM and ORPC, and CORBA are designed to be language, architecture, and (except for Microsoft) operating system independent.

- While those capabilities are lost, the gain is that RMI fits cleanly into the language and has no need for standardized data representations (Java uses the same byte ordering everywhere).

The Design Goals for Java RMI are:

- It should fit the language, be integrated into the language, and be simple to use
- Support seamless remote invocation of objects
- Support callbacks from servers to applets
- Preserve safety of the Java object environment
- Support distributed garbage collection
- Support multiple transports

3. Third Generation RPCs: Web Services and the XML

XML RPC

- XML-RPC, the protocol, was created in 1998 by Dave Winer of UserLand Software and Microsoft. As new functionality was introduced, the standard evolved into what is now SOAP.

- XML-RPC is a Remote Procedure Call (RPC) protocol which uses XML to encode its calls and HTTP as a transport mechanism. "XML-RPC" also refers generically to the use of XML for remote procedure call, independently of the specific protocol.

- XML-RPC works by sending a HTTP request to a server implementing the protocol. The client in that case is typically software wanting to call a single method of a remote system. Multiple input parameters can be passed to the remote method, one return value is returned.

- The parameter types allow nesting of parameters into maps and lists, thus larger structures can be transported.

- Therefore XML-RPC can be used to transport objects or structures both as input and as output parameters.

- Identification of clients for authorization purposes can be achieved using popular HTTP security methods. Basic access authentication is used for identification; HTTPS is used when identification (via certificates) and encrypted messages are needed. Both methods can be combined.

SOAP

- SOAP, originally defined as Simple Object Access Protocol, is a protocol specification for exchanging structured information in the implementation of Web Services in computer networks.

- It relies on Extensible Markup Language (XML) for its message format, and usually relies on other Application Layer protocols, most notably Hypertext Transfer Protocol (HTTP) and Simple Mail Transfer Protocol (SMTP), for message negotiation and transmission.

- SOAP can form the foundation layer of a web services protocol stack, providing a basic messaging framework upon which web services can be built.

- This XML based protocol consists of three parts: an envelope, which defines what is in the message and how to process it, a set of encoding rules for expressing instances of application-defined data types, and a convention for representing procedure calls and responses.

- SOAP has three major characteristics: Extensibility (security and WS-routing are among the extensions under development), Neutrality (SOAP can be used over any transport protocol such as HTTP, SMTP or even TCP), and Independence (SOAP allows for any programming model).

- As an example of how SOAP procedures can be used, a SOAP message could be sent to a web site that has web services enabled, such as a real-estate price database, with the parameters needed for a search.

- The site would then return an XML-formatted document with the resulting data, e.g., prices, location, features.

- With the data being returned in a standardized machine-parseable format, it can then be integrated directly into a third-party web site or application.

2.8.5 Failure Handling

- The RPC API provides a consistent error handling mechanism for all routines. Each routine includes a status output argument, which is used to return error status codes.

- These codes may be passed to the dce_error_inq_text() routine to extract error message text from a message catalogue. RPC calls return protocol and run-time error status codes through fault status and comm_status parameters, as described in Interface Definition Language . These status codes are consistent with the status codes returned from the RPC API and may be passed to dce_error_inq_text () to obtain error message text.

- The dce_error_inq_text() routine may be used by RPC applications to return message text corresponding to a status value

2.9 JAVA RMI

- RMI applications often comprise two separate programs, a server and a client. A typical server program creates some remote objects, makes references to these objects accessible, and waits for clients to invoke methods on these objects.

- A typical client program obtains a remote reference to one or more remote objects on a server and then invokes methods on them.

- RMI provides the mechanism by which the server and the client communicate and pass information back and forth. Such an application is sometimes referred to as a *distributed object application.*

Distributed Object Applications need to do the Following:

- Locate remote objects. Applications can use various mechanisms to obtain references to remote objects. For example, an application can register its remote objects with RMI's simple naming facility, the RMI registry.

- Alternatively, an application can pass and return remote object references as part of other remote invocations.

- Communicate with remote objects. Details of communication between remote objects are handled by RMI. To the programmer, remote communication looks similar to regular Java method invocations.

- Load class definitions for objects that are passed around. Because RMI enables objects to be passed back and forth, it provides mechanisms for loading an object's class definitions as well as for transmitting an object's data.

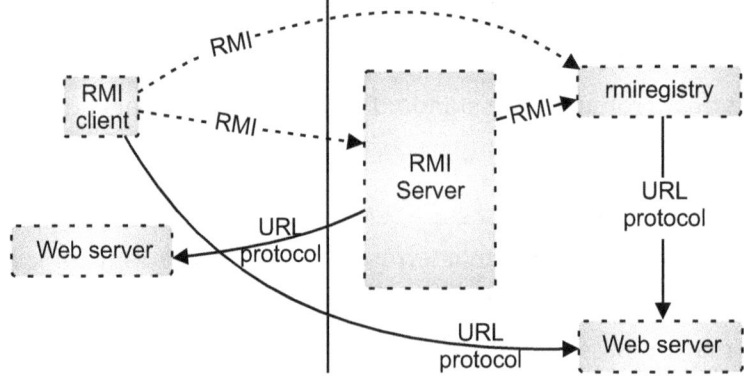

Fig. 2.4: RMI registry

- The Fig. 2.4 illustration depicts an RMI distributed application that uses the RMI registry to obtain a reference to a remote object. The server calls the registry to associate (or bind) a name with a remote object. The client looks up the remote object by its name in the server's registry and then invokes a method on it. The illustration also shows that the RMI system uses an existing web server to load class definitions, from server to client and from client to server, for objects when needed.

2.9.1 Dynamic Code Loading Advantage

One of the central and unique features of RMI is its ability to download the definition of an object's class if the class is not defined in the receiver's Java virtual machine. All of the types and behaviour of an object, previously available only in a single Java virtual machine, can be transmitted to another, possibly remote, Java virtual machine. RMI passes objects by their actual classes, so the behaviour of the objects is not changed when they are sent to another Java virtual machine. This capability enables new types and behaviours to be introduced into a remote Java virtual machine, thus dynamically extending the behaviour of an application. The compute engine example in this trail uses this capability to introduce new behaviour to a distributed program.

2.9.2 Remote Interfaces, Objects, and Methods

- The Java application, a distributed application built by using Java RMI is made up of interfaces and classes. The interfaces declare methods.

- The classes implement the methods declared in the interfaces and, perhaps, declare additional methods as well. In a distributed application, some implementations might reside in some Java virtual machines but not others.

- Objects with methods that can be invoked across Java virtual machines are called *remote objects*.

An object becomes remote by implementing a *remote interface*, which has the following characteristics:

A remote interface extends the interface java.rmi. Remote. Each method of the interface declares java.rmi. Remote Exception in its throws clause, in addition to any application-specific exceptions.

- RMI treats a remote object differently from a non-remote object when the object is passed from one Java virtual machine to another Java virtual machine. Rather than making a copy of the implementation object in the receiving Java virtual machine, RMI passes a remote *stub* for a remote object. The stub acts as the local representative, or proxy, for the remote object and basically is, to the client, the remote reference.

- The client invokes a method on the local stub, which is responsible for carrying out the method invocation on the remote object. A stub for a remote object implements the same set of remote interfaces that the remote object implements. This property enables a stub to be cast to any of the interfaces that the remote object implements. However, *only* those methods defined in a remote interface are available to be called from the receiving Java virtual machine.

2.9.3 Creating Distributed Applications by Using RMI

Using RMI to develop a distributed application involves these general steps:

1. Designing and implementing the components of your distributed application.
2. Compiling sources.
3. Making classes network accessible.
4. Starting the application.

1. Designing and Implementing the Application Components:

- First, determine your application architecture, including which components are local objects and which components are remotely accessible. This step includes Defining the remote interfaces.

- A remote interface specifies the methods that can be invoked remotely by a client. Clients program to remote interfaces, not to the implementation classes of those interfaces.

- The design of such interfaces includes the determination of the types of objects that will be used as the parameters and return values for these methods. If any of these interfaces or classes do not yet exist, you need to define them as well.

- Implementing the remote objects. Remote objects must implement one or more remote interfaces.

- The remote object class may include implementations of other interfaces and methods that are available only locally.

- If any local classes are to be used for parameters or return values of any of these methods, they must be implemented as well. Implementing the clients.

- Clients that use remote objects can be implemented at any time after the remote interfaces are defined, including after the remote objects have been deployed.

2. Compiling Sources:

- As with any Java program, you use the javac compiler to compile the source files.

- The source files contain the declarations of the remote interfaces, their implementations, any other server classes, and the client classes.

3. Making Classes Network Accessible:

- In this step, you make certain class definitions network accessible, such as the definitions for the remote interfaces and their associated types, and the definitions for classes that need to be downloaded to the clients or servers.

- Classes definitions are typically made network accessible through a web server.

4. Starting the Application:

- Starting the application includes running the RMI remote object registry, the server, and the client. The rest of this section walks through the steps used to create a compute engine.

2.9.4 Building a Generic Compute Engine

- This trail focuses on a simple, yet powerful, distributed application called a *compute engine*. The compute engine is a remote object on the server that takes tasks from clients, runs the tasks, and returns any results.

- The tasks are run on the machine where the server is running.

- This type of distributed application can enable a number of client machines to make use of a particularly powerful machine or a machine that has specialized hardware.

- The novel aspect of the compute engine is that the tasks it runs do not need to be defined when the compute engine is written or started.

- New kinds of tasks can be created at any time and then given to the compute engine to be run.

- The only requirement of a task is that its class implements a particular interface.

- The code needed to accomplish the task can be downloaded by the RMI system to the compute engine.

- Then, the compute engine runs the task, using the resources on the machine on which the compute engine is running.

- The ability to perform arbitrary tasks is enabled by the dynamic nature of the Java platform, which is extended to the network by RMI. RMI dynamically loads the task code into the compute engine's Java virtual machine and runs the task without prior knowledge of the class that implements the task.

- Such an application, which has the ability to download code dynamically, is often called a *behaviour-based application*.

- Such applications usually require full agent-enabled infrastructures. With RMI, such applications are part of the basic mechanisms for distributed computing on the Java platform.

2.9.5 Writing an RMI Server

- The compute engine server accepts tasks from clients, runs the tasks, and returns any results.

- The server code consists of an interface and a class. The interface defines the methods that can be invoked from the client. Essentially, the interface defines the client's view of the remote object.

- The class provides the implementation.

Designing a Remote Interface: This section explains the Compute interface, which provides the connection between the client and the server. You will also learn about the RMI API, which supports this communication.

Implementing a Remote Interface: This section explores the class that implements the Compute interface, thereby implementing a remote object. This class also provides the rest of the code that makes up the server program, including a main method that creates an instance of the remote object, registers it with the RMI registry, and sets up a security manager.

2.9.5.1 Designing a Remote Interface

- At the core of the compute engine is a protocol that enables tasks to be submitted to the compute engine, the compute engine to run those tasks, and the results of those tasks to be returned to the client.

- This protocol is expressed in the interfaces that are supported by the compute engine. The remote communication for this protocol is illustrated in the following Fig. 2.5.

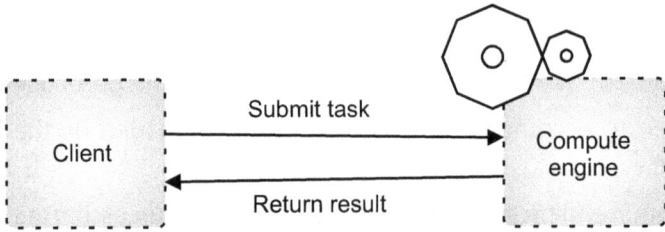

Fig. 2.5: Remote communication

- Each interface contains a single method. The compute engine's remote interface, Compute, enables tasks to be submitted to the engine. The client interface, Task, defines how the compute engine executes a submitted task.

- The compute. Compute interface defines the remotely accessible part, the compute engine itself. Here is the source code for the Compute interface

```
package compute ;
import java.rmi.remote;
import java.rmi.RemoteException;
public interface Compute extends Remote {
<T> T executeTask(Task<T> t) throws RemoteException;
}
```

- By extending the interface java.rmi.Remote, the Compute interface identifies itself as an interface whose methods can be invoked from another Java virtual machine. Any object that implements this interface can be a remote object.

- As a member of a remote interface, the execute task method is a remote method. Therefore, this method must be defined as being capable of throwing a java.rmi.RemoteException. This exception is thrown by the RMI system from a remote method invocation to indicate that either a communication failure or a protocol error has occurred.

- A RemoteException is a checked exception, so any code invoking a remote method needs to handle this exception by either catching it or declaring it in its throws clause.

- The second interface needed for the compute engine is the task interface, which is the type of the parameter to the execute task method in the compute interface. The compute, task interface defines the interface between the compute engine and the work that it needs to do, providing the way to start the work.

- Here is the source code for the task interface:

```
package compute;

public interface Task<T> {

T execute ();

}
```

- The task interface defines a single method, execute, which has no parameters and throws no exceptions. Because the interface does not extend Remote, the method in this interface doesn't need to list java.rmi.RemoteException in its throws clause.

- The task interface has a type parameter, T, which represents the result type of the task's computation. This interface's execute method returns the result of the computation and thus its return type is T.

- The compute interface's executeTask method, in turn, returns the result of the execution of the task instance passed to it. Thus, the executeTask method has its own type parameter, T that associates its own return type with the result type of the passed Task instance.

- RMI uses the Java object serialization mechanism to transport objects by value between Java virtual machines.

- For an object to be considered serializable, its class must implement the java.io.Serializable marker interface.

- Therefore, classes that implement the Task interface must also implement Serializable, as must the classes of objects used for task results.

- Different kinds of tasks can be run by a Compute object as long as they are implementations of the task type.

- The classes that implement this interface can contain any data needed for the computation of the task and any other methods needed for the computation.

- Here is how RMI makes this simple compute engine possible. Because RMI can assume that the task objects are written in the Java programming language, implementations of the task object that were previously unknown to the compute engine are downloaded by RMI into the compute engine's Java virtual machine as needed.
- This capability enables clients of the compute engine to define new kinds of tasks to be run on the server machine without needing the code to be explicitly installed on that machine.
- The compute engine, implemented by the Compute Engine class, implements the compute interface, enabling different tasks to be submitted to it by calls to its executeTask method. These tasks are run using the task's implementation of the execute method and the results, are returned to the remote client.
- The Task interface defines a single method, execute, which has no parameters and throws no exceptions. Because the interface does not extend Remote, the method in this interface doesn't need to list java.rmi.Remote Exception in its throws clause. The Task interface has a type parameter, T, which represents the result type of the task's computation. This interface's execute method returns the result of the computation and thus its return type is T.
- The Compute interface's executeTask method, in turn, returns the result of the execution of the Task instance passed to it. Thus, the executeTask method has its own type parameter, T that associates its own return type with the result type of the passed Task instance. RMI uses the Java object serialization mechanism to transport objects by value between Java virtual machines. For an object to be considered serializable, its class must implement the java.io.Serializable marker interface. Therefore, classes that implement the Task interface must also implement Serializable, as must be classes of objects used for task results.
- Different kinds of tasks can be run by a Compute object as long as they are implementations of the Task type.
- The classes that implement this interface can contain any data needed for the computation of the task and any other methods needed for the computation.
- Here is how RMI makes this simple compute engine possible.
- Because RMI can assume that the Task objects are written in the Java programming language, implementations of the Task object that were previously unknown to the compute engine are downloaded by RMI into the compute engine's Java virtual machine as needed.
- This capability enables clients of the compute engine to define new kinds of tasks to be run on the server machine without needing the code to be explicitly installed on that machine. The compute engine, implemented by the Compute Engine class, implements the Compute interface, enabling different tasks to be submitted to it by calls to its executeTask method.
- These tasks are run using the task's implementation of the execute method and the results, are returned to the remote client.

2.9.5.2 Implementing a Remote Interface

In this section we discuss the task of implementing a class for the compute engine. In general, a class that implements a remote interface should at least do the following:

- Declare the remote interfaces being implemented,
- Define the constructor for each remote object,
- Provide an implementation for each remote method in the remote interfaces.

An RMI server program needs to create the initial remote objects and *export* them to the RMI runtime, which makes them available to receive incoming remote invocations. This setup procedure can be either encapsulated in a method of the remote object implementation class itself or included in another class entirely. The setup procedure should do the following:

- Create and install a security manager,
- Create and export one or more remote objects.

Register at least one remote object with the RMI registry (or with another naming service, such as a service accessible through the Java Naming and Directory Interface) for bootstrapping purposes

The complete implementation of the compute engine follows. The engine. Compute Engine class implements the remote interface Compute and also includes the main method for setting up the compute engine. Here is the source code for the Compute Engine class:

```
package engine ;
import java.rmi.RemoteException;
import java.rmi.registry.LocateRegistry ;
import java.rmi.registry.Registry ;
import java.rmi.server.UnicastRemoteobject ;
import compute.Compute ;
import compute.Task ;
public class ComuteEngine implements Compute {
    public ComputeEngine ( ) {
        super ( ) ;
    }
    public <T> T executeTask (Task<T> t)  {
        return t.execute ( ) ;
    }
```

```
public static void main (String [ ] args) {
if  (System.getSecurityManager () = = null ) {
System.getSecurityManager (new SecurityManager ( )) ;
}
try {
    String name = "Compute" ;
    Compute engine = new ComputeEngine ( );
    Compute stub =
        (Compute) UnicastremoteObject.exportObject (engine, 0) ;
        Registry registry = LocateRegistry.getRegistry ( );
        registry.rebind(name, stub) ;
        System.out.println ("ComputeEngine bound") ;
    }   catch (Exception e) {
        System.err,prinln ("ComputeEngine exception ;") ;
        e.printStackTrace ( ) ;
    }
}
}
```

The following sections discuss each component of the compute engine implementation.

Declaring the Remote Interfaces Being Implemented:

- The implementation class for the compute engine is declared as follows: public class ComputeEngine implements Compute this declaration states that the class implements the Compute remote interface and therefore can be used for a remote object.

- The ComputeEngine class defines a remote object implementation class that implements a single remote interface and no other interfaces. The ComputeEngine class also contains two executable program elements that can only be invoked locally. The first of these elements is a constructor for ComputeEngine instances.

- The second of these elements is a main method that is used to create a ComputeEngine instance and make it available to clients.

Defining the Constructor for the Remote Object:

- The ComputeEngine class has a single constructor that takes no arguments. The code for the constructor is as follows: public ComputeEngine() { super(); }.

- This constructor just invokes the super class constructor, which is the no-argument constructor of the Object class.

- Although the super class constructor gets invoked even if omitted from the ComputeEngine constructor, it is included for clarity.

Providing Implementations for Each Remote Method:

- The class for a remote object provides implementations for each remote method specified in the remote interfaces.

- The Compute interface contains a single remote method, executeTask, which is implemented as follows:

```
public <T> T executeTask(Task<T> t)
{ return t.execute(); }
```

- This method implements the protocol between the ComputeEngine remote object and its clients. Each client provides the ComputeEngine with a Task object that has a particular implementation of the Task interface's execute method.

- The ComputeEngine executes each client's task and returns the result of the task's executing method directly to the client.

2.9.5.3 Passing Objects in RMI

- Arguments to or return values from remote methods can be of almost any type, including local objects, remote objects, and primitive data types.

- More precisely, any entity of any type can be passed to or from a remote method as long as the entity is an instance of a type that is a primitive data type, a remote object, or a *serializable* object, which means that it implements the interface java.io.Serializable.

- Some object types do not meet any of these criteria and thus cannot be passed to or returned from a remote method.

- Most of these objects, such as threads or file descriptors, encapsulate information that makes sense only within a single address space.

- Many of the core classes, including the classes in the packages java.lang and java.util, implement the Serializable interface. The rules governing how arguments and return values are passed are as follows:

- Remote objects are essentially passed by reference. A *remote object reference* is a stub, which is a client-side proxy that implements the complete set of remote interfaces that the remote object implements.

- Local objects are passed by copy, using object serialization. By default, all fields are copied except fields that are marked static or transient. Default serialization behavior can be overridden on a class-by-class basis.

- Passing a remote object by reference means that any changes made to the state of the object by remote method invocations are reflected in the original remote object.

- When a remote object is passed, only those interfaces that are remote interfaces are available to the receiver.

- Any methods defined in the implementation class or defined in non-remote interfaces implemented by the class are not available to that receiver.

- **For example**, if you were to pass a reference to an instance of the Compute Engine class, the receiver would have access only to the compute engine's execute Task method.

- That receiver would not see the Compute Engine constructor, its main method, or its implementation of any methods of java.lang.Object.

- In the parameters and return values of remote method invocations, objects that are not remote objects are passed by value.

- Thus, a copy of the object is created in the receiving Java virtual machine. Any changes to the object's state by the receiver are reflected only in the receiver's copy, not in the sender's original instance.

- Any changes to the object's state by the sender are reflected only in the sender's original instance, not in the receiver's copy.

2.8.5.4 Implementing the Server's Main Method

- The most complex method of the ComputeEngine implementation is the main method. The main method is used to start the ComputeEngine and therefore needs to do the necessary initialization and housekeeping to prepare the server to accept calls from clients.

- This method is not a remote method, which means that it cannot be invoked from a different Java virtual machine. Because the main method is declared static, the method is not associated with an object at all but rather with the class ComputeEngine.

2.9.6 Creating a Client Program

- The compute engine is a relatively simple program: it runs tasks that are handed to it. The clients for the compute engine are more complex.

- A client needs to call the compute engine, but it also has to define the task to be performed by the compute engine.

- Two separate classes make up the client in our example. The first class, Compute Pi, looks up and invokes a Compute object. The second class, Pi, implements the Task interface and defines the work to be done by the compute engine.

- The job of the Pi class is to compute the value of to some number of decimal places.

The non-remote Task interface is defined as follows:

```
Package compute ;
Public interface Task <T> {
    T execute ( ) ;
}
```

- The code that invokes a Compute object's methods must obtain a reference to that object, create a Task object, and then request that the task be executed.

- The definition of the task class Pi is shown later. A Pi object is constructed with a single argument, the desired precision of the result. The result of the task execution is a java.math.BigDecimal representing calculated to the specified precision.

- Here is the source code for client.ComputePi, the main client class:

```
package client ;
import java.rmi.registry.LocateRegistry ;
import java.rmi.registry.Registry ;
import java.math.BigDecimal ;
import compute.Compute ;
public class ComputePi {
    public static void main (String arge [ ]) {
        if  (System.getSecurityManager ( ) = = null) {
            System.setSecrityManager (new SecrityManager ( )) ;
        }
        try {
            String name = "Compute" ;
            Registry registry = LocateRegistry.getRegistry (args [0]) ;
            Compute comp = (Compute) registry.lokup (name) ;
            Pi task = new Pi (Integer.parseInt (args [1])) ;
            BigDecimal pi = comp.executeTask (task) ;
            System.out.prinln(pi) ;
        }   catch (Exception e) {
            System.err.println ("Compute Pi exception:");
```

```
        e.printStackTrace ( );
    }
  }
}
```

- Like the ComputeEngine server, the client begins by installing a security manager. This step is necessary because the process of receiving the server remote object's stub could require downloading class definitions from the server.

- For RMI to download classes, a security manager must be in force. After installing a security manager, the client constructs a name to use to look up a Compute remote object, using the same name used by ComputeEngine to bind its remote object.

- Also, the client uses the LocateRegistry.getRegistry API to synthesize a remote reference to the registry on the server's host.

- The value of the first command-line argument, args[0], is the name of the remote host on which the Compute object runs.

- The client then invokes the lookup method on the registry to look up the remote object by name in the server host's registry.

- The particular overload of LocateRegistry.getRegistry used, which has a single String parameter, returns a reference to a registry at the named host and the default registry port, 1099. You must use an overload that has an int parameter if the registry is created on a port other than 1099.

- Next, the client creates a new Pi object, passing to the Pi constructor the value of the second command-line argument, args[1], parsed as an integer.

- This argument indicates the number of decimal places to use in the calculation.

- Finally, the client invokes the executeTask method of the Compute remote object.

- The object passed into the executeTask invocation returns an object of type Big Decimal, which the program stores in the variable result. Finally, the program prints the result.

- The following Fig. 2.6 depicts the flow of messages among the ComputePi client, the rmiregistry, and the ComputeEngine.

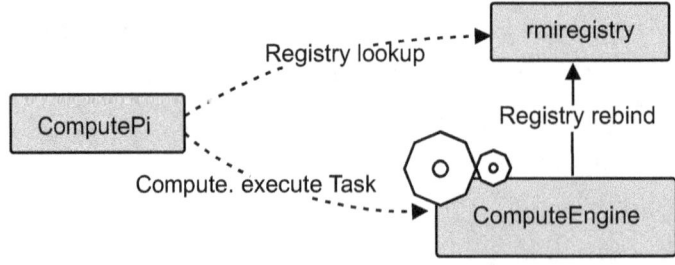

Fig. 2.6 : Flow messages client to RMI register

2.9.7 Client Program Creation

- The Pi class implements the Task interface and computes the value of to a specified number of decimal places.
- For this example, the actual algorithm is unimportant. What is important is that the algorithm is computationally expensive, meaning that you would want to have it executed on a capable server.
- Here is the source code for client.Pi, the class that implements the Task interface

```
package client ;
import compute.Task ;
import java.io.Serializable ;
import java.match.BigDecimal ;
public class Pi implements Task <BigDecimal>, Serializable {
    private static final long serialVersionUTD = 227L;
    /** constants used in pi computation */
    private static finalBigDecimal FOUR =
    BigDecimal.valueof (4) ;
/** rounding mode to use during pi computation */
private static final introundingMode =
    BigDecimal.ROUND_HALF_EVEN ;
/** digits of precision after the decimal point */
private final int digits ;
/**
* construct a task to calculate pi to the specified
*precision.
*/
public Pi (int digits)          {
    this.digits = digits ;
}
/**
* Compute the value of pi to the specified number of
* digits after the decimal point. The value is
* computed using Machin's formula:
```

```
*
*       pi/4 = 4*arctan (1/5) – arctan (1/239)
*
*   and a power series expansion of arctan (x) to
*     sufficient precision.
*/
public static BigDecimalcomputePi (int digits) {
    int scale = digits + 5;
    BigDecimal arctan1_5 = arctan (5, scale) ;
    BigDecimal arctan1_239 = arctan (239, scale) ;
    BigDecimal pi = arctan1_5.multiply (FOUR). Subtract ( arctan1_239).multiply(FOUR)
;

    Return pi.setScale (digits, BigDecimal.ROUND_HALF_UP) ;
}
/**
* Compute the value, in radians, of the arctangent of
* the inverse of thesupplied integer to the specified
*number of digits after the decimal point. The value
* is computed using the power series expansion for the
* arc tangent:
*
* arctab (x) = x – (x^3)/3 + (x^5)/5 – (x^7)/7 +
*   (x^9)/9 ...
*/
public static BigDecimalarctan (intinverseX, int scale)
{
    BigDecimal result, numer, term;
    BigDecimalbinvX = BigDecimal.valueOf (inverseX) ;
    BigDecimal invX2 =
        BigDecimal.valueOf (inverseX * inverseX) ;
    numer = BigDecimal.ONE.divide (invX, scale, roundingMode) ;
```

```
result – number ;
inti = 1 ;
do {
    number.divide (intX2, scale, roundingMode) ;
intdenom = 2 * i + 1;
term =
    number.divide (BigDecimal.valueOf (denom), scale, roundingMode) ;
if ((i % 2) ! = 0 ) {
    result = result.subtract (term) ;
} else {
    result = result.add (term) ;
}
i++;
} while (term.compareTo (BigDecimal.ZERO) ! = 0) ;
return result ;
```

Note: All serializable classes, whether they implement the Serializable interface directly or indirectly, must declare a private static final field named serialVersionUID to guarantee serialization compatibility between versions.

- If no previous version of the class has been released, then the value of this field can be any long value, similar to the 227L used by Pi, as long as the value is used consistently in future versions.

- If a previous version of the class has been released without an explicit serialVersionUID declaration, but serialization compatibility with that version is important, then the default implicitly computed value for the previous version must be used for the value of the new version's explicit declaration.

- The serial tool can be run against the previous version to determine the default computed value for it.

- The most interesting feature of this example is that the Compute implementation object never needs the Pi class's definition until a Pi object is passed in as an argument to the executeTask method.

- At that point, the code for the class is loaded by RMI into the Compute object's Java virtual machine, the execute method is invoked, and the task's code is executed.

- The result, which in the case of the Pi task is a Big Decimal object, is handed back to the calling client, where it is used to print the result of the computation.

- The fact that the supplied Task object computes the value of Pi is irrelevant to the ComputeEngine object.

- You could also implement a task that, for example, generates a random prime number by using a probabilistic algorithm. That task would also be computationally intensive and therefore a good candidate for passing to the ComputeEngine, but it would require very different code.

- This code could also be downloaded when the Task object is passed to a Compute object. In just the way that the algorithm for computing is brought in when needed, the code that generates the random prime number would be brought in when needed.

- The Compute object knows only that each object it receives implements the execute method.

- The Compute object does not know, and does not need to know, what the implementation does.

2.9.8 Compiling and Running the Program

Now that the code for the compute engine example has been written, it needs to be compiled and run.

Compiling the Programs: In this section, you learn how to compile the server and the client programs that make up the compute engine example.

Running the Programs: Finally, you run the server and client programs and consequently compute the value of π.

2.9.8.1 Compiling the Programs

- In a real-world scenario in which a service such as the compute engine is deployed, a developer would likely create a Java Archive (JAR) file that contains the Compute and Task interfaces for server classes to implement and client programs to use.

- Next, a developer, perhaps the same developer of the interface JAR file, would write an implementation of the Compute interface and deploy that service on a machine available to clients.

- Developers of client programs can use the Compute and the Task interfaces, contained in the JAR file, and independently develop a task and client program that uses a Compute service. In this section, you learn how to set up the JAR file, server classes, and client classes.

- You will see that the client's Pi class will be downloaded to the server at runtime. Also, the Compute and Task interfaces will be downloaded from the server to the registry at runtime. This example separates the interfaces, remote object implementation, and client code into three packages:

- **Compute:** Compute and Task interfaces,

- **Engine:** ComputeEngine implementation class,

- **Client:** ComputePi client code and Pi task implementation.

- First, you need to build the interface **JAR file** to provide to server and client developers.

2.9.8.2 Building a JAR File of Interface Classes

- First, you need to compile the interface source files in the compute package and then build a JAR file that contains their class files.

- Assume that user waldo has written these interfaces and placed the source files in the directory   c:\home\waldo\src\compute   on   Windows   or   the   directory /home/waldo/src/compute on Solaris OS or Linux.

- Given these paths, you can use the following commands to compile the interfaces and create the JAR file:

Microsoft Windows:

```
cd c:\home\waldo\src

javac compute\Compute.java compute\Task.java

jar cvf compute.jar compute\*.class
```

Solaris OS or Linux:

```
cd /home/waldo/src

javac compute/compute.java compute/Task.java

jar cvf compute.jar compute/*.class
```

- The jar command displays the following output due to the -v option:

```
added manifest

adding: compute/Compute.class (in = 307) (out = 201) (deflated 34%)

adding: compute/Task.class (in = 217) (out = 149) (deflated 31 %)
```

- Now, you can distribute the compute.jar file to developers of server and client applications so that they can make use of the interfaces.

- After you build either server-side or client-side classes with the javac compiler, if any of those classes will need to be dynamically downloaded by other Java virtual machines, you must ensure that their class files are placed in a network-accessible location.

- In this example, for Solaris OS or Linux this location is /home/*user*/public_html/classes because many web servers allow the accessing of a user's public_html directory through an HTTP URL constructed as http://host/~*user*/. If your web server does not support this convention, you could use a different location in the web server's hierarchy, or you could use a file URL instead.

- The file URLs take the form file:/home/*user*/public_html/classes/ on Solaris OS or Linux and the form file:/c:/home/*user*/public_html/classes/ on Windows. You may also select another type of URL, as appropriate.

2.9.8.3 Building the Server Classes

- The engine package contains only one server-side implementation class, ComputeEngine, the implementation of the remote interface Compute.

- Assume that user ann, the developer of the ComputeEngine class, has placed ComputeEngine.java in the directory c:\home\ann\src\engine on Windows or the directory /home/ann/src/engine on Solaris OS or Linux.

- Here, we deploying the class files for clients to download in a subdirectory of her public_html directory, c:\home\ann\public_html\classes on Windows or /home/ann/public_html/classes on Solaris OS or Linux. This location is accessible through some web servers as http://*host:port*/~ann/classes/.

- The ComputeEngine class depends on the Compute and Task interfaces, which are contained in the compute.jar JAR file.

- Therefore, you need the compute.jar file in your class path when you build the server classes. Assume that the compute.jar file is located in the directory c:\home\ann\public_html\classes on Windows or the directory /home/ann/public_html/classes on Solaris OS or Linux. Given these paths, you can use the following commands to build the server classes.

Microsoft Windows:

```
cd c:\home\waldo\src
javac -cp c:\home\ann\public_html\classes\compute.jar
    engine\ComputeEngine.java
```

Solaris OS or Linux:

```
cd /home/ann/src
javac -cp c:\home\ann\public_html\classes\compute.jar
    engine/ComputeEngine.java
```

- The stub class for ComputeEngine implements the Compute interface, which refers to the Task interface. So, the class definitions for those two interfaces need to be network-accessible for the stub to be received by other Java virtual machines such as the registry's Java virtual machine.

- The client Java virtual machine will already have these interfaces in its class path, so it does not actually need to download their definitions.

- The compute.jar file under the public_html directory can serve this purpose. Now, the compute engine is ready to deploy. You could do that now, or you could wait until after you have built the client.

2.9.8.4 Building the Client Classes:

- The client package contains two classes, ComputePi, the main client program, and Pi, the client's implementation of the Task interface.

- Assume that user Suresh, the developer of the client classes, has placed ComputePi.java and Pi.java in the directory c:\home\jones\src\client on Windows or the directory /home/suresh/src/client on Solaris OS or Linux. He is deploying the class files for the compute engine to download in a subdirectory of his public_html directory, c:\home\suresh\public_html\classes on Windows or /home/suresh/public_html/classes on Solaris OS or Linux. This location is accessible through some web servers as http://host:port/~suresh/classes/.

- The client classes depend on the Compute and Task interfaces, which are contained in the compute.jar JAR file. Therefore, you need the compute.jar file in your class path when you build the client classes. Assume that the compute.jar file is located in the directory c:\home\suresh\public_html\classes on Windows or the directory /home/Suresh/public_html/classes on Solaris OS or Linux.

- Given these paths, you can use the following commands to build the client classes:

Microsoft Windows:

```
cd c:\home\waldo\src
javac –cp c:\home\suresh\public_html\classes\compute.jar
    client\ComputePi.java client\Pi.java
mkdir c:\home\suresh\public_html\classes\client
cp client\Pi.class
    c:\home\suresh\public_html\classes\client
```

Solaris OS or Linux:

```
cd /home/suresh/src
javac –cp c/home/suresh/public_html/classes/compute.jar
```

```
    client/ComputePi.java client/Pi.java
mkdir/home/suresh/public_html/classes/client
cp client/Pi.class
    /home/suresh/public_html/classes/client
```

2.9.8.5 Running the Programs

A Note about Security:

- The server and client programs run with a security manager installed. When you run either program, you need to specify a security policy file so that the code is granted the security permissions it needs to run. Here is an example policy file to use with the server program:

```
{
    permission java.security.AllPermission ;
};
```

Here is an example policy file to use with the client program:

```
    permission java.security.AllPermission;
};
```

- For both example policy files, all permissions are granted to the classes in the program's local class path, because the local application code is trusted, but no permissions are granted to code downloaded from other locations.

- Therefore, the compute engine server restricts the tasks that it executes (whose code is not known to be trusted and might be hostile) from performing any operations that require security permissions.

- The example client's Pi task does not require any permissions to execute. In this example, the policy file for the server program is named server.policy, and the policy file for the client program is named client.policy.

2.9.8.6 Starting the Server

- Before starting the compute engine, you need to start the RMI registry. The RMI registry is a simple server-side bootstrap naming facility that enables remote clients to obtain a reference to an initial remote object.

- It can be started with the rmiregistry command.

- Before you execute rmiregistry, you must make sure that the shell or window in which you will run rmiregistry either has no CLASSPATH environment variable set or has a CLASSPATH environment variable that does not include the path to any classes that you want downloaded to clients of your remote objects.

- To start the registry on the server, execute the rmiregistry command. This command produces no output and is typically run in the background.

2.9.8.7 Building a JAR File of Interface Classes

- First, you need to compile the interface source files in the compute package and then build a JAR file that contains their class files.

- Assume that user Suresh has written these interfaces and placed the source files in the directory c:\home\waldo\src\compute on Windows or the directory /home/suresh/src/compute on Solaris OS or Linux. Given these paths, you can use the following commands to compile the interfaces and create the JAR file:

Microsoft Windows (use javaw if start is not available):

```
start rmiregistry

Solaries OS or Linux:

Rmiregistry
```

- By default, the registry runs on port 1099. To start the registry on a different port, specify the port number on the command line. Do not forget to unset your CLASSPATH environment variable.

Microsoft Windows:

```
Start rmiregistry 2001

Solaris OS or Linux:

Rmiregistry 201 &
```

- Once the registry is started, you can start the server. You need to make sure that both the compute.jar file and the remote object implementation class are in your class path. When you start the compute engine, you need to specify, using the java.rmi.server.codebase property, where the server's classes are network accessible.

- In this example, the server-side classes to be made available for downloading are the Compute and Task interfaces, which are available in the compute.jar file in the public_html\classes directory of user Suresh. The compute engine server is started on the host zaphod, the same host on which the registry was started.

Microsoft Windows:

```
java -cp c: \home\suresh\src;c:\home\ann\public_html\classes\compute.jar

Djava.rmi.server.codebase=file:/c:/home/suresh/public_html/classes/compute.jar
```
- Djava.rmi.server.hostname=zaphod.east.sun.com
- Djava.security.policy=server.policy
```
engine.CompteEngine
```

Solaris OS or Linux:

java   -cp /home/suresh/src:/home/ann/public_html/classes/compute.jar

Djava.rmi.server.codebase=http://zaphod/~suresh/classes/compute.jar

   -Djava.rmi.server.hostname=zaphod.east.sun.com

   -Djava.security.policy=server.policy

engine.CompteEngine

The above java command defines the following system properties:

- The **java.rmi.server.codebase:** Property specifies the location, a codebase URL, from which the definitions for classes originating *from* this server can be downloaded. If the codebase specifies a directory hierarchy (as opposed to a JAR file), you must include a trailing slash at the end of the codebase URL.

- The **java.rmi.server.hostname:** Property specifies the host name or address to put in the stubs for remote objects exported in this Java virtual machine. This value is the host name or address used by clients when they attempt to communicate remote method invocations. By default, the RMI implementation uses the server's IP address as indicated by the java.net.InetAddress.getLocalHost API. However, sometimes, this address is not appropriate for all clients and a fully qualified host name would be more effective. To ensure that RMI uses a host name (or IP address) for the server that is routable from all potential clients, set the java.rmi.server.hostname property. The java.security.policy property is used to specify the policy file that contains the permissions you intend to grant.

2.9.8.8 Starting the Client

- Once the registry and the compute engine are running, you can start the client, specifying the following: The location where the client serves its classes (the Pi class) by using the java.rmi.server.codebase property

- The java.security.policy property, which is used to specify the security policy file that contains the permissions you intend to grant to various pieces of code As command-line arguments, the host name of the server (so that the client knows where to locate the Compute remote object) and the number of decimal places to use in the calculation Start the client on another host (a host named ford, for example) as follows:

Microsoft Windows:

java   -cp c: \home\jsuresh\src;c:\home\jones\public_html\classes\compute.jar

   - Djava.rmi.server.codebase=file:/c:/home/suresh/public_html/classes/

   - Djava.security.policy=client.policy

     client.ComputePi zaphod.east.sun.com 60

Solaris OS or Linux:

java   -cp /home/suresh/src:/home/suresh/public_html/classes/compute.jar

  – Djava.rmi.server.codebase=http://ford/~suresh/classes/

  -Djava.security.policy=server.policy

    clinet.ComputePi zaphod.east.sun.com 45

Note: The class path is set on the command line so that the interpreter can find the client classes and the JAR file containing the interfaces. Also note that the value of the java.rmi.server.codebase property, which specifies a directory hierarchy, ends with a trailing slash.

After you start the client, the following output is displayed:

   3.141592653589793238462643383279502884197169399

The following Fig. 2.7 illustrates where the **rmiregistry**, the **ComputeEngine** server, and the **ComputePi** client obtain classes during program execution

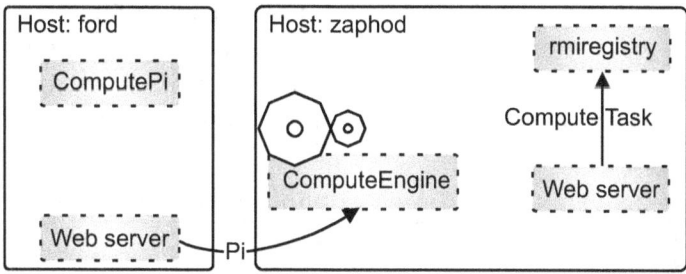

Fig 2.7: RMI registry

• When the ComputeEngine server binds its remote object reference in the registry, the registry downloads the Compute and Task interfaces on which the stub class depends.

• These classes are downloaded from either the ComputeEngine server's web server or file system, depending on the type of codebase URL used when starting the server.

• Because the ComputePi client has both the Compute and the Task interfaces available in its class path, it loads their definitions from its class path, not from the server's codebase.

• Finally, the Pi class is loaded into the ComputeEngine server's Java virtual machine when the Pi object is passed in the execute Task remote call to the ComputeEngine object.

• The Pi class is loaded by the server from either the client's web server or file system, depending on the type of codebase URL used when starting the client.

2.10 INDIRECT COMMUNICATION

• *Indirect communication* is well-defined as communication among entities in a distributed system through an intermediary with no direct coupling between the sender and the receiver(s)

- The techniques considered in RMI and RPC are all based on a direct coupling between a sender and a receiver, and this leads to a some amount of inflexibility in the system in terms of dealing with change.

- To explain this, consider a simple client-server communication. Because of the direct coupling, it is more difficult to replace a server with a substitute one offering equivalent functionality. Likewise, if the server fails, this straight away affects the client, which must openly deal with the fiasco.

- In contrast, indirect communication dodges this direct coupling and hence receives exciting properties. The two key properties stopping from the use of an intermediary:

- Space Uncoupling: In which the sender does not know or need to know the uniqueness of the receiver(s), and vice versa. Because of this space uncoupling, the system developer has many degrees of freedom in dealing with change: participants (senders or receivers) can be replaced, updated, replicated or migrated.

- Time Uncoupling: In which the sender and receiver(s) can have self-governing lifetimes, the sender and receiver(s) do not need to exist at the same time to communicate. This has important profits, for example, in more instable environments where senders and receivers may come and go. Hence, indirect communication is often used in distributed systems where change is expected for example, in mobile environments where users may rapidly connect to and disconnect from the global network and must be coped to provide more dependable services.

Table 2.2 : Space and Time Coupling in Distributed Systems

	Time Coupled	**Time- Uncoupled**
Space Coupling	**Properties:** Communication directed towards a given receiver or receivers; receiver(s) must exist at that moment in time **Examples:** Message passing, remote invocation	**Properties:** Communication directed towards a given receiver or receivers; sender(s) and receiver(s) can have free lifetimes
Space uncoupling	**Properties:** Sender does not need to know the identity of the receiver(s); receiver(s) must exist at that moment in time **Examples:** IP multicast	**Properties:** Sender does not need to know the identity of the receiver(s); sender(s)and receiver(s) can have independent lifetimes **Examples:** Most indirect communication paradigms covered in this chapter

2.11 GROUP COMMUNICATION

- Groups of computers to communicate with one another using the existing network is referred to as group communication. It is considerably more efficient to convey information to an entire group than separately to each member of the group.

- The typical group communication applications are video conferencing, distance learning, distributed databases, data replication, multi-party games, distributed simulation; network broadcast services and many others.

2.11.1 Types of Communication

In this section we discuss the different types of group communication; there are various types of communication which can be differentiated, depending on the number of senders and receivers involved. A distinction is made between the following basic types of communication:

- Unicast(1:1)
- Multicast(1:n)
- Concast(m:1)
- Multipeer/Multipoint(m:n)

The notation in the brackets should be interpreted as follows: The first number (m) refers to the number of senders; the second (n) refers to the number of receivers. The special case of a single sender or receiver is denoted by the number 1.

1. Unicast Communication

First type of group communication is Unicast which is equivalent to traditional point-to-point communication in which there is exactly one sender and one receiver. Point-to-point communication between two people in a group can be viewed as a special case of group communication. Fig. 2.8 illustrates a simple unicast communication within a group. The nodes shaded in green (receivers) and red (sender) represent members of a group. The nodes in yellow represent non-members of a group.

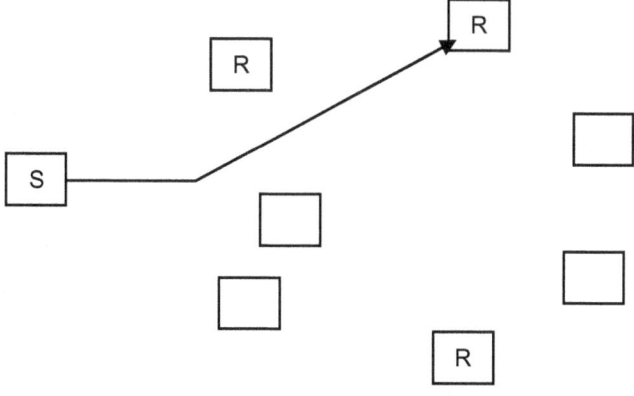

Fig. 2.8: Unicast communication

- As shown in the example above, the sender (S) communicates receiver (R) using unicast communication. The communication may be a simplex wherein one participant is the sender of data and the other participant is receiver of the data or duplex communication wherein both the participants are active senders as well as active receivers.
- Traditional applications like File Transfer Protocol (FTP), electronic mail, chat etc. make use of unicast communication.
- If unicast is used to support group communication, then two unicast communication relationships have to be established between two members in a group.
- The number of transmissions for a packet delivery linearly increases with group size.
- Since there is no scalability with respect to group size, unicast communication is not feasible option for large groups.

2. Multicast Communication

- Multicast communication is basically used with the new emerging applications like video-conferencing, shared whiteboards; multi-user games etc. getting into the life of an average computer user, a mode of communication called multicast.
- These applications require that the data should be sent only to a set of participants (green shaded nodes), not to every other end points (yellow shaded nodes) as shown in Fig. 2.9.
- Hence, to fulfill the requirements where the communication is restricted to only a set of participants (a group), the multicast communication emerged in the computer communications arena.
- When compared to traditional IP unicasting and broadcasting, IP multicasting is more efficient and economical, consumes less bandwidth and processing power, scales better, and does not lead to network congestion as the number of clients grows.
- Multicasting operates over any network technology that can support Transmission Control Protocol/Internet Protocol (TCP/IP), including Ethernet, Asynchronous Transfer Mode (ATM), frame relay, and satellite.

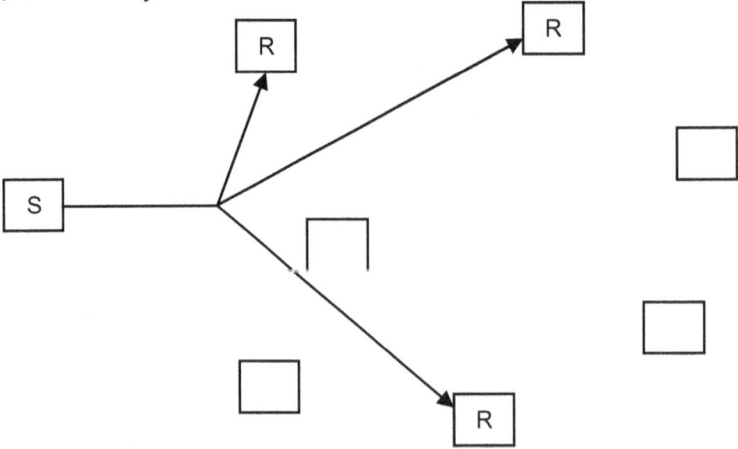

Fig. 2.9: Multicast communication

3. Concast Communication

- In a concast communication several senders are able to send user data to a single receiver. This involves an m:1 communication in which data is sent on a unidirectional basis from the senders to the receiver.

- Concast communication is used in the field of open distance learning when students forward their homework assignments to their teachers or tutors.

4. Multipeer Communication

- Multipeer communication takes place when several senders are able to send user data to the group members. This corresponds to an m:n type of communication and is frequently referred to as multipoint communication.

- Multipeer is the most diverse form of group communication because it places no restrictions on the number of senders and receivers that can communicate.

- Multipeer communication is very difficult to implement but can be emulated through the simultaneous operation of several multicast communications.

- To this end, a multicast communication is established for each sender to all the other members of the group. This technical implementation is frequently selected as an option today.

2.11.2 Other Types of Communication

- As we discuss the basic types of group communication in previous section there are other types of communication also available. Unicast can be viewed as an exception in group communication types since it does not really involve more than two communication partners.

- Other two types of communication are also used today:

  - **Anycast**

  - **Broadcast**

- Anycast also makes use of the group concept. However, in this case the group is not used for the actual exchange of data; this takes place with the available unicast mechanisms or with new anycast mechanisms.

- The receiver is selected from a group of potential candidates. In anycast, there is also a one-to-many association between network addresses and network endpoints. The destination address identifies a set of receiver endpoints, but only one of them is chosen at any given time to receive information from any given sender. This is shown in Fig. 2.10.

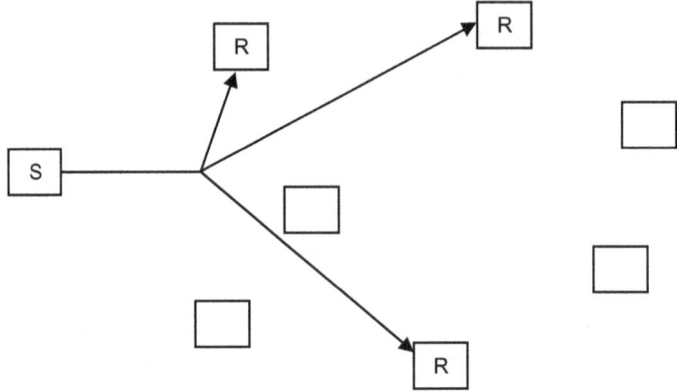

Fig. 2.10: Anycast communication

- In this example, though the receivers are identified by single address, sender S sends data to only one receiver. Anycast is generally used as a way to provide high availability and load balancing for stateless services such as access to replicated data; for example, Domain Name System (DNS) service is a distributed service over geographically dispersed servers.

- In broadcast communication, there are one or more senders that send data to every other receiver in the network as shown in Fig. 2.11 and there is no restriction with respect to the group of receivers. In this sense broadcast is a simplified version of multicast because it does not require the establishment, addressing or administration of a group.

- There are packet radio networks, satellite networks and bus local networks that use broadcast communication.

- However, IP broadcasting sends a copy of a message simultaneously to every client on the network, including those who don't want to receive it.

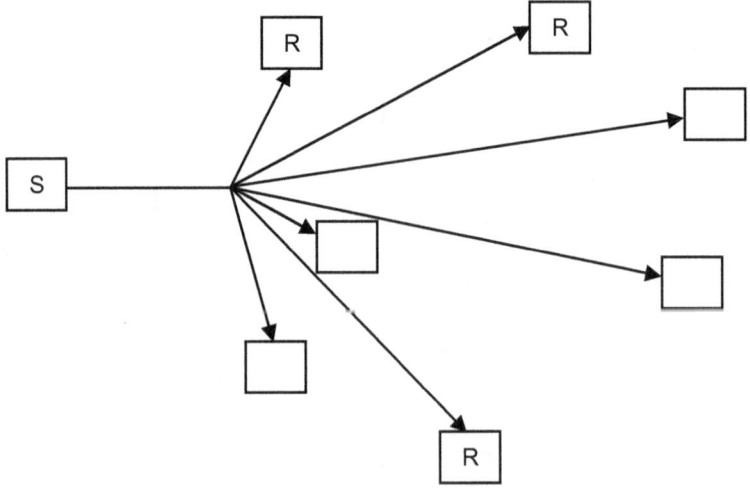

Fig. 2.11: Broadcast communication

- For example in Fig. 2.11, yellow shaded nodes also receive the packets without cause. In data communication, broadcast tends to play a less important role, at least for wide-area networks. Applications of group communication are listed in Table 2.3.

Table 2.3: Applications of Group Communication

Types of Communication	No. of Senders	No. of Receivers	Applications
Unicast	1	1	FTP, electronic mail, chat.
Multicast	1	n	Database Updates, Push media, Live Concerts, Newsfeeds, Lectures and Announcements.
Concast	M	1	Resource Discovery, Auctions, Data Collection and Polling.
Multipeer	M	n	Multimedia Conferencing , Synchronized Resources , Concurrent Processing, Chat Groups, Distance Learning , Multi-player Games and Distributed Interactive Simulations.
Broadcast	1	All	Television, Radio, Ethernet and Address Resolution Protocol (ARP).
Anycast	1	1 (anyone of the designated receiver in a group)	Domain Name System.

2.12 PUBLISH-SUBSCRIBE SYSTEMS

- A publish-subscribe system is a scheme where publishers publish structuredevents to an event service and subscribers express interest in particular events throughsubscriptions which can be random patterns over the structured events.

- For example, asubscriber could express an interest in all events related to buying early edition of some book, such as theavailability of a new edition or updates to the related web site.

- The job of the publishsubscribesystem is to tie subscriptions alongside published events and guarantee theright delivery of event notifications.

- A given event will be delivered to potentiallymany subscribers, and hence publish-subscribe is fundamentally a one-to-manycommunications model

Applications of Publish-Subscribe Systems

Publish-subscribe systems are used in avaried variety of application domains, particularly those related to the large-scaledistribution of events. Examples include:• financial information systems;other areas with live feeds of real-time data (including RSS feeds);

- Support for cooperative working, where a number of participants need to beinformed of events of shared interest;

- Support for ubiquitous computing, including the management of events emanatingfrom the ubiquitous infrastructure (for example, location events);

- A broad set of monitoring applications, including network monitoring in theInternet.

- Publish-subscribe is also a key component of Google's infrastructure, including forexample the distribution of events related to advertisements, such as 'ad clicks', tointerested parties.

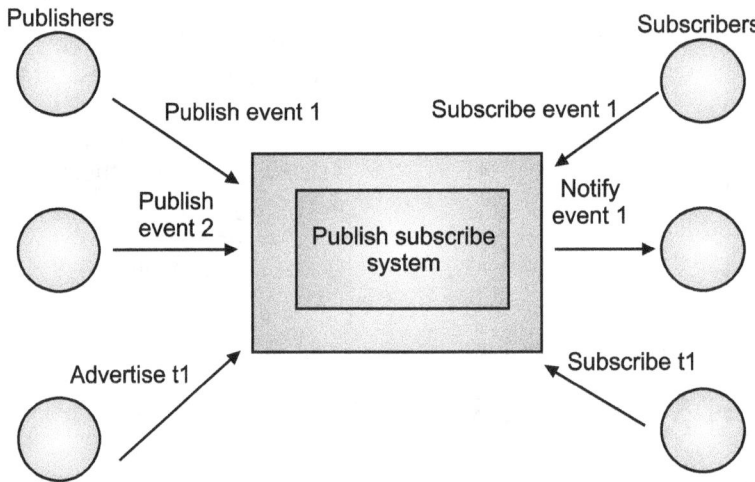

Fig. 2.12: The publish-subscribe model

2.12.1 Programming Model

- The programming model in publish-subscribe systems is based on a small set of operations. Publishers disseminate an event and subscribers express an interest in a set of events through subscriptions.

- Some systems complement the above set of operations by introducing the concept of advertisements.

- With advertisements, publishers have the option of declaring the nature of future events.

- The advertisements are defined in terms of the types of events of interest (these happen to take the same form as filters).

- In other words, subscribers declare their interests in terms of subscriptions and publishers optionally declare the styles of events they will generate through advertisements.

- The expressiveness of publish-subscribe systems is determined by the subscription (filter) model, with a number of schemes defined and considered here in increasing order of sophistication:

Channel-Based: In this approach, publishers publish events to named channels and subscribers then subscribe to one of these named channels to receive all events sent to that channel. This is a rather primitive scheme and the only one that defines a physical channel; all other schemes employ some form of filtering over the content of events as we shall see below. Although simple, this scheme has been used successfully in the CORBA Event Service

Topic-Based (Also Referred to as Subject-Based): In this approach, we make the assumption that each notification is expressed in terms of a number of fields, with one field denoting the topic. Subscriptions are then defined in terms of the topic of interest. This approach is equivalent to channel-based approaches, with the difference that topics are implicitly defined in the case of channels but explicitly declared as one of the fields in topic-based approaches. The expressiveness of topic based approaches can also be enhanced by introducing hierarchical organization of topics. For example, let us consider a publish-subscribe system for this book. Subscriptions could be defined in terms of indirect_communicationorindirect_communication/publish-subscribe. Subscribers expressing interest in the former will receive all events related to this chapter, whereas with the latter subscribers can instead express an interest in the more specific topic of publish subscribe.

Content-Based: Content-based approaches are a generalization of topic-based approaches allowing the expression of subscriptions over a range of fields in an event notification. More specifically, a content-based filter is a query defined in terms of compositions of constraints over the values of event attributes. For example, a subscriber could express interest in events that relate to the topic of publish-subscribe systems, where the system in question is the 'CORBA Event Service' and where the author is 'Tim Kindberg' or 'Gordon Blair'. The sophistication of the associated query languages varies from system to system, but in general this approach is significantly more expressive than channel- or topic-based approaches, but with significant new implementation challenges (discussed below).

Type-Based: These approaches are intrinsically linked with object-based approaches where objects have a specified type. In type-based approaches, subscriptions are defined in terms of types of events and matching is defined in terms of types or subtypes of the given filter. This approach can express a range of filters, from coarse grained filtering based on overall type names to more fine-grained queries defining attributes and methods of a given object. Such fine-grained filters are similar inexpressiveness to content-based approaches. The advantages of type-based approaches are that they can be integrated elegantly into programming languages and they can check the type correctness of subscriptions, eliminating some kinds of subscription errors.

2.13 MESSAGE QUEUES

- *Message queues* are a further significant category of indirect communication systems. Whereas groups and publish subscribe provide a one-to-many style of communication, message queues provide a *point-to-point* service using the concept of a message queue as an indirection, thus accomplishing the anticipated properties of space and time uncoupling.

- They are point-to-point in that the sender places the message into a queue, and it is then removed by a single process. Message queues are also referred to as Message-Oriented Middleware.

2.13.1 Programming Model

Especially, producer processes can *send* messages to a definite queue and other (consumer) processes can then receive messages from this queue. Three types of receive are usually maintained:

- A *blocking receive*, which will block till an suitable message is available;

- A *non-blocking receive* (a polling operation), which will check the status of the queue and return a message if available, or a not available indication otherwise;

- A *notify* operation, which will issue an event notification when a message is available in the associated queue.

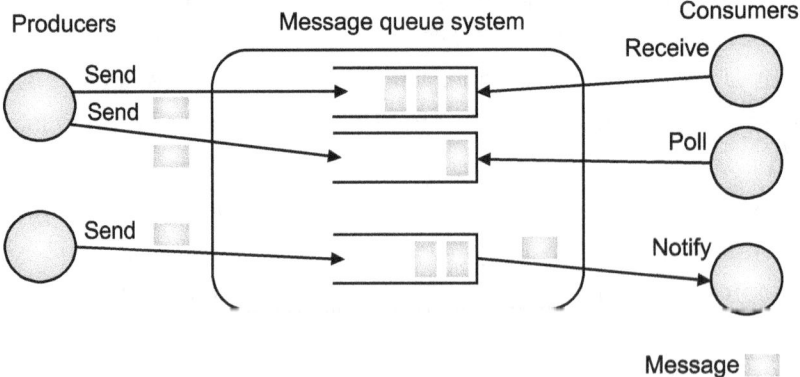

Fig. 2.13: The message queue paradigm

- A number of processes can send messages to the same queue, and similarly a number of receivers can eliminate messages from a queue.

- The queuing policy is usually first-in-first-out (FIFO), but most message queue operations also support the concept of priority, with higher-priority messages delivered first.

- Consumer processes can also select messages from the queue based on properties of a message.

- A message consists of a destination (that is, a unique identifier designating the destination queue), metadata associated with the message, including fields such as the priority of the message and the delivery mode, and also the body of the message

2.14 SHARED MEMORY APPROACHES

2.14.1 Distributed Shared Memory

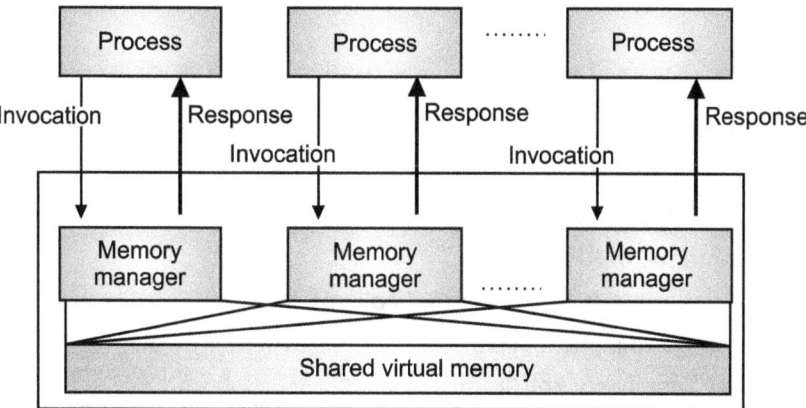

Distributed shared memory

Fig. 2.14: The Shared Memory Approach

- Distributed shared memory (DSM) is an abstraction used for sharing data between computers that do not share physical memory.

- Processes access DSM by reads and updates to what appears to be ordinary memory within their address space.

- However, an underlying runtime system ensures transparently that processes executing at different computers observe the updates made by one another.

- The main point of DSM is that it spares the programmer the concerns of message passing when writing applications that might otherwise have to use it. DSM is primarily a tool for parallel applications or for any distributed application or group of applications in which individual shared data items can be accessed directly.

- DSM is in general less appropriate in client-server systems, where clients normally view server-held resources as abstract data and access them by request (for reasons of modularity and protection).

- Message passing cannot be avoided altogether in a distributed system: in the absence of physically shared memory, the DSM runtime support has to send updates in messages between computers.

- DSM systems manage replicated data: each computer has a local copy of recently accessed data items stored in DSM, for speed of access.

REVIEW QUESTIONS

1. What is marshalling?
2. State and explain MPI.
3. Write a short note on
   (1) RPC
   (2) JAVA RMI
   (3) Group communication
4. State and discuss issues in implementing RPC.
5. Publish subscribe system state and explain.
6. State the advantages of RPC.
7. Message Quening models explain with diagrams.
8. Use of group communication in DS.
9. What is socket? Specify socket primitives.

UNIVERSITY QUESTIONS

May 2012

1. What is marshaling? List out the different approaches of external data representation and discuss each approach in detail.   [8]
2. The Internet enables users to access services and run application over a heterogeneous collection of computers and networks. How to apply heterogeneity for networks, computer hardware, operating systems and programming languages in distributed systems.   [8]
3. Write a C function for adding two integers and call it using RPC and identify the contents generated by stub.   [6]
4. Explain the purpose of following with respect to RMI.   [6]
   (i) Dispatcher
   (ii) Reflection and
   (iii) Registry in RMI

5. List and explain the steps involved in doing remote computation through RPC. **[6]**
6. Compare static and dynamic remote method invocation with the help of suitable example. **[6]**
7. Explain Message Queuing model with suitable example. **[6]**

Oct. 2012

8. What is RPC? Explain role of client and server stub procedures in RPC in the context of a procedural language. **[8]**
9. What is socket? Explain the difference between connection oriented socket and connectionless socket? **[8]**
10. What is pipe? How pipe is used for inter-process communication? **[8]**

May 2013

11. List out different types of transparencies associated in a Distributed System. Compare Distributed Operating System with Network Operating System in terms of transparencies associated. **[8]**
12. Define Remote Object. Explain Distributed Objects with working of client side proxy and server side skeleton to provide remote access to methods of an object. **[8]**
13. What is marshalling? How marshalling and serialization is used in communication between a client and a server? **[8]**
14. Explain working of Remote Procedure Call with neat diagram showing various RPC components and their interactions with each other. **[8]**
15. How Lightweight Remote Procedure Call technology is used to provided communication between domains in a single machine. What are the basic feature of LRPC? **[8]**

Dec. 2013

16. Explain steps involved in doing remote computation through RPC with suitable diagram. **[8]**
17. What is persistence and synchronicity in communication? Explain different forms of message oriented communication. **[10]**
18. What is group communication? What is its use in distributed computing? **[6]**
19. Give a short note on each of the following : **[12]**
    (i) Asynchronous RPC
    (ii) Doors
    (iii) Interface Definition language
20. Describe distributed shared memory architecture. **[3]**

May 2014

21. Explain General Architecture of Message Queuing System along with roles of message broker. **[8]**

22. What are sockets? Specify socket primitives? Draw a diagram specifying connection oriented socket communication.   **[8]**
23. Explain different "RPC invocation semantics".   **[8]**
24. Explain design and implementation issues of Distributed Shared Memory in details. **[8]**
25. Explain   **[8]**
    (i) Flat and Hierarchical groups
    (ii) Open and closed groups
26. Explain basic reliable multicasting. How it could be made scalable?   **[10]**

Dec. 2014

27. Discuss the concept of request/reply message handling using HTTP protocol and TCP protocol. Compare the working, limitations and advantages of both protocols.   **[8]**
28. What is primary motivation behind the development of a lightweight RPC System? Describe the four techniques used in a LRPC system that makes more efficient than a conventional RPC system.   **[8]**
29. Write a short note on   **[8]**
    (i) Sun RPC
    (ii) CORBA

May 2015

30. What is Remote Method Invocation? How would you incorporate persistent asychoronous communication into model of communication based on RMIs to remote object ?   **[8]**
31. What is socket ? What is the difference between connection-oriented socket and connection-less socket?**[8]**
32. Compare local method invocation and remote method invocation. Explain the role of proxy and skeleton in remote method invocation in detail.   **[8]**

MIDDLEWARE

3.1 OBJECT ORIENTED DISTRIBUTED COMPUTING TECHNOLOGIES

3.1.1 Introduction

- The idea of distributed objects is an extension of the concept of remote procedure calls. In a remote procedure call system (Sun RPC, DCE RPC, and Java RMI), code is executed remotely via a remote procedure call.

- The unit of distribution is the procedure/function/method which is used as synonym. So the client has to import a client stub (either manually as in RPC or automatically as in RMI) to allow it to connect to the server offering the remote procedure.

3.1.2 Distributed Object

The term **distributed objects** usually refers to software modules that are designed to work together, but reside either in multiple computers connected via a network or in different processes inside the same computer. One object sends a message to another object in a remote machine or process to perform some task. The results are sent back to the calling object.

Distributed Object Examples:

- DCOM (Distributed Common Object Model), developed by Microsoft, but also available on other platforms. Built on top of DCE's RPC, interacts with COM.

- CORBA (Common Object Request Broker Architecture), defined by the Object Management Group, an industry consortium. CORBA is available for most major operating systems

- JINI ("Genie," JINI is not initials a joke; JINI actually doesn't stand for anything.) JINI is developed on top of Java. JINI was released by Sun in January, 1999.

3.1.3 Local Vs Distributed Object

Local and distributed objects differ in many respects. Here are some of them:

- **Life Cycle:** Creation, migration and deletion of distributed objects is different from local objects

- **Reference:** Remote references to distributed objects are more complex than simple pointers to memory addresses

- **Request Latency:** A distributed object request is orders of magnitude slower than local method invocation

- **Object Activation:** Distributed objects may not always be available to serve an object request at any point in time

- **Parallelism:** Distributed objects may be executed in parallel.

- **Communication:** There are different communication primitives available for distributed objects requests

- **Failure:** Distributed objects have far more points of failure than typical local objects

- **Security:** Distribution makes them vulnerable to attack.

3.1.4 Distributed Object Model

- Distributed systems require entities which reside in different address spaces, potentially on different machines, to communicate.

- The model we describe is based on objects. Objects are used to structure both applications programs and operating system kernels. They also provide the application interface to the operating system kernel, and access to hardware devices for both kernels and applications.

- By providing structuring mechanisms for large (distributed) objects, we believe that applications will be are easier to build.

- At the same time we provide flexibility by allowing extensions of operating system kernels and applications with new objects at run time, and by providing a way to bind to objects dynamically.

- An important aspect of a distributed system is the scalability of the system. A scalable system should not depend on centralized resources or on algorithms that need global information.

- At the same time, a flexible system can use different algorithms depending on the situation.

- For example, the use of broadcasting and multicasting on a local Ethernet can be quite effective but should be avoided on a world wide scale.

3.1.4.1 Distributed Objects

- The objects which call as a local object are limited to one address space. This implies that both the state and the interface instances are in a single address space.

- To be able to create objects that span multiple address spaces we introduce distributed objects.

- So we define the distributed object as "A **distributed object** is an object that can have interface instances in multiple address spaces, or can have its state spread out over multiple address spaces, or both."

- Distributed objects can be implemented in different ways depending on the partitioning and replication of the state and on the way in which the overall state is kept consistent.

- The state is said to be **partitioned** if it is split up in a number of disjunct parts that are stored in different address spaces. The state can be **replicated** by storing copies in different address spaces.

- These two techniques can be combined by replicating partitions.

- To have distributed objects, one needs communication to keep an object consistent if the state of the object is replicated.

- It is also needed if a method is invoked on an object but not all the state of the object that is needed by the method implementation is available in the address space in which the method was invoked.

- For example, a simple distributed object might keep its state in one address space and have multiple interfaces instances in other address spaces.

- A method can then be invoked in an address space where the state is not locally available, so it needs to be forwarded (e.g. using RPC) to the address space which keeps the state of the object.

- Another example is an object with fully replicated state. In this case, each address space with an interface instance also contains a full copy of the object's state.

- When a method is invoked that changes the state of the object, all other address spaces that keep a copy of the state must be informed about the change. When this happens is object dependent.

- We structure distributed objects as a collection of communicating local objects. In Fig. 3.1 (a) we see a distributed object which spans 4 address spaces: A1 through A4. Each of these address spaces contains a local object that *represents* the distributed object, by providing the interfaces of the distributed object.

- Together, these local objects implement the distributed object. Method invocation on a distributed object is only possible in a given address space if that address space contains a local object that is part of the distributed object.

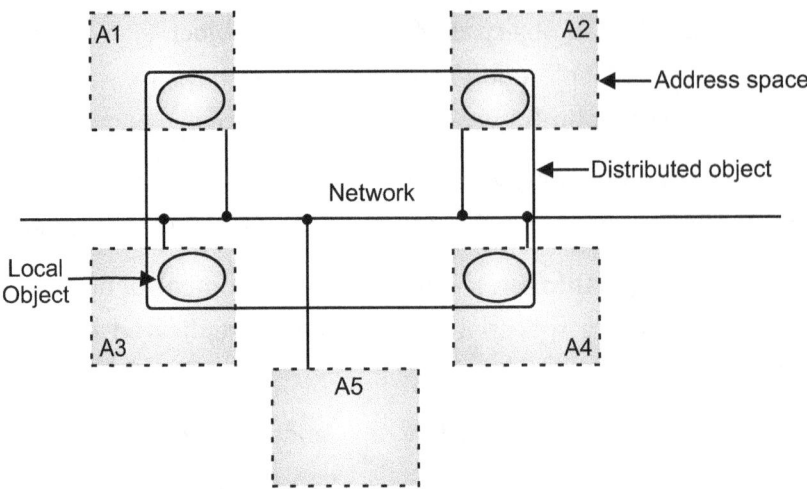

Fig. 3.1 (a): A distributed object

- "The process of installing and initializing such an object in an address space is called **binding**."

Two Aspects of the Implementation of the Local Objects are:

- The structure of the distributed object and the role the local object plays in the distributed object, and

- The communication protocols which are supported by the local object. The first aspect comes from the fact that distributed objects vary in partitioning, replication, etc. This is reflected in the implementations of the local object. The second aspect is due to the varying communication demands of distributed objects. For example, small distributed objects with centralized state can be implemented best using a low-latency RPC protocol. Distributed objects with many replicas work best with multicast and/or group communication protocols, and objects that move large amounts of state back and forth benefit from bulk data transfer protocols.

Note: The best communication protocol depends on the internal structure of a distributed object, and not primarily on its type. A simple file object can be implemented in various ways: with many replicas and a voting mechanism, or partitioned, or just stored in one place.

- This means that multiple communication protocols should be supported in a transparent way.

- The *user* of the object should not be concerned with these details: the user only invokes methods on the object. Fig. 3.1 (b) shows a distributed object with local objects in two address spaces.

- The local object in address space 1 supports two protocol stacks; one based on TCP/IP and the other one based on X.25.

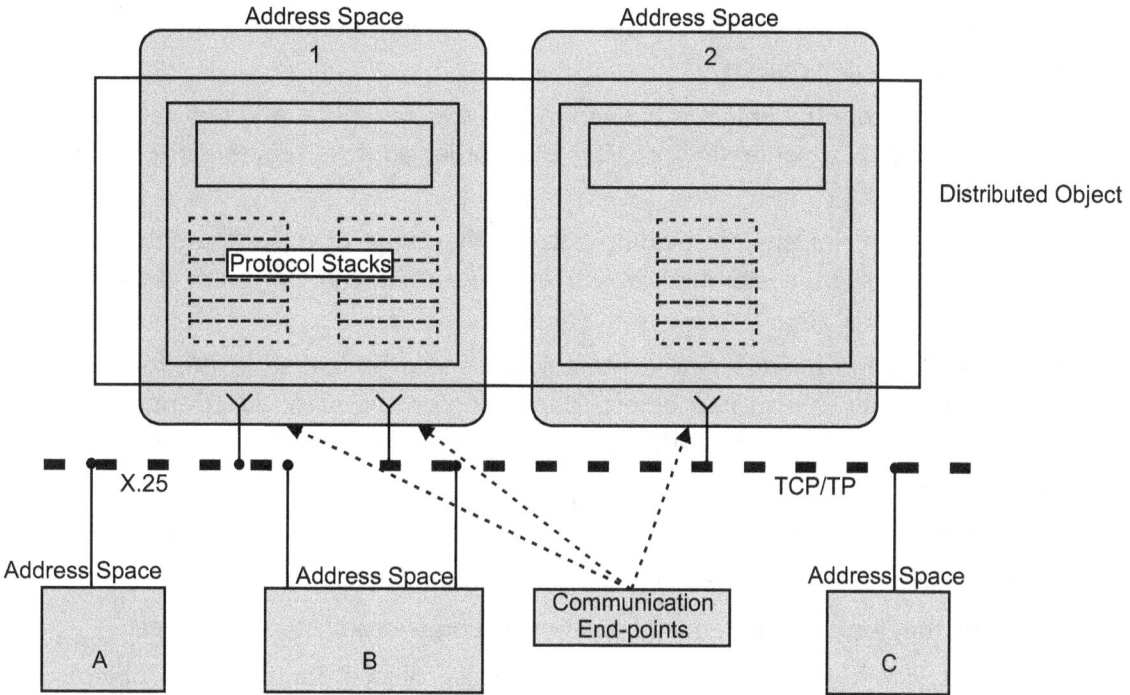

Fig. 3.1 (b): A distributed object with multiple protocol stacks

- The local object in address space 2 supports only TCP/IP. In many cases the upper communication layers of a protocol stack (the layers that deal with data representation, consistency of replicas, etc.), are independent from the lower layers (that deal with host addressing, routing, etc.). We call instances of these lower layers **communication end-points**.

- The distributed object in our example can be reached at three communication end-points, one X.25 endpoint in address space 1, and two TCP/IP end-points in address spaces 1 and 2. In the Fig. 3.1 (b) we see the address spaces, A and B, connected to the X.25 network.

- Address space B is also connected to the TCP/IP network together with address space C. Different communication end-points can be used depending on the address space from which the binding takes place.

- Address space A can only use the X.25 end-point, address space B can use all three end-points, and address space C can use the two TCP/IP end-points.

- Note that if we bind to the distributed object from address space A, we need a local object that can communicate using X.25. If we bind from address space C we need a local object that speaks TCP/IP. Depending on the communication protocols we may need different implementations of the local objects, but the interface which is presented to the user of a distributed object is always the same.

- In the remainder of this section we will describe an algorithm for the naming of and the binding to distributed objects.

- In general, a distributed object is created in one address space, and registered under a certain name with a name service. After that, other address spaces can bind to that distributed object.

- The function that implements binding accepts the name of a distributed object, and returns a pointer to a standard object interface that can be used to access the distributed object.

- During this binding process new executable code can be loaded in the form of class objects. The ability to load new objects depending on the particular distributed object that is accessed allows straightforward object implementations without leading to inflexible systems.

Basically, the Binding System Should:

- Provide a way to refer to (to name) existing distributed objects.

- Determine the "location" (in terms of communication end-points) of the object.

- Select and load a suitable implementation (class object) for the local object, and instantiate and initialize this local object.

3.1.5 Communication between Distributed Object

- **Distributed Object Communication** realizes communication between distributed objects in the distributed computing environment.

- The main role is to interconnect objects residing in non-local memory space and allowing them to perform remote calls and exchange data.

- The widely used approach on how to implement the communication channel is realized by using stubs and skeletons.

- They are generated objects whose structure and behavior depends on chosen communication protocol, but in general provide additional functionality that ensures reliable communication over the network.

- When a caller wants to perform remote call on the called object, it delegates requests to its stub which initiates communication with the remote skeleton. Consequently, the stub passes caller arguments over the network to the server skeleton.

- The skeleton then passes received data to the called object, waits for a response and returns back the result to the client stub.

- Note, there is no direct communication between the caller and the called object.

The Communication Process Consists of Several Steps as Follows:

- Caller calls a local procedure implemented by the stub.

- Stub Marshalls call type and input arguments into a request message.

- Client stub sends the message over the network to the server and blocks the current execution thread.

- Server skeleton receives the request message from the network.

- Skeleton unpacks call type from the request message and looks up the procedure on the called object.

- Skeleton unmarshalls procedure arguments.

- Skeleton executes the procedure on the called object.

- Called object performs a computation and returns the result.

- Skeleton packs the output arguments into a response message.

- Skeleton sends the message over the network back to the client.

- Client stub receives the response message from the network.

- Stub unpacks output arguments from the message.

- Stub passes output arguments to the caller, releases execution thread and caller then continues in execution.

The advantage of this architecture is that neither the caller nor the called object has to implement network related logic. This functionality, that ensures reliable communication channel over the network, has been moved to the stub and the skeleton layer.

3.1.6 Events and Notification

- **Distributed Systems** have a number of advantages over conventional, centralized systems.

- They can support a larger number of users at a smaller cost and the overall availability of the system is higher than of a centralized solution.

- Increased performance of the system can be provided to the users by adding small, inexpensive components as the systems grow. However, the cost to be paid for these benefits is the increased complexity of the system which has to be managed.

- This complexity mainly comes from the fact that a potentially large set of autonomous and heterogeneous components are part of the distributed system.

- In order to simplify the problem, middleware platforms were developed that run on top of heterogeneous operating systems and provide a homogeneous, abstract view of the entire distributed system.

- Today, most middleware systems like CORBA or Java RMI are invocation-based and thus follow a request/reply paradigm: A client requests a particular service from a server by either sending a request message or performing a Remote Method Invocation (RMI) and then receives a reply in return.

- Although such a mode of operation works well in a Local Area Network (LAN) context with a moderate number of clients and servers, it does not scale to large networks like the Internet.

- This is mainly because the request/reply paradigm only supports one-to-one communication where a single client interacts with a single server. In contrast, large-scale systems benefit from many-to-many communication since the client does not have to decide on the best communication partner.

- Another problem is the tight-coupling of request/reply middleware.

- The method invocation is synchronous forcing the client and server to couple at one particular point in time.

- Such a behaviour is clearly not desirable on the Internet because of the large number of potential communication partners and the dynamic nature of the system with new clients joining and servers failing.

- A different underlying communication paradigm for building large-scale distributed systems on top of a middleware seems to be necessary.

- In this paper, we argue that event-based communication is a viable new alternative for doing this.

In an Event-Based System, Events are the Basic Communication Mechanism:

- Event subscribers, i.e. clients, express their interest in receiving certain events in the form of an event subscription.

- Event publishers, i.e. servers, publish events which will be delivered to all interested subscribers.

Event-Based Middleware

- An event-based middleware is a traditional publish/subscribe systems have very limited application scenarios like stock quote dissemination or instant messaging middleware functionality, such as type-checking of invocations, reliability, access control, transactions, and so on, is often neglected.

- Here we focus on providing a scalable event-based middleware that is powerful enough to be the building layer for any large-scale distributed application that would traditionally be implemented with an invocation-based middleware.

- We envision a world with global e-commerce and business applications, and complex systems like an active city with thousands of components.

- We have identified a number of important middleware and publish/subscribe features that must be provided in an event-based middleware system.

- **Scalability:** It is a crucial requirement for Internet-wide applications. A system is only scalable if all its components are which means that the implementation of the middleware system must not rely on any centralized services. Moreover, algorithms must not keep any global state, and resources like network bandwidth and memory must be consumed efficiently.

- **Interoperability:** It should allow the integration of a variety of components with the middleware. The event model and the subscription language must be language- and platform-independent. The middleware must not rely on any particular support from the underlying network that is not universally available like IP multicast. However, it should take advantage of available services for performance reasons.

- **Reliability:** When delivering events may be one of the quality of service (QoS) requirements requested by event clients or servers. The middleware must support a range of QoS guarantees, from ``best-effort'' to ``guaranteed and timely'' event delivery. Fault-tolerance mechanisms such as *persistent events* stored in a database allow the middleware to operate in the light of client and server failures.

- **Expressiveness:** It is an important requirement when specifying events and subscriptions. Subscriptions must allow filtering depending on the content of events (content-based filtering). Composite event expressions that detect patterns in the event stream are an intuitive and powerful higher-level abstraction that helps event subscribers to express their information need. Nevertheless, there is always a trade-off between expressiveness and efficiency

- **Usability:** It means that the middleware is easy to handle. It should cleanly integrate with the application programming language. For instance, events should be typed objects that are mapped transparently to programming language objects. Linguistic supports involves type-checking of events and subscriptions and tools for the construction of complex composite event expressions.

3.2 CASE STUDY : CORBA

3.2.1 Introduction to CORBA

- CORBA, which stands for Common Object Request Broker Architecture, is an industry standard developed by the OMG (a consortium of more than 700 companies) to aid in distributed objects programming. CORBA is just a specification for creating and using distributed objects; CORBA is not a programming language.

- The CORBA architecture is based on the object model. This model is derived from the abstract core object model defined by the OMG in the Object Management Architecture Guide, which can be found at http://www.omg.org.

- The model is abstract in the sense that it is not directly realized by any particular technology; this allows applications to be built in a standard manner using basic building blocks such as objects.

- Therefore, a CORBA-based system is a collection of objects that isolates the requestors of services (clients) from the providers of services (servers) by a well-defined encapsulating interface.

It is important to note that CORBA objects differ from typical programming objects in three ways:

- CORBA objects can run on any platform.
- CORBA objects can be located anywhere on the network.
- CORBA objects can be written in any language that has IDL mapping.

3.2.2 CORBA Architecture

- The OMG's Object Management Architecture (OMA) tries to define the various high-level facilities that are necessary for distributed object-oriented computing. The core of the OMA is the Object Request Broker (ORB), a mechanism that provides object location transparency, communication, and activation.
- Based on the OMA, the CORBA specification which provides a description of the interfaces and facilities that must be provided by compliant ORBs was released.
- CORBA is composed of five major components: ORB, IDL, Dynamic Invocation Interface (DII), Interface Repositories (IR), and Object Adapters (OA). These are discussed in the following sections.

The Object Request Broker

The CORBA specification must have software to implement it. The software that implements the CORBA specification is called the ORB. The ORB, which is the heart of CORBA, is responsible

For all the mechanisms required to perform these tasks:

- Find the object implementation for the request.
- Prepare the object implementation to receive the request.
- Communicate the data making up the request.

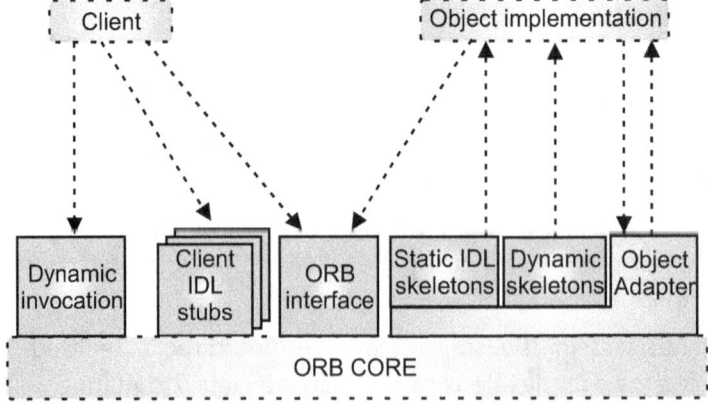

Fig. 3.2(a): The structure of the CORBA 2.0 ORB

- A number of implementations exist in the market today, including ORBIX from IONA Technologies (http://www.iona.ie), VisiBroker from Inprise (http://www.inprise.com), and JavaIDL from JavaSoft (http://java.sun.com/products/jdk.idl).

- Throughout this part of the book, we will use the VisiBroker ORB for Java, version 3.1. Fig. 3.2 (b) shows how the five major components of CORBA fit together.

- Fig. 3.2 (b) shows a request being sent by a client to an object implementation. The client is the entity that wishes to perform an operation on the object, and the object implementation is the actual code and data that implements the object.

- Note that in this Fig. 3.2(b), the client, ORB, and object implementation are all on a single machine (meaning they're not separated by a network).

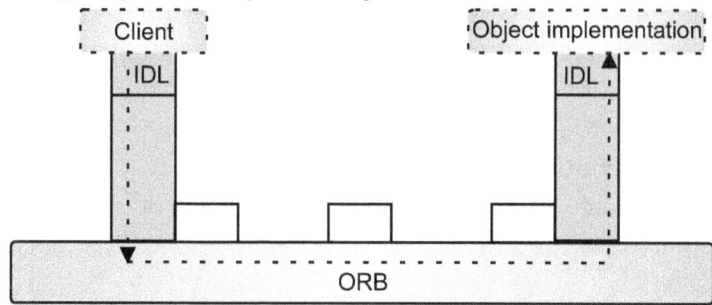

Fig. 3.2 (b): A request from a client to an object implementation

- There are two important things to note about the CORBA architecture and its computing model: Both the client and the object implementation are isolated from the ORB by an IDL interface.

- All requests are managed by the ORB. This means that every invocation (whether it is local or remote) of a CORBA object is passed to an ORB. In the case of a remote invocation, however, the invocation passed from the ORB of the client to the ORB of the object implementation as shown in Fig. 3.2 (c).

Different Vendors and Different ORBs

- Since there is more than one CORBA implementation, and these implementations are from different vendors, a good question at this point would be whether objects implemented in different ORBs from different vendors would be able to communicate with each other.

- The answer is this: all CORBA 2.0 (and above) compliant ORBs are able to interoperate via the Internet Inter-ORB Protocol, or IIOP for short. This was not true for CORBA 1.0 products, however. The whole purpose of IIOP is to ensure that your client will be able to communicate with a server written for a different ORB from a different vendor.

Interface Definition Language

- As with RMI, CORBA objects are to be specified with interfaces, which are the contract between the client and server. In CORBA's case, however, interfaces are specified in the special definition language IDL.

- The IDL defines the types of objects by defining their interfaces. An interface consists of a set of named operations and the parameters to those operations. Note that IDL is used to describe interfaces only, not implementations.
- Despite the fact that IDL syntax is similar to C++ and Java, IDL is not a programming language.
- Through IDL, a particular object implementation tells its potential clients what operations are available and how they should be invoked.
- From IDL definitions, the CORBA objects are mapped into different programming languages. Some of the programming languages with IDL mapping include C, C++, Java, Smalltalk, Lisp, and Python.
- Thus, once you define an interface to objects in IDL, you are free to implement the object using any suitable programming language that has IDL mapping. And, consequently, if you want to use that object, you can use any programming language to make remote requests to the object.

Dynamic Invocation Interface

- Invoking operations can be done through either static or dynamic interfaces. Static invocation interfaces are determined at compile time, and they are presented to the client using stubs.
- The DII, on the other hand, allows client applications to use server objects without knowing the type of those objects at compile time.
- It allows a client to obtain an instance of a CORBA object and make invocations on that object by dynamically constructing requests.
- DII uses the interface repository to validate and retrieve the signature of the operation on which a request is made. CORBA supports both the dynamic and the static invocation interfaces.

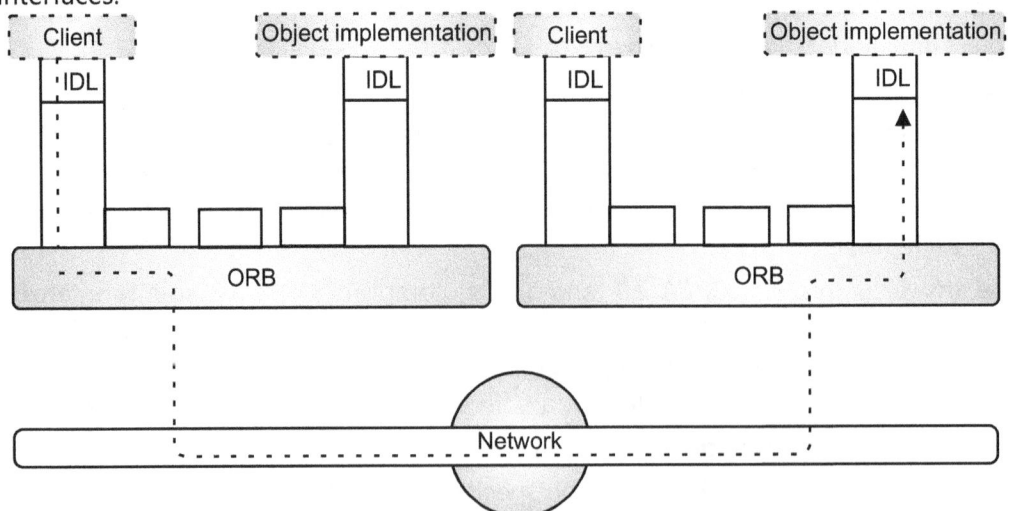

Fig. 3.2 (c): A request from a client to an object implementation within a network

Dynamic Skeleton Interface

- Analogous to the DII is the server-side dynamic skeleton interface (DSI), which allows servers to be written without having skeletons, or compile-time knowledge, for the objects being implemented.

- Unlike DII, which was part of the initial CORBA specification, DSI was introduced in CORBA 2.0. Its main purpose is to support the implementation of gateways between ORBs which utilize different communication protocols.

- However, DSI has many other applications beside interoperability. These applications include interactive software tools based on interpreters and distributed debuggers.

Interface Repository

- The IR provides another way to specify the interfaces to objects. Interfaces can be added to the interface repository service.

- Using the IR, a client should be able to locate an object that is unknown at compile time, find information about its interface, then build a request to be forwarded through the ORB.

Object Adapters

- An object adapter is the primary way that an object implementation accesses services provided by the ORB.

- Such services include object reference generation and interpretation, method invocation, security of interactions, and object and implementation activation and deactivation.

3.2.3 Corba RMI

- The impact of Java on the computing world is beyond doubt; just look at the bookshelves in the computing section of any bookstore, or attend any conference in the software industry.

- There are good reasons. The near-perfect portability of Java applications is a great boon in a multi-platform world; the ability to download Java applets and the close integration of Java with Web browsers make it an ideal medium for Web- and Internet-based development; its ease of use compared to its most popular object-oriented predecessor, C++, makes it accessible to a much wider range of developers and speeds the development process measurably.

- Java's praises having been sung, it behooves us to ask, what are its limitations? What role will Java's rising star play in the expanding universe of distributed computing? How will Java coexist with other pre-existing or simultaneously emerging technologies? In particular, what roles will Java and CORBA play, with respect to each other? Will they compete, or be complementary?

Java and CORBA:

- Java and CORBA, to a great extent, appear to be made for each other.

- "Java is the first step toward creating an Object Web, but it is still not enough. Java offers tremendous flexibility for distributed application development, but it currently does not support a client/server paradigm.

- To do this, Java needs to be augmented with a distributed object infrastructure, which is where OMG's CORBA comes into the picture. CORBA provides the missing link between the Java portable application environment and the world of intergalactic back-end services. The intersection of Java and CORBA object technologies is the natural next step in the evolution of the Object Web."

- The respective object models of Java and CORBA correspond closely to one another- they both support the notion of abstract interfaces distinct from implementations or classes; CORBA IDL data types map very naturally to Java data types; their interface inheritance mechanisms are nearly identical; CORBA name spaces-modules-map directly onto Java packages; the list could continue. Beyond having highly compatible object models, the architectural roles they play in building systems are naturally complementary.

- Simply put, Java allows you to create portable objects and easily distribute them; CORBA allows you to connect them together and to integrate them with rest of you computing environment-databases, legacy systems, objects or applications written in other languages, what have you.

3.2.3.1 RMI

- With the release of JDK version 1.1, Java has its own, built-in native ORB, called RMI (Remote Method Invocation). Though RMI is an ORB in the generic sense that it supports making method invocations on remote objects, it's not a CORBA-compliant ORB.

- RMI is native to Java. It is, in essence, an extension to the core language. RMI depends on many of the other features of Java-object serialization, portable, down-loadable object implementations, and Java interface definitions, among others. The resulting mechanism is very natural for Java programmers to use.

- They never have to leave the Java programming environment or learn any new "foreign" technology. On the other hand, RMI has some limitations, principle among which is a consequence of its greatest strength-its tight integration with Java makes it impractical for use with objects or applications written in any other language.

3.2.3.2 RMI AS Programming Technology

- Java (with RMI by extension) is a concrete programming technology. It is primarily designed to solve the problems of writing and organizing executable code, programs. It achieves this end admirably. As such, it constitutes a specific point in the space of programming technologies. .

- The chasm that exists between programming languages is always painful to cross. That pain may vary (metaphorically speaking) from that of a hangnail to that of a limb amputation, depending on the languages being used and their relative differences.

- In this respect, programming technologies are like islands, or peaks separated by deep canyons as shown in Fig. 3.3. Building systems in multiple languages requires that you somehow bridge these canyons, which is a non-trivial programming task at best, as shown in Fig. 3.3.

- The techniques and skills required depend to a great extent on the particular pair of languages being used together, so that the techniques used to make Java call Ada code are somewhat different from those used to call C++, and so on. This causes the complexity of building systems in a multilingual environment to increase significantly (sometimes non-linearly) with the number of languages being used.

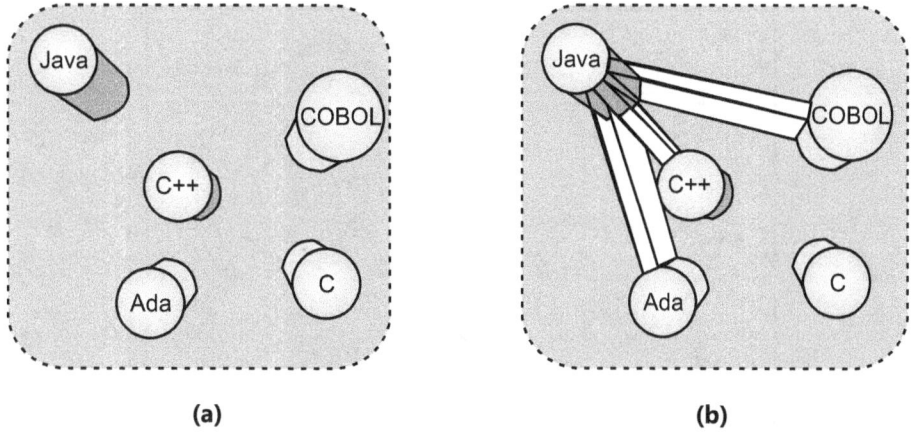

(a)   (b)

Fig. 3.3: Java concept

- Java supplies an API called JNI, or Java Native Interface, that allows Java code to call and be called by routines in other languages. It is primarily geared toward inter-operating with C and C++, and it is a rather difficult interface to master.

- RMI is a Java-to-Java technology. If you want a Java client to use RMI to communicate with a remote object in another language, you must do it by way of a Java intermediary that is co-located with the "foreign" remote object, as shown in Fig. 3.4.

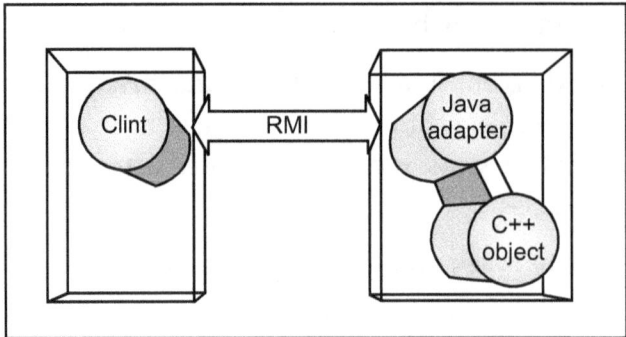

Fig. 3.4: Remote object

- The underlying problem here is that Java is a *programming* technology that, by definition, works within the boundaries of the languages itself.

- Using a programming language to solve the problem of crossing gaps between programming languages is like using rats to kill mice-at the end of the day, you still have a rodent problem. By contrast, CORBA is an *integration* technology, not a *programming* technology. It is specifically designed to be the glue that binds disparate programming technologies together.

- It does not exist as a point in the programming space; by design, it occupies the spaces *between* the peaks representing individual languages, as shown in Fig. 3.5.

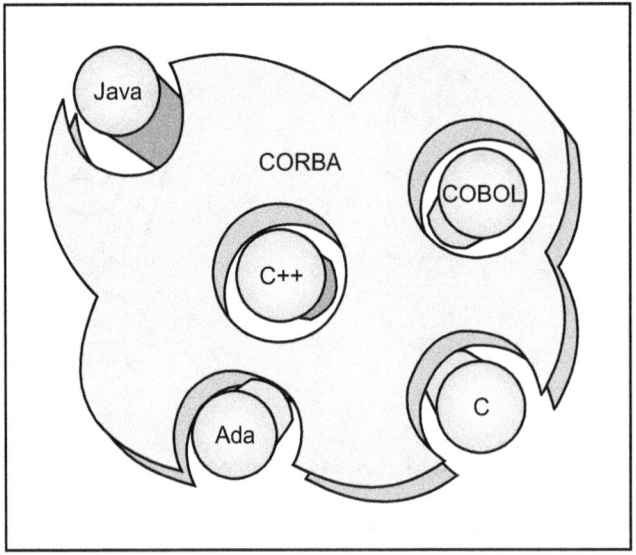

Fig. 3.5: CORBA as a integration technology

- When a Java client uses CORBA technology to communicate with a C++ object, for example, both the C++ programmer are the Java programmer work completely within their respective language environments.

- The CORBA ORB presents the Java client with a Java stub interface and the C++ programmer with a C++ skeleton interface ,as shown in Fig. 3.6. CORBA takes care of the cross-language issues automatically.

- This picture reflects the fact that CORBA is specifically designed as an *integration* technology, not a *programming* technology.

- The medium that CORBA uses to perform this integration is OMG IDL (Interface Definition Language). IDL isn't a programming language.

- It describes *interfaces* between distributed components. It doesn't depend on any particular programming language technology. From IDL interface descriptions, an ORB product automatically generates code in the language of your choice to effect integration and distribution-the "glue" that connects components and manages communication between them.

- You may ask, "why should I have to Learn Development Language (IDL) in order to use CORBA technology ?". First, note that IDL is an extremely simple language. Since it only describes interfaces, almost all of the complex issues faced by programming languages-control flow, memory management, functional composition, and so on-are absent from IDL.

- Learning and using IDL is trivial in comparison to using a new programming language. Second, having a single descriptive language as the basis for agreeing on interfaces is extremely important. Other approaches, such as the attempt to describe POSIX APIs separately in both C and FORTRAN, usually lead to subtle but troublesome differences in behavior.

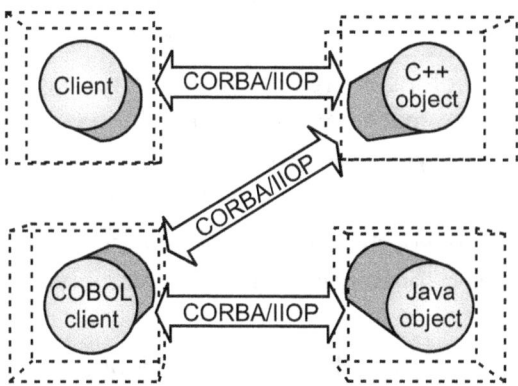

Fig. 3.6: Cross-language issues

- Finally, IDL can be generated from some programming languages' native interface descriptions. This capability is currently available is some ORB products, such as Visigenic's Caffeine product, or IBM's Direct to SOM compilers.

- By taking this approach, it is possible to get the benefits of IDL's language neutrality and power as an integration medium without leaving your favorite programming language.

3.2.3.3 But Won't I Write Everything In Java, Anyway?

- In light of the programming herd's stampede towards Java, this is a fair question, deserving serious consideration. There are a lot of good reasons for writing programs in Java. Does Java's popularity spell the demise of all other programming languages, for all time?

- Not likely. Though Java will undoubtedly have a large share of the market for new software development, there are several reasons why it won't be the only language you will have to accommodate in your systems, including:

- Legacy Systems-There is billions of dollars invested in software written in languages other than Java. In fact, the largest problem faced by most large enterprises in the immediate future is the integration of their existing stovepipe applications, not creating new applications.

- Most of the new applications being written in corporate IT shops today are not isolated systems; they are subsystems that live in the context of existing legacy systems. In addition to legacy systems, IT organizations also have large investments in legacy tools, legacy application libraries, and-perhaps most troublesome of all-legacy programmers.

- This railroad train of investment in technology and skills will not be suddenly de-railed by the advent of new language, however titillating it may be.

- Performance-Java's extreme portability is gained, to some extent, at the cost of performance. Java programs are executed by a virtual machine, a machine being simulated by software on your computer. While much can do to improve the performance of execution on a software virtual machine, it will never perform as well as equivalent code executing directly on the hardware; it's a theoretical impossibility.

- While JIT compilers can potentially reduce these performance penalties by converting the Java byte code to native machine code, the resulting code is no longer portable, and the cost of compiling the byte code is only worth paying if the resulting program is executed often enough for the savings to offset that cost.

- In addition to execution speed, there is also the matter of predictability. Java eliminates most of the programming problems related to memory management by providing automatic garbage collection.

- The Java virtual machine continuously executes a low-priority thread that scours memory for blocks that are no longer in use, and returns them to the free memory pool. This is one of Java's major advantages, in terms of programming simplicity, but it also creates performance-related problems.

- When the memory available to a Java application grows small or runs out, the Java virtual machine is forced to stop processing long enough to collect garbage, i.e., to recover unused memory. This causes the application to suspend, which is not practical in time-critical systems.

- Moreover, it is generally the case that applications use memory in proportion to the amount of work they are doing; as the workload increases, so does the memory usage. In systems that rely on garbage collection, this effect tends to force the system to interrupt processing the application most often when the application is most heavily loaded-precisely when it is least desirable.

- Although a great deal of effort is being invested in improving Java's performance, many system architects remain sceptical about Java's suitability for high-volume, heavily-loaded server environments, or environments with critical real-time execution constraints.

- **It Won't Last Forever:** Today's Java will be the next big legacy problem that the computing world has to face. Even the best technologies eventually become obsolete. Some day Java's successor will appear, and (perhaps) take the world by storm, much as Java has done. To the extent that organizations have planned (or failed to plan) for that day, they will spare themselves (or incur) enormous costs and pain, perhaps even save their businesses.

- To say this won't happen is to be naive. Consider the mindset of IT managers who made total commitments to large mainframe systems with 3270 terminals. At the time, these managers either completely failed to consider what might happen when these systems became obsolete, or they made naive assumptions about the cost of evolving or replacing the systems.

- As a consequence, the IT industry faces a continuing crisis of rising maintenance costs, and extremely high costs of integrating legacy systems. This crisis has also given rise to an entire sub-industry of bizarre technology such as screen-scrapers- Rube Goldberg software contraptions to connect to a rigid, un-accommodating technology to which organizations swore eternal allegiance, but now hangs like an albatross around their necks.

- You may well point out that these statements apply equally well to CORBA technology. They do, but in a very different sense. Yes, of course, CORBA will eventually be obviated.

- All things must pass. However, it is open integration technology like CORBA that provides the best defence against system obsolescence.

- The main reason that software becomes obsolete is not that it "wears out". It fails to adapt to the changing environment around it. It won't integrate with new applications and evolving technology.

- It fails because more development effort was spent on building the program's internals, and very little was spent on building the program's interfaces to the rest of the world.

- Historically, the software development processes followed by the IT world view applications as closed systems, large boxes of functionality to be filled with lines of code.

- Very little thought or effort has been devoted to packaging applications as flexible components that live in the context of larger, changing systems. This is a programming-oriented view of application architecture.

- By contrast, CORBA offers an integration-oriented point of view, where design efforts focus on the boundaries between elements of the system.

- The underlying interface technologies (IDL, IIOP, Interface Repository, etc.) are designed to make those boundaries as flexible, adaptive, and programming technology-independent as possible.

- Interface technologies such as CORBA not only have longer half-lives than programming technologies, they are the best prophylactic against the aging and death of applications due to dependence on obsolete programming technology.

3.2.3.4 Infrastructure

- Real-world distributed object computing requires much more than a communication mechanism; it requires infrastructure.

- Applications need to find objects that are migrating about the network; objects that the applications need may be dormant and require activation; applications need to obtain services based on general property descriptions rather than specific identities; applications need transactional integrity among groups of distributed objects; the software components that constitute a distributed system need to be administered and managed through standard interfaces; the underlying mechanisms that support communication, location, and other basic services must be reliable, able to recover from errors and re-configure themselves as necessary to provide high availability; the list goes on.

- These requirements are met by a distributed computing infrastructure, architecture of underlying mechanisms and basic services that provide a stable, powerful platform upon which applications can be built. The OMG Object Management Architecture (OMA) provides this platform, including the core CORBA ORB specification and a set of object services (called CORBA services).

3.2.3.5 CORBA Core

- The core ORB specification itself does not detect a specific implementation architecture. It describes an abstract model for ORB semantics and a set of standard interfaces, extensible through a standard Interface Definition Language.

- ORB implementers are free to construct their ORBs in any way they choose, as long as they support the proper interfaces and semantics. This freedom is extremely important to ORB users.

- It means:

- ORBs can be tailored to specific run-time environments or unique system requirements. For example, several vendors offer ORBs specialized for embedded real-time requirements, where an ORB designed for workstations in a client-server system would be completely inappropriate.

- Though ORBs may have diverse implementations, they can still inter-operate, and applications will still be ported among them.

- In contrast, RMI is, in essence, a single, specific implementation architecture. If its one-size-fits-all approach doesn't work for you, or your requirements are evolving in ways you might not be able to predict, you're out of luck.

- ORB implementations can evolve rapidly to offer increased performance, reliability, and saleability without breaking applications. For example, many ORB vendors have begun to integrate their products with high-performance, highly-reliable middleware messaging systems.

- These ORBs offer builders of large enterprise systems very high quality-of-service communication, with logging, persistent queuing, and so on. Because CORBA is an interface specification and not a concrete code base, ORBs are free to evolve in this way.

- CORBA ORBs have been subjected to strong evolutionary pressures for several years now. A diverse, flexible range of products has emerged, ranging from small-footprint "ORBlets" for widely distributed web-based clients, to industrial-strength ORBs suitable for high volume, mission-critical transactional systems. In comparison, RMI, while quite useful, can best be described as a lightweight mechanism suited for a narrower range of tasks.

3.2.3.6 Difference between RMI and CORBA

- RMI is completely Java based, where CORBA is language independent. There are many adapters for CORBA, and programs can call processes written in any language that has a CORBA interface.

- CORBA has many more features documented in the specification than just process communication.

- RMI is easier to implement if you already know Java - it looks just the same as calling a process locally - but it's limited to only calling other Java applications.

- RMI is a technology that was released with Java 1.1 to make JVM to remote JVM calls possible. RMI uses stubs a skeletons, a little RMI server that has its own, sexy little naming type service, and the RMI protocol for marshalling requests back and forth from JVM to JVM.

- CORBA is an entire infrastructure, almost like J2EE before the Java Gods created J2EE. Actually, lots of J2EE stuff is just totally stolen from CORBA, er, I mean, based on CORBA. CORBA defines a naming service, transaction service, and even a social housing service. CORBA was very progressive.

3.2.3.7 CORBA Services

CORBA provides the services like,

- Naming Service

- Event Service

- Security Service

The CORBA standard is really a collection of standards and definitions. In addition to the core specifications for the Object Request Broker (ORB) and inter-ORB communication protocols such as IIOP, CORBA also includes specifications for services that distributed objects may require, such as naming services, security measures, etc. Taken as a whole, these specifications, backed up by solid implementations, provide a very powerful environment for the distributed application developer.

Here we discuss overview of some of the key services currently included in the CORBA Services specification. Some of these services are similar in nature to features provided inherently by Java. In these cases, we discuss the contrasts between the Java-native service and the CORBA service.

(A) Naming Service

- The Naming Service is arguably the most commonly used service in the CORBA family. The Naming Service provides a means for objects to be referenced by name within a given naming context. A naming context is a scoping mechanism for names, similar in philosophy to class packages in Java. Within a particular context, names must be unique, and contexts can be nested to form compound contexts and names.

- Fig. 3.7 shows two naming contexts in the form of Venne diagrams: one, whose topmost context is named "BankServices," defines names for objects in a banking application; the other, named "LANResources," defines names for network resources such as printers, compute servers, data servers, etc.

- The "BankServices" naming context contains a single object named "AuthorizationAgent," and a subcontext named "CorporateAccount." The "LANServices" context contains a "DataServer" context and a "Printer" context, and each of these contains two named objects.

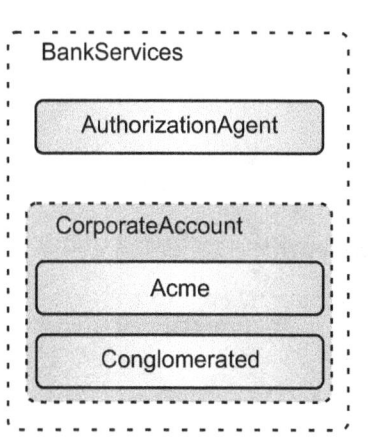 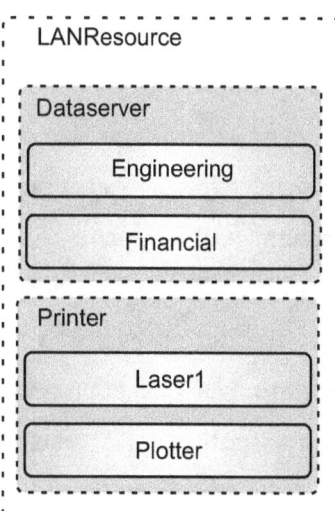

Fig. 3.7: Sample naming contexts

- Agents in a distributed system can add named objects to the Naming Service by binding objects to a particular name within a context. Other agents can then look up these objects by resolving their names into object references.

- The name of an object is made up of a sequence of name components that specify the subcontext that the object falls within. So, for example, the "Laser1" object in the "LANResources" context would be fully specified with a name made up of the ordered components "LANResources," "Printer," and "Laser1."

- All of the interfaces making up the Naming Service are contained in the CosNaming module.

- The interface to the central Naming Service functions is the NamingContext interface, which provides methods for binding, rebinding, and unbinding objects to names, as well resolving object references from names.

- Using a Java implementation of the CORBA Naming Service, the "LANResources" context and all of its object "contents" might be built up as follows:

```
// Get handle on base naming context from the ORB
NamingContext base = ...
// Get references to the objects to be registered in Naming Service
omg.CORBA.Object engDataBaseRef = ...
omg.CORBA.Object finDataBaseRef = ...
omg.CORBA.Object laserPrinterRef = ...
omg.CORBA.Object plotterRef = ...
// Build up subcontexts for LAN resources
```

```
NameComponent lan = new NameComponent("LANResources", "");
NameComponent data = new NameComponent("DataServer", "");
NameComponent print = new NameComponent("Printer", "");
// Create context for LAN resources
NameComponent path[] = {lan};
NamingContext lanContext = base.bind_new_context(path);
// Bind all of the data servers to their names within the new context
path = {lan, data, new NameComponent("Engineering", "")};
lanContext.bind(path, engDataBaseRef);
path = {lan, data, new NameComponent("Financial", "")};
lanContext.bind(path, finDataBaseRef);
// Bind the printers to their names
path = {lan, print, new NameComponent("Laser1", "")};
lanContext.bind(path, laserPrinterRef);
path = {lan, print, new NameComponent("Plotter", "")};
lanContext.bind(path, plotterRef);
```

- In this example, a new context is established first for the LAN resource objects. The bind_new_context() method of the NamingContext interface takes an array of NameComponents, which specify the fully qualified name for the new context. In this case, we simply need a single NameComponent to give the new context the name "LANResources."

- Next, the object references are bound to their names within this new context. In each case, we create an array of NameComponents specifying the compound name for the object, then bind the object to its name by calling the bind() method on the NamingContext.

- Agents that want to use these named objects can look them up by getting a reference to the NamingContext and resolving the object references from their full names:

```
NamingContext base = ...
NameComponent printerName =    {new NameComponent("LANResources", ""),
                        new NameComponent("Printer", ""),
                        new NameComponent("Laser1", "")};
omg.CORBA.Object printerRef = base.resolve(printerName);
```

(B) Event Service

- The Event Service provides asynchronous communications between cooperating, remote objects. The CORBA Event Service is based on a model involving suppliers and consumers of events, connected by event channels that carry events back and forth between the two. An event channel can support multiple event suppliers and multiple event consumers.

- The Event Service also supports two event propagation styles for both consumers and suppliers of events: push style and pull style.

- A push-style consumer has events pushed to it by its event suppliers, while a pull-style consumer explicitly pulls events from its suppliers. On the other end of the event channel, a push-style supplier pushes events to its consumers, while a pull-style supplier waits for its consumers to pull events from it.

- Fig. 3.8 shows the relationship between event suppliers, consumers, and channels. In the Fig. 3.8, arrows indicate flow of events, and the location of the head of the arrow indicates which entity drives the event transfer.

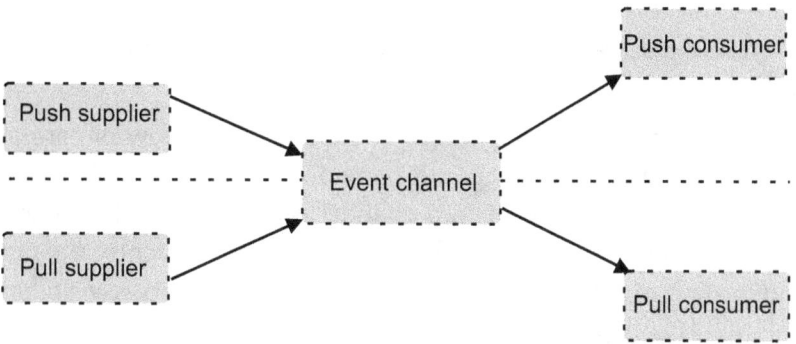

Fig. 3.8: Propagation model in the event services

- Although the event channel provides a physical connection between consumers and suppliers in the Event Service model, logically each consumer attaches itself to one or more suppliers, and each supplier attaches itself to one or more consumers.

- Each consumer and supplier attaches itself to an event channel by attaching itself to a proxy supplier or consumer that the event channel exports. An event channel can be thought of as supporting both the supplier and consumer interfaces, simultaneously.

- So here's the typical execution plan that an agent follows when using the CORBA Event Service:

- A reference to an event channel object is obtained, either using the Naming Service to look up a remote event channel object reference, or by invoking an operation on an existing remote object reference that dynamically opens an event channel.

- If the agent has any event suppliers, they register themselves with the event channel by attaching themselves to proxy consumers obtained from the channel. Pull-style suppliers attach themselves to proxy pull consumers created from the channel, and push-style suppliers attach themselves to proxy push consumers created from the channel.

- If the agent has any event consumers, they register themselves with the event channel in a similar way. Pull-style consumers attach themselves to proxy pull suppliers and push-style consumers attach themselves to proxy push suppliers.

- When suppliers on the agent's side of the channel generate events, the events are carried through the event channel to any consumers attached remotely to the channel. Push suppliers push their events through the channel by calling push() methods on the proxy consumers obtained from the channel.

- Pull suppliers wait for their proxy consumers to pull events from them through the channel.

- Consumers on the agent's side of the channel receive events from remote suppliers attached to the channel. Pull-style consumers pull events through the channel from their proxy suppliers by calling pull() methods on them.

- Push-style consumers wait for their proxy suppliers to give them events received through the channel.

- The consumers and suppliers attached to a channel don't know or care about the type or implementation details of their counterparts on the other end of the event channel. A push consumer might attach itself to a channel with only a pull supplier on the other end; the event channel is responsible for ensuring that events are pulled from the supplier and pushed to the consumer, so that the flow of events is maintained.

- The same is the case when a pull consumer is attached to a push supplier--the event channel accepts the events pushed to it by the supplier, and buffers them until the consumer pulls them. Regardless of the types of suppliers and consumers attached to an event channel at any given time, you should assume that event delivery by the channel is asynchronous.

- The Event Service specification provides both generic and typed event communication. In the generic case, the type of the event data is not specified in the interfaces for the suppliers, consumers, or channels.

- Event data is represented using the CORBA any data type, and suppliers and consumers call generic push() and pull() methods on each other to propagate events through the distributed system.

- In typed event communication, the interfaces for the suppliers, consumers, and channels can include type-specific event propagation methods and type-specific event representations.

Quality of Service for Channels:

- Any given implementation of the event channel interface can support a particular quality of service. Some implementations may guarantee delivery of every event to every consumer attached to the channel, while others may just guarantee to make a best effort to deliver the events generated by its suppliers.

- The Event Service specification leaves the implementation open to these different levels of service to allow for different application requirements.

- The trade-offs here are similar to those found at a lower level, in choosing between TCP and UDP packet delivery over IP network connections.

- Guaranteed event delivery typically means reduced net throughput. Best-effort event delivery can potentially provide higher event throughput, but at the cost of potentially undelivered events, or events delivered to only some of the consumers attached to the channel.

Interface Specifics:

- The Event Service includes several modules that provide IDL interfaces for suppliers, consumers, and event channels.

- The CosEventComm module contains interface definitions for push and pulls consumers and suppliers of events:

Push Supplier

- The Push Supplier interface has only one method, disconnect_push_supplier() , which releases the supplier from its event communication link.

- There's no exported method for getting events from the supplier, since it's responsible for pushing events to its attached consumer(s).

Push Consumer

- The Push Consumer has a push() method, which accepts a single input argument of type any that represents the event data.

- The any type is an IDL language feature used to mark data that can be of any type. The receiver of the event is responsible for determining the actual data type.

- The Push Consumer also has a disconnect_push_consumer() method for releasing it from the event communication channel.

Pull Supplier

- This interface has two methods for pulling event data from the supplier: pull() and try_pull().

- A consumer can choose to do a blocking event pull by calling pull(), or it can do a nonblocking polling of the event supplier by calling try_pull(). There is also a disconnect_pull_supplier() method.

Pull Consumer

- The Pull Consumer just has a disconnect_pull_consumer() method, since it's responsible for internally pulling events from its suppliers.

- The CosEventChannelAdmin module contains interfaces for event channels and their proxy consumers and suppliers:

Event Channel

- This interface has three methods: for_consumers() , for_suppliers() , and destroy() . The for_consumers() method returns a reference to a ConsumerAdmin object, which can be used by consumers to get references to proxy suppliers.

- Likewise, the for_suppliers() method returns a SupplierAdmin object, which can be used by suppliers to get references to proxy consumers. The destroy() method destroys the channel and any communication resources it had been using.

Consumer Admin

- This interface allows consumers to get references to proxy suppliers from an event channel. The obtain_push_supplier() method returns a reference to a Proxy Push Supplier object, and the obtain_pull_supplier() method returns a reference to a Proxy Pull Supplier object.

Supplier Admin

- The Supplier Admin interface allows suppliers to get references to proxy consumers from the channel. The obtain_push_consumer() method returns a Proxy Push Consumer reference, and obtain_pull_consumer() returns a Proxy Pull Consumer reference.

Proxy Push Supplier

- This interface derives from the Push Supplier interface in the CosEventComm module. It adds a method, connect_push_consumer(), which allows a local Push Consumer to attach itself to the supplier.

- The method takes a single argument: a reference to a Push Consumer. Attaching a consumer to the proxy supplier sets up a path for events to flow from the remote suppliers attached to the channel, through the channel, to the local proxy supplier, and finally to the local consumer.

Proxy Pull Supplier

- This derives from Pull Supplier and adds a connect_pull_consumer() method, which accepts a Pull Consumer reference.

Proxy Push Consumer

- This derives from Push Consumer and adds a connect_push_supplier() method, which accepts a Push Supplier reference.

- Attaching a supplier to a proxy consumer sets up a path for events to flow from the local suppliers attached to the channel to the local proxy consumer, through the channel, and finally to remote consumers attached to the channel.

Proxy Pull Consumer

- This derives from Pull Consumer and adds a connect_pull_supplier() method, which accepts a Pull Supplier reference.

(c) Security Service

The CORBA Security Service specification is one of the more complicated and detailed of the CORBA services. This is in large part due to the inherent complexity of security, and also to the fact that the Security Services specification includes security models and interfaces for application development, security administration, and the implementation of security services themselves.

In this section we'll only provide a brief overview of the security model and interfaces provided within the CORBA Security Services for application development.

3.2.3.8 Service Types

The CORBA Security Services provide interfaces for the following:

- Authenticating and generating credentials for principals, including the delegation of credentials to intermediary principals

- Performing secure transactions (e.g., method invocations, data transfers, etc.) between objects

- Auditing secure transactions for later review

- Non-repudiation facilities that generate evidence of transactions, to prevent principals involved in a secure transaction from denying that the action ever took place (e.g., the sender of a message denies ever sending it, or the receiver denies receipt)

All of these services and their interfaces are specified in an implementation-neutral manner. So the authentication service interface does not depend on the use of symmetric or asymmetric keys, and the interface to a principal's credentials is not dependent on the use of a particular certificate protocol like X.509.

3.2.3.9 Security Model

- The model used by the CORBA Security Services specification involves principals that are authenticated using a PrincipalAuthenticator object. Once authenticated, a principal is associated with a Credential object, which contains information about its authenticated identity and the access rights that it has under this identity.

- These credentials are then used in secure transactions, to verify the access privileges of the parties involved, and to register identities for actions that are audited or carried out in a non-repudiation mode.

- A CORBA remote object request run under the security services is outlined in Fig. 3.20. The client requests a remote object through a local reference. The client's Credentials (generated earlier by authenticating the user using the PrincipalAuthenticator interface) are attached to the request by the Security Services present in the ORB, and sent along with the request over the transport mechanism in use.

- The remote object receives the request through its ORB, along with the client's Credentials. The target object can decide whether to honor the request or not, based on the access rights of the client's identity.

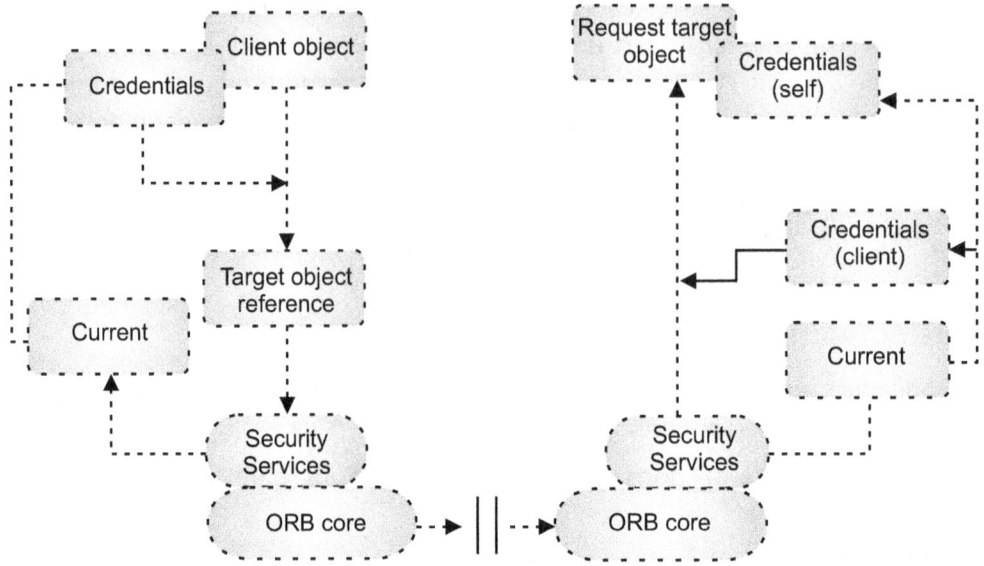

Fig. 3.9: A secure CORBA request

- When a request is received from a remote agent, its right to access the resources requested can be checked through an Access Decision object, which can be used to compare the remote principal's credentials against access control settings, like an ACL. There typically isn't a default access-control policy that the Security Services will enforce for requests, since checking access rights is usually very application-specific (e.g., "Is the client principal in the `Credit Admin' group?", or "Has this principal tried and failed to access this resource more than x times?").

- The target of a request can also explicitly audit the transaction using the Audit Channel interface, or just check to see if auditing is required by the current security policy by calling the audit_needed() method on the AuditDecision interface. If non-repudiation services are available, then evidence of the action can be generated using the NRCredentials interface.

3.2.3.10 Other Key CORBA Services

In addition to the Naming, Event, and Security services that we discussed here, the CORBA Services Specification defines several other services, including:

- **Persistent Object Services**

  Services for generating, retrieving, and maintaining persistent object states. This service is intended to be an interface between CORBA applications and object databases or other persistent object technologies.

- **Transaction Service**

  A service that supports issuing transactions across a distributed system. A transaction can be as simple or complex as needed, from a single remote-object request to a collection of multiple requests among many distributed objects. The side effects of all the requests comprising a transaction are not realized until the transaction is completed and committed.

- **Query Service**

  This service has similar goals to JDBC. It provides an interface for querying and modifying collections of objects, including selecting, updating, inserting, or deleting objects from these collections. The most obvious implementation for this service would be an interface between CORBA applications and SQL-based relational databases or object databases.

3.3 CASE STUDY: ENTERPRISE JAVABEANS AND FRACTAL

- Enterprise JavaBeans (EJB) [java.sun.com XII] is a specification of a server-side, managed component architecture and a major element of the Java Platform, Enterprise Edition (Java EE), a set of specifications for client-server programming. Other specifications include Java RMI and JMS.

- EJB is defined as a *server-side component model* because it supports the development of the classic style of application, where potentially large numbers of clients interact with a number of services realized through components or configuration of components.

- The components, which are known as *beans* in EJB, are intended to capture the application (or business) logic. EJB is *managed* in the sense that the container pattern is used to provide support for key distributed systems services including transactions, security and lifecycle support.

- Typically, the container injects appropriate calls to the associated services to provide the required properties, and the use of a transaction manager or security services is completely hidden from the developer of the associated beans (*container-managed*). It is also possible for the bean developer to take more control over these operations (*bean-managed*).

- The goal of EJB is to maintain a strong separation of concerns between the various roles involved in developing distributed applications. The EJB specification identifies the following key roles:

- The *bean provider*, who develops the application logic of the component(s);

- The *application assembler*, who assembles beans into application configurations;

- The *deployer*, who takes a given application assembly and ensures it can be correctly deployed in a given operational environment;

- The *service provider*, who is a specialist in fundamental distributed system services such as transaction management and establishes the desired level of support in these areas;

- The *persistence provider*, who is a specialist in mapping persistent data to underlying databases and in managing these relationships at runtime;

- The *container provider*, who builds on the above two roles and is responsible for correctly configuring containers with the required level of distributed systems support in terms of non-functional properties related to, for example, transactions and security as well as the desired support for persistence;

- The *system administrator*, who is responsible for monitoring a deployment at runtime and making any adjustments to ensure its correct operation.

Note: EJB is a *heavyweight* component architecture in the sense introduced above.

There is significant software complexity, particularly associated with the management of containers. As such, the approach is prescriptive and intended for certain classes of application only. As mentioned above, EJB is particularly suited to applications that follow the three-tier architecture based on a back-end database accessed via a service interface offered by the middle tier (the application logic). For example, this style of architecture is common in many eCommerce applications where the database maintains information on stock items, prices and availability, while the middle tier offers interfaces to browse the stock and purchase selected items. These are typically large and complex systems that require support in terms of distributed system services, and hence the overhead associated with container management is fully justified. We will use the example of an *eShop* throughout this section as motivation and to illustrate the use of EJB in this setting. Other classes of application will not follow this pattern, and hence EJB is an inappropriate technology for such applications. Examples include peer-to-peer structures that simply do not follow this tiered model and more lightweight applications running on embedded devices where the overhead of EJB cannot be justified.

3.3.1 The EJB Component Model

- A *bean* in EJB is a component offering one or more *business interfaces* to potential clients of that component, where interfaces can be either *remote*, requiring the use of appropriate communication middleware (such as RMI or JMS), or *local*, in which case more direct, and hence efficient, bindings are possible.

    Relating back to the terminology introduced in Section 8.4, a business interface is equivalent to a *provided interface* (we will see how EJB supports required interfaces below, in the subsection on dependency injection). A given bean is represented by the set of remote and local business interfaces together with an associated *bean class* that implements the interfaces. Two main styles of bean are supported in the EJB 3.0 specification:

Session Beans: A session bean is a component implementing a particular task within the application logic of a service, for example to make a purchase in our *eShop* application. A session bean persists for the duration of a service and maintains a running conversation with the client for the duration of the session. Session beans can be either *stateful*, maintaining associated conversational state (such as the current status of the eCommerce transaction), or *stateless*, in which case no state is maintained. Stateful session beans imply a conversation with a single client and maintain the state of that conversation. In contrast, stateless beans can have many concurrent conversations with different clients. The state associated with stateful beans may or may not be persistent, as we discuss below.

Message-Driven Beans: Clients interact with session beans using local or remote invocation. We have seen throughout this book that other communication paradigms are also important for distributed systems development, including indirect communication paradigms. The concept of a message-driven bean was introduced in EJB 2.0 to support indirect communication and, in particular, the possibility to interact with components using either message queues or topics, building directly on the functionality offered by JMS (remember that both queues and topics are firstclass entities in JMS representing alternative intermediaries for messages – see Section 6.4.3). In a message-drive bean, a business interface will be realized as a listener-style interface reflecting the event-driven nature of the associated bean.

POJOs and Annotations

- The task of programming in EJB has been simplified significantly through the use of *Enterprise JavaBeanPOJOs* (plain old Java objects) together with Java *Enterprise JavaBean annotations*.

- A bean (that is the implementation of the bean's business interfaces) is a plain old Java object: it consists of the application logic written simply in Java with no other code relating to it being a bean. Annotations are then used to ensure the correct behaviour in the EJB context. In other words, a bean is a POJO supplemented by annotations.

- Annotations were introduced in Java 1.5 as a mechanism for associating metadata with packages, classes, methods, parameters and variables. This metadata can then be used by frameworks to ensure the right behaviour or interpretation is associated with that part of the program.

- As an example, annotations are used to introduce a bean of a particular style. For example, the following are examples of annotated bean definitions (representing the main styles of bean in EJB 3.0):

@Stateful public class eShop implements Orders {...}

@Stateless public class CalculatorBean implements Calculator {...}

@MessageDriven public class SharePrice implements MessageListener {...}

- Annotations are also used to indicate whether business interfaces are remote (@Remote) or local (@Local).

- The following example introduces the Orders interface as a remote interface and the Calculator interface from the CalculatorBean as a local interface only:

@Remote public interface Orders {...}

@Local public interface Calculator {...}

- As will become apparent, annotations are used throughout EJB, providing a specification of how a program should be interpreted in an EJB context.

- In the description that follows we will develop the eShop example as an illustration of the extensive use of annotations in programming bean objects (in this cas, a session bean).

Enterprise JavaBean containers in EJB

- Beans are deployed to containers, and the containers provide implicit distributed system management using interception. In this way, the container provides the necessary policies in areas including transaction management, security, persistence and lifecycle management allowing the bean developer to focus exclusively on the application logic.

- Containers must therefore be configured with the necessary level of support. In the current version, EJB is preconfigured with common default policies and the developer need only take action if these defaults are insufficient (referred to as configuration by exception in the specification [java.sun.com XII]).

Enterprise JavaBean Interception

- The Enterprise JavaBeans specification enables the programmer to intercept two types of operation on beans in order to alter their default behaviour:

- Method calls associated with a business interface;

- Lifecycle events.

We look at each in turn below.

Interception of Methods: This mechanism is used where it is necessary to associate a particular action or set of actions with an incoming call on a business interface. This applies equally to incoming invocations on a session bean or incoming events on a message-driven bean. As we have already seen, interception is used widely in the EJB architecture to provide implicit management. This allows the application developer to extend the use of interception to more domain-specific concerns not provided by the container.

Consider the running example of the *eShop*. Suppose there is a need within the *eShop* to implement logging of all operations carried out in the system, for example for auditing purposes. Interception allows the programmer to introduce such a service without changing the application logic contained in the bean. As a second example, the interception mechanism could be used to prevent certain customers from making purchases in the *eShop* (for example, if they have defaulted on previous payments).

There are several ways of associating interceptors with a given bean, including associating an interception class with a given bean class or individual method (using the annotation *@Interceptors*), or associating an interception method with a given class (using the annotation *@AroundInvoke*). For the sake of simplicity, we focus on the latter mechanism and return to our example of an *eShop*:

```
@Stateful
public class eShop implements Orders {
public void MakeOrder (...) {

...
}
@AroundInvoke
public Object log(InvocationContext ctx) throws Exception {
System.out.println ("The following method was invoked: " +
ctx.getMethod().getName());
return invocationContext.proceed();
}
}
```

The annotation *@AroundInvoke* introduces an interceptor on the *eShop* bean class. The interceptor method must have the following syntax:

```
Object <methodName>(javax.ejb.InvocationContext)
```

This method is then called whenever any of the business methods are called on *eShop*. The associated parameter adds significantly to the capabilities of interceptors by providing both metadata associated with the invocation being intercepted (for example, references to the bean, the method invoked and the actual parameters associated with the invocation) and also limited capabilities to intercede that is, to change the parameters before the method is executed. The last line of the method, the call to *proceed*, returns control back to the intercepted method (or to the next interceptor in the chain if more than one interceptor is defined).

3.3.2 Fractal

- As mentioned above, Fractal is a lightweight component model that brings the benefits of component-based programming to the development of distributed systems [Bruneton *et al.* 2006, fractal.ow2.org I].

- Fractal provides support for *programming with interfaces*, with the associated benefits in terms of the separation of interface and implementation (benefits also provided by distributed objects).

- Fractal goes further, though, and supports the *explicit representation* of the software architecture of the system, avoiding the problem of implicit dependencies.

- The approach is deliberately minimal, with no support for additional component-related functionality such as deployment, the full container pattern or the enriched programming model offered by application servers.

- Fractal is used to construct more complex software systems using the component model as the basic building block, resulting in software that has a clear component-based architecture and that is *configurable* and also *reconfigurable* at runtime to match the current operational environment and requirements.

- Fractal defines a programming model and, as such, is programming language–agnostic. Implementations of this model are available in several different languages, including:

- Julia and AOKell (Java-based, with the latter also offering support for aspect oriented programming);

- Cecilia and Think (C-based);

- FracNet (.NET-based);

- FracTalk (Smalltalk-based);

- Julio (Python-based).

Julia and Cecilia are Treated as the Reference Implementations of Fractal.

- Fractal is supported by the OW2 consortium [www.ow2.org], an open source software community for distributed systems middleware that encourages and promotes the component-based philosophy for the construction of such software.

- To date, Fractal has been used in the construction of a wide range of middleware platforms including think (a configurable operating system kernel), DREAM (a middleware platform supporting various forms of indirect communication), Jasmine (a tool supporting the monitoring and management of SOA platforms), GOTM (offering flexible transaction management) and Proactive (a middleware platform for Grid computing).

- Fractal is also the basis of the Grid Component Model (GCM), which has been influential in the development of associated ETSI standards [Baude *et al.* 2009].

- Further details of all these projects can be found on the OW2 web site [www.ow2.org].

Note: A some other lightweight component models have been developed specifically for distributed systems. We feature two – OpenCOM and OSGI in the box on the next page.

The Core Component Model

- A component in Fractal offers one or more interfaces, with two types of interfaces available:

- **Server Interfaces:** Which support incoming operational invocations

- **Client Interfaces:** Which support outgoing invocations (equivalent to required interfaces).

An interface is an implementation of an *interface type*, which defines the operations that are supported by that interface.

- **Bindings in Fractal:** To enable composition, Fractal supports *bindings* between interfaces. Two styles of binding are supported by the model:

- **Primitive Bindings:** The simplest style of binding is a *primitive binding*, which is a direct mapping between one client interface and one server interface within the same address space, assuming the types are compatible. Primitive bindings can be implemented efficiently in a given language environment, for example through direct object references.

- **Composite Bindings:** Fractal also supports *composite bindings*, which are arbitrarily complex software architectures (that is consisting of components and bindings) implementing communication between a number of interfaces potentially on different machines. For example, if you were implementing a CORBA connection in Fractal, the binding would be composed of components representing the core architectural elements in CORBA, including proxies, the ORB core, object adapters, skeletons and servants Composite bindings are themselves components in Fractal, and this is important for two reasons:

- A system developed using Fractal is fully configurable in terms of the components *and* their interconnections. For example, a configuration can be established wherein components interact using a composite binding implementing any of the communication. If a given communication paradigm is not already provided, it can be developed in Fractal and then made available to future developers as a component.

- Once established, any aspect of the software architecture can be reconfigured at runtime, including composite bindings. It is very useful to be able to adapt communication structures at runtime, for example to introduce added levels of security or to alter the implementation to be more scalable as a system grows in size.

3.4 WEB SERVICES

- A web service provides a service interface enabling clients to interact with servers in a more general way than web browsers do.

- Clients access the operations in the interface of a web service by means of requests and replies formatted in XML and usually transmitted over HTTP.

- Web services are increasingly important in distributed systems: they support interoperability across the global Internet, including the key area of business-to-business integration and also the emergent 'mashup' culture enabling third-party developers to creative innovative software on top of the existing service base.

- Web services also provide the underlying middleware for both the Grid and cloud computing.

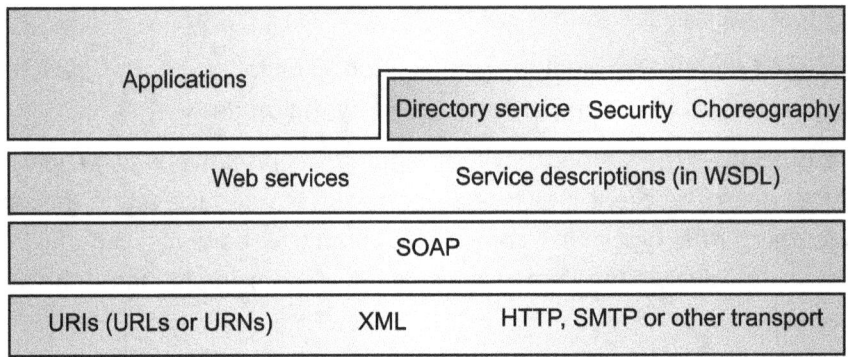

Fig. 3.10 : Web service infrastructure

3.4.1 Service Descriptions and IDL for Web Services

- Interface definitions are needed to allow clients to communicate with services. For web services, interface definitions are provided as part of a more general service description, which specifies two other additional characteristics how the messages are to be communicated (for example, by SOAP over HTTP) and the URI of the service.

- To cater for use in a multi-language environment, service descriptions are written in XML.

- A service description forms the basis of an agreement between a client and a server as to the service on offer. It assembles all of the facts concerning the service that are relevant to its clients.

- Service descriptions are generally used to generate client stubs that automatically implement the correct behaviour for the client.

- The IDL-like component of a service description is more flexible than other IDLs, in that a service may be specified either in terms of the types of messages that it will send and receive or in terms of the operations it supports, to allow for both document exchange and request-reply-style interactions.

- A variety of different methods of communication can be used by web services and their clients.

- Therefore the method of communication is left to be decided by the service provider and specified in the service description, rather than built into the system, as it is in CORBA, for example.

- The ability to specify the URI of a service as a part of the service description avoids the need for the separate binder or naming service used by most other middleware.

- It has the implication that the URI cannot be changed once the service description has been made available to potential clients, but the URN scheme does cater for a change of location by allowing for an indirection at the reference level.

- In contrast, in the binder approach, the client uses a name to look up the service reference at runtime, allowing the service references to change over time.

- This approach requires an indirection from a name to a service reference for all services, even though many of them may always remain at the same location.

- In the web services context, the Web Services Description Language (WSDL) is commonly used for service descriptions.

- The current version, WSDL 2.0 [www.w3.org XI], became a W3C Recommendation in 2007.

- It defines an XML schema for representing the components of a service description, which include, for example, the element names definitions, types, message, interface, bindings and services.

3.4.2 A Directory Service for use of Web Service

Any organization that plans to base its applications on web services will find it more convenient to use a directory service to make these services available to clients. This is the purpose of the Universal Description, Discovery and Integration Service (UDDI) [Bellwood et al. 2003], which provides both a name service and a directory service.

Data Structures:

- The data structures supporting UDDI are designed to allow all the above styles of access and can incorporate any amount of human-readable information.

The data is organized in terms of the four structures business Entity describes the organization that provides these web services, giving its name, address and activities, etc.; business Services stores information about a set of instances of a web service, such as its name and a description of its purpose (for example, travel agent or bookseller); binding Template holds the address of a web service instance and references to service descriptions;

Model holds service descriptions, usually WSDL documents, stored outside the database and accessed by means of URLs.

Lookup

- UDDI provides an API for looking up services based on two sets of query operations:

- The get_xxx set of operations includes get_BusinessDetail, get_ServiceDetail, get_bindingDetail and get_tModelDetail; they retrieve an entity corresponding to a given key.

- The find_xxx set of operations includes find_business, find_service, find_binding and find_tModel; they retrieve the set of entities that matches a particular set of search criteria, providing a summary of names, descriptions, keys and URLs.

Thus clients in possession of a particular key may use a get_xxx operation to retrieve the corresponding entity directly, and other clients may use browsing to assist with searches, starting with a large set of results and gradually narrowing it down. For example, they may start by using the find_business operation in order to get a list containing a summary of information on matching providers. From this summary, the user may use the find_service operation to narrow the search by matching the sort of service required. In both cases, they will find the key of a suitable bindingTemplate and thereby find the

URL for retrieving the WSDL document for a suitable service. In addition, UDDI provides a notify/subscribe interface by which clients register interest in a particular set of entities in a UDDI registry and get change notifications, either synchronously or asynchronously.

Publication

- UDDI provides an interface for publishing and updating information about web services. The first time that a data structure is published at a UDDI server, it is given a key in the form of a URI – for example, uddi:cdk5.net:213 and that server becomes its owner.

Registries

- The UDDI service is based on replicated data stored in registries. A UDDI registry consists of one or more UDDI servers, each of which has a copy of the same set of data. The data is replicated between the members of a registry.

- Each of them may respond to queries and publish information.

- Changes to a data structure must be submitted to its owner that is, the server at which it was first published.

- It is possible for an owner to pass on the ownership to another UDDI server in the same registry.

Replication Scheme: The members of a registry propagate copies of data structures to one another as follows: a server that has made changes notifies the other servers in the registry, which then request the changes. A form of vector timestamp is used to determine which of the changes should be propagated and applied. The scheme is simple in comparison with other replication schemes that use vector timestamps, such as Gossip or Coda for two reasons:

- All changes to a particular data structure are made at the same server.

- Updates from a particular server are received in sequential order by the other members, but no particular ordering is imposed between update operations made by different servers.

Interaction between servers: As described above, servers interact with one another to carry out the replication scheme. They can also interact in order to transfer ownership of data structures. However, the response to a lookup operation is made by a single server without any interaction with other servers in the registry, unlike in the X.500 directory service, in which data is partitioned between servers that cooperate with one another in finding the relevant server for a particular request.

3.4.3 XML Security

- XML security consists of a set of related W3C designs for signing, key management and encryption. It is intended for use in cooperative work over the Internet involving documents whose contents may need to be authenticated or encrypted.

- Typically the documents are created, exchanged, stored and then exchanged again, possibly after being modified by a series of different users.

- To allow for the new type of usage outlined above, the security must be specified within the document itself and applied to the document rather than as a property of the channel that will convey it from one user to another.

- This is possible in XML or other structured document formats, in which metadata can be used. XML tags can be used to define the properties of the data in the document.

- In particular, XML security depends on new tags that can be used to indicate the beginning and end of sections of encrypted or signed data and of signatures.

- Once the necessary security has been applied within a document, it may be sent to a variety of different users, even by means of multicast.

Basic Requirements

- XML security should provide at least the same level of protection as TLS. That is:

- To be able to encrypt either an entire document or just some selected parts of it: For example, consider the information about a financial transaction, which includes a person's name, the type of transaction and details about the credit or debit card being used.

- In one case, just the card details could be hidden, making it possible to identify the transaction before decrypting the record.

- In another case, the type of transaction could also be hidden, so that outsiders cannot tell whether it is, for example, an order or a payment.

- To be able to sign either an entire document or just some selected parts of it: When a document is intended to be used for cooperative work by a group of people, there can be some critical parts of the document that should be signed in order to guarantee that they were made by a particular person or that they have not been changed.

- But it is also useful to be able to have other parts that can be altered during the use of the document these should not be signed.

Additional Basic Requirements

Further requirements arise from the need to store documents, possibly to modify them and then to send them on to a variety of different recipients:

- *To add to a document that is already signed and to sign the result*: For example, Alice may sign a document and pass it on to Bob, who 'witnesses her signature' by adding a remark to that effect and then signing the entire document

- *To authorize different users to view different parts of a document*: In the case of a medical record, a researcher can view some particular section of the medical data, an administrator can view personal details and a doctor can view both.

- *To add to a document that already contains encrypted sections and to encrypt part of the new version, possibly including some of the already encrypted sections.*

- The flexibility and structuring capabilities of XML notation make it possible do all of the above, without any additions to the scheme derived from the basic requirements.

Requirements Concerning Algorithms

XML secure documents are signed and/or encrypted well in advance of any consideration as to who will be accessing them. If the originator is no longer involved, it is not possible to negotiate the protocols and whether to use authentication or encryption. Therefore:

- *The standard should specify a suite of algorithms to be provided in any implementation of XML security*: At least one encryption and one signature algorithm should be mandatory, to enable the widest possible interoperability.

- Other optional algorithms should be provided for use within smaller groups.

- *The algorithms used for encryption and authentication of a particular document must be selected from that suite and the names of the algorithms in use must be referenced within the XML document itself.*

- If the places where the document will be used cannot be predicted, then one of the required protocols should be used.

- XML security defines the names of elements that can be used to specify the URI of the algorithm in use for signing or encryption. So as to be able to select a variety of algorithms within the same XML document, an element that specifies an algorithm is generally nested inside an element containing signed information or encrypted data.

Requirements for Finding Keys

When a document is created and each time that it is updated, appropriate keys must be chosen, without any negotiation with those parties that may access the document in the future. This leads to the following requirements:

- *To help the users of secure documents with finding the necessary keys*: For example, a document that includes signed data should contain information as to the public key to be used to validate the signature, such as a name that can be used to obtain the key, or a certificate. A *KeyInfo* element can be used for this purpose.

- *To make it possible for cooperating users to help one another with keys*: Provided that the *KeyInfo* element is not cryptographically bound to the signature itself, information may be added without breaking the digital signature.

- For example, suppose Alice signs a document and sends it to Bob with a *KeyInfo* element that specifies only the name of the key. When Bob receives the document he retrieves the information needed to validate the signature and adds this to the *KeyInfo* element when he passes the document to Carol.

The KeyInfo Element

- XML security specifies a *KeyInfo* element for indicating the key to be used to validate a signature or to decrypt some data.

- It may contain, for example, certificates, the names of keys or key agreement algorithms.

- Its use is optional: the signer may not want to reveal any key information to all of the parties that access the document, and in some cases the application using XML security may already have access to the keys in use.

Canonical XML

- Some applications may make changes that have no effect on the actual information content of an XML document.

- This arises because there are a variety of different ways of representing what is logically the same XML document.

- For example, attributes may be in different orders and differing character encodings may be used, yet the information content is equivalent. Canonical XML [www.w3.org X] was designed for use with digital signatures, which are used to guarantee that the information content of a document has not been changed. XML elements are canonicalized before being signed and the name of the canonicalization algorithm is stored, together with the signature.

- This enables the same algorithm to be used when the signature is validated.

- The canonical form is a standard serialization of XML as a stream of bytes. It adds default attributes and removes superfluous schemas, putting the attributes and schema declarations in lexicographic order in each element. It uses a standard form for line breaks and the UTF-8 encoding for characters.

- Any two equivalent XML documents have the same canonical form.

- When a subset of an XML document say an element is canonicalized, the canonical form includes the ancestor context, that is, the namespaces declared and the values of the attributes.

- Thus when canonical XML is used in conjunction with digital signatures, the signature of an element will not pass its validation if that element is placed in a different context.

- A variation of this algorithm, called Exclusive Canonical XML, omits the context from the serialization. This could be used if the application intends a particular signed element to be used in different contexts.

Use of Digital Signatures in XML

The specification for digital signatures in XML [www.w3.org XII] is a W3C recommendation that defines new XML element types to hold signatures, the names of algorithms, keys and references to signed information. The names provided in this specification are defined in the XML Signature schema which

The KeyInfo Element

- XML security specifies a *KeyInfo* element for indicating the key to be used to validate a signature or to decrypt some data.

- It may contain, for example, certificates, the names of keys or key agreement algorithms.

- Its use is optional: the signer may not want to reveal any key information to all of the parties that access the document, and in some cases the application using XML security may already have access to the keys in use.

3.4.4 Coordination of Web Services

- The SOAP infrastructure supports single request-response interactions between clients and web services. However, many useful applications involve several requests that need to be done in a particular order.

- For example, when booking a flight, the price and availability information is collected before the reservations are made.

- When a user interacts with web pages by means of a browser, for example, to book a flight or to make a bid in an auction, the interface provided by the browser (which is based on the information provided by the server) controls the sequence in which the operations are performed.

- Atomic transactions suit the requirements of applications using web services. However, activities such as those of the travel agent take a long time to complete, and it would be impractical to use a two-phase commit protocol to carry them out because it involves keeping resources locked for long periods of time.

- An alternative is to use a more relaxed protocol in which each participant makes changes to persistent state as they occur. In the case of failure, an application-level protocol is used to undo these actions.

- In conventional middleware, the infrastructure provides a simple request-reply protocol, leaving other services such as transactions, persistency and security to be implemented as separate higher-level services that can be used when they are needed.

- The same is true for web services, where the W3C and others have been putting in effort towards the definition of higher-level services.

- It has coordinator and participant roles that are able to act out particular protocols, for example, to carry out a distributed transaction.

- This work, which is called WSCoordination, is described by Langworthy [2004]. The same group has also shown how transactions may be carried out within this model. For a comprehensive study of web services coordination protocols, see Alonso et al. [2004].

- Consider the fact that it would be possible to describe all of the possible valid alternative paths through the set of interactions between pairs of web services working together in a joint task such as the travel agent scenario. If such a description were available, it could be used as an aid to the coordination of joint tasks. It could also be used as a specification to be followed by new instances of a service, such as a new flight booking service wishing to join a collaboration.

- The W3C uses the term choreography to refer to a language based on WSDL for defining coordination. For example, the language might specify constraints on the order and the conditions in which messages are exchanged by participants. A choreography is intended to provide a global description of a set of interactions, showing the behavior of each member of a set of participants, with a view to enhancing interoperability.

Requirements for Choreography

- Choreography is intended to support interactions between web services which are generally managed by different companies and organizations.

- A collaboration involving multiple web services and clients should be described in terms of the sets of observable interactions between pairs of them.

- Such a description might be seen as a contract between the participants, and could be used for the following purposes:

- To generate code outlines for a new service that wants to participate;

- As a basis for generating test messages for a new service;

- To promote a common understanding of the collaboration;
- To analyze the collaboration, for example to identify possible deadlock situations.

3.4.5 Applications of Web Services

3.4.5.1 Service-Oriented Architecture

- Service-Oriented Architecture (SOA) is a set of design principles whereby distributed systems are developed using sets of loosely coupled services that can be dynamically discovered and then communicate with each other or are coordinated through choreography to provide enhanced services.

- Service-oriented architecture is an abstract concept that can be implemented using a variety of technologies including the distributed object or component-based approaches.

3.4.5.2 The Grid

- The name 'Grid' is used to refer to middleware that is designed to enable the sharing of resources such as files, computers, software, data and sensors on a very large scale.

- The resources are shared typically by groups of users in different organizations who are collaborating on the solution of problems requiring large numbers of computers to solve them, either by the sharing of data or by the sharing of computing power. These resources are necessarily supported by heterogeneous computer hardware, operating systems, programming languages and applications. Management is needed to coordinate the use of resources to ensure that clients get what they need and that services can afford to supply it.

Requirements of Grid Applications

- The World-Wide Telescope is typical of a range of data-intensive Grid applications, wherein:
- Data is collected by means of scientific instruments;
- The data is stored in archives at separate sites whose locations can be in different places throughout the world;
- The data is managed by teams of scientists belonging to separate organizations;
- An immense and increasing quantity (terabytes or petabytes) of raw data is generated from the instruments;
- Computer programs are used to analyze and make summaries of the raw data, for example, to classify, calibrate and catalogue the raw data representing celestial objects.

The Internet makes all of these data archives potentially available to scientists throughout the world, enabling them to get data from different instruments gathered at different times and at different sites. However, a particular scientist using this data for their own research will be interested in just a subset of the objects in the archives.

3.4.5.3 Cloud Computing

- Cloud computing is defined as a type of computing that relies on *sharing computing resources* rather than having local servers or personal devices to handle applications. Cloud computing is comparable to grid computing, a type of computing where unused processing cycles of all computers in a network are harnesses to solve problems too intensive for any stand-alone machine.

- In cloud computing, the word cloud (also phrased as "the cloud") is used as a metaphor for "*the Internet*," so the phrase *cloud computing* means "a type of Internet-based computing," where different services such as servers, storage and applications are delivered to an organization's computers and devices through the Internet.

How Cloud Computing Works

- The goal of cloud computing is to apply traditional supercomputing, or high-performance computing power, normally used by military and research facilities, to perform tens of trillions of computations per second, in consumer-oriented applications such as financial portfolios, to deliver personalized information, to provide data storage or to power large, immersive online computer games.

- To do this, cloud computing uses networks of large groups of servers typically running low-cost consumer PC technology with specialized connections to spread data-processing chores across them.

- This shared IT infrastructure contains large pools of systems that are linked together.

- Often, virtualization techniques are used to maximize the power of cloud computing.

3.5 PEER-TO-PEER SYSTEMS

- Peer-to-peer systems represent a paradigm for the construction of distributed systems and applications in which data and computational resources are contributed by many hosts on the Internet, all of which participate in the provision of a uniform service.

- Their emergence is a consequence of the very rapid growth of the Internet, embracing many millions of computers and similar numbers of users requiring access to shared resources.

- A key problem for peer-to-peer systems is the placement of data objects across many hosts and subsequent provision for access to them in a manner that balances the workload and ensures availability without adding undue overheads.

- We describe several recently developed systems and applications that are designed to achieve this.

- Peer-to-peer middleware systems are emerging that have the capacity to share computing resources, storage and data present in computers 'at the edges of the Internet' on a global scale.

- They exploit existing naming, routing, data replication and security techniques in new ways to build a reliable resource-sharing layer over an unreliable and untrusted collection of computers and networks.

- Peer-to-peer applications have been used to provide file sharing, web caching, information distribution and other services, exploiting the resources of tens of thousands of machines across the Internet.

- They are at their most effective when used to store very large collections of immutable data.

- Their design diminishes their effectiveness for applications that store and update mutable data objects.

- Peer-to-peer systems aim to support useful distributed services and applications using data and computing resources available in the personal computers and workstations that are present in the Internet and other networks in ever-increasing numbers.

- This is increasingly attractive as the performance difference between desktop and server machines narrows and broadband network connections proliferate.

Peer-to-Peer Systems Share these Characteristics:

- Their design ensures that each user contributes resources to the system.

- Although they may differ in the resources that they contribute, all the nodes in a peer-to-peer system have the same functional capabilities and responsibilities.

- Their correct operation does not depend on the existence of any centrally administered systems.

- They can be designed to offer a limited degree of anonymity to the providers and users of resources.

- A key issue for their efficient operation is the choice of an algorithm for the placement of data across many hosts and subsequent access to it in a manner that balances the workload and ensures availability without adding undue overheads.

3.6 PEER-TO-PEER MIDDLEWARE

- The third generation is characterized by the emergence of middleware layers for the application-independent management of distributed resources on a global scale. Several research teams have now completed the development, evaluation and refinement of peer-to-peer middleware platforms and demonstrated or deployed them in a range of application services.

- These platforms are designed to place resources (data objects, files) on a set of computers that are widely distributed throughout the Internet and to route messages to them on behalf of clients, relieving clients of any need to make decisions about placing resources and to hold information about the whereabouts of the resources they require.

- Unlike the second-generation systems, they provide guarantees of delivery for requests in a bounded number of network hops.

- They place replicas of resources on available host computers in a structured manner, taking account of their volatile availability, their variable trustworthiness and requirements for load balancing and locality of information storage and use.

- Peer-to-peer middleware systems are designed specifically to meet the need for the automatic placement and subsequent location of the distributed objects managed by peer-to-peer systems and applications.

Functional Requirements

- The function of peer-to-peer middleware is to simplify the construction of services that are implemented across many hosts in a widely distributed network.

- To achieve this it must enable clients to locate and communicate with any individual resource made available to a service, even though the resources are widely distributed amongst the hosts.

- Other important requirements include the ability to add new resources and to remove them at will and to add hosts to the service and remove them.

- Like other middleware, peer-to-peer middleware should offer a simple programming interface to application programmers that is independent of the types of distributed resource that the application manipulates.

Non-Functional Requirements

- To perform effectively, peer-to-peer middleware must also address the following non-functional requirements:

- **Global Scalability:** One of the aims of peer-to-peer applications is to exploit the hardware resources of very large numbers of hosts connected to the Internet. Peer-to-peer middleware must therefore be designed to support applications that access millions of objects on tens of thousands or hundreds of thousands of hosts.

- **Load Balancing:** The performance of any system designed to exploit a large number of computers depends upon the balanced distribution of workload across them. For the systems we are considering, this will be achieved by a random placement of resources together with the use of replicas of heavily used resources.

- **Optimization for Local Interactions between Neighbouring Peers:** The 'network distance' between nodes that interact has a substantial impact on the latency of individual interactions, such as client requests for access to resources. Network traffic loadings are also impacted by it. The middleware should aim to place resources close to the nodes that access them the most.

- **Accommodating to Highly Dynamic Host Availability:** Most peer-to-peer systems are constructed from host computers that are free to join or leave the system at any time.

- The hosts and network segments used in peer-to-peer systems are not owned or managed by any single authority; neither their reliability nor their continuous participation in the provision of a service is guaranteed. A major challenge for peer-to-peer systems is to provide a dependable service despite these facts. As hosts join the system, they must be integrated into the system and the load must be redistributed to exploit their resources. When they leave the system whether voluntarily or involuntarily, the system must detect their departure and redistribute their load and resources.

3.7 CASE STUDY: SQUIRREL

Squirrel

- The Squirrel web caching service performs the same functions using a small part of the resources of each client computer on a local network. The SHA-1 secure hash function is applied to the URL of each cached object to produce a 128-bit Pastry GUID.

- Since the GUID is not used to validate the contents, it need not be based on the entire object contents, as it is in other Pastry applications.

- The authors of Squirrel base their justification for this on the end-to-end argument, arguing that the authenticity of a web page may be compromised at many points in its journey from the host to the client; authentication of cached pages adds little to any overall guarantee of authenticity and the HTTPS protocol (incorporating end-to-end Transport Layer Security,) should be used to achieve a much better guarantee for those interactions that require it.

- In the simplest implementation of Squirrel which proved to be the most effective one the node whose GUID is numerically closest to the GUID of an object becomes that object's *home node*, responsible for holding the cached copy of the object when there is one.

- Client nodes are configured to include a local Squirrel proxy process, which takes responsibility for both local and remote caching of web objects.

- If a fresh copy of a required object is not in the local cache, Squirrel routes a *Get* request or a *Get* request (when there is a stale copy of the object in the local cache) via Pastry to the home node.

- If the home node has a fresh copy, it directly responds to the client with a *not-modified* message or a fresh copy, as appropriate. If the home node has a stale copy or no copy of the object, it issues a *Get* or a *Get* to the origin server, respectively.

- The origin server may respond with a *not-modified* message or a copy of the object.

- In the former case, the home node revalidates its cache entry and forwards a copy of the object to the client.

- In the latter case, it forwards a copy of the new value to the client and places a copy in its local cache if the object is cacheable.

Evaluation of Squirrel

- Squirrel was evaluated by simulation using modelled loads derived from traces of the activity of existing centralized proxy web caches in two real working environments within Microsoft, one with 105 active clients (in Cambridge) and the other with more than 36,000 (in Redmond). The evaluation compared the performance of a Squirrel web cache with a centralized one in three respects:

- **The Reduction in Total External Bandwidth Used:** The total external bandwidth is inversely related to the hit ratio, since it is only cache misses that generate requests to external web servers. The hit ratios observed for centralized web cache servers were 29% (for Redmond) and 38% (for Cambridge). When the same activity logs were used to generate a simulated load for the Squirrel cache, with each client contributing 100 Mbytes of disk storage, very similar hit ratios of 28% (Redmond) and 37% (Cambridge) were achieved. It follows that the external bandwidth would be reduced by a similar proportion.

- **The Latency Perceived by Users for Access to Web Objects:** The use of a routing overlay results in several message transfers (routing hops) across the local network to transmit a request from a client to the host responsible for caching the relevant object (the home node). The mean numbers of routing hops observed in the simulation were 4.11 hops to deliver a GET request in the Redmond case and 1.8 hops in the Cambridge case, whereas only a single message transfer is required to access a centralized cache service.

  However local transfers take only a few milliseconds with modern Ethernet hardware, including TCP connection setup time, whereas wide area TCP message transfers across the Internet require 10–100 ms. The Squirrel authors therefore argue that the latency for access to objects found in the cache is swamped by the much greater latency of access to objects not found in the cache, giving a similar user experience to that provided with a centralized cache.

- **The Computational and Storage Load Imposed on Client Nodes:** The average number of cache requests served for other nodes by each node over the whole period of the evaluation was extremely low, at only 0.31 per minute (Redmond), indicating that the overall proportion of system resources consumed is extremely low.

  Based on the measurements described above, the authors of Squirrel concluded that its performance is comparable to that of a centralized cache. Squirrel achieves a reduction in the observed latency for web page access close to that achievable by a centralized cache server with a similarly sized dedicated cache. The additional load imposed on client nodes is low and likely to be imperceptible to users. The Squirrel system was subsequently deployed as the primary web cache in a local network with 52 client machines using Squirrel, and the results confirmed their conclusions.

REVIEW QUESTIONS

1. State and explain CORBA.

2. State and explain application of web service.

3. State and explain squirrel.

4. Comment about XML security.

5. Short note on

    (1) SOAP

    (2) WSDL

    (3) EJB

    (4) Peer-to-Peer system

6. Define distributed system.

7. Draw and explain EJB architecture.

UNIVERSITY QUESTIONS

May 2012

1. State and explain the Invocation models supported in CORBA.   **[6]**

October 2012

2. Explain CORBA callback and polling model for asynchronous method invocation.   **[8]**

May 2013

3. Describe the working of Distributed System based upon middleware software systems. Also clearly describe the roles played by middleware in Distributed System.   **[8]**

May 2014

4. What is CORBA? Describe the general organization of CORBA system with the help of neat diagram.   **[8]**

May 2015

5. Describe the working of distributed system based upon middleware software systems. Also clearly describe the roles played by middleware in distributed system.   **[9]**

6. What is CORBA? Describe the general organization of CORBA system with help of a neat diagram.   **[8]**

✠ ✠ ✠

DISTRIBUTED ALGORITHMS

4.1 TIME AND GLOBAL STATES

4.1.1 Clocks, Events and Process States

- In this unit we discuss the important concept of timing that is nothing but synchronization between the devices connected to each other within the distributed system basically, the absence of common memory and a system wide common clock is an inherent problem in distributed systems.
- In the absence of global time, it becomes difficult to talk about temporal order of events.
- Without a shared memory, up-to-date information about the state of the system is not available to every process via a simple memory lookup.
- The state information must therefore be collected through communication.
- The combination of communication delays and the lack of global time in a distributed system make it difficult to know how up-to-date collected state information really is.

No Global Clock

- In a distributed system each system is having their own clock. The clocks are coordinated to keep them somewhat consistent but no one clock has the exact time.
- Even if the clocks were somewhat in synchronous, the individual clocks on each component may run at a different rate or granularity leading to them being out of synchronization only after one local clock cycle.
- Time is only known within a given precision. At frequent intervals, a clock may synchronize with a more trusted clock.
- However, the clocks are not precisely the same because of time lapses due to transmission and execution.
- If a group of people going to a meeting. Each person has a watch. Each watch has a similar, but having different time. Even with the error in time, the group is able to meet and conduct business.
- This is how distributed time works. This is in contrast to a clock on a single system. Here there is only one clock and it provides a unified time for all sub components on this individual system.
- Communication between elements is inherently asynchronous in a distributed system. There is no global clock or consistent clock rate.
- Each computer processes independently of others. Some computers in the system have fast clock cycles while others have slower clock cycles.

- Even if time was precisely the same on every element in the distributed system, each element would still process the communication at different rates, thus making the commutation asynchronous.
- It is impossible to synchronize the clocks of different processors precisely because of uncertainty in communication delays between them.
- As a result, it is rare to use physical clocks for synchronization in distributed systems.

Shared Memory

- Shared memory is memory that is simultaneously accessed by multiple programs, it provide communication among them or avoid redundant copies.
- Depending on context, programs may run on a single processor or on multiple separate processors. Using memory for communication inside a single program, for example among its multiple threads, is generally not referred to as shared memory.
- In computer hardware, shared memory can be accessed by different central processing units (CPUs) in a multiple-processor computer system.
- A shared memory system is relatively easy to program since all processors share a single view of data and the communication between processors can be as fast as memory accesses to a same location.
- The issue with shared memory systems is that many CPUs need fast access to memory and will likely cache memory, which has two complications:
  - CPU-to-memory connection becomes a bottleneck: Shared memory computers cannot scale very well. Most of them have ten or fewer processors.
  - Cache coherence problem: When cache is updated with information that may be used by other processors, the change needs to be reflected to the other processors, otherwise the different processors will be working with incoherent data.
- The lack of common memory a system wide common clock is an inherent problem in distributed systems. In the absence of global time, it becomes difficult to talk about temporal order of events. Without a shared memory, up-to-date information about the state of the system is not available to every process via a simple memory lookup. The state information must therefore be collected through communication.
- The combination of unpredictable communication delays and the lack of global time in a distributed system make it difficult to know how up-to-date collected state information really is.
- In a distributed system, it is impossible for anyone processor to know the global state of the system. As a result, it is difficult to observe any global property of the system. The example below Fig. 4.1 illustrates this problem and underscores the need for a coherent global state.

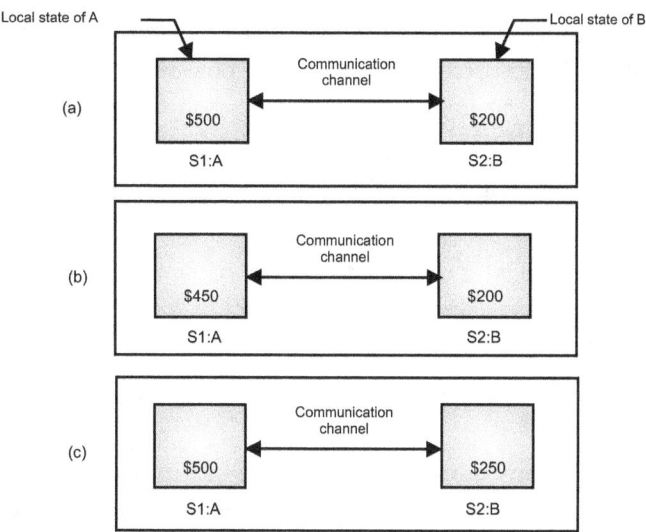

Fig. 4.1: A distributed system with two sites

- Consider that S1 and S2 are two different entities (sites) of a distributed system which maintain bank accounts A and B, respectively.

- Three is a requirement of knowledge related to global state of the system to compute the net balance of both accounts. The initial state of the two accounts is shown in Fig. 4.1 (a).

- Let site S1 transfer, say $ 50 from account A to account B. During the collection of a global state, if site S1 records the state of a immediately after the debit has occurred, and site S2 saves the state of B before the fund transfer message has reached B, then the global system state will show $50 missing as shown in Fig. 4.1 (b).

- The communication channel cannot record its state by itself. Hence, sites have to coordinate their state recording activities in order to record the channel state.

- On the other hand, if A's state is recorded immediately before the transfer and B's state is recorded after account B has been credited $50, then the global system state will show an extra $50 as shown in Fig. 4.1 (c)

4.1.1.1 Universal Coordinated Time (UTC)

- In this section we discuss the time coordination system The international time scale is an atomic time scale distributed by various telecommunication systems throughout the world known as Coordinated Universal Time (UTC).

- UTC is defined by the International Telecommunication Union (ITU-R) and is maintained by the International Bureau of Weights and Measures (BIPM) in cooperation with the International Earth reference and Rotation Service (IERS).

- Contributed measurements from timing centres around the world are used in the determination of UTC, which is adjusted to within 0.9 s of Earth rotation time (UT1) by IERS-determined values of the Earth rotation.

- The adjustments, made in one second steps known as leap seconds, were implemented in 1972 to permit UT1 to be recovered from broadcast values of UTC for celestial navigation. Current telecommunication and navigation systems utilize continuous timing for their data transmissions; consequently, deliberations have been on-going within the ITU-R on the issue of modifying the definition of UTC to a continuous time scale.

Leap Second:

- A leap second is a second which is added to Coordinated Universal Time (UTC) in order to keep it synchronized with astronomical time. UTC is an atomic time scale, based on the performance of atomic clocks that are more stable than the Earth's rotational rate.

- Astronomical time (UT1), or mean solar time, is based on the rotation of Earth, which is irregular.

- There are two main reasons because of that leap seconds occur. The first reason is that the atomic second was originally defined by comparing atomic clocks to the ephemeris second, which is slightly shorter than the mean solar second and which is no longer used.

- This made the atomic second slightly shorter than the mean solar second to begin with.

- The second reason is that the rotation of Earth varies and is gradually slowing down, so the mean solar second is gradually getting longer. All of these factors contribute to the difference between UTC and UT1.

International Atomic Time (TAI):

- TAI is the basis for Coordinated Universal Time (UTC), which is used for civil timekeeping all over the Earth's surface, and for Terrestrial Time, which is used for astronomical calculations.

- Since 2008-12-31 when the last leap second was added, TAI has been exactly 34 seconds ahead of UTC. 34 seconds results from the initial difference of 10 seconds at the start of 1972, plus 24 leap seconds in UTC since 1972.

- A new leap second is scheduled to be added on July 1st, 2012.

- Time coordinates on the TAI scales are conventionally specified using traditional means of specifying days, carried over from non-uniform time standards based on the rotation of the Earth.

- TAI in this form was synchronised with Universal Time at the beginning of 1958, and the two have drifted apart ever since, due to the changing motion of the Earth.

Mean Solar Time

- Mean solar time is in relation to the mean sun. The mean sun is a point which moves uniformly around the earth along the plane of the ecliptic, but is usually not is the same position as the real sun.

- The real sun, as viewed from earth, does not move uniformly because of the elliptical nature of the earth's orbit and because of the slight variations in the earth's rotation period.

- A mean solar day contains 24 solar hours, the time it takes for the mean sun to be on a point's celestial meridian, the mean noon, twice. It is measured from midnight to midnight with midnight being hour 0.

- A solar day is divided into 24 solar hours, each solar hour is divided into 60 solar minutes, and solar minutes are divided into 60 solar seconds.

- A solar year is the time the earth takes to make a revolution around the sun, from one vernal equinox to the next.

- A solar year is sometimes called a tropical year and is equal to 365 days, 5 hours, 48 minutes, and 45.51 seconds, or 365.24219 days, in solar time.

- A solar year is affected by the precession of the equinox. A solar month is one twelfth of a solar year.

- The moon also creates an interval of time known as a synodic, or lunar, month. A lunar month is the time between two new moons and is equal to about 29.53 days.

4.1.1.2 Clock Synchronization

- In distributed system clock synchronization deals with understanding the temporal ordering of events produced by concurrent processes. It is useful for synchronizing senders and receivers of messages, controlling joint activity, and the serializing concurrent access to shared objects.

- The goal is that multiple unrelated processes running on different machines should be in agreement with and be able to make consistent decisions about the ordering of events in a system.

- For these kinds of events, we introduce the concept of a logical clock, one where the clock need not have any bearing on the time of day but rather be able to create event sequence numbers that can be used for comparing sets of events, such as a messages, within a distributed system.

- Another aspect of clock synchronization deals with synchronizing time-of-day clocks among groups of machines. In this case, we want to ensure that all machines can report the same time, regardless of how imprecise their clocks may be or what the network latencies are between the machines.

A Consistent View of Time

- In distributed system application for making time-based decisions we can relay upon a time-of-day clock. Most computers have them and it would seem to be a simple matter to throw on a time-of-day timestamp to any message or other event where we would need to mark its time and possibly compare it with the time of other events.

- This method is known as global time ordering. There are a couple of problems with this approach.

- The first is that we have no assurance that clocks on different machines are synchronized.
- If machine A generates a message at 4:15:00 and machine B generates a message at 4:15:20, it's quite possible that machine B's message was generated prior to that of machine A if B's clock was over 20 seconds too fast. Even if we synchronize periodically, it's quite possible (even likely) that the clocks may run at different speeds and drift apart to report different times.
- The second problem is that two events on two different systems may actually occur at exactly the same time (to the precision of the clock, at least) and thus be tagged with identical timestamps.
- If we have algorithms that compare messages to pick one over another and rely on them coming up with the same answer on all systems, we have a problem as there will be no unique way to select one message over another consistently.

4.1.1.3 Logical Clock

- If we want to assigning sequence numbers ("timestamps") to events upon which all cooperating processes can agree.
- What matters in these cases is not the time of day at which the event occurred but that all processes can agree on the order in which related events occur.
- Our interest is in getting event sequence numbers that make sense system-wide. These clocks are called logical clocks.
- If we can do this across all events in the system, we have something called **total ordering:** every event is assigned a unique timestamp (number), every such timestamp is unique.
- However, we don't always need total ordering. If processes do not interact then we don't care when their events occur.
- If we only care about assigning timestamps to related (causal) events then we have something known as partial ordering.
- **Leslie Lamport** developed a "happens before" notation to express the relationship between events: a→b means that a happens before b. If a represents the timestamp of a message sent and b is the timestamp of that message being received, then a→b must be true; a message cannot be received before it is sent.
- This relationship is transitive. If a→b and b→then a→c. If a and b are events that take place in the same process the a→b is true if a occurs before b.
- The importance of measuring logical time is in assigning a time value to each event such that everyone will agree on the final order of events.
- That is, if a→b then clock(a)< clock(b) since the clock (timestamp) must never run backwards.
- If a and b occur on different processes that do not exchange messages (even through third parties) then a→b is not true. These events are said to be concurrent: there is no way that a could have influenced b.

- Consider the sequence of events in Fig. 4.2 taking place between three processes. Each event is assigned a timestamp by its respective process.

- The process simply maintains a global counter that is incremented before each event gets a timestamp.

- If we examine the timestamps from our global perspective, we can observe a number of peculiarities.

- Event g, the event representing the receipt of the message sent by event a, has the exact same timestamp as event a when it clearly had to take place after event a.

- Event e has an earlier time stamp (1) than the event that sent the message b, with a timestamp of(2).

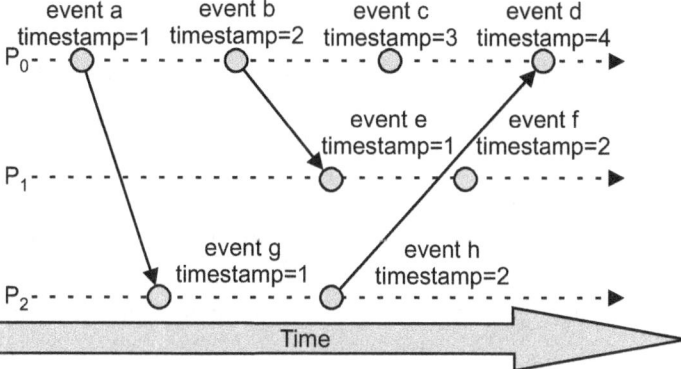

Fig. 4.2: Unsequenced event stamps

4.2 LAMPORT'S LOGICAL CLOCK IN DISTRIBUTED SYSTEMS

- In a distributed system, it is not possible to synchronize time across entities within the system, hence, the entities can use the concept of a logical clock based on the events through which they communicate.

- If two entities do not exchange any messages, then they probably do not need to share a common clock, events occurring on those entities are termed as concurrent events.

- Among the processes on the same local machine we can order the events based on the local clock of the system. When two entities communicate by message passing, then the send event is said to 'happen before' the receive event, and the logical order can be established among the events.

- A distributed system is in partial order if we can have a partial order relationship among the events in the system.

- If 'totality', i.e., causal relationship among all events in the system can be established, then the system is said to have total order. In light of the need for ordering events, Lamport proposed a scheme using logical clocks.

- While it remains true in general that the order of two events occur at two different computers cannot be determined based on the local time at which they occur, events that have certain causal dependencies can be ordered. Lamport's logical clocks are designed to capture those dependencies where two events are causally related by a "happened before" relation as defined below.

Happened Before Relation ($\rightarrow$). The relation $\rightarrow$ is defined as follows:

$a \rightarrow b$, if a and b are events in the same process and a occurred before b.

$a \rightarrow b$, if a is the event of sending a message m in a process and b is the event of receiving the same message m by another process.

If $a \rightarrow b$ and $b \rightarrow c$, then $a \rightarrow c$, i.e., "$\rightarrow$" relation is transitive.

- The *happened before* relation captures the causal dependencies between events, i.e., whether two events are causally related or not. Event a *causally affects* event b if $a \rightarrow b$.

- Two events a and b are said to be concurrent (denoted as $a||b$) if $not(a \rightarrow b \text{ or } b \rightarrow a)$.

- In other words, concurrent events do not causally affect each other. For any two events a and b in a system, either $a \rightarrow b$, $b \rightarrow a$, or $a \| b$.

- Consider that, e_{11}, e_{12}, e_{13} and e_{14} are events in process p_1 and e_{21}, e_{22}, e_{23} and e_{24} are events in process p_2. The arrow is used to represent transferring of message between the processes. i.e. arrow e_{12} e_{23} is used to represent that message sent from process p_1 to process p_2, e_{12} is the event of sending the message at p_1 and e_{23} is the event of receiving the same message at p_2.

- As shown in Fig. 4.3 $e_{22} \rightarrow e_{13}$ and $e_{13} \rightarrow e_{14}$ therefore we say that $e_{22} \rightarrow e_{14}$. Note that whenever a $\rightarrow$ b holds for two events a and b, there exists a path from a to b which moves only forward along the time axis in the space-time diagram.

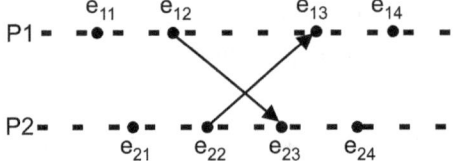

Fig. 4.3: Space-time diagram

Important Condition to be Satisfied by Lamport's Logical Clocks for any event a and b:

IF a→b ,then C(a)<C(b)

The happened before relation "$\rightarrow$" can now be realized by using the logical clocks if the following conditions are met:

Condition 1:

For any two events a and b in a process P_i, if a occurs before b, then $C_i(a) < C_i(b)$.

Condition 2:

If a is the event of sending a message m in process P_i and b is the event of receiving the same message m at process P_j, then $C_i(a) < C_j(b)$.

These two conditions are guaranteed with the following implementation rules(IR):

Implementation Rules 1:

Clock C_i is incremented between any two successive events in process P_i as follows:

$$C_i: = C_i + d, \text{ where } d > 0.$$

Implementation Rules 2:

- If event a is the sending of message m in process P_i, then message m is assigned a timestamp $t_m = C_i (a)$. On receiving the same message m by process P_j, C_j is first set using [IR1], then set to a value greater than or equal to the new C_j and greater than t_m, i.e., $C_j := \max (C_j, t_m + d)$, where $d > 0$.

- With these two implementation rules, two causally related events a and b such that $a \to b$ will have $C(a) < C(b)$, and two successive events a and b in process Pi will yield $Ci(b) = Ci(a) + d$.

- Lamport's system of logical clocks implements an approximation to global/physical time that is referred to as *virtual time*.

- The virtual time advances along with the progression of events and is therefore discrete.

- The virtual time is defined based on an irreflexive partial order "$\to$", and can be used to totally order events in a distributed system (hence produces a total order relation "$\Rightarrow$") as follows:

- If a is any event at process Pi and b is any event at process P_j, then $a \Rightarrow b$ if and only if either

$$C_i (a) < C_j (b), \text{ or}$$
$$C_i (a) = C_j (b) \text{ and } P_i < P_j$$

- Where $<$ is any arbitrary relation that totally orders the processes to break ties (e.g., process id $i < j$ implies $P_i < P_j$).

- It should be noted that $a \Rightarrow b$ does not necessarily imply $a \to b$. And this is known to be a major limitation of Lamport's logical clocks: If $a \to b$ then $C(a) < C(b)$, but the converse is not necessarily true.

4.3 VECTOR CLOCKS

- A vector clock is an algorithm which is used for generating a partial ordering of events in a distributed system and detecting causality violations.

- Just as in Lamport timestamps, inter-process messages contain the state of the sending process's logical clock.

- A vector clock of a system of N processes is an array of N logical clocks, one per process, a local copy of which is kept in each process with the following rules for clock updates:

  - Initially all clocks are zero.

  - Each time a process experiences an internal event, it increments its own logical clock in the vector by one.

- Each time a process prepares to send a message, it increments its own logical clock in the vector by one and then sends its entire vector along with the message being sent.
- Each time a process receives a message, it increments its own logical clock in the vector by one and updates each element in its vector by taking the maximum of the value in its own vector clock and the value in the vector in the received message (for every element).

Partial Ordering Property:

Vector clocks allow for the partial causal ordering of events. Defining the following:

VC(x) denote the vector clock of event x

Statement in partial ordering property:

$$VC\ (x) < VC\ (y) \Leftrightarrow \forall z\ [VC\ (x)Z \le VC\ (y)Z] \cap \exists z'\ [VC\ (x)Z' < VC\ (y)Z']$$

$$GS = \left\{ \underset{i}{U}\ L\ S_i, \ \underset{i\ j}{U}\ SC_{ij} \right\}$$

C_1: Send $(m_{ij} > \in LS_t \Rightarrow m_{ij} \in SC_{ij} \oplus rec\ (m_{ij}) \in LS_j$ ($\oplus$ is EX-OR operator)

C_2: Send $(m_{ij}) \notin LS_t \Rightarrow m_{ij} \in SC_{ij} \wedge rec\ (m_{ij}) \notin LS_i$.

$O\ (rn^2)$

In English: VC(x) is less than VC(y) if and only if VC(x)[z] is less than or equal to VC(y)[z] for all indices z and there exists an index z' such that VC(x)[z'] is strictly less than VC(y)[z']. denote event x happened before event y. It's defined as: if , then VC(x) < VC(y)

Properties:

If VC(a) < VC(b), then

Antisymmetry: If VC(a) < VC(b), then $\downarrow$ VC(b) < VC(a)

Transitivity: If VC(a) < VC(b) and VC(b) < VC(c), then VC(a) < VC(c) or if and then

Each process P_i in a distributed system with n processes is equipped with a vector clock C_i. The clock C_i consists of an integer vector of length n, and can be viewed as a function that assigns a vector C_i (a) to any event a at P_i as the event's timestamp. C_i $[i]$, the i th entry of C_i, corresponds to P_i's own logical time. C_i $[j]$, $j \ne i$, indicates the time of occurrence of the last event at P_j that "happened before" the current point in time at P_i.

It therefore represents P_i's best guess of the logical time at P_j, and must satisfy the assertion of C_i $[j] \le C_j$ $[j]$.

The vector clocks can be implemented with the following implementation rules:

Implementation Rules 1:

Clock C_i is incremented between any two successive events in process P_i as follows:

$$C_i\ [i] := C_i\ [i] + d, \text{ where } d > 0.$$

Implementation Rules 2:

If event a is the sending of message m in process P_i, then message m is assigned a timestamp $t_m = C_i$ (a). On receiving the same message m by process P_j, C_j $[j]$ is first incremented as in [IR1], then C_j is updated as follows:

$$\forall k,\ C_j\ [k] := max\ (C_j\ [k], t_m\ [k]).$$

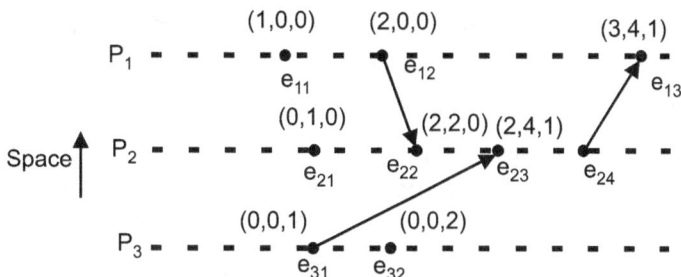

Fig. 4.4: Examples of how vector clocks advance as events occur

With vector clocks, $a \rightarrow b$ iff $t_a < t_b$, where t_a and t_b denote the vector timestamps of events a and b, respectively. In other words, vector clocks allow us to order events in a distributed system and decide whether two events are causally related based simply on the timestamps of the events.

4.4 GLOBAL STATE

Because of lack of shared memory and a global clock, and communication delays are unpredictable, one cannot count on simultaneous observations of states in all the individual computers in an asynchronous distributed system. Consequently, one cannot determine a global state in such a system in a conventional manner.

We can use the 2-site system given in Fig. 4.5 to illustrate the difficulty.

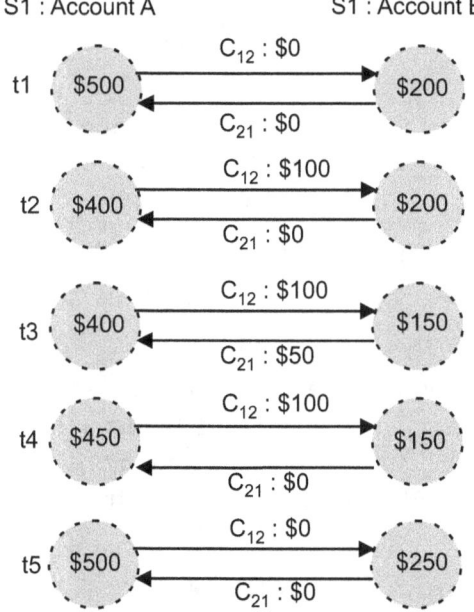

Fig. 4.5: A banking example

Let S1 and S2 be two distinct sites of a distributed system which maintain bank accounts A and B, respectively. A site refers to a process in this example.

Let the communication channels from site S1 to site S2 and from site S2 to site S1 be denoted by C_{12} and C_{21}, respectively. Consider the following sequence of actions,

- Initially, Account A = $500, Account B = $200, C_{12} = $0, C_{21}= $0.
- Site SI initiates a transfer of $100 from Account A to Account B. Account A is decremented by $100 to $400 and a request for $100 credit to Account B is sent on Channel C_{12} to site S2. Account A = $400, Account B = $200, C_{12}= $100, C_{21} = $0.
- Site S2 initiates a transfer of $50 from Account B to Account A. Account B is decremented by $50 to $150 and a request for $50 credit to Account A is sent on Channel Czl to site S1. Account A = $400, Account B = $150, C_{12}= $100, C_{21} = $50.
- Site S1 receives the message for a $50 credit to Account A and updates Account A. Account A = $450, Account B = $150, C_{12} = $100, C_{21} = $0.
- Site S2 receives the message for a $100 credit to Account B and updates Account B. Account A = $450, Account B = $250, C_{12} = $0, C_{21} = $0.

Suppose the local state of Account A is recorded at the end of step 1 to show $500 and the local state of Account B and channels C_{12} and C_{21} are recorded at the end of step 3 to show $150, $100, and $50, respectively.

Then the recorded global state shows $800 in the system. An extra of $100 appears in the system. The reason for the inconsistency is that Account A's state was recorded before the $100 transfer to Account B using channel C_{12} was initiated, whereas channel C_{12}'s state was recorded after the $100 transfer was initiated.

This simple example shows that recording a consistent global state of a distributed system is not a trivial task.

The global state of a distributed system is a collection of the local states of the processes and the channels. Notationally, a global state GS is defined as

$$GS = \{U \; LSi, \; U \; SC_{ij} \}$$

A global state GS is a consistent global state iff it satisfies the following two conditions:

C_1: send(mij) $\in$ $LSt=>$ $m_{ij} \in SC_{ij}$rec(m_{ij}) E LSj. (is Ex-OR operator.)

C_2: send(mij) $LSi=>m_{ij} \in SC_{ij} \wedge$ rec(m_{ij}) LSj.

In a consistent global state, every message that is recorded as received is also recorded as sent and such a state captures the notion of causality that a message cannot be received if it was not sent. Consistent global states are meaningful global states and inconsistent global states are not meaningful in the sense that a distributed system can never be in an inconsistent state.

4.4.1 Issues in Recording a Global State

- In this section we discuss the issue in recording a global state. If a global physical clock were available, the following simple procedure could be used to record a consistent global snapshot of a distributed system:

- The initiator of the snapshot collection decides a future time at which the snapshot is to be taken and broadcasts this time to each process.
- All processes take their local snapshots at that instant in the global time. The snapshot of channel C_{ij} includes all the messages that process j receives after taking the snapshot and whose timestamp is smaller than the time of the snapshot. (All messages are times tamped with the sender's time).
- Clearly, if channels are not FIFO, a termination detection scheme will be needed to determine when to stop waiting for messages on channels.
- However, a global physical clock is not available in a distributed system and the following two issues need to be addressed in recording a consistent global snapshot of a distributed system:

I_1: How to distinguish between the messages to be recorded in the snapshot (either in a channel state or a process state) from those not to be recorded. The answer to this comes from conditions C_1 and C_2 as follows:

Any message that is sent by a process before recording its snapshot must be recorded in the global snapshot (from C_1).

Any message that is sent by a process after recording its snapshot must not be recorded in the global snapshot (from C_2).

I_2: How to determine the instant when a process takes its snapshot. The answer to this comes from condition C_2:

A process j must record its snapshot before processing a message m_{ij} that was sent by process i after recording its snapshot.

4.5 COORDINATION AND AGREEMENT

4.5.1 Distributed Mutual Exclusion

- In distributed system when a particular process has to read or update certain shared data structures, it first enters a critical region to achieve mutual exclusion and ensure that no other process will use the shared data structures at the same time.
- Mutual Exclusion is the state in which only one process can access critical region of the parallel and distributed environment at a single instance of time.
- Mutual exclusion ensure that critical region is being access or enter by a single process and makes other processes wait or busy who want to access or enter that same critical region while one process is already in that critical region. so, mutual exclusion requires some communication between processes to avoid race condition.
- Race condition is said to be occurred when more than one process access and manipulate same critical region at a same instance of time.
- This type of communication between processes is referred as Interprocess communication. Inter-Process Communication (IPC) is necessary to achieve synchronization between every process in distributed environment. All processes must have to communicate with other process to be synchronized to avoid race condition, deadlock or starvation.

- To avoid these parameters, IPC has different approaches or different ways to communicate with processes. Those approaches or mechanism are: Pipes, First In First Out (FIFO), Shared Memory, Mapped Memory, and Message Queues.

- In the mutual exclusion, whenever a process enters critical region, it simply has to test or check the lock of that critical region and if it is set free then and then that process can enter or access that critical region of the memory in distributed environment. Lock is a data structure in which process fills its own parameter to set lock.

- A process can enter only if lock is set by itself.

- If any other process has set lock for a critical region for which current process wants to enter or access, in such scenario that requesting process has to wait until the lock is set free by presently accessing critical region.

- After accessing critical region or on completing critical region execution, process set lock to free for that critical region so that any other process which has been in queue to enter or to access that critical region.

- As process exit from the critical region, it notifies all other processes by sending message that critical region are free to access.

- So, all waiting processes enter that critical region according to smallest timestamp of the request.

- There is one data structure or queue which maintains request of other processes with the time stamp of the request when one process is using that critical region. Thus, after setting that critical region free, process sends message to all other waiting procedures that resource or critical region is free to enter.

- Fig. 4.6 (a) shows illustration of entering a critical region and Fig 4.6 (b) shows illustration of exiting a critical region.

- There may be a case of process failure in the critical region. In such case, presently residing process may dead in the critical region and hence setting lock free is still left. In this scenario, all other processes have to wait until the current process completes it task and sets lock free.

- This may lead to infinite time of wait if that process will not recovered or that critical region's lock is not set free. There may be a case of deadlock in such situation.

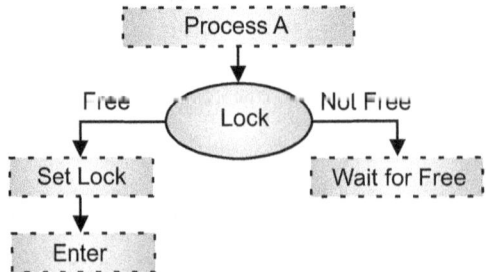

(a) Scenario of entering critical region by a process

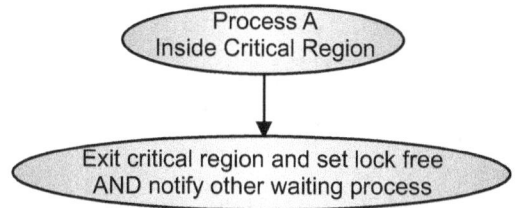

(b) Scenario of exiting critical region by a process

Fig. 4.6

4.5.1.1 Basic Requirements for a Mutual Exclusion Mechanism

- In distributed system to implement the mutual exclusion mechanism there are two basic requirement i.e. Safty and liveness.

- **Safety:** at most one process may execute in the critical section (CS) at a time;

- **Liveness:** a process requesting entry to the CS is eventually granted it (so long as any process executing the CS eventually leaves it).Liveness implies freedom of deadlock and starvation.

4.5.1.2 Classification of Distributed Mutual Exclusion

The distributed mutual exclusion is basically classified into two types

- Non-token-based
- Token-based:

In Non-token-based each process freely and equally competes for the right to use the shared resource; requests are arbitrated by a central control site or by distributed agreement. and in Token-based a logical token representing the access right to the shared resource is passed in a regulated fashion among the processes; whoever holds the token is allowed to enter the critical section.

1. Non-Token-Based Mutual Exclusion:

Non-Token-Based Mutual Exclusion is further classified into two types

(a) Central Coordinator Algorithm

(b) Ricart-Agrawala Algorithm

(a) Central Coordinator Algorithm:

- In this algorithm we discuss how mutual exclusion is done in a one-processor system. We use one concept of process called as the coordinator (e.g., the one running on the machine with the highest network address). Whenever a process wants to enter a critical region, it sends a request message to the coordinator stating which critical region it wants to enter and asking for permission. If no other process is currently in that critical region, the coordinator sends back a reply granting permission, as shown in Fig. 4.7 (a).

- When the reply arrives, the requesting process enters the critical region

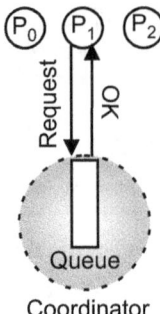

**Fig. 4.7: (a) Process 1 asks the coordinator for permission
to enter a critical region. Permission is granted**

- Now suppose that another process, 2 in Fig. 4.7 (b), asks for permission to enter the same critical region.

- The coordinator knows that a different process is already in the critical region, so it cannot grant permission.

- The exact method used to deny permission is system dependent. Process 2 then asks permission to enter the same critical region. The coordinator does not reply.

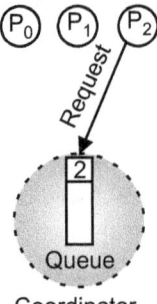

**Fig. 4.7 (b): Process 2 then asks permission
to enter the same critical region. The coordinator does not reply**

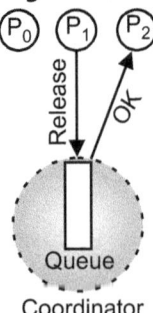

**Fig. 4.7 (c) When process 1 exits the critical region,
it tells the coordinator, which then replies to 2**

- As shown in Fig 4.7 (c) When process 1 exits the critical region, it sends a message to the coordinator releasing its exclusive access.

- The coordinator takes the first item off the queue of deferred requests and sends that process a grant message.
- If the process was still blocked (i.e., this is the first message to it), it unblocks and enters the critical region. If an explicit message has already been sent denying permission, the process will have to poll for incoming traffic or block later. Either way, when it sees the grant, it can enter the critical region.

It is easy to see that the algorithm guarantees mutual exclusion: the coordinator only lets one process at a time into each critical region. It is also fair, since requests are granted in the order in which they are received. No process ever waits forever (no starvation). The scheme is easy to implement, too, and requires only three messages per use of a critical region (request, grant, release). It can also be used for more general resource allocation rather than just managing critical regions.

The centralized approach also has some disadvantages.

- The coordinator is a single point of failure, so if it crashes, the entire system may go down.
- If processes normally block after making a request, they cannot distinguish a dead coordinator from "permission denied" since in both cases no message comes back in a large system, a single coordinator can become a performance bottleneck. The scheme is simple and easy to implement. The strategy requires only three messages per use of a CS (request, OK, release).

Problems with this:

- The coordinator can become a performance bottleneck. It is a critical point of failure, if the coordinator crashes, a new coordinator must be created. The coordinator can be one of the processes competing for access; an election algorithm has to be run in order to choose one and only one new coordinator.

(b) Ricart-Agrawala Algorithm:

Rule for Process Initialization:

/* Performed by each process P_i at initialization */

Rule 1: state P_i:= RELEASED.

Rule for Access Request to CS:

/* Performed whenever process Pi requests an access to the CS */

Rule 1: state P_i:= REQUESTED.

TP$_i$:= the value of the local logical clock corresponding to this request.

Rule 2: P_i sends a request message to all processes; the message is of the form (TP$_i$, i), where i is an identifier of P_i.

Rule 3: P_i waits until it has received replies from all other n – 1 processes.

Rule for Executing the CS:

/* Performed by P_i after it received the n – 1 replies */

Rule 1: state P_i:= HELD.

P_i enters the CS.

Rule for Handling Incoming Requests:

/* Performed by P_i whenever it received a request (TP_j, j) from P_j */

Rule 1: if state P_i = HELD or ((state P_i = REQUESTED)

and $((TP_i, i) < (TP_j, j)))$ then

Queue the request from Pj without replying.

else

Reply immediately to P_j.

end if.

Rule for Releasing a CS:

/* performed by P_i after it finished work in a CS */

Rule 1: state P_i:= RELEASED.

P_i replies to all queued requests.

- In a distributed environment it is more natural to implement mutual exclusion, based upon distributed agreement - not on a central coordinator. It is assumed that all processes keep a (Lamport's) logical clock which is updated according to the rules discussed above.

- The algorithm requires a total ordering of requests, requests are ordered according to their global logical timestamps; if timestamps are equal, process identifiers are compared to order them.

- The process that requires entry to CS multicasts the request message to all other processes competing for the same resource; it is allowed to enter the CS when all processes have replied to this message.

- The request message consists of the requesting process' timestamp (logical clock) and its identifier.

- Each process keeps its state with respect to the CS: released, requested, or held. A request issued by a process P_j is blocked by another process P_i only if P_i is holding the resource or if it is requesting the resource with a higher priority (this means a smaller timestamp) then P_j.

Problems with this Algorithm:

- The algorithm is expensive in terms of message traffic; it requires 2(n – 1) messages for entering a CS: (n – 1) requests and (n – 1) replies. The failure of any process involved makes progress impossible if no special recovery measures are taken.

2. Token-Based Mutual Exclusion:

Token-Based Mutual Exclusion is further classified into two types:

- (a) Ricart-Agrawala Second Algorithm
- (b) Token Ring Algorithm

(a) Ricart-Agrawala Second Algorithm:

- A process is allowed to enter in a critical section when it got the token. In order to get the token it sends a request to all other processes competing for the same resource.

- The request message consists of the requesting process' timestamp (logical clock) and its identifier. Initially the token is assigned arbitrarily to one of the processes.

When a process P_i leaves a critical section it passes the token to one of the processes which are waiting for it; this will be the first process P_j, where j is searched in order [i+1, i+2, ..., n, 1, 2, ..., i – 2, i – 1] for which there is a pending request. If no process is waiting, P_i retains the token (and is allowed to enter the CS if it needs); it will pass over the token as result of an incoming request.

How does P_i find out if there is a Pending Request?

Each process P_i records the timestamp corresponding to the last request it got from process P_j, in request P_i [j]. In the token itself, token[j] records the timestamp (logical clock) of P_j's last holding of the token. If request P_i [j] > token[j] then P_j has a pending request.

The Algorithm:

Rule for Process Initialization:

/* performed at initialization */

Rule1: *state P_i:=* NO-TOKEN for all processes P_i, except *one single process P_x* for which *state P_x:=* TOKEN-PRESENT.

Rule 2: *token[k]* initialized 0 for all elements *k* = 1 ..*n. request P[k]* initialized 0 for all processes P_i and all elements *k* = 1 .. *n.*

Rule for Access Request and Execution of the CS:

/* performed whenever process P_i requests an access to the CS and when it finally gets it; in particular P_i can already possess the token */

Rule1: **if** *state P_i =* NO-TOKEN **then**

P_i sends a request message to all processes;

the message is of the form (*TP_i, i*), where

TP_i= CP i is the value of the local logical clock,

and *i* is an identifier of P_i.

P_i waits until it receives the token.

end if.

state P_i = TOKEN-HELD.

P_i enters the CS.

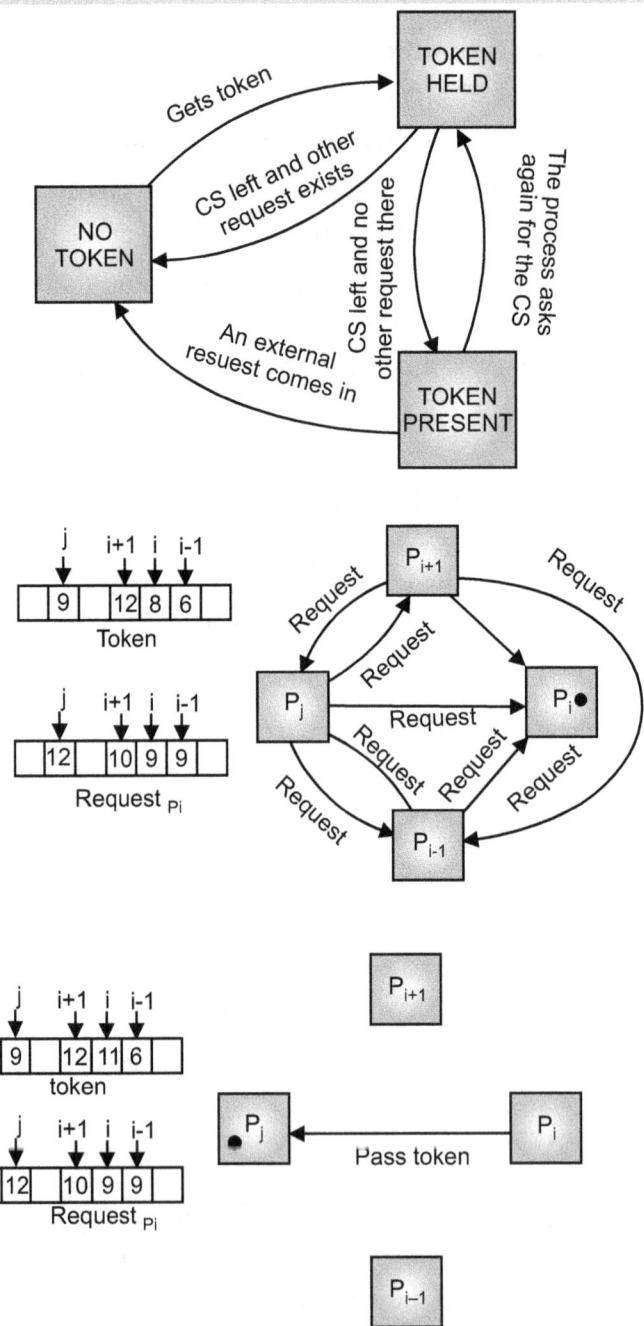

Fig 4.8: Ricart-agrawala second algorithm

Rule for Handling Incoming Requests:

/* performed by P_i whenever it received a request (TP_j, j) from P_j*/

    Rule 1: request[j]:= max(request[j], TP_j).

    Rule 2: **if** state P_i = TOKEN-PRESENT **then**

        P_i releases the resource (see rule RR2).

           end if.

Rule for Releasing a CS:

    /* performed by P_i after it finished work in a CS or when it holds a token without using it and it got a request */

    Rule 1 state P_i = TOKEN-PRESENT.

    Rule 2: **for** k = [i+1, i+2, ...,n, 1, 2, ..., i-2, i-1] **do**

        if request [k] > token[k] **then**

        state P_i:= NO-TOKEN.

        token[i]:= CP_i, the value of the local

           logical clock.

        P_i sends the token to P_k.

        break. /* leave the for loop */

           end if.

           end for.

Each process keeps its state with respect to the token: NO-TOKEN, TOKEN-PRESENT, TOKEN-HOLD.

The complexity is reduced compared to the (first) Ricart-Agrawala algorithm: it requires n messages for entering a CS: (n − 1) requests and one reply. The failure of a process, except the one which holds the token, doesn't prevent progress.

4.6 A TOKEN RING ALGORITHM

- The Token Ring Algorithm is basically used to achieving mutual exclusion in a distributed system is illustrated in Fig. 4.9. Here we have a bus network, as shown in Fig. 4.9 (a), with no inherent ordering of the processes e.g., Ethernet. IN software. In Fig. 4.9 (b) a logical ring is constructed in which each process is assigned a position in the ring.

- The ring positions may be allocated in numerical order of network addresses or some other means. It does not matter what the ordering is. All that matters is that each process knows who is next in line after itself.

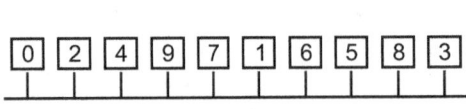

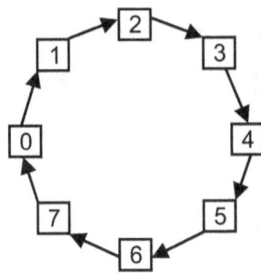

(a) An unordered group of processes on a network

(b) A logical ring constructed in software

Fig 4.9

- When the ring is initialized, process 0 is given a token. The token circulates around the ring. It is passed from process k to process k +1 (modulo the ring size) in point-to-point messages.

- When a process acquires the token from its neighbour, it checks to see if it is attempting to enter a critical region. If so, the process enters the region, does all the work it needs to, and leaves the region. After it has exited, it passes the token along the ring. It is not permitted to enter a second critical region using the same token.

- If a process is handed the token by its neighbour and is not interested in entering a critical region, it just passes it along. As a consequence, when no processes want to enter any critical regions, the token just circulates at high speed around the ring. The correctness of this algorithm is easy to see.

- Only one process has the token at any instant, so only one process can actually be in a critical region. Since the token circulates among the processes in a well-defined order, starvation cannot occur.

- Once a process decides it wants to enter a critical region, at worst it will have to wait for every other process to enter and leave one critical region.

- This algorithm has some problems, if the token is ever lost, it must be regenerated. In fact, detecting that it is lost is difficult, since the amount of time between successive appearances of the token on the network is unbounded.

- The fact that the token has not been spotted for an hour does not mean that it has been lost; somebody may still be using it.

- The algorithm also runs into trouble if a process crashes, but recovery is easier than in the other cases.

- If we require a process receiving the token to acknowledge receipt, a dead process will be detected when its neighbour tries to give it the token and fails.

- At that point the dead process can be removed from the group, and the token holder can throw the token over the head of the dead process to the next member down the line, or the one after that, if necessary. Of course, doing so requires that everyone maintains the current ring configuration.

4.7 A COMPARISON OF THE THREE ALGORITHMS

- In this section we compare the three algorithms centralized distributed and token ring. Table 4.1 below shows Comparison of algorithms with three key properties: the number of messages required for a process to enter and exit a critical region, the delay before entry can occur (assuming messages are passed sequentially over a network), and some problems associated with each algorithm.

Table 4.1: A Comparison of Three Mutual Exclusion Algorithms

Algorithm	Messages per Entry/Exit	Delay before Entry (in Message Times)	Problems
Centralized	3	2	Coordinator crash
Distributed	$2 (n - 1)$	$2 (n - 1)$	Crash of any process
Token ring	1 to ∞	0 to $n - 1$	Lost token, process crash

- The centralized algorithm is simplest and also most efficient. It requires only three messages to enter and leave a critical region: a request, a grant to enter, and a release to exit. The distributed algorithm requires $(n - 1)$ request messages, one to each of the other processes, and an additional $(n - 1)$ grant messages, for a total of $2(n - 1)$. (We assume that only point-to-point communication channels are used.)

- With the token ring algorithm, the number is variable. If every process constantly wants to enter a critical region, then each token pass will result in one entry and exit, for an average of one message per critical region entered.

- At the other extreme, the token may sometimes circulate for hours without anyone being interested in it. In this case, the number of messages per entry into a critical region is unbounded.

- The delay from the moment a process needs to enter a critical region until its actual entry also varies for the three algorithms.

- When critical regions are short and rarely used, the dominant factor in the delay is the actual mechanism for entering a critical region. When they are long and frequently used, the dominant factor is waiting for everyone else to take their turn.

- In Table 4.1 we show the former case. It takes only two message times to enter a critical region in the centralized case, but $2(n - 1)$ message times in the distributed case, assuming that messages are sent one after the other. For the token ring, the time varies from 0 (token just arrived) to $(n - 1)$ (token just departed).

- All three algorithms suffer badly in the event of crashes. Special measures and additional complexity must be introduced to avoid having a crash bring down the entire system. It is ironic that the distributed algorithms are even more sensitive to crashes than the centralized one. In a fault-tolerant system, none of these would be suitable, but if crashes are very infrequent, they might do.

4.8 ELECTION ALGORITHMS

- Many systems require one process to act as a coordinator It does not matter which process is the coordinator as long as all of them agree on this. We assume that each process has a unique number.

- In general, election algorithms attempt to select the process with the highest number. It is assumed that every process knows the process number of any other process, Processes do not know which process is currently running and which ones have crashed.

- The goal of the election algorithms is to ensure that at the end all processes agree on who the new coordinator is

4.8.1 The Bully Algorithm

When any process notices that the coordinator is down, it can initiate the election process

A process P holds an election as follows:

- P sends an election message to all process with higher numbers
- If no one responds, P wins and becomes the coordinator
- If one of the higher-ups answers, it takes over. P's job is done

When a process receives an election message it replies with a OK to indicate he is alive and will take over The receiver then starts an election unless it is already holding one. Eventually, all the processes give up except one, which is the new coordinator. The winning process announces the victory by sending a message to all the process telling them that it is the new coordinator. When a crashed process comes up, it holds an election.

Fig 4.10 shows the bully election algorithm, in this ,

- Process 4 holds an election.
- Process 5 and 6 respond, telling 4 to stop.
- Now 5 and 6 each hold an election.
- Process 6 tells 5 to stop.
- Process 6 wins and tells everyone.

Fig 4.10 (a): The bully algorithm

4.8.2 Ring Algorithm

- For understanding the ring algorithm we assume that the processes are physically or logically ordered each process knows who its successor is When a process notices not functioning coordinator, it sends an election message with its number to its successor; If successor down, send the message to the next one.

- At each step the sender adds its own number to the list in the message thus making itself a candidate.

- When the message gets back to the originating process, the message type is changed to coordinator and circulated once again in the ring everybody is informed who the new coordinator is. Fig. 4.11 shows the Election algorithm using a ring.

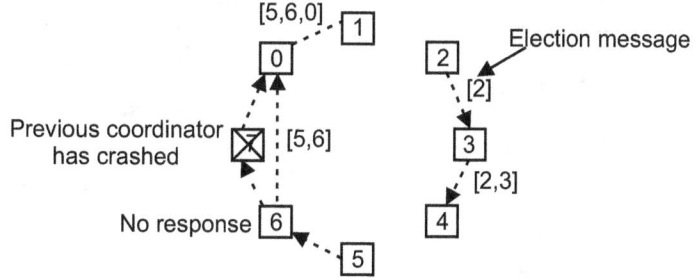

Fig. 4.11: Election algorithm using a ring

Elections in Wireless Environments:

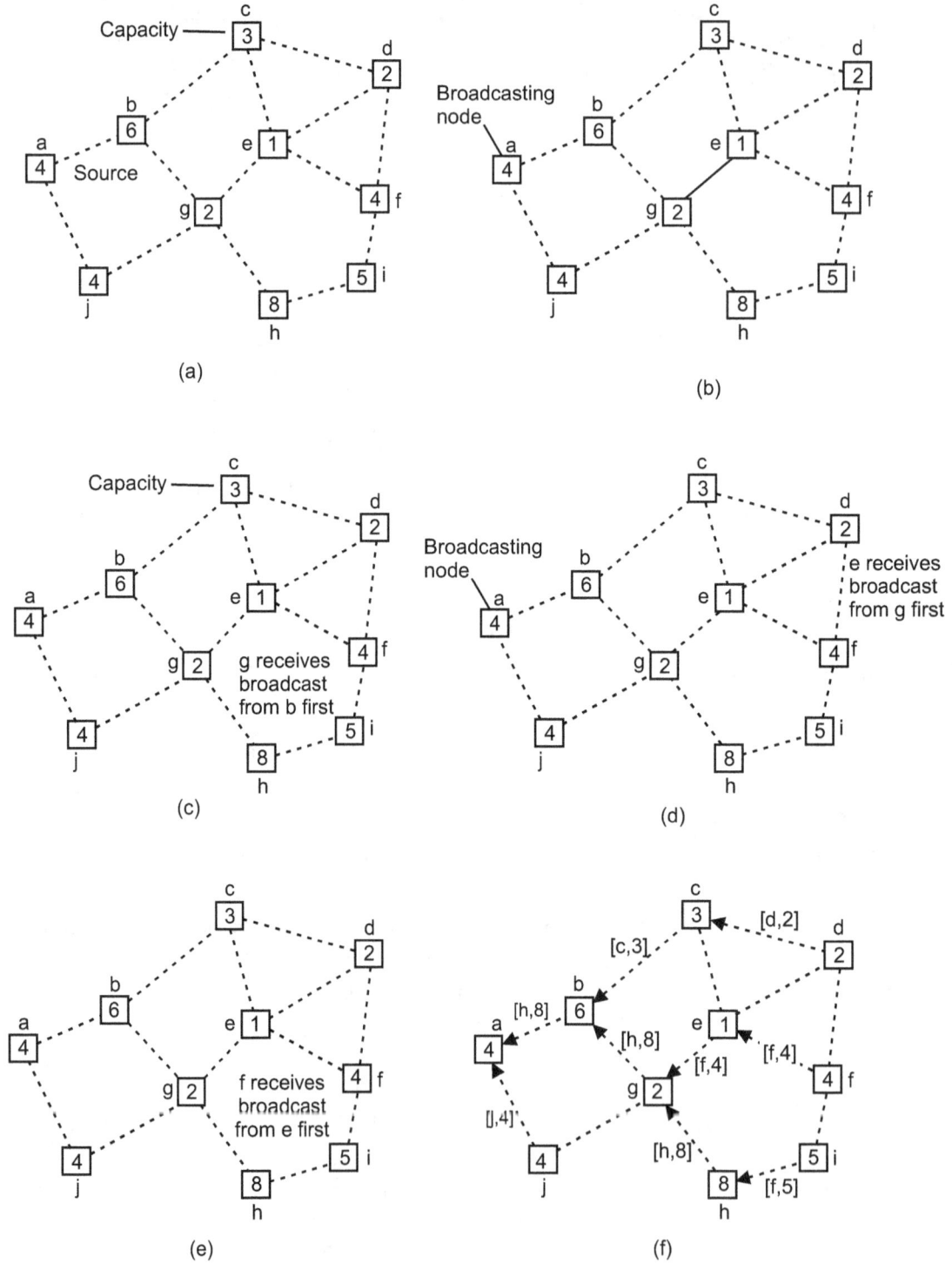

Fig 4.12: Election algorithm in a wireless network

- Traditional election algorithm based on assumptions such as reliable message passing and fixed topology, which are not always true for wireless environments Best leader elected (not an arbitrary node). Any node can initiate the process by sending an election message to all its neighbors.

When election msg received, sender marked as a parent and an election message is send to all the neighbors but the parent. Leaf nodes immediately respond with ACK, which also contains information about battery lifetime and resource capacity. When all ACKs received from children, data aggregated and best node picked and its info send back to the current parent, until the initiating node is reached. At the end the source node has information about the best node.

Fig. 4.12 below shows Election algorithm in a wireless network, with node a as the source. Fig. 4.12 (a) is a Initial network, Fig. 4.12 (b) to 4.12 (e) is the build-tree phase and Fig. 4.12 (f) shows Reporting of best node to source.

4.8.3 Elections in Large-Scale Systems

Requirements for Superpeer Selection:

- Normal nodes should have low-latency access to superpeers.
- Superpeers should be evenly distributed across the overlay network.
- There should be a predefined portion of superpeers relative to the total number of nodes in the overlay network.
- Each superpeer should not need to serve more than a fixed number of normal nodes.

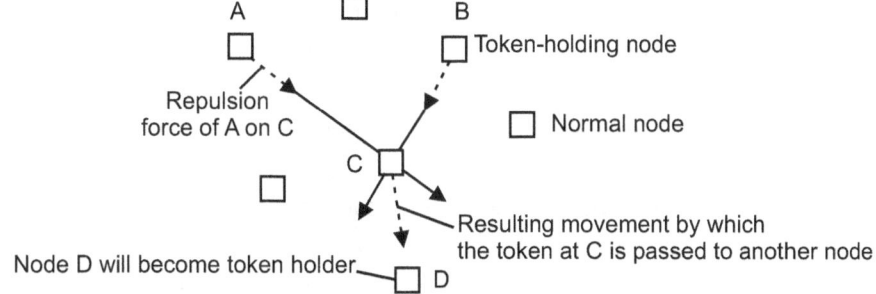

Fig. 4.13: Moving tokens in a two-dimensional space using repulsion forces

4.9 BASIC CONCEPT OF REPLICATION

4.9.1 Introduction

- **Replication** is the process of sharing information so as to ensure consistency between redundant resources, such as software or hardware components, to improve reliability, fault-tolerance, or accessibility.
- It could be *data replication* if the same data is stored on multiple storage devices or *computation replication* if the same computing task is executed many times.

- A computational task is typically *replicated in space*, i.e. executed on separate devices, or it could be *replicated in time*, if it is executed repeatedly on a single device.
- Replication has been studied in many areas, especially in distributed systems (mainly for fault tolerance purposes) and in databases (mainly for performance reasons).
- In these two fields, the techniques and mechanisms used are similar, and yet, comparing the protocols developed in the two communities is a frustrating exercise that many researchers have unsuccessfully attempted.
- Due to the many subtleties involved mechanisms that are conceptually identical, area and apply them in the other. End up being very different in practice. As a result, it is very difficult to take results from one.

4.9.2 Reason for Replication

- **Replication** is the process of copying and maintaining database objects, such as tables, in multiple databases that make up a distributed database system. Changes applied at one site are captured and stored locally before being forwarded and applied at each of the remote locations.
- Advanced Replication is a fully integrated feature of the Oracle server; it is not a separate server.
- Replication uses distributed database technology to share data between multiple sites, but a replicated database and a distributed database are not the same.
- In a distributed database, data is available at many locations, but a particular table resides at only one location.
- For example, the employees table resides at only the ny.world database in a distributed database system that also includes the hk.world and la.world databases. Replication means that the same data is available at multiple locations. For example, the employees table is available at ny.world, hk.world, and la.world.

Here Some of the Common Reasons for using Replication:

Availability:	<ul><li>Replication improves the availability of applications because it provides them with alternative data access options.</li><li>If one site becomes unavailable, then users can continue to query or even update the remaining locations.</li><li>In other words, replication provides excellent failover protection.</li></ul>
Performance:	<ul><li>Replication provides fast, local access to shared data because it balances activity over multiple sites.</li><li>Some users can access one server while other users access different servers, thereby reducing the load at all servers.</li><li>Also, users can access data from the replication site that has the lowest access cost, which is typically the site that is geographically closest to them.</li></ul>

... Contd

Disconnected Computing:	• A **materialized view** is a complete or partial copy (replica) of a target table from a single point in time.
	• Materialized views enable users to work on a subset of a database while disconnected from the central database server.
	• Later, when a connection is established, users can synchronize (refresh) materialized views on demand.
	• When users refresh materialized views, they update the central database with all of their changes, and they receive any changes that may have happened while they were disconnected.
Network Load Reduction:	• Replication can be used to distribute data over multiple regional locations.
	• Then, applications can access various regional servers instead of accessing one central server.
	• This configuration can reduce network load dramatically.
Mass Deployment:	• Increasingly, organizations need to deploy many applications that require the ability to use and manipulate data.
	• With Advanced Replication, deployment templates enable you to create multiple materialized view environments quickly.
	• You can use variables to customize each materialized view environment for its individual needs.
	• For example, you can use deployment templates for sales force automation. In this case, the template could contain variables for various sales regions and salespersons.

Applications of Replication

• Replication supports a variety of applications that often have different requirements. Some applications allow for relatively autonomous individual materialized view sites.

• For example, sales force automation, field service, retail, and other mass deployment applications typically require data to be periodically synchronized between central database systems and a large number of small, remote sites, which are often disconnected from the central database. Members of a sales force must be able to complete transactions, regardless of whether they are connected to the central database.

• In this case, remote sites must be autonomous.

• On the other hand, applications such as call centers and Internet systems require data on multiple servers to be synchronized in a continuous, nearly instantaneous manner to ensure that the service provided is available and equivalent at all times.

• For example, a retail Web site on the Internet must ensure that customers see the same information in the online catalog at each site.

• Here, data consistency is more important than site autonomy.

4.9.3 Functional Model

- Here we discuss the functional model basically A replication protocol can be described using five generic phases.

- These phases represent important steps in the protocol and will be used to characterise the different approaches.

- As we will later show, some replication techniques may skip some phases, order them in a different manner, iterate over some of them, or merge them into a simpler sequence.

- Thus, the protocols can be compared by the way they implement each one of the phases and how they combine the different phases. In this regard, an abstract replication protocol can be described as a sequence of the following five phases (see Fig. 4.14).

  - **Request (RE):** The client submits an operation to one (or more) replicas.

  - **Server Coordination (SC):** The replica servers coordinate with each other to synchronise the execution of the operation.

  - **Execution (EX):** The operation is executed on the replica servers.

  - **Agreement Coordination (AC):** The replica servers agree on the result of the execution.

  - **Response (END):** The outcome of the operation is transmitted back to the client.

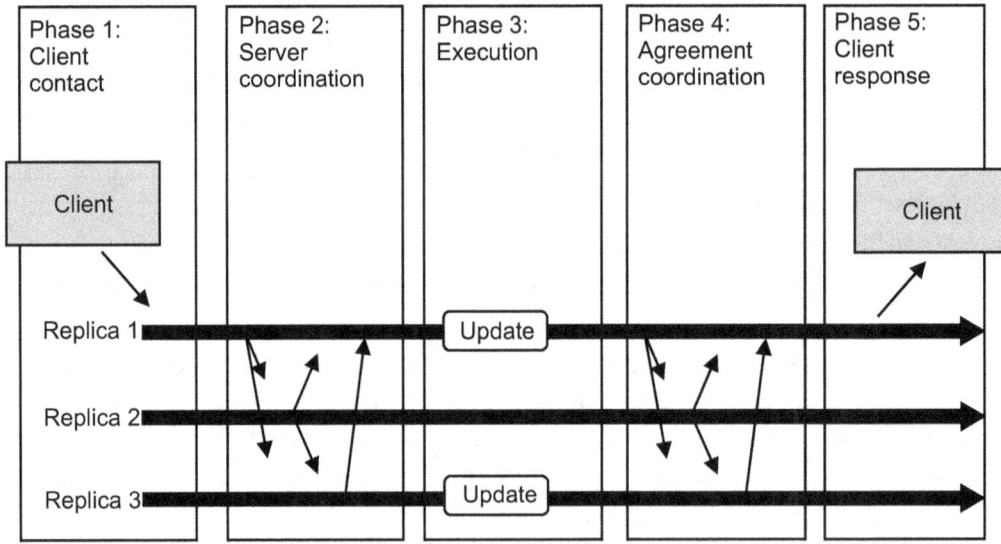

Fig. 4.14: Functional model with the five phases

- This functional model represents the basic steps of replication: submission of an operation, coordination among the replicas (e.g., to order concurrent operations), execution of the operation, further coordination among the replicas (e.g., to guarantee atomicity), and response to the client.

- The differences between protocols arise due to the different approaches used in each phase which, in some cases, obviate the need for some other phase (e.g., when messages are ordered based on an atomic broadcast primitive, the agreement coordination phase is not necessary since it is already performed as part of the process or ordering the messages).

- Within this framework, we will first consider transactions composed of a single operation. This can be a single read or write operation, a more complex operation with multiple parameters, or an invocation on a method.

1. Request Phase:

- During the request phase, a client submits an operation to the system. This can be done in two ways: the client can directly send the operation to all replicas or the client can send the operation to one replica which will them send the operation to all others as part of the server coordination phase.

- This distinction, although apparently simple, already introduces some significant differences between databases and distributed systems. In databases, clients never contact all replicas, and always send the operation to one copy.

- The reason is very simple: replication should be transparent to the client. Being able to send an operation to all replicas will imply the client has knowledge about the data location, schema, and distribution which is not practical for any database of average size. This is knowledge intrinsically tied to the database nodes, thus, client must always submit the operation to one node which will then send it to all others.

- In distributed systems, however, a clear distinction is made between replication techniques depending on whether the client sends the operation directly to all copies (e.g. active replication) or to one copy (e.g. passive replication).

- It could be argued that in both cases, the request mechanisms can be seen as contacting a *proxy* (a database node in one case, or a communication module in the other), in which case there are no significant differences between the two approaches.

- Conceptually this is true. Practically, it is not a very helpful abstraction because of its implications as it will be discussed below when the different protocols are compared.

- For the moment being, note that distributed systems deal with *processes* while database deal with *relational schemas*. A list of processes is simpler to handle that a database schema, i.e., a communication module can be expected to be able to handle a list of processes but it is not realistic to assume it can handle a database schema.

- In particular, database replication requires to understand the operation that is going to be performed while in distributed systems, operation semantics usually play no role.

- Finally, distributed systems distinguish between deterministic and non-deterministic replica behaviour. Deterministic replica behaviour assumes that when presented with the same operations in the same order, replicas will produce the same results.

- Such an assumption is very difficult to make in a database.

- Thus, if the different replicas have to communicate anyway in order to agree on a result, they can as well exchange the actual operation.
- By shifting the burden of broadcast the request to the server, the logic necessary at the client side is greatly simplified at the price of (theoretically) reducing fault tolerance.
- If fault tolerance is necessary, a back-up system can be used, but this is totally transparent to the client.

2. Server Coordination Phase:

- During the server coordination phase, the different replicas try to find an order in which the operations need to be performed.
- This is the point where protocols differ the most in terms of ordering strategies, ordering mechanisms, and correctness criteria.
- In terms of ordering strategies, databases order operations according to data dependencies. That is, all operations must have the same data dependencies at all replicas.
- It is because of this reason that operation semantics play an important role in database replication: an operation that only reads a data item is not the same as an operation that modifies that data item since the data dependencies introduced are not the same in the two cases.
- If there are no direct or indirect dependencies between two operations, they do not need to be ordered because the order does not matter. Distributed systems, on the other hand, are commonly based on very strict notions of ordering.
- From causality, this is based on potential dependencies without looking at the operation semantics, to total order (either causal or not) in which all operations are ordered regardless of what they are.
- In terms of correctness, database protocols use serializability adapted to replicated scenarios: one-copy serializability. It is possible to use other correctness criteria but, in all cases, the basis for correctness is data dependencies.
- Distributed systems use *linearisability* and *sequential consisten*. Linearisability is strictly stronger than sequential consistency.
- Linearisability is based on *real-time* dependencies, while sequential consistency only considers the order in which operations are performed on every individual process.
- Sequential consistency allows, under some conditions, to read *old values*. In this respect, sequential consistency has similarities with one-copy serializability, but strictly speaking, the two consistency criteria are different.
- The distributed system replication techniques presented in this paper all ensure Linearisability.

3. Execution Phase:

- The execution phase represents the actual performing of the operation. It does not introduce many differences between protocols, but it is a good indicator of how each approach treats and distributes the operations.

- This phase only represents the actual execution of the operation; the applying of the update is typically done in the agreement coordination phase, even though applying the update to other copies may be done by re-executing the operations.

4. Agreement Coordination Phase:

- During this phase, the different replicas make sure that they all do the same thing. This phase is interesting because it brings up some of the fundamental differences between protocols.

- In databases, this phase usually corresponds to a Two Phase Commit Protocol (2PC) during which it is decided whether the operation will be committed or aborted.

- This phase is necessary because in databases, the server coordination phase takes care only of ordering operations. Once the ordering has been agreed upon, the replicas need to ensure everybody agrees to actually committing the operation.

- Note that being able to order the operations does not necessarily mean the operation will succeed.

- In a database, there can be many reasons why an operation succeeds at one site and not at another (load, consistency constraints, and interactions with local operations).

- This is a fundamental difference with distributed systems where once an operation has been successfully ordered (in the Server Coordinator phase) it will be delivered (i.e., "performed") and there is no need to do any further checking.

5. Client Response Phase:

- The client response phase represents the moment in time when the client receives a response from the system.

- There are two possibilities: either the response is sent only after everything has been settled and the operation has been executed, or the response is sent right away and the propagation of changes and coordination among all replicas is done afterwards.

- In the case of databases, this distinction leads to 1) the so called eager or synchronous (no response until everything has been done) and 2) lazy or asynchronous (immediate response, propagation of changes is done afterwards) protocols.

- In the distributed systems case, the response takes place only after the protocol has been executed and no discrepancies may arise.

- The client response phase is of increasing importance given the proliferation of applications for *mobile* users, where a copy is not always connected to the rest of the system and it does not make sense to wait until updates take place to let the user see the changes made.

4.9.4 Distributed Systems Replication

- In this section, we describe the model and the communications abstractions used by replication protocols in distributed systems so we will start with replication model and abstraction.

Replication Model and Abstractions

- We consider a distributed system modelled as a set of services implemented by servers processes and invoked by clients processes. The specification of the service defines the set of invocations that can be issued by the clients.

- Each server process has a local state that is modified through invocations. We consider that invocations modify the state of a server in an atomic way, that is, the state changes resulting from an invocation are not applied partially.

- The isolation between concurrent invocations is the responsibility of the server, and is typically achieved using some local synchronisation mechanism.

- This model is similar to "one operation" transactions in databases (e.g., stored procedure). In order to tolerate faults, services are implemented by multiple server processes or replicas.

- To cope with the complexity of replication, the notion of *group* (of servers) and *group communication primitives* have been introduced.

- The notion of *group* acts as a logical addressing mechanism, allowing the client to ignore the degree of replication and the identity of the individual server processes of a replicated service. *Group communication primitives* provide one-to-many communication with various powerful semantics.

- These semantics hide much of the complexity of maintaining the consistency of replicated servers.

- The two main group communication primitives are *Atomic Broadcast* (or ABCAST) and *View Synchronous Broadcast* (or VSCAST).

- We give here an informal definition of these primitives. A more formal definition of ABCAST can be found in and of VSCAST can be found in.

- Group communication properties can also feature FIFO order guarantees, that is, if a process broadcasts a message m before a message **m'**, then no process delivers **m'** before m.

- **Atomic Broadcast (ABCAST):** Atomic Broadcast provides *atomicity* and *total order*. Let m and m' be two messages that are ABCAST to the same group g of servers.

- The atomicity property ensures that if one member of g delivers m (respt. m'), then all (not crashed) members of g eventually deliver m (respt. m').

- The order property ensures that if two members of g deliver both m and m', they deliver them in the same order.

View Synchronous Broadcast (VSCAST): The definition of View Synchronous Broadcast is more complex. It is defined in the context of a group g, and is based on the notion of *a sequence of views* v0(g), v1(g), . . . , vi(g), . . . of group g. Each view vi(g) defines the composition of the group at same time t, i.e. the members of the group that are perceived as being correct at time t. Whenever a process p in some view vi(g) is suspected to have crashed, or some process q wants to join, a new view vi+1(g) is installed, which reflects the membership change. Roughly speaking, VSCAST of message m by some member of the group g currently in view vi(g) ensures the following property: if one process p in vi(g) delivers m before installing view vi+1(g), than no process installs view vi+1(g) before having first delivered m.

4.9.5 Object Replication and Scaling Technique

4.9.5.1 Object Replication

- The technique of data replication in distributed systems is typically used to increase the availability and reliability of the data in the presence of processor failures and network partitions.

- For example, if multiple copies of the same logical data are stored on different processors, the data can still be accessed if some of the processors are down.

- In contrast, we use replication primarily for speeding up access to shared data and for decreasing the communication overhead involved in sharing data. The general idea is to replicate an object on those processors that frequently access it.

- A copy may be accessed by all processes running on the same processor, without sending any messages, as shown in Fig. 4.15.

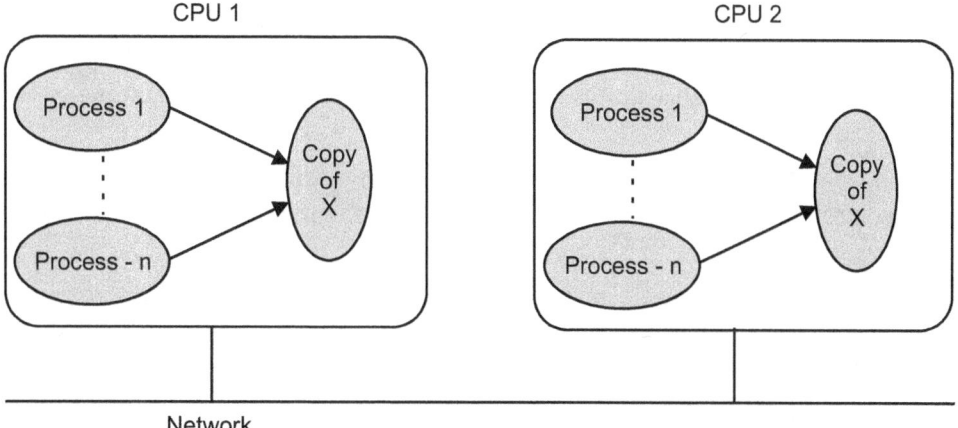

Fig. 4.15: Replication of data-objects in a distributed system.

- Each processor contains multiple processes running in pseudo-parallel. These processes belong to a single job and run in a single address space, so they can share copies of objects.

- It is useful to distinguish between *read* operations and *write* operations on replicated data: a read operation does not modify the data, while a write operation (potentially) does.
- For our model, we define a read operation as an operation that does not change the internal data of the object it is applied to.
- The primary goal of replicating shared data-objects is to apply read operations to a local copy of the object, if available, without doing any interprocess communication.
- On a write operation, all copies of the object except the one just modified must be invalidated or updated.
- To deal with this problem, communication will be needed, so write operations involve communication. This is a departure from most of the replication techniques cited above, which in general need interprocess communication for every read and write operation.
- The second goal of replication is to increase parallelism. If an object is stored on only one processor, each operation must be executed by that processor.
- This processor may easily become a sequential bottleneck.
- With replicated objects, on the other hand, all processors can simultaneously read their own copies. Since a read operation does not change its object, it can be executed concurrently with other read operations without violating the serializability principle.
- The effectiveness of replication depends on many factors. One important factor is the ratio of read and write operations on objects, which is determined by the user application. Another factor is the overhead in execution time for reading or writing objects. These costs are determined by the implementation of the model they depend on:
    - The action undertaken after each writes. If each write operation *invalidates* all copies, a subsequent read operation will need to do communication. If, on the other hand, all copies are *updated*, this disadvantage disappears, but write operations will become more expensive
    - The protocol used for invalidating or updating copies. Many protocols exist (e.g., owner protocols, two-phase update protocols), each with their own advantages and disadvantages.
    - The replication strategy. If an object is replicated everywhere, each read operation can be applied to a local copy, which is much cheaper than doing the operation remotely. On the other hand, writing an object that has many copies will be more expensive than writing a non-replicated object.

4.9.5.2 Object Replication Techniques

- Redundancy is a common practice form asking the failures of individual components of a system. With redundant copies, a replicated object can continue to provide a service in spite of the failure of some of its copies, without affecting its clients.

- In distributed systems, the two best known replication techniques are *active* and *passive* replication. Each of these techniques has its own advantages, and they are thus complementary.
- A brief description of both techniques is given below.

1. Active Replication:

- Active replication also called the state machine approach is a general protocol for replication management that has no centralized control.
- All copies of the replicated object play the same role: they all receive each request, process it, update their state, and send a response back to the client [Fig. 4.16 (a)]. Since the invocations are always sent to every replica, the failure of one of them is transparent to the client.

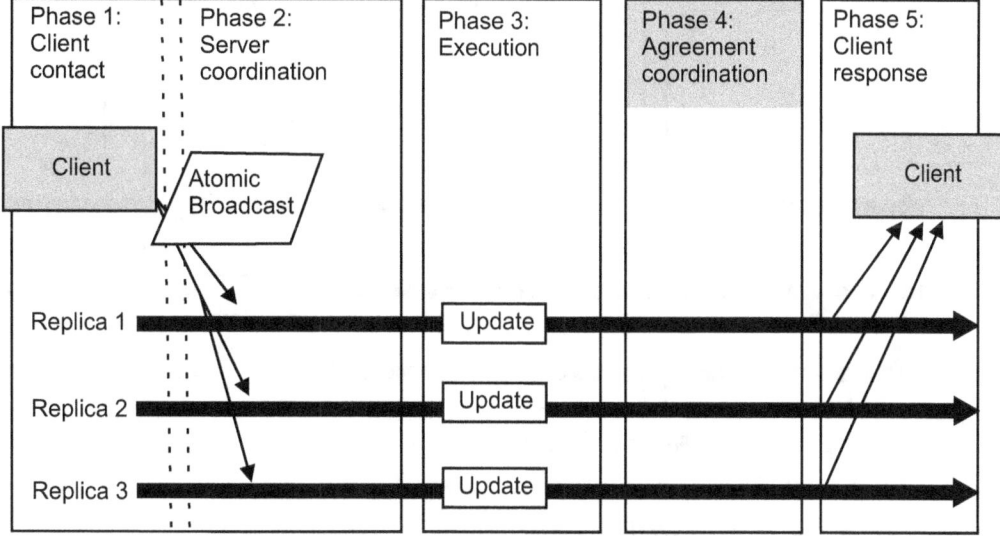

Fig. 4.16 (a): Active replication

- From the point of view of a client, all correct replicas should appear as having the same state. In order to guarantee this, all invocations sent by the clients should be treated in the same order by all correct replicas.
- This is ensured by a *total order multicast* primitive also called *atomic multicast* that provides total ordering of messages sent to a set of destinations.

The following Steps are Involved in the Processing of an Update Request in the Active Replication

- The client sends the request to the servers using an Atomic Broadcast.
- Server coordination is given by the total order property of the Atomic Broadcast.
- All replicas execute the request in the order they are delivered.
- No coordination is necessary, as all replica process the same request in the same order. Because replicas are deterministic, they all produce the same results.

- All replica send back their result to the client, and the client typically only waits for the first answer (the others are ignored)

2. Passive Replication:

- With passive replication also called primary backup replication one server is designated as the primary, while all other are backups. The clients send their requests to the primary only.

- The primary executes the request, atomically updates the other copies, and sends the response to the client [Fig. 4.16 (b)]. If the primary fails, then one of the backups takes over.

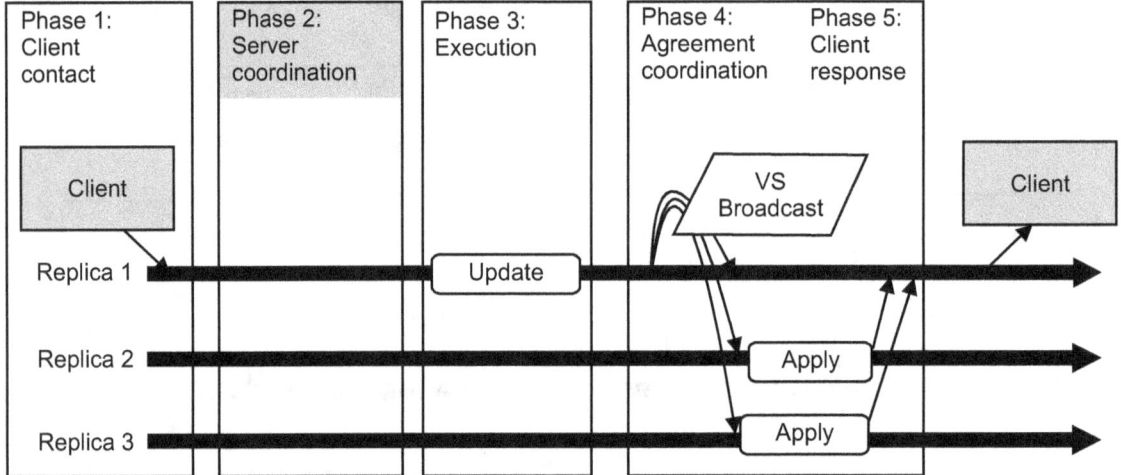

Fig. 4.16 (b): Passive replication

The Five Steps of our Framework are the Following:

- The client sends the request to the primary.
- There is no initial coordination.
- The primary executes the request.
- The primary coordinates with the other replicas by sending the update information to the backups.
- The primary sends the answer to the client.

4.9.5.3 Which Replication Technique is Better?

- Active replication requires the operations on the replicated object to be *deterministic*. Determinism means that the outcome of an operation depends only on the initial state of the object, and on the sequence of operations performed by the object (history).

- If the operations on the replicated object are deterministic, the shared state of the replicated object remains consistent and all responses sent back to the client are identical.

- Thus, the client can simply wait for the first reply from any replica. An interesting property of active replication lies in the fact that a crash does not increase the latency experienced by a client.
- Unlike active replication, passive replication does not waste extra resources through redundant processing, and permits *non-deterministic* operations.
- However, a crash of the primary may significantly increase the latency of an invocation.
- Furthermore, passive replication requires additional application support for the primary to update the state of the other copies.
- There is a tradeoff between both replication techniques. Active replication provides a more predictable and generally faster response time than passive replication, and requires less application support.
- On the other hand, passive replication is more flexible since it does not require the servers to be deterministic. Since active and passive replication are complementary, *supporting both techniques* is a major benefit that permits the application developer to choose the technique best adapted to his problem.

4.9.5.4 System Support for Replicated Objects

- This section presents the basic components that provide the system support for object replication. These components define replication protocols, as well as facilities for managing the structure, addressing, and invocation of replicated objects. They are used as a generic infrastructure for marrying active and passive replication in a unified framework.
- As depicted in Fig. 4.17, the OGS replication infrastructure essentially consists of three basic components:
  - The consensus service is the building block that provides the common algorithmic infrastructure for both replication techniques.

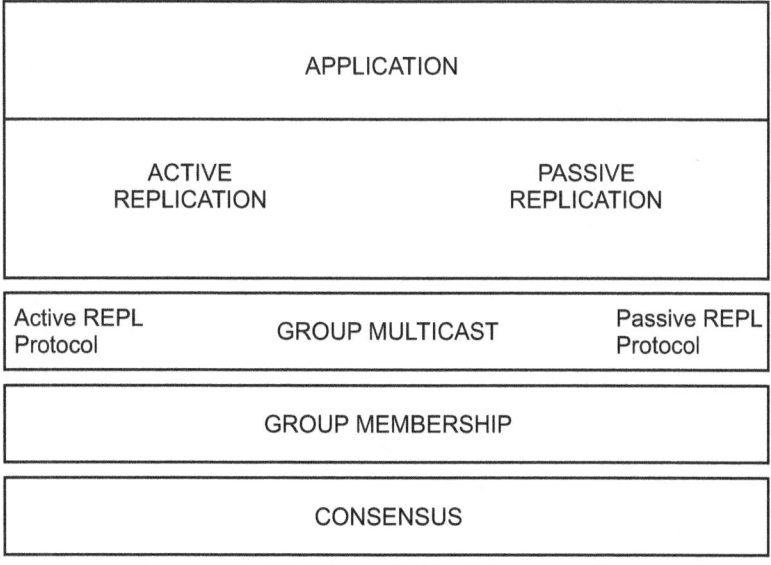

Fig. 4.17: Components architectural overview

- The group membership service manages the changes in the composition of groups.
- The group multicast service provides the communication protocols required for active and passive replication. These protocols allow the client to issue requests to a group of actively or passively replicated objects.
- These components are packaged as Distributed services, entirely defined in terms of IDL interfaces and usable between heterogeneous objects. They are not exclusive to object replication, and may be used in very different contexts.
- The OGS replication infrastructure is original in that active and passive replication invocation protocols are based on a common consensus algorithm, and are thus unified *at the protocol level.*
- The choice of the replication technique can be performed by the application developer on a per operation basis.1. In other words, this choice can be driven by the operation semantics, depending for instance on whether the operation is deterministic or not.

4.9.5.5 Managing Replicated Objects

- The key idea of *group communication* is to gather a set of processes or objects into a logical group, and to provide primitives for sending messages to all group members at the same time with various ordering guarantees.
- A group constitutes a logical addressing facility since messages can be issued to groups without having to know the number, identity, or location of individual members (Fig. 4.18). Groups have proven to be very useful for providing *high availability* through *replication*: a set of replicas constitutes a group, viewed by clients as a single entity in the system.

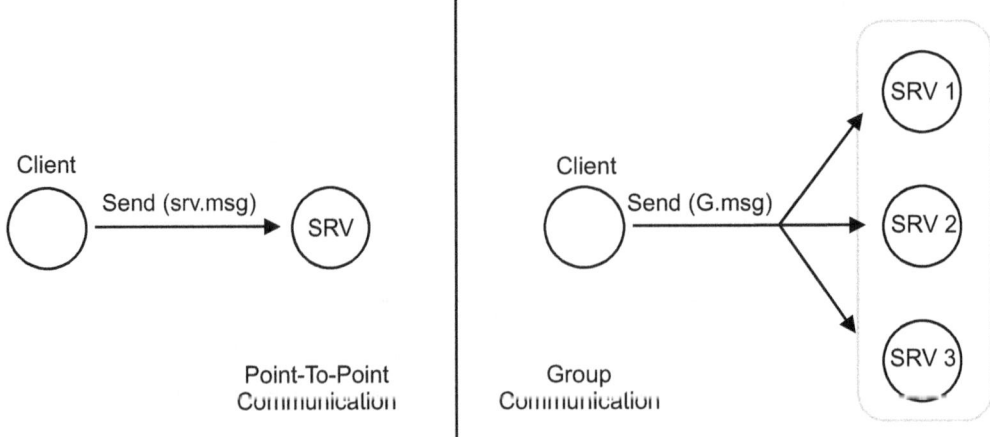

Fig. 4.18: Point-to-Point vs. group communication

- In order to provide group communication in a distributed environment, we have specified and implemented a generic group service, which defines interfaces for gathering sets of distributed objects into logical groups.

- The group service implements essentially two functionalities: *group membership* and *group multicast*.

- Group membership manages the life cycle of object groups. It maintains the updated list of all correct group members and provides support for joining and leaving groups, and for view change notification.

- The *view change protocol* occurs each time the composition of a group changes, and ensures that every correct member of the group receives a *view change notification*, indicating the new composition of the group as a list of group members with mutually consistent rankings.

- Group multicast provides primitives for sending invocations to groups instead of singleton objects. OGS provides a rich set of group multicast primitives, adapted to various types of applications.

- OGS implements groups as open structures, allowing non-member objects to issue multicast invocations to groups. Multicast primitives can be classified according to their degree of *reliability* and their *ordering* guarantees.

- A reliable multicast guarantees that all correct group members deliver the same set of messages *(agreement)*, that this set includes all messages multicast to the group by correct objects *(validity)*, and that no spurious messages are ever delivered *(integrity)*.

- Reliable multicast, in itself, does not ensure that group consistency is preserved; it is generally combined with an ordering guarantee. As a matter of fact, the state of an object generally depends on the order in which it receives requests.

- OGS provides several types of multicast primitives with various reliability and ordering guarantees. In particular, two protocols are essential for active and passive replication.

- The *active replication protocol* is based on a totally ordered multicast, which guarantees that reliable multicasts are delivered in the same order to all target objects. In addition, it ensures that the client receives a reply.

- The *passive replication protocol* guarantees that one copy (the primary) receives and handles the original invocation, that all other copies (the backups) receive an update message from the primary, and that the client receives a reply.

- In OGS, a protocol may be associated with any operation of a server's interface, without the knowledge of the client.

- This scheme provides more flexibility that in comparable systems since it allows the developer to choose a protocol that matches the operation's semantics.

- OGS provides group transparency to clients through its typed invocation interface. Clients can issue invocations to an object group as if they were invoking a single object. The client directly invokes operations of the server's interface using static stubs, and OGS delivers multicasts by directly invoking the relevant operation of the server, using static skeletons. OGS transparently filters messages and returns a single reply to the client.

- This scheme is very useful when using groups for replication, since it permits to hide *replication* and not only the *replication technique* from the client.
- The application can invoke a single object or an object group without even a recompilation of the client's code.
- In addition, the application developer does not need to perform the marshaling and unmarshaling of the request (these operations are performed transparently by OGS), and can benefit from the type safety of CORBA's static invocation interface.

4.10 SCALING TECHNIQUES

4.10.1 Introduction

- In recent years scale has become an increasingly important factor in the design of distributed systems. Large computer networks such as the Internet have broadened the pool of resources from which distributed systems can be constructed.
- Building a system to fully use such resources requires an understanding of the problems of scale.
- A system is said to be scalable if it can handle the addition of users and resources without suffering a noticeable loss of performance or increase in administrative complexity.
- Scale has three components: the number of users and objects that are part of the system, the distance between the farthest nodes in the system, and the number of organizations that exert administrative control over pieces of the system.
- If a system is expected to grow, its ability to scale must be considered when the system is designed.
- Naming, authentication, authorization, accounting, communication, and the use of remote resources are all affected by scale.
- Scale also affects the user's ability to easily interact with the system. Grapevine was one of the earliest distributed computer systems consciously designed to scale. More recent projects such as the Internet Domain Naming System (IDNS), Kerberos, Sprite, and DEC's Global Naming and Authentication Services have concentrated on particular subsystems. Other projects have at- tempted to provide complete scalable systems.

4.10.2 Scalability Techniques

Many developers of modern distributed system easily use the adjective "scalable" without making clear how and why their system actually scales. For this we have consider following three components:

- Number of users and/or processes (size scalability),
- Maximum distance between nodes (geographical scalability),
- Number of administrative domains (administrative scalability).

Most systems account only, to a certain extent, for size scalability. The (non)solution: powerful servers today, the challenge lies in geographical and administrative scalability.

Techniques for Scaling:

1. **Hide Communication Latencies: Avoid Waiting for Responses; do Something else:**
   - Make use of asynchronous communication.
   - Have separate handler for incoming response.
   - Problem: not every application fits this model.

2. **Distribution: Partition Data and Computations Across Multiple Nodes:**
   - Move computations to clients (Java applets).
   - Decentralized naming services (DNS).
   - Decentralized information systems (WWW).

3. **Replication/Caching: Make Copies of Data Available at Different Nodes:**
   - Replicated file servers and databases.
   - Mirrored Web sites.
   - Web caches (in browsers and proxies).
   - File caching (at server and client).

Scaling Examples

1. **Hiding Latency:** To avoid waiting for responses to remote service requests (e.g. do other useful work at the requester's side).

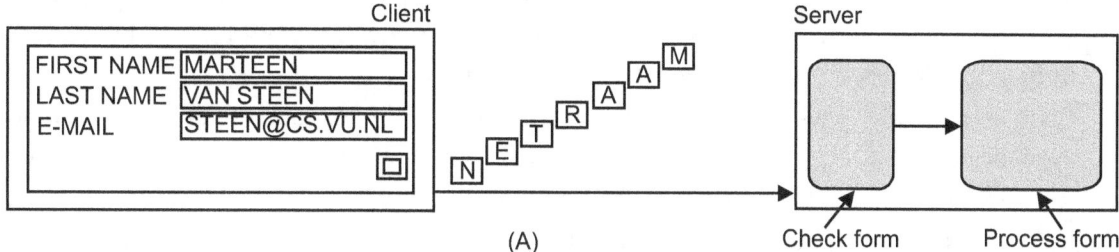

(A)

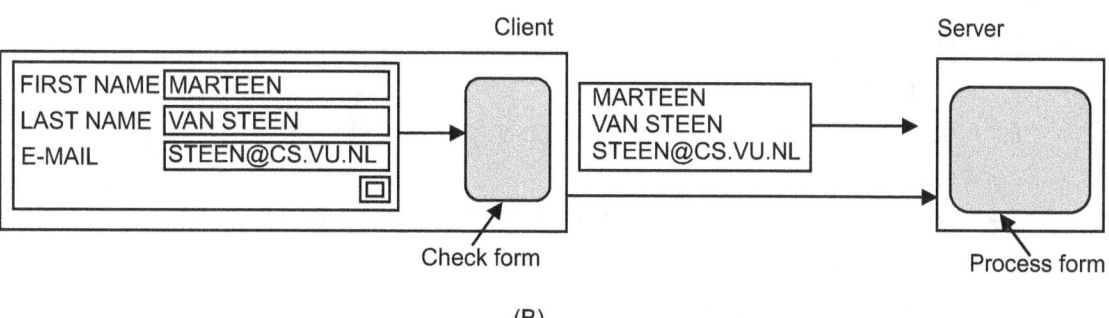

(B)

Fig. 4.19: (a) The difference between letting (a) a server or (b) a client check forms as they are being filled.

2. **Distribution:** Another important scaling technique is distribution, e.g. Domain Name System (DNS): The DNS name space is hierarchically organized into a tree of domains, which are divided into non-overlapping zones.

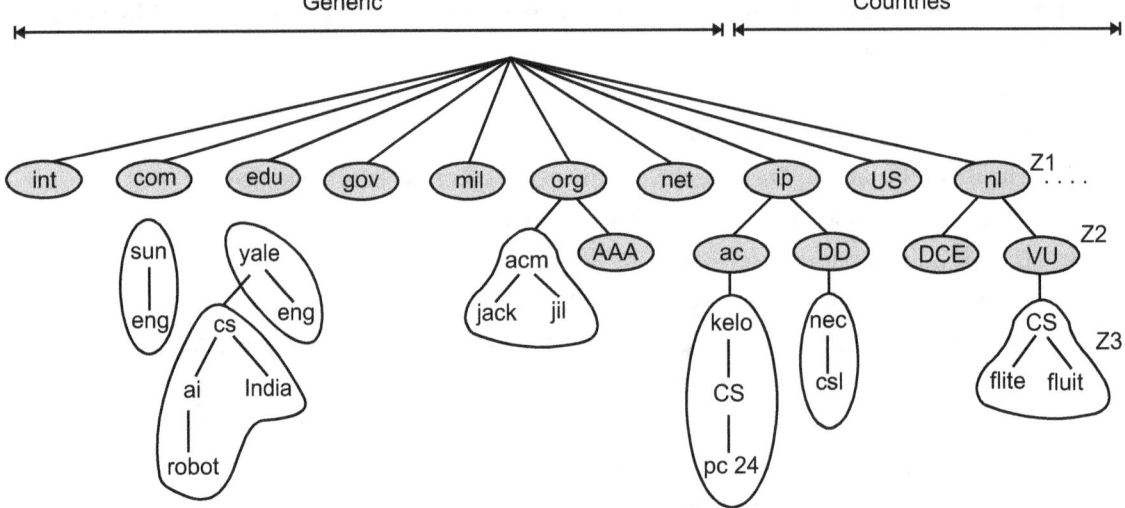

Fig. 4.20: An example of dividing the DNS name space into zones.

4.11 CODA FILE SYSTEM

- In this section we discuss the coda file system basically Coda has been developed at Carnegie Mellon University (CMU) in the 1990s, and is now integrated with a number of popular UNIX-based operating systems such as Linux.

- Coda is in many ways different from NFS, notably with respect to its goal for high availability. This goal has led to advanced caching schemes that allow a client to continue operation despite being disconnected from a server.

4.11.1 Features of Coda File System

Coda has many features that are desirable for network file systems some of the features are as follows:

- Disconnected operation for mobile computing.
- Is freely available under a liberal license.
- High performance through client side persistent caching.
- Server replication.
- Security model for authentication, encryption and access control.
- Continued operation during partial network failures in server network.
- Network bandwidth adaptation.
- Good scalability.
- Well defined semantics of sharing, even in the presence of network failures.

- Coda uses a local cache to provide access to server data when the network connection is lost. During normal operation, a user reads and writes to the file system normally, while the client fetches, or "hoards", all of the data the user has listed as important in the event of network disconnection.

- If the network connection is lost, the Coda client's local cache serves data from this cache and logs all updates.

- This operating state is called disconnected operation. Upon network reconnection, the client moves to reintegration state; it sends logged updates to the servers.

- Then it transitions back to normal connected-mode operation.

- Also different from AFS is Coda's data replication method. AFS uses a pessimistic replication strategy with its files, only allowing one read/write server to receive updates and all other servers acting as read-only replicas.

- Coda allows all servers to receive updates, allowing for a greater availability of server data in the event of network partitions, a case which AFS cannot handle.

- These unique features introduce the possibility of semantically diverging copies of the same files or directories, known as "conflicts".

- Disconnected operation's local updates can potentially clash with other connected users' updates on the same objects, preventing reintegration. Optimistic replication can potentially cause concurrent updates to different servers on the same object, preventing replication.

- The former case is called a "local/global" conflict, and the latter case a "server/server" conflict. Coda has extensive repair tools, both manual and automated, to handle and repair both types of conflicts.

4.11.2 Overview of Coda

- Basically Coda was designed to be a scalable, secure, and highly available distributed file system.

- An important goal of coda is to achieve a high degree of naming and location transparency so that the system would appear to its users very similar to a pure local file system. By also taking high availability into account, the designers of Coda have also tried to reach a high degree of failure transparency.

- Coda is a descendant of version 2 of the Andrew File System (AFS), which was also developed at, and inherits many of its architectural features from AFS. AFS was designed to support the entire CMU community, which implied that approximately 10,000 workstations would need to have access to the system.

- To meet this requirement, AFS nodes are partitioned into two groups. One group consists of a relatively small number of dedicated vice file servers, which are centrally administered.

- The other group consists of a very much larger collection of Virtue workstations that give users and processes access to the file system, as shown in Fig. 4.21.

- Coda follows the same organization as AFS. Every Virtue workstation hosts a user-level process called Venus, whose role is similar to that of an NFS client. A

- Venus process is responsible for providing access to the files that are maintained by the Vice file servers. In Coda, Venus is also responsible for allowing the client to continue operation even if access to the file servers is (temporarily) impossible.

- This additional role is a major difference with the approach followed in NFS. The internal architecture of a Virtue workstation is shown in Fig. 4.21 (a).

- The important issue is that Venus runs as a user-level process. Again, there is a separate Virtual File System (VFS) layer that intercepts all calls from client applications, and forwards these calls either to the local file system or to Venus, as shown in Fig. 4.21 (a).

- This organization with VFS is the same as in NFS. Venus, in turn, communicates with Vice file servers using a user-level RPC system.

- The RPC system is constructed on top of UDP datagrams and provides at-most-once semantics. There are three different server-side processes.

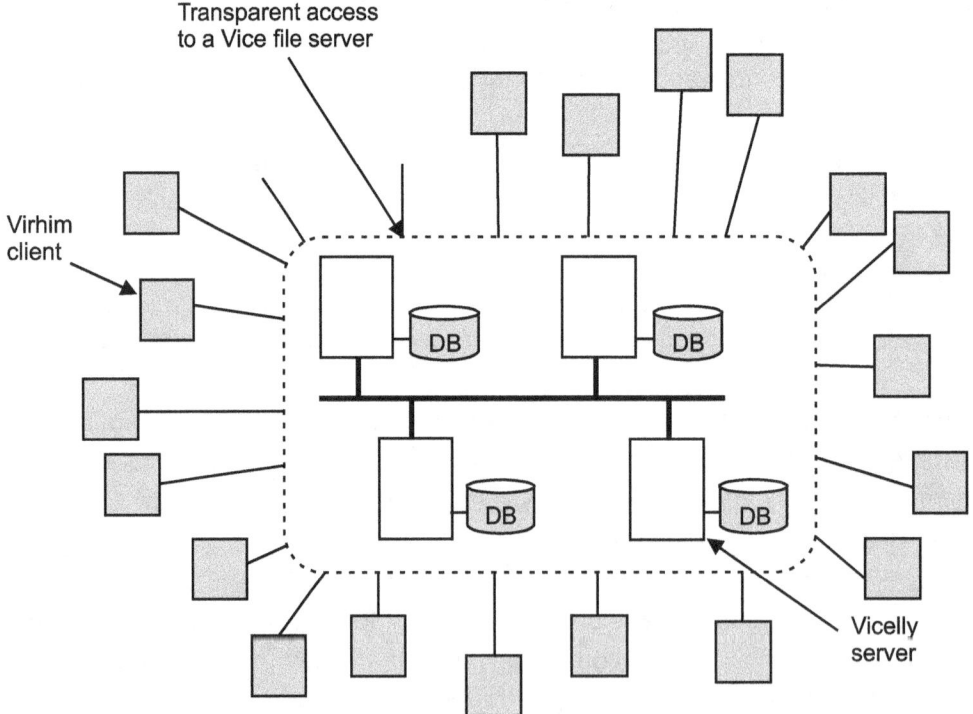

Fig. 4.21: The overall organization of AFS

- The great majority of the work is done by the actual Vice file servers, which are responsible for maintaining a local collection of files.

- Like Venus, a file server runs as a user-level process. In addition, trusted Vice machines are allowed to run an authentication server, which we discuss in detail later.

- Finally, update processes are used to keep meta information on the file system consistent at each Vice server.

4.11.3 Communication in Coda File System

- Inter process communication in Coda is performed using RPCs. However, the RPC2 system for Coda is much more sophisticated than traditional RPC systems such as ONC RPC, which is used by NFS. RPC2 offers reliable RPCs on top of the (unreliable) UDP protocol.

- Each time a remote procedure is called, the RPC2 client code starts a new thread that sends an invocation request to the server and subsequently blocks until it receives an answer.

Virtual client machanism

Fig. 4.22 (a): The internal organization of a Virtue workstation

- As request processing may take an arbitrary time to complete, the server regularly sends back messages to the client to let it know it is still working on the request.

- If the server dies, sooner or later this thread will notice that the messages have ceased and report back failure to the calling application.

- An interesting aspect of RPC2 is its support for side effects.

- A side effect is a mechanism by which the client and server can communicate using an application-specific protocol. Consider, for example, a client opening a file at a video server.

- What is needed in this case is that the client and server set up a continuous data stream with an isochronous transmission mode.

- In other words, data transfer from the server to the client is guaranteed to be within a minimum and maximum end-to-end delay.

- RPC2 allows the client and the server to set up a separate connection for transferring the video data to the client on time. Connection setup is done as a side effect of an RPC call to the server. For this purpose, the RPC2 runtime system provides an interface of side-effect routines that is to be implemented by the application developer.

- For example, there are routines for setting up a connection and routines for transferring data.

- These routines are automatically called by the RPC2 runtime system at the client and server, respectively, but their implementation is otherwise completely independent of RPC2.

- This principle of side effects is shown in Fig. 4.22 (b). Another feature of RPC2 that makes it different from other RPC systems is its support for multicasting. As we explain in detail below, an important design issue in Coda is that servers keep track of which clients have a local copy of a file.

- When a file is modified, a server invalidates local copies by notifying the appropriate clients through an RPC. Clearly, if a server can notify only one client at a time, invalidating all clients may take some time, as illustrated in Fig. 4.22 (c).

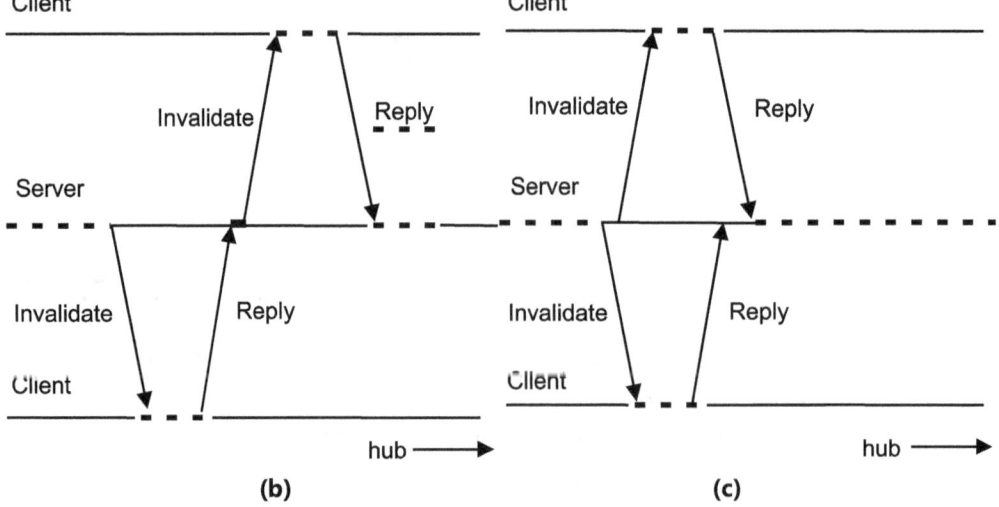

Fig. 4.22: (b) Sending an invalidation message one at a time,
(c) Sending invalidation messages in parallel

- The problem is caused by the fact that an RPC may fail. Invalidating files in a strict sequential order may be delayed considerably because the server cannot reach a possibly crashed client, but will give up on that client only after a relatively long expiration time. Meanwhile, other clients will still be reading from their local copies.

- A better solution is shown in Fig. 4.22. Instead of invalidating each copy one-by-one, the server sends an invalidation message to all clients in parallel.

- As a consequence, all non-failing clients are notified in the same time as it would take to do an immediate RPC. Also, the server notices within the usual expiration time that certain clients are failing to respond to the RPC, and can declare such clients as being crashed.

4.11.4 Processes

- Coda maintains a clear distinction between client and server processes. Clients are represented by Venus processes; servers appear as Vice processes. Both types of processes are internally organized as a collection of concurrent threads. Threads in Coda are non-preemptive and operate entirely in user space.

- To account for continuous operation in the face of blocking I/O requests, a separate thread is used to handle all I/O operations, which it implements using low-level asynchronous I/O operations of the underlying operating system. This thread effectively emulates synchronous I/O without blocking an entire process.

4.11.5 Naming

- Coda maintains a naming system similarly to that of UNIX. Files are grouped into units referred to as volumes. A volume is similar to a UNIX disk partition (i.e., an actual file system), but generally has a much smaller granularity.

- It corresponds to a partial sub-tree in the shared name space as maintained by the Vice servers.

- Usually a volume corresponds to a collection of files associated with a user. Examples of volumes include collections of shared binary or source files, and so on. Like disk partitions, volumes can be mounted.

- Volumes are important for two reasons. First, they form the basic unit by which the entire name space is constructed.

- This construction takes place by mounting volumes at mount points. A mount point in Coda is a leaf node of a volume that refers to the root node of another volume.

- Considering the granularity of volumes, it can be expected that a name lookup will cross several mount points. In other words, a path name will often contain several mount points. To support a high degree of naming transparency, a Vice file server returns mounting information to a Venus process during name lookup.

- This information will allow Venus to automatically mount a volume into the client's name space when necessary.

- This mechanism is similar to crossing mount points as supported in NFS version 4. It is important to note that when a volume from the shared name space is mounted in the client's name space, Venus follows the structure of the shared name space.

- To explain, assume that each client has access to the shared name space by means of a subdirectory called */afs*.

- When mounting a volume, each Venus process ensures that the naming graph rooted at */afs* is always a sub-graph of the complete name space jointly maintained by the Vice servers, as shown in Fig. 4.23. In doing so, clients are guaranteed that shared files indeed have the same name, although name resolution is based on a locally-implemented name space. Note that this approach is fundamentally different from that of NFS.

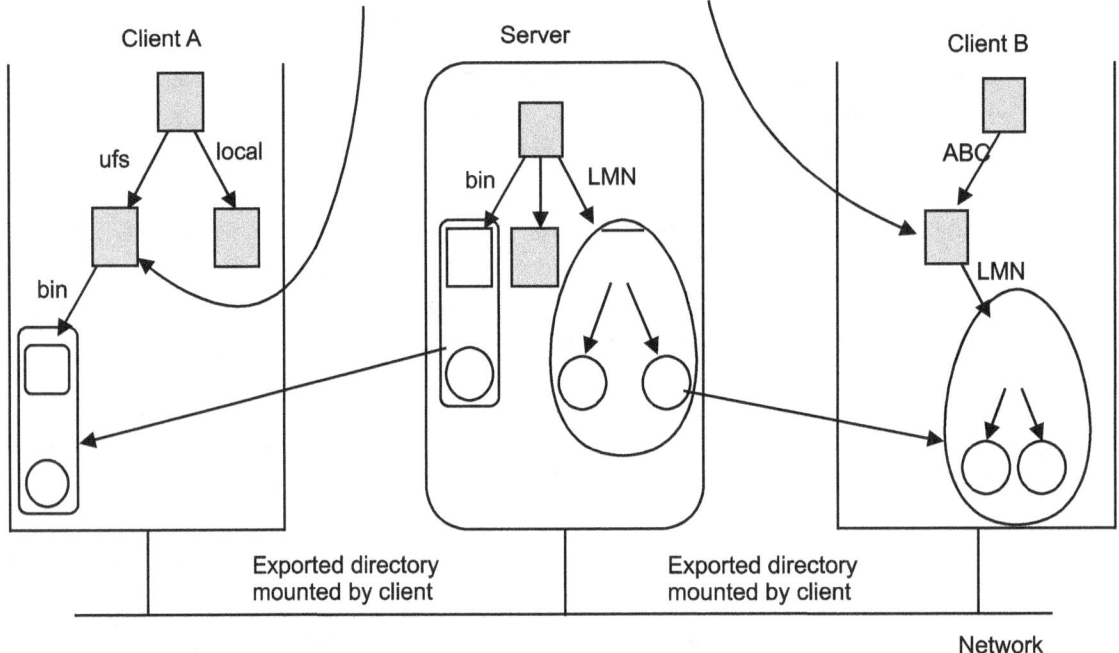

Fig. 4.23: Clients in Coda have access to a single shared name space

4.11.6 File Identifiers

- Here we discuss the file identifier used in the coda file system Considering that the collection of shared files may be replicated and distributed across multiple Vice servers, it becomes important to uniquely identify each file in such a way that it can be tracked to its physical location, while at the same time maintaining replication and location transparency Each file in Coda is contained in exactly one volume.

- As we mentioned above, a volume may be replicated across several servers. For this reason, Coda makes a distinction between logical and physical volumes.

- A logical volume represents a possibly replicated physical volume, and has an associated Replicated Volume Identifier(RVID). An RVID is a location and replication independent volume identifier.

- Multiple replicas may be associated with the same RVID.

- Each physical volume has its own Volume Identifier(VID), which identifies a specific replica in a location independent way.

- The approach followed in Coda is to assign each file a 96-bit file identifier. A file identifier consists of two parts as shown in Fig. 4.24.

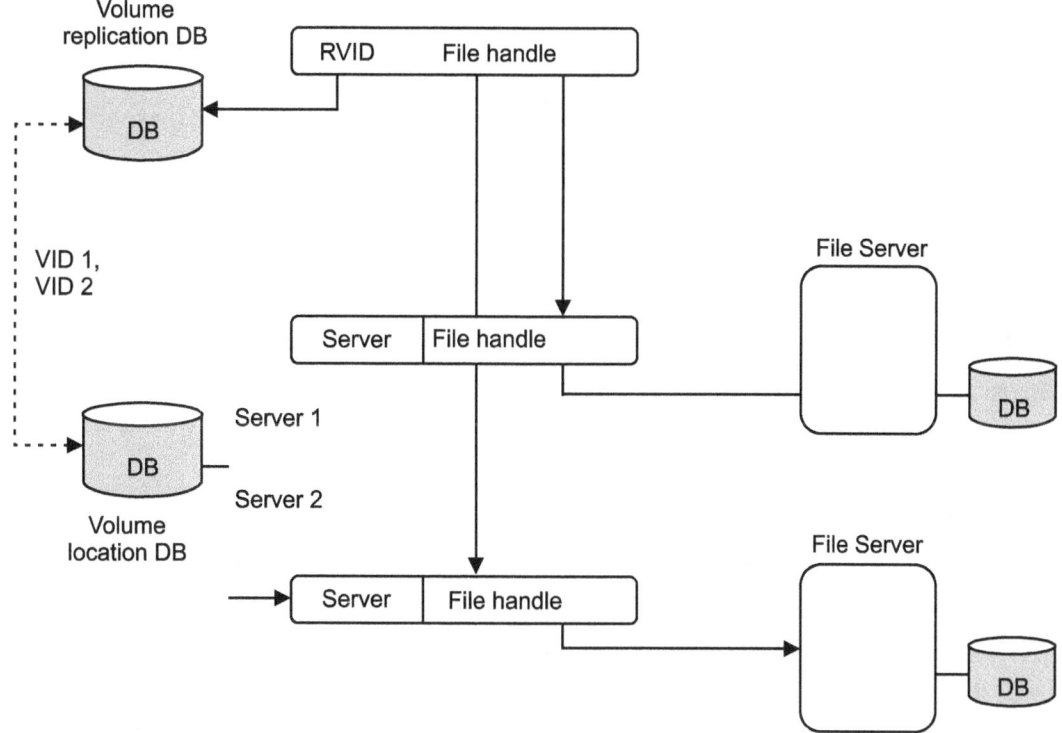

Fig. 4.24: The implementation and resolution of a Coda file identifier

- The first part is the 32-bit RVID of the logical volume that the file is part of. To locate a file, a client first passes the RVID of a file identifier to a volume replication database, which returns the list of VIDs associated with that RVID. Given a VID, a client can then look up the server that is currently hosting the particular replica of the logical volume.

- This lookup is done by passing the VID to a volume location database which returns the current location of that specific physical volume.

- The second part of a file identifier consists of a 64-bit file handle that uniquely identifies the file within a volume. In reality, it corresponds to the identification of an index node as represented within VFS. Such a v node as it is called is similar to the notion of an i node in UNIX systems.

4.11.7 Synchronization in Coda File System

- Many distributed file systems, including Coda's ancestor, AFS, do not provide UNIX file-sharing semantics but instead support the weaker session semantics. Given its goal to achieve high availability, Coda takes a different approach and makes an attempt to support transactional semantics, albeit a weaker form than normally supported by transactions.

- The problem that Coda wants to solve is that in a large distributed file system it may easily happen that some or all of the file servers are temporarily unavailable. Such unavailability can be caused by a network or server failure, but may also be the result of a mobile client deliberately disconnecting from the file service.

- Provided that the disconnected client has all the relevant files cached locally, it should be possible to use these files while disconnected and reconcile later when the connection is established again.

4.11.8 Caching and Replication

- Caching and replication play an important role in Coda. In fact, these two approaches are fundamental for achieving the goal of high availability as set out by the developers of Coda.

- In the following, we first take a look at client-side caching, which is crucial in the face of disconnected operation. We then take a look at server-side replication of volumes.

4.11.8.1 Client Caching

- Client-side caching is crucial to the operation of Coda for two reasons. First, and in line with the approach followed in AFS, caching is done to achieve scalability.

- Second, caching provides a higher degree of fault tolerance as the client becomes less dependent on the availability of the server.

- For these two reasons, clients in Coda always cache entire files. In other words, when a file is opened for either reading or writing, an entire copy of the file is transferred to the client, where it is subsequently cached.

- Unlike many other distributed file systems, cache coherence in Coda is maintained by means of callbacks. For each file, the server from which a client had fetched the file keeps track of which clients have a copy of that file cached locally. A server is said to record a **callback promise** for a client.

- When a client updates its local copy of the file for the first time, it notifies the server, which, in turn, sends an invalidation message to the other clients.

- Such an invalidation message is called a **callback break**, because the server will then discard the callback promise it held for the client it just sent invalidation.

- The interesting aspect of this scheme is that as long as a client knows it has an outstanding callback promise at the server, it can safely access the file locally. In particular, suppose a client opens a file and finds it is still in its cache.
- It can then use that file provided the server still has a callback promise on the file for that client.
- The client will have to check with the server if that promise still holds. If so, there is no need to transfer the file from the server to the client again. This approach is illustrated. When client A starts session SA, the server records a callback promise. The same happens when B starts session SB.
- However, when B closes SB, the server breaks its promise to callback client A by sending A a callback break. Note that due to the transactional semantics of Coda, when client A closes session SA, nothing special happens; the closing is simply accepted as one would expect.
- The consequence is that when A later wants to open session S'A, it will find its local copy of f to be invalid, so that it will have to fetch the latest version from the server.
- On the other hand, when B opens session S'B, it will notice that the server still has an outstanding call back promise implying that B can simply re-use the local copy it still has from session SB.

4.11.8.2 Server Replication

- Coda allows file servers to be replicated; the unit of replication is a volume. The collection of servers that have a copy of a volume, are known as that volume's volume storage group, or simply VSG. In the presence of failures, a client may not have access to all servers in a volume's VSG.
- A client's Accessible Volume Storage Group (AVSG) for a volume consists of those servers in that volume's VSG that the client can contact. If the AVSG is empty, the client is said to be disconnected.

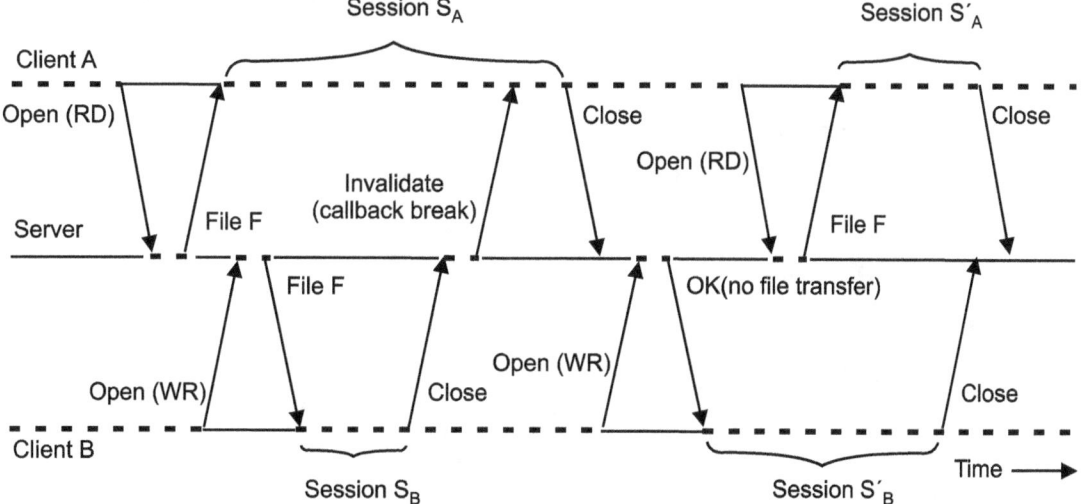

Fig. 4.25 (a): The use of local copies when opening a session in Coda

- Coda uses a replicated-write protocol to maintain consistency of a replicated volume.
- In particular, it uses a variant of Read-One, Write-All (ROWA When a client needs to read a file, it contacts one of the members in its AVSG of the volume to which that file belongs.
- However, when closing a session on an updated file, the client transfers it in parallel to each member in the AVSG. This parallel transfer is accomplished by means of multi RPC.
- This scheme works fine as long as there are no failures, that is, for each client, that client's AVSG of a volume is the same as its VSG.
- However, in the presence of failures, things may go wrong. Consider a volume that is replicated across three servers S_1, S_2, and S_3. For client A, assume its AVSG covers servers S_1 and S_2 whereas client B has access only to server S_3, as shown in Fig. 4.25 (b).

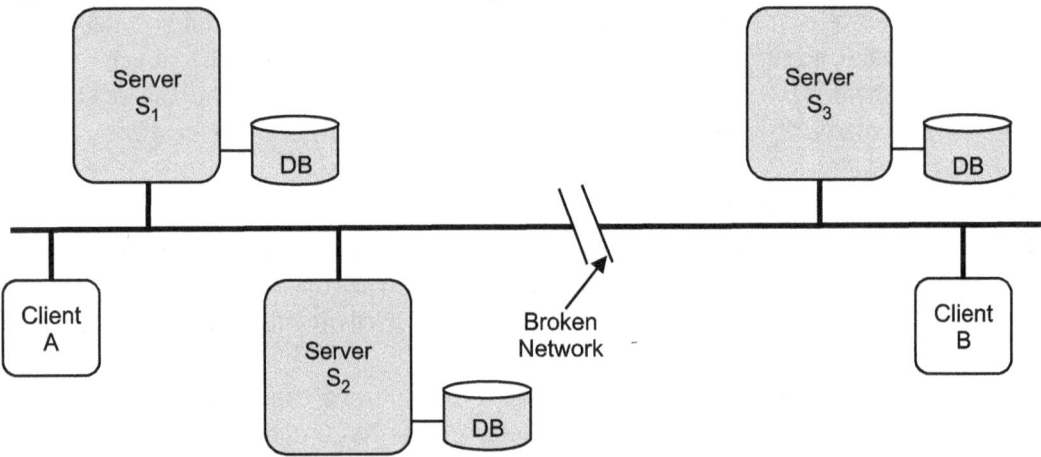

Fig. 4.25 (b): Two clients with a different AVSG for the same replicated file.

- Coda uses an optimistic strategy for file replication. In particular, both A and B will be allowed to open a file, f, for writing, update their respective copies, and transfer their copy back to the members in their AVSG.
- Obviously, there will be different versions of f stored in the VSG. The question is how this inconsistency can be detected and resolved.

4.11.9 Fault Tolerance

- In this section we discuss the process of fault tolerance in coda file system basically Coda has been designed for high availability, which is mainly reflected by its sophisticated support for client-side caching and its support for server replication.
- We have discussed both in the preceding sections.
- An interesting aspect of Coda that needs further explanation is how a client can continue to operate while being disconnected, even if disconnection lasts for hours or days.

4.11.9.1 Disconnected Operation

- As we mentioned above, a client is said to be disconnected with respect to a volume, if its AVSG for that volume is empty. In other words, the client cannot contact any of the servers holding a copy of the volume. In most file systems (e.g., NFS), a client is not allowed to proceed unless it can contact at least one server.

- A different approach is followed in Coda. There, a client will simply resort to using its local copy of the file that it had when it opened the file at a server.

- Closing a file (or actually, the session in which the file is accessed) when disconnected will always succeed. However, it may be possible that conflicts are detected when modifications are transferred to a server when connection is established again.

- In case automatic conflict resolution fails, manual intervention will be necessary.

- Practical experience with Coda has shown that disconnected operation generally works, although there are occasions in which reintegration fails due to unresolvable conflicts.

- The success of the approach followed in Coda is mainly attributed to the fact that, in practice, *write-sharing* a file hardly occurs.

- In other words, in practice it is rare for two processes to open the same file for writing of course, sharing files for only reading happens a lot, but that does not impose any conflicts.

- These observations have also been made for other file systems Furthermore, the transactional semantics underlying Coda's file-sharing model also makes it easy to handle the case in which there are multiple processes only reading a shared file at the same time that exactly one process is concurrently modifying that file.

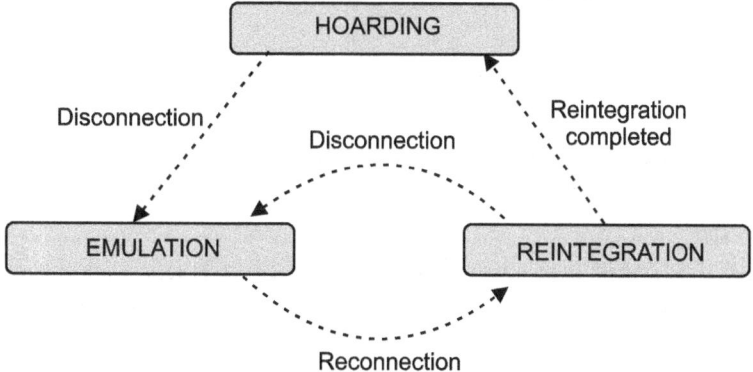

Fig. 4.26: The state-transition diagram of a coda client with respect to a volume

- The main problem that needs to be solved to make disconnected operation a success, is to ensure that a client's cache contains those files that will be accessed during disconnection. If a simple caching strategy is followed, it may turn out that a client cannot continue as it lacks the necessary files.

- Filling the cache in advance with the appropriate files is called hoarding. The overall behaviour of a client with respect to a volume (and thus the files in that volume) can now be summarized by the state-transition diagram shown in Fig. 4.26.

- Normally, a client will be in the *HOARDING* state. In this state, the client is connected to (at least) one server that contains a copy of the volume. While in this state, the client can contact the server and issue file requests to perform its work.

- Simultaneously, it will also attempt to keep its cache filled with useful data (e.g., files, file attributes, and directories). At a certain point, the number of servers in the client's AVSG will drop to zero, bringing it into an *emulation* state in which the behaviour of a server for the volume will have to be emulated on the client's machine.

- In practice, this means that all file requests will be directly serviced using the locally cached copy of the file.

- Note that while a client is in its *emulation* state, it may still be able to contact servers that manage other volumes. In such cases, disconnection will generally have been caused by a server failure rather than that the client has been disconnected from the network.

- Finally, when reconnection occurs, the client enters the *reintegration* state in which it transfers updates to the server in order to make them permanent. It is during reintegration that conflicts are detected and, where possible, automatically resolved.

4.11.10 Security

- Coda inherits its security architecture from AFS, which consists of two parts. The first part deals with setting up a secure channel between a client and a server using secure RPC and system-level authentication.

- The second part deals with controlling access to files. We will not examine each of these in turn.

4.11.10.1 Secure Channels

- Coda uses a secret-key cryptosystem for setting up a secure channel between a client and a server.

- The protocol followed in Coda is derived from the Needham-Schroeder authentication protocol. A user is first required to obtain special tokens from an Authentication Server (AS), as we explain shortly.

- These tokens are somewhat comparable to handing out a ticket in the Needham-Schroeder protocol in the sense that they are used to subsequently set up a secure channel to a server.

- All communication between a client and server is based on Coda's secure RPC mechanism, which is shown in Fig. 4.27 (a).

- If Alice (as client) wants to talk to Bob (as server), she sends her identity to Bob, along with a challenge RA, which is encrypted with the secret key KA, B shared between Alice and Bob. This is shown as message 1.

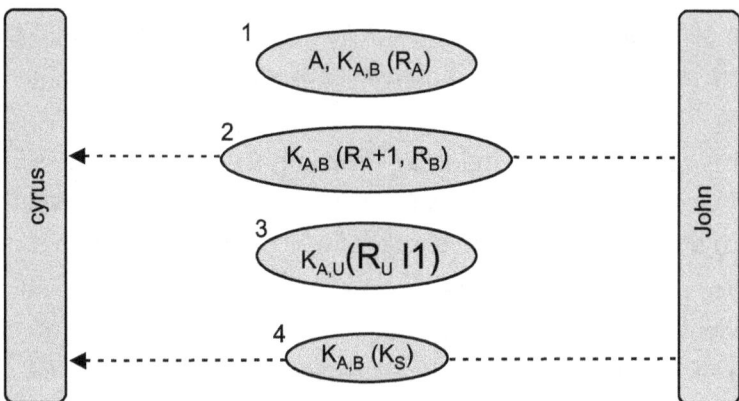

Fig. 4.27 (a): Mutual authentication in RPC2

- Bob responds by decrypting message 1 and returning $R_A + 1$, proving that he knows the secret key and thus that he is Bob. He returns a challenge R_B (as part of message 2), which Alice will have to decrypt and return as well (shown as message 3).

- When mutual authentication has taken place, Bob generates a session key KS that can be used in further communication between Alice and Bob.

- Secure RPC in Coda is used only to set up a secure connection between a client and a server; it is not enough for a secure login session that may involve several servers and which may last considerably longer.

- Therefore, a second protocol is used that is layered on top of secure RPC, in which a client obtains authentication tokens from the AS briefly mentioned above.

- An **authentication token** is somewhat like a ticket in Kerberos. It contains an identifier of the process that obtained it, a token identifier, a session key, timestamps telling when the token becomes valid and when it expires. A token may be cryptographically sealed for integrity.

- For example, if T is a token, K_{vice} a secret key shared by all Vice servers, and H a hash function, then $[T,H(K_{vice}, T)]$ is a cryptographically sealed version of T.

- In other words, despite the fact that T is sent as plaintext over an insecure channel, it is impossible for an intruder to modify it such that a Vice server would not notice the modification.

- When Alice logs into Coda, she will first need to get authentication tokens from the AS. In this case, she does a secure RPC using her password to generate the secret key $K_{A, AS}$ she shares with the AS, and which is used for mutual authentication as explained before. The AS returns two authentication tokens.

- A **cleartoken** $CT = [A, T_{ID}, K_S, T_{start}, T_{end}]$ identifying Alice and containing a token identifier T_{ID}, a session key K_S, and two timestamps T_{start} and T_{end} indicating when the token is valid.

- In addition, it sends a **secret token** $ST = K_{vice}$ ([CT] K_{vice}), which is CT cryptographically sealed with the secret key K_{vice} that is shared between all Vice servers, and encrypted with that same key.

- A Vice server is capable of decrypting ST revealing CT and thus the session key K_S. Also, because only Vice servers know K_{vice}, such a server can easily check whether CT has been tampered with by doing an integrity check (of which the computation requires K_{vice}).

- Whenever Alice wants to set up a secure channel with a Vice server, she uses the secret token ST to identify herself as shown in Fig. 4.27 (b). The session key K_S that was handed to her by the AS in the clear token is used to encrypt the challenge RA she sends to the server.

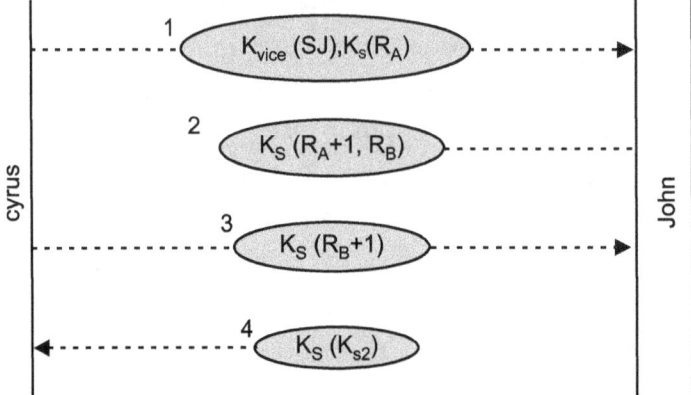

Fig. 4.27 (b): Setting up a secure channel between a (Venus) client and a Vice server in Coda

- The server, in turn, will first decrypt ST using the shared secret key K_{vice}, giving CT. It will then find K_S, which it subsequently uses to complete the authentication protocol.

- Of course, the server will also do an integrity check on CT and proceed only if the token is currently valid.

4.11.10.2 Access Control

- Let us briefly consider protection in Coda. As in AFS, Coda uses access control lists to ensure that only authorized processes have access to files.

- For reasons of simplicity and scalability, a Vice file server associates an access control list only with directories and not with files. All normal files in the same directory (i.e., excluding subdirectories) share the same protection rights.

- Coda distinguishes access rights with respect to the types of operations shown in Fig. 4.28.

- Note that there is no right with respect to executing a file. There is simple reason for this omission: execution of files takes place at clients and is thus out of the scope of a Vice file server.

- Once a client has downloaded a file there is no way for Vice to even tell whether the client is executing it or just reading it.
- Coda maintains information on users and groups. Besides listing the rights a user or group has, Coda also supports the listing of negative rights. In other words, it is possible to explicitly state that a specific user is *not* permitted certain access rights.
- This approach has shown to be convenient in the light of immediately revoking access rights of a misbehaving user, without having to first remove that user from all groups.

Classification of file and directory operations recognized by Coda with respect to access control

Operation	Description
Read	Read any file in the directory
Write	Modify any file in the directory
Lookup	Look up the status of any file
Insert	Add a new file to the directory
Delete	Delete an existing file
Administer	Modify the ACL of the directory

REVIEW QUESTIONS

1. Short notes on
   (1) Clock synchronization
   (2) Mutual exclusion
   (3) Bully algorithm
   (4) Token ring algorithm
2. Why do we need a global clock?
3. Define :
   (1) Drift rate
   (2) Physical clock
   (3) Global stale
   (4) Clock skew
4. Explain centralized and distributed algorithm used to achieve mutual exclusion.
5. State and explain fault tolerance issues in DS.
6. How security is implemented in CODA file system.
7. How does CODA file system used for replication?
8. Explain Ricart and Agrawala's algorithm for ME.

UNIVERSITY QUESTIONS

May 2012

1. Discuss following with an examples :   **[8]**
   (i) Logical Clock
   (ii) Physical Clock and
   (iii) Clock Skew

2. Write Lamport's time stamp algorithm in pseudo C and explain it with suitable example.
   [8]

3. Write Bully algorithm for electing a coordinator in pseudo C and explain it with suitable example.   **[8]**

4. List and compare various algorithms used to achieve Mutual exclusion in a Distributed Systems with respect to.   **[8]**
   (i) Messages per entry/exit
   (ii) Delay before entry
   (iii) Time complexity
   (iv) Problems

5. How does the CODA file system used for replication strategy?   **[5]**

6. Consider the following set of concurrently executing processes   **[5]**

P1	P2	P3
x = 1;	y = 1;	z = 1;
print (y, z);	print (x, z);	print (x, y);

   Is 001110 a legal output for a sequentially consistent memory? Explain your answer. **[5]**

7. Explain following consistency models with suitable examples: **[6]**
   (i) Causal   (ii) FIFO

8. Describe object replication and scaling technique in distributed shared memory systems.   **[5]**

9. In a fault tolerant distributed system how check-pointing is used. Describe following check-pointing: **[8]**
   (i) Independent check-pointing
   (ii) Coordinated check-pointing

10. Consider a web browser that returns an outdated cached page instead of a more recent one that had been updated at the server. Is this a failure and if so, what kind of failure? **[4]**

11. Draw and explain triple modular redundancy. **[4]**

Oct. 2012

12. What is Election algorithm? Suppose that two processes detect the demise of the coordinator simultaneously and both decide to hold an election using Bully algorithm. What happens? **[10]**

13. Explain global state? What are the different types of global states? **[8]**

14. What do you understand by logical time and logical clocks? What is Lamport's contribution for it? Discuss. **[10]**

15. What are advantages and drawbacks of multi-version timestamp ordering in comparison with the ordering timestamp ordering? **[8]**

16. Why is it difficult to implement the casual memory consistency model for DSM system?

[8]

17. What is difference between the unit of replication and the granularity of coherence? What are the advantages of small granularity? **[8]**

18. Discuss the relative merits and demerits of write - update and write-invalidate protocols. **[8]**

19. Discuss design and implementation issues of distributed shared memory. **[8]**

20. Define the following: **[10]**

    (i) Arbitrary Failures.

    (ii) Timing Failures.

    (iii) Backward Recovery

    (iv) Forward Recovery

    (v) Check pointing

21. What is use of stable storage? How stable storage technique is used in recovery. **[8]**

22. What is process resilience? Explain different design issues of process resilience. **[10]**

23. What is recovery line? Draw and explain domino effect in detail. **[8]**

May 2013

24. A Why should time be synchronized in a Distributed System? How network Time Protocol (NTP) work to synchronize the clocks of computers in internet? Compare clock synchronization in centralized and Distributed Systems. **[10]**

25. Discuss happens-before relationship in a set of events occur in various processes. How happens-before relationship is used in Lamport's logical clock synchronization?   **[8]**

26. Explain the working of coordinator selection algorithm. How Bully and Ring algorithms are used to handle the workload after crash of the current coordinator in Distributed System.   **[10]**

27. Explain centralized and distributed algorithms used to achieve mutual exclusion.   **[8]**

28. Explain following points related to fault tolerance issues in distributed systems: **[10]**

    (i)   Availability

    (ii) Reliability

    (iii) Failure models

    (iv) Triple Modular Redundancy.

29. How check pointing is used in fault tolerance in Distributed Systems? Explain independent check pointing and coordinated check pointing.   **[8]**

30. Explain following points related to recovery for providing fault tolerance capacities: **[10]**

    (i)   Backward recovery

    (ii) Forward recovery

    (iii) Receive based logging

    (iv) Receive based logging

    (v)   Stable storage

31. How failure masking is used to provide fault tolerance capability in distributed system?

    [8]

Dec. 2013

32. What is global state of a distributed system? Give suitable application where global state of the system is used.   **[8]**

33. Discuss distributed approach for mutual exclusion. Discuss Ricart and Agrawala algorithm that supports mutual exclusion.   **[8]**

34. What are physical clocks and logical clocks? Explain Berkeley Algorithm for clock synchronization.   **[8]**

35. Explain in detail vector timestamp method for logical clock synchronization.   **[8]**

36. Explain three-phase commit protocol in detail.   **[8]**

May 2014

37. How might the clocks in two computers that are linked by a local network be synchronized without reference to an external time source? What factors limit the accuracy of the procedure you have described? How could the clocks in large number of computers connected by Internet be synchronized?   **[8]**

38. Describe Cristian algorithm for clock synchronization.   **[8]**

39. Show the instances where we cannot conclude C(a) < C(b) or C(b) < C(a). Draw appropriate timing diagram.   **[8]**

40. Compare Centralized, Distributed and Token ring algorithms of mutual exclusion with their performance measures.   **[8]**

41. How is security implemented in CODA file system.   **[8]**

42. Write a short note on caching and replication in CODA file system.   **[8]**

43. What is consistency model? Explain Monotonic writes and Writes follow reads client centric consistency model?   **[8]**

44. What is replication? Explain main reasons for replication?   **[8]**

45. Why replicas must be consistent? Explain following Data Centric Consistency Models.

                    [8]

    (i) Sequential

    (ii) Weak

46. What is check pointing? Explain independent check pointing and co-ordinated check pointing.   **[8]**

47. Explain Byzantine Generals Problem. Why do we need to have 3m +1 total processes for system to work correctly, assuming non-faulty commander?   **[10]**

Dec. 2014

48. Compare Centralized, Decentralized, Distributed and Token ring mutual exclusion algorithms.   **[8]**

49. Explain network time protocol to distribute time information over Internet.   **[8]**

50. Explain following protocols: **[8]**

    (i)   One-Phase Commit

    (ii) Two-Phase Commit

    (iii) Three-Phase commit

May 2015

51. Explain the concept of logic clock and their importance in distributed system. A clock of a computer system must never run backward. Explain how this issue can be handled in an implementation.   **[8]**

52. Explain Ricart and Agrawala's algorithm for mutual exclusion in detail.   **[8]**

53. Suppose that the coordinator crashes. Does this always brings the system down? If not, under what a circumstances does this happened? Is there any way to avoid the problem and tolerate the crash of the coordinator?   **[8]**

54. Define global state. Explain consistent cut and inconsistent cut with suitable example.

                                                                                      [8]

55. What is Byzatine's general problem? Discuss Lamport's algorithm to solve this problem.

                                                                                      [8]

56. Explain following points related to fault tolerate issues in distributed systems: **[8]**

    (1) Availability

    (2) Reliability

    (3) Failure models

    (4) Triple modulator redundancy

57. Explain basic reliable multicasting. How it could be made scalable.   **[8]**

58. Draw state transition diagram for two phase commit protocol and highlight the state where the participant is get blocked. Also mention the drawbacks of 2PC.   **[8]**

DISTRIBUTED STORAGE AND MULTIMEDIA SYSTEMS

5.1 INTRODUCTION TO FILE SYSTEM

- In this unit we discuss the basic concept of file system basically File systems are abstraction that enables users to read, manipulate and organize data.

- Typically the data is stored in units known as files in a hierarchical tree where the nodes are known as directories.

- The file system enables a uniform view, independent of the underlying storage devices which can range between anything from floppy drives to hard drives and flash memory cards. Since file systems evolved from stand-alone computers the connection between the logical file system and the storage device was typically a one-to-one mapping.

- Even software RAID that is used to distribute the data on multiple storage devices is typically implemented below the file system layer.

5.1.1 Definition of Distributed Files System

- "A Distributed File System (DFS) is a file system with data stored on a server. The data is accessed and processed as if it was stored on the local client machine. The DFS makes it convenient to share information and files among users on a network in a controlled and authorized way. The server allows the client users to share files and store data just like they are storing the information locally. However, the servers have full control over the data and give access control to the clients."

- A distributed file system is a client/server-based application that allows clients to access and process data stored on the server as if it were on their own computer.

- When a user accesses a file on the server, the server sends the user a copy of the file, which is cached on the user's computer while the data is being processed and is then returned to the server.

- Basically, a distributed file system organizes file and directory services of individual servers into a global directory in such a way that remote data access is not location-specific but is identical from any client.

- All files are accessible to all users of the global file system and organization is hierarchical and directory-based.

- Since more than one client may access the same data simultaneously, the server must have a mechanism in place (such as maintaining information about the times of access) to organize updates so that the client always receives the most current version of data and that data conflicts do not arise.

- Distributed file systems typically use file or database replication (distributing copies of data on multiple servers) to protect against data access failures.

5.2 CHARACTERISTICS OF DISTRIBUTED FILE SYSTEM

Distributed file system having the following characteristics

1. **Access Transparency**

   Clients are unaware that files are distributed and can access them in the same way as local files are accessed.

2. **Location Transparency**

   A consistent name space exists encompassing local as well as remote files. The name of a file does not give it location.

3. **Concurrency Transparency**

   All clients have the same view of the state of the file system. This means that if one process is modifying a file, any other processes on the same system or remote systems that are accessing the files will see the modifications in a coherent manner.

4. **Failure Transparency**

   The client and client programs should operate correctly after a server failure.

5. **Heterogeneity**

   File service should be provided across different hardware and operating system platforms.

6. **Scalability**

   The file system should work well in small environments (1 machine, a dozen machines) and also scale gracefully to huge ones (hundreds through tens of thousands of systems).

7. **Replication transparency**

   To support scalability, we may wish to replicate files across multiple servers. Clients should be unaware of this. Migration transparency

   Files should be able to move around without the client's knowledge.

8. **Support Fine-Grained Distribution of Data**

   To optimize performance, we may wish to locate individual objects near the processes that use them.

9. **Tolerance for Network Partitioning**

   The entire network or certain segments of it may be unavailable to a client during certain periods (e.g. disconnected operation of a laptop). The file system should be tolerant of this.

5.3 FILE SERVICE ARCHITECTURE

The file service architecture is an architecture that offers a clear separation of the main concerns in providing access to files is obtained by structuring the file service as three basic components as follows:

A Flat File Service

- Operate on the contents of files
- Unique file identifier (UFID)

A Directory Service

- Provide a mapping between text names to UFIDs

A Client Module

- Support applications accessing remote file service transparently.
- E.g. iterative request to directory service, cache files.

The relevant modules and their relationship are The Client module implements exported interfaces by flat file and directory services on server side.

5.3.1 File Service Architecture

In this section we discuss the file service architecture Fig. 5.1 shows the architecture of file service architecture

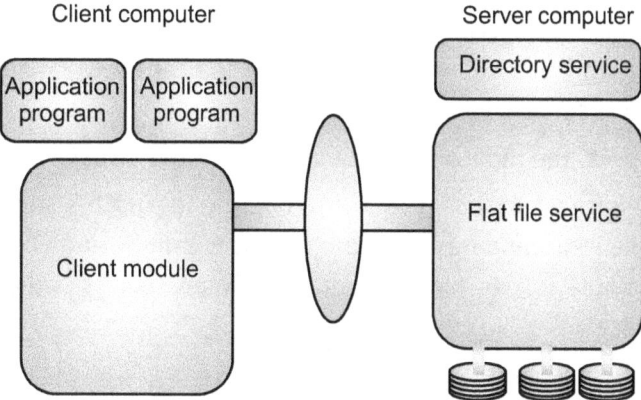

Fig. 5.1 :File service architecture

Flat File Service:

- Concerned with the implementation of operations on the contents of file.
- Unique File Identifiers (UFIDs) are used to refer to files in all requests for flatfile service operations. UFIDs are long sequences of bits chosen so that each file has a unique among all of the files in a distributed system.

Directory Service:

- Provides mapping between text names.
- For the files and their UFIDs. Clients may obtain the UFID of a file by quoting its text name to directory service. Directory service supports functions needed generate directories, to add new files to directories.

Client Module:

- It runs on each computer and provides integrated service (flat file and directory) as a single API to application programs.
- For example, in UNIX hosts, a client module emulates the full set of UNIX file operations.
- It holds information about the network locations of flat-file and directory server processes; and achieves better performance through implementation of a cache of recently used file blocks at the client.

5.4 DISTRIBUTED FILE SYSTEM ARCHITECTURE

- Here we discuss the architecture of DSF basically Distributed File System (DFS) is a set of client and server services that allow an organization using servers to organize many distributed SMB(Server Message Block) file shares into a distributed file system.
- DFS provides location transparency and redundancy to improve data availability in the face of failure or heavy load by allowing shares in multiple different locations to be logically grouped under one folder, or DFS root.
- DFS has two major logical components. First, DFS namespaces provide an abstraction layer for SMB network file shares, allowing one logical network path to be served by multiple physical file servers.
- Second, DFS supports the replication of data between the servers.
- There is no requirement to use the two components of DFS together; it is perfectly possible to use the logical namespace component without using DFS file replication, and it is perfectly possible to use file replication between servers without combining them into one namespace

There are two ways of implementing DFS on a server:

(a) **Standalone DFS Namespace:** Allow for a DFS root that exists only on the local computer, and thus does not use Active Directory. A Standalone DFS can only be accessed on the computer on which it is created. It doesn't offer any fault tolerance and cannot be linked to any other DFS. This is the only option available on Windows NT 4.0 Server systems. Standalone DFS roots are rarely encountered because of their limited utility.

(b) **Domain-Based DFS Namespace:** Stores the DFS configuration within Active Directory, the DFS namespace root is accessible at \\domainname\<dfsroot> or \\fq.domain.name\<dfsroot>. The namespace roots do not have to reside on domain controllers, they can reside on member servers, if domain controllers are not used as the namespace root servers, then multiple member servers should be used to provide full fault tolerance.

- Ideally, files can be stored at any machine (or computer) and computation (file access operations) can be performed at any machine.
- However, for higher performance, several machines, referred to as *file servers*, are dedicated to storing files and performing storage and retrieval operations.

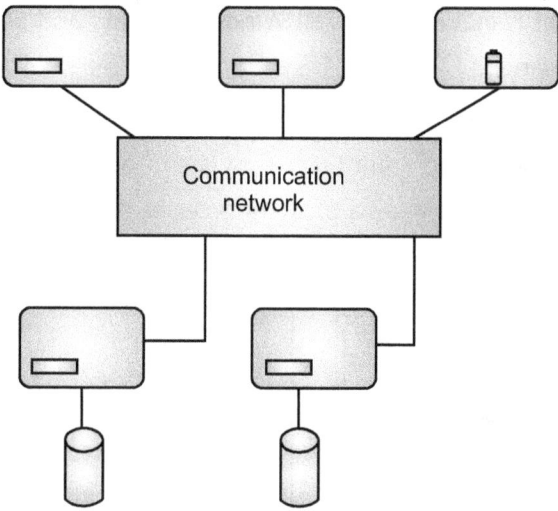

Fig. 5.2 : Distributed file system architecture

- The rest of the machines in the system can be used solely for computational purposes. These machines are referred to as *clients* and they access the files stored on servers.
- Some client machines may also be equipped with a local disk storage that can be used for caching remote files, as a swap area, or as a storage area.
- The two most important services present in a distributed file system are the *name server* and *cache manager.*
- A name server is a process that maps names specified by clients to stored objects such as files and directories.
- The mapping (also referred to as name resolution) occurs when a process references a file or directory for the first time.
- A cache manager is a process that implements file caching. In a file caching, a copy of data stored at a remote file server is brought to the client's machine when referenced by the client. Subsequent accesses to the data are performed locally at the client, thereby reducing the access delays due to network latency.
- Cache managers can be present at both clients and file servers. Cache managers at the servers cache files in the memory to reduce delays due to disk latency.
- If multiple clients are allowed to cache a file and modify it, the copies become inconsistent.
- To avoid this inconsistency problem, cache manager at both servers and clients coordinate to perform data storage and retrieval operations.

5.4.1 Working Principle of Distributed File System

- The distributed file system work on the basis of DFS service which consists of a client component and a server component.

- The client component is included with all Windows clients and allows the client to make requests to the DFS server.

- The server component is included with Windows NT, Windows 2000, and Windows Server products. The DFS server component receives a client request and redirects or refers it to a physical target, similar to the way a browser receives a DNS call and refers the client to a Web site.

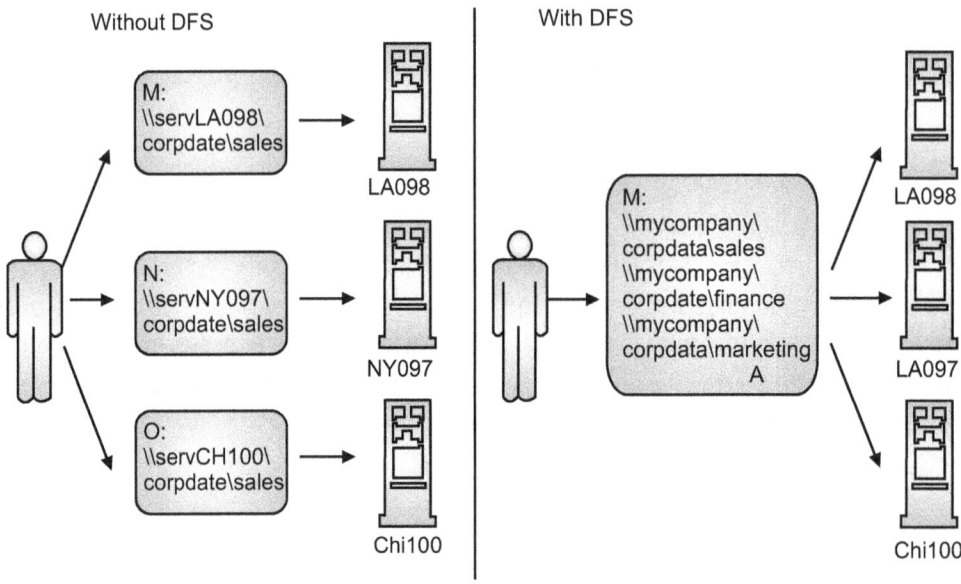

Fig.5.3 (a) DFS simplifies access to frequently accessed file shares with a unified namespace

- The view of shared folders on different servers is called the DFS namespace. Another way to think of a DFS namespace is as an intuitive view of shared folders on different servers. Or think of it as a virtual UNC path.

- A namespace is much easier to use as Fig. 5.3 (a) below shows. For example, an administrator can create a single namespace for commonly accessed corporate documents called \\myCompany.com\corpdata\Sales that maps to physical resources residing on multiple servers that could be located just about anywhere

- When DFS is not used, users are able to select file servers without regard to geography or user load, much less logical namespace shown below in Fig. 5.3 (b).

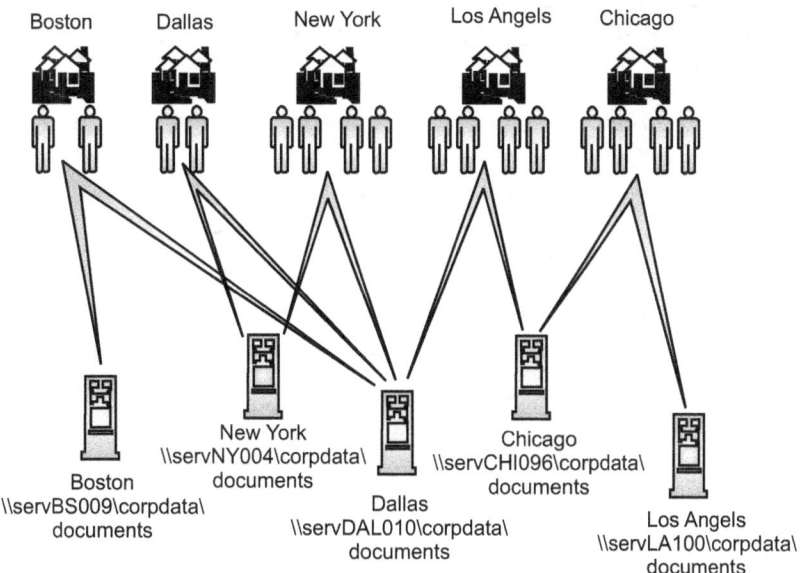

Fig. 5.3 (b) : Before implementing a DFS namespace

- After DFS is implemented, however, users are automatically routed to the closest server, as Figure 5.3 (c) shows.
- Moreover, if a server becomes unavailable, DFS ensures that users are routed to the next closest server by using site-costing.
- This capability is available when using Windows Server 2003 in either a stand-alone or domain-based DFS configuration.
- Windows Server 2003 will also use the site and costing information in Active Directory to determine whether sites are linked by inexpensive, high-speed links or by expensive WAN links.

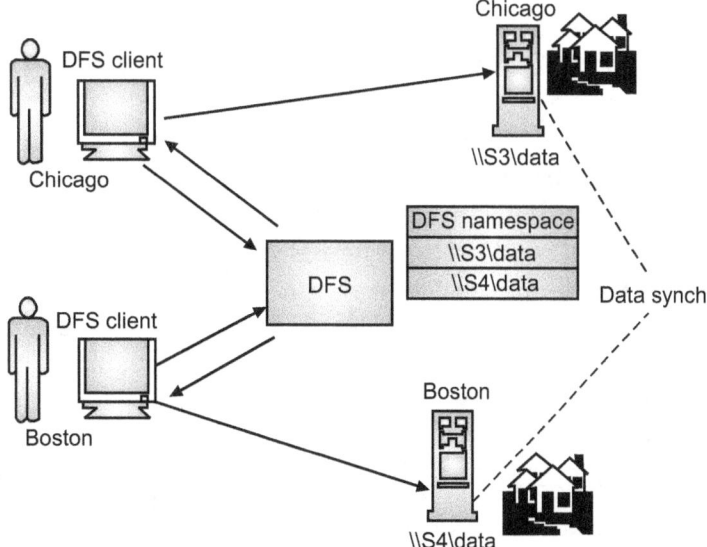

Fig. 5.3 (c) :With DFS, users are automatically routed to the closest server

5.5 DISTRIBUTED FILE BUILDING MECHANISM

- In this section we discuss the basic mechanism for distributed file system that takes advantages over the previous file system that are mounting, name server, availability

5.5.1 Mounting

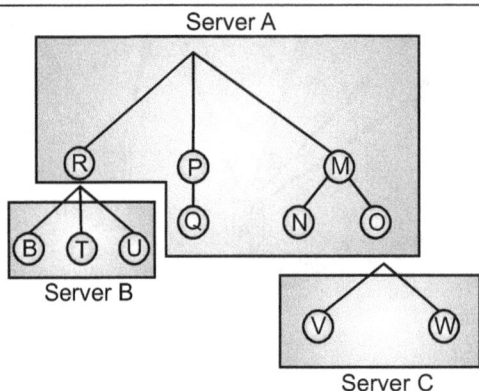

Fig. 5.4: Name space hierarchy

- A mount mechanism allows the binding together of different filename spaces to form a single hierarchically structured name space. Even though mounting is UNIX specific, it is worthwhile to study this mechanism as most of the existing distributed file systems are based on UNIX.
- A name soace (or a collection of files) can be bounded to or mounted at an internal node or a leaf node od a name space tree.
- A node onto which a name space is mounted is known as a *mount point*.
- In Fig. 5.4, nodes *a* and *i* are mount points at which directories stored at server Y and server Z are mounted. Note that a andi are internal nodes in the name space tree.
- The kernel maintains a structure called the *mount table*, which maps mount points to appropriate storage devices. In the case of DFS, the file systems maintained by remote servers are mounted at the clients.
- There are two approaches to maintain the mount information:
- (a) Mount information can be maintained at clients, in which case each client has to individually mount every required file system. This approach is employed in the Sun network file system, every client need not necessarily see an identical filename space;
- (b) Mount information can be maintained at servers, in which case it is possible that every client sees an identical filename space. If files are moved to a different server, then mount information need only be updated at the servers. In the first approach, every client needs to update its mount table.

5.5.2 Name Server

- In distributed systems, *name servers* are responsible for name resolution. The easiest approach to name resolution in distributed systems is for all clients to send their queries to a single name server which maps names to objects.

- This approach has the following serious drawbacks: first, if the name server crashes, the entire system is drastically affected.
- Second, the name server may become a bottleneck and seriously degrade the performance of the system.
- The second approach involves having several name servers (on different hosts) wherein each server is responsible for mapping objects stored in different domains.
- This approach is commonly used in the distributed file systems operating today. When a name (usually with many components such as "a/b/c") is to be mapped to an object, the local name server (such as a table maintained in the kernel) is queried.
- The local name server may point to a remote name server to further mapping of the name. For example, querying /a/b/c may require a remote server mapping the /b/c part of the filename.
- This procedure is repeated until the name is completely resolved. By replacing the tables used by name servers, one can achieve fault tolerance and higher performance.

5.5.3 Availability

- The failure of servers or the communication network can severely affect the availability of files. *Replication* is the primary mechanism used for enhancing the availability of files in DFS.

5.5.3.1 Replication

- Under replication, many copies or replicas of files are maintained at different servers. Replication is inherently expensive because of extra storage space required to store the replicas and the overhead incurred in maintaining all the replicas up to date.
- Some typical situations that cause inconsistency among replicas are:
  (a) a replica is not updated due to the failure of the server storing the replica and
  (b) all the file servers storing the replicas of a file are not reachable from all the clients due to network partition, and the replicas of a file in different partitions are updated differently.

5.5.3.2 Unit of Replication

- The most basic unit is a *file*. While this unit allows the replication of only those files that need to have higher availability, it makes overall replica management harder.
- For example, the protection rights associated with a directory have to be individually stored with each replica; replicas of files belonging to a common directory may not have common file servers and hence require extra name resolutions to locate the replicas in the case of modifications to the directory or the file.
- Alternatively, the replication unit can be a group of all the files of a single user or the files that are ina server, etc.
- The group of files is referred to as a *volume*. The main advantage of volume replication is that replica management is easier.

- Protection rights can be assosiated with the volume instead of with each individual file replica.
- However, volume replication may be wasteful as a user typically needs higher availability for only a few files in the volume.
- A compromise scheme captures the advantages of the above two schemes. All the files of a user constitute a file group called a *primary pack*. A replica of a primary pack, called a pack, is allowed to contain a subset of the files in the primary pack.
- With this arrangement, a different degree of replication for each file in the primary pack can be obtained by creating one or more packs of the primary pack.

5.5.4 Replica Management

- In distributed file system Replica management is concerned with the maintenance of replicas and in making use of them to provide increased availability.
- Replica management depends on whether consistency is garanteed by the distributed file system.
- Here we are concerned with the consistency among replicas only (which is also known as *mutual consistency*), and not with the consistency within a file.
- We will look at two well-known algorithms that solve the problem of replicas modification. The first one is called *primary copy replication*. When it is used, one server is designated as the primary. All the others are secondaries. When a replicated file is to be updated, the change is sent to the primary server, which makes the change locally, and then sends commands to the secondaries, ordering them to change too. Reads can be done from any copy, primary or secondary.
- Although the method is straightforward, it has the disadvantage that if the primary is down, no updates can be performed.

5.6 NAME SERVICE AND DOMAIN NAME SYSTEM

- In a distributed system, names are used to refer to a wide variety of resources such as computers, services, remote objects and files, as well as to users. Names enable communication and resource sharing.
- A name is required to request a computer system to act upon a specific resource chosen out of many; for example, a name in the form of a URL is needed to access a specific web page.
- Sometimes clients do not know the name of the particular entity that they seek, but they do have some information that describes it.
- They may require a service and know some of its characteristics but not what entity implements it.
- This section presents name services, which provide clients with data about named objects in distributed systems, and the related concept of directory services, which provide data about objects that satisfy a given description.

- Name management is separated from other services because of the openness of distributed systems, which brings the following impetus:

Unification: It is suitable for resources managed by different services to use the same naming scheme. URIs are a good example of this.

Integration: It is not possible to predict the scope of sharing in a distributed system. It may become necessary to share and therefore name resources that were created in different administrative domains. Without a common name service, the administrative domains may use entirely different naming conventions.

5.6.1 Name Spaces

- A name space is the group of all suitable names known by a particular service. The service will try to look up a valid name, even though that name may prove not to correspond to any object i.e., to be unbound.

- Name spaces require a syntactic definition to separate valid names from invalid names.

- The URL name space also includes comparative names such as ../images/figure1.jpg. When a browser or other web client encounters such a relative name, it uses the resource in which the relative name is embedded to determine the server host name and the directory to which this pathname refers.

- DNS names are strings called domain names. The DNS name space has a hierarchic structure: a domain name consists of one or more strings called name components or labels, separated by the delimiter '.'. There is no delimiter at the beginning or end of a domain name, although the root of the DNS name space is sometimes referred to as '.' for administrative purposes. The name components are non-null printable strings that do not contain '.'. In general, a prefix of a name is an initial section of the name that contains only zero or more entire components. For example, in DNS www and www.nirali are both prefixes of www.nirali.net. DNS names are not case-sensitive, so www.nirali.net and www.nirali.net have the same meaning.

- DNS servers do not recognize relative names: all names are referred to the global root. However, in practical implementations, client software keeps a list of domain names that are appended automatically to any single-component name before resolution.

- For example, the name www presented in the domain nirali.net probably refers to www.nirali.net; client software will append the default domain nirali.net and attempt to resolve this name.

- If this fails, then further default domain names may be appended; finally, the (absolute) name www will be presented to the root for resolution (an operation that will of course fail in this case).

- Names with more than one component, however, are normally presented intact to the DNS, as absolute names.

5.6.2 Domain Name System

- The Domain Name System is a name service design whose main naming database is used across the Internet.
- DNS replaced the original Internet naming scheme, in which all host names and addresses were held in a single central master file and downloaded by FTP to all computers that required them [Harrenstien et al. 1985].

This original scheme was soon seen to suffer from three major short comings:

- It did not scale to large numbers of computers.
- Local organizations wished to administer their own naming systems.
- A general name service was needed not one that serves only for looking up computer addresses.

- The objects named by the DNS are primarily computers for which mainly IP addresses are stored as attributes and what we have referred to in this chapter as naming domains are called simply domains in the DNS.
- In principle, however, any type of object can be named, and its architecture gives scope for a variety of implementations. Organizations and departments within them can manage their own naming data.
- The DNS is designed for use in many implementations, each of which may have its own name space. In practice, however, only one is in widespread use, and that is the one used for naming across the Internet. The Internet DNS name space is partitioned both organizationally and according to geography. The names are written with the highest-level domain on the right. The original top-level organizational domains (also called generic domains) in use across the Internet were:

com : Commercial organizations.

edu : Universities and other educational institutions.

gov : US governmental agencies.

mil : US military organizations.

net : Major network support centres.

org : Organizations not mentioned above.

int : International organizations.

- New top-level domains such as biz and mobi have been added since the early 2000s. A full list of current generic domain names is available from the Internet Assigned Numbers Authority [www.iana.org I].
- In addition, every country has its own domains:

us : United States

uk : United Kingdom

fr : France

... − ...

- Countries, particularly those other than the US often use their own subdomains to distinguish their organizations. The UK, for example, has domains co.uk and ac.uk, which correspond to com and edu respectively (ac stands for 'academic community').

5.6.3 Directory Services

- A service that stores collections of bindings between names and attributes and that looks up entries that match attribute-based specifications is called a directory service.

- A directory service returns the sets of attributes of any objects found to match some specified attributes. So, for example, the request 'Telephone Number = 020 555 5555' might return {'Name =ABC XYZ, 'TelephoneNumber = 020 555 5555', 'emailAddress = abc@nirali.ac.in', ...}.

- The client may specify that only a subset of the attributes is of interest – for example, just the email addresses of matching objects. X.500 and some other directory services also allow objects to be looked up by conventional hierarchic textual names.

5.7 CASE STUDY : SUN NETWORK FILE SYSTEMS

5.7.1 The Sun Network File Systems

- In this section we study the basic concept sun network file system like design goal, implementation basic operation.

- The Sun Network File System (NFS) provides transparent, remote access to file systems. Unlike many other remote file system implementations under UNIX, NFS is designed to be easily portable to other operating systems and machine architectures.

- It uses an External Data Representation (XDR) specification to describe protocols in a machine and system independent way. NFS is implemented on top of a Remote Procedure Call Package (RPC) to help simplify protocol definition, implementation, and maintenance.

- In order to build NFS into the UNIX kernel in a way that is transparent to applications, we decided to add a new interface to the kernel which separates generic file system operations from specific file system implementations.

- The "file system interface" consists of two parts: the Virtual File System (VFS) interface defines the operations that can be done on a file system, while the virtual node (vnode) interface defines the operations that can be done on a file within that file system.

- This new interface allows us to implement and install new file systems in much the same way as new device drivers are added to the Kernel.

- In this section we discuss the design and implementation of the file system interface in the UNIX kernel and the NFS virtual file system.

- We compare NFS to other remote file system implementations, and describe some interesting NFS ports that have been done, including the IBM PC implementation under MS/DOS and the VMS server implementation.

- We also describe the user-level NFS server implementation which allows simple server ports without modification to the underlying operating system.
- We conclude with some ideas for future enhancements.
- In this section we use the term *server* to refer to a machine that provides resources to the network; a *client* is a machine that accesses resources over the network; a *user* is a person "logged in" at a client; an *application* is a program that executes on a client; and a *workstation* is a client machine that typically supports one user at a time.

5.7.1.1 Design Goals

- NFS was designed to simplify the sharing of file system resources in a network of non-homogeneous machines.
- Our goal was to provide a way of making remote files available to local programs without having to modify, or even relink, those programs. In addition, we wanted remote file access to be comparable in speed to local file access.

The Overall Design Goals of NFS were:

Machine and Operating System Independence:

- The protocols used should be independent of UNIX so that an NFS server can supply files to many different types of clients. The protocols should also be simple enough that they can be implemented on low-end machines like the PC.

Crash Recovery:

- When clients can mount remote file systems from many different servers it is very important that clients and servers be able to recover easily from machine crashes and network problems.

Transparent Access:

- We want to provide a system which allows programs to access remote files in exactly the same way as local files, without special pathname parsing, libraries, or recompiling.
- Programs should not need or be able to tell whether a file is remote or local.

UNIX Semantics Maintained on UNIX Client:

- In order for transparent access to work on UNIX machines, UNIX file system semantics have to be maintained for remote files.

Reasonable Performance:

- People will not use a remote file system if it is no faster than the existing networking utilities, such as *rcp*, even if it is easier to use. Our design goal was to make NFS as fast as a small local disk on a SCSI interface.

Basic Design:

- The NFS design consists of three major pieces:
  1. The protocol.
  2. The server side.
  3. The client side.

1. NFS Protocol:

- The NFS protocol uses the Sun Remote Procedure Call (RPC) mechanism 1. For the same reasons that procedure calls simplify programs, RPC helps simplify the definition, organization, and implementation of remote services.

- The NFS protocol is defined in terms of a set of procedures, their arguments and results, and their effects. Remote procedure calls are synchronous, that is, the client application blocks until the server has completed the call and returned the results.

- This makes RPC very easy to use and understand because it behaves like a local procedure call.

- NFS uses a stateless protocol. The parameters to each procedure call contain all of the information necessary to complete the call, and the server does not keep track of any past requests.

- This makes crash recovery very easy; when a server crashes, the client resends NFS requests until a response is received, and the server does no crash recovery at all.

- When a client crashes, no recovery is necessary for either the client or the server.

- If state is maintained on the server, on the other hand, recovery is much harder. Both client and server need to reliably detect crashes.

- The server needs to detect client crashes so that it can discard any state it is holding for the client, and the client must detect server crashes so that it can rebuild the server's state.

- A stateless protocol avoids complex crash recovery. If a client just resends requests until a response is received, data will never be lost due to a server crash. In fact, the client cannot tell the difference between a server that has crashed and recovered, and a server that is slow.

- Sun's RPC package is designed to be transport independent.

- New transport protocols, such as ISO and XNS, can be "plugged in" to the RPC implementation without affecting the higher level protocol code.

- NFS currently uses the DARPA User Datagram Protocol (UDP) and Internet Protocol (IP) for its transport level. Since UDP is an unreliable datagram protocol, packets can get lost, but because the NFS protocol is stateless and NFS requests are idempotent, the client can recover by retrying the call until the packet gets through.

- The most common NFS procedure parameter is a structure called a file handle (fhandle or fh) which is provided by the server and used by the client to reference a file.

- The fhandle is opaque, that is, the client never looks at the contents of the fhandle, but uses it when operations are done on that file.

- An outline of the NFS protocol procedures is given below.
  - **null**() returns ()
    Do nothing procedure to ping the server and measure round trip time.

- **lookup** (dirfh, name) returns (fh, attr)

  Returns a new fhandle and attributes for the named file in a directory.

- **create** (dirfh, name, attr) returns (newfh, attr)

  Creates a new file and returns its fhandle and attributes.

- **remove** (dirfh, name) returns (status)

  Removes a file from a directory.

- **getattr** (fh) returns (attr)

  Returns file attributes. This procedure is like a stat call.

- **setattr**(fh, attr) returns (attr)

  Sets the mode, uid, gid, size, access time, and modify time of a file. Setting the size to zero truncates the file.

- **read** (fh, offset, count) returns (attr, data)

  Returns up to *count* bytes of data from a file starting *offset* bytes into the file. read also returns the attributes of the file.

- **write**(fh, offset, count, data)

  Returns (attr) Writes *count* bytes of data to a file beginning *offset* bytes from the beginning of the file. Returns the attributes of the file after the write takes place.

- **rename**(dirfh, name, tofh, toname) returns (status)

  Renames the file *name* in the directory *dirfh,* to *to name* in the directory *tofh.*

- **link**(dirfh, name, tofh, to name) returns (status)

  Creates the file *to name*in the directory *tofh,* which is a link to the file *name* in the directory *dirfh.*

- **symlink**(dirfh, name, string) returns (status)

  Creates a symbolic link *name* in the directory *dirfh* with value *string*. The server does not interpret the *string* argument in any way, just saves it and makes an association to the new symbolic link file.

- **readlink**(fh) returns (string)

  Returns the string which is associated with the symbolic link file.

- **mkdir**(dirfh, name, attr)

  returns (fh, newattr)Creates a new directory *name* in the directory *dirfh*and returns the new fhandle and attributes.

- **rmdir**(dirfh, name) returns(status)

  Removes the empty directory *name* from the parent directory *dirfh*.readdir(dirfh, cookie, count) returns(entries) Returns up to *count* bytes of directory entries from the directory *dirfh*. Each entry contains a file name, file id, and an opaque pointer to the next directory entry called a *cookie*. The *cookie* is used in subsequent readdircalls to start reading at a specific entry in the directory. A readdircall with the *cookie* of zero returns entries starting with the first entry in the directory.

- **statfs**(fh) returns (fsstats)

  Returns file system information such as block size, number of free blocks, etc. New fhandles are returned by thelookup, create, andmkdirprocedures which also take an fhandle as an argument. The first remote fhandle, for the root of a file system, is obtained by the client using the RPC based MOUNT protocol. The MOUNT protocol takes a directory pathname and returns an fhandle if the client has access permission to the file system which contains that directory. The reason for making this a separate protocol is that this makes it easier to plug in new file system access checking methods, and it separates out the operating system dependent aspects of the protocol. Note that the MOUNT protocol is the only place that UNIX pathnames are passed to the server. In other operating system implementations the MOUNT protocol can be replaced without having to change the NFS protocol.

- The NFS protocol and RPC are built on top of the Sun External Data Representation (XDR) specification XDR defines the size, byte order and alignment of basic data types such as string, integer, union, boolean and array.

- Complex structures can be built from the basic XDR data types. Using XDR not only makes protocols machine and language independent, it also makes them easy to define.

- The arguments and results of RPC procedures are defined using an XDR data definition language that looks a lot like C declarations.

- This data definition language can be used as input to an XDR protocol compiler which produces the structures and XDR translation procedures used to interpret RPC protocols.

2. **Server Side:**

- Because the NFS server is stateless, when servicing an NFS request it must commit any modified data to stable storage before returning results.

- The implication for UNIX based servers is that requests which modify the file system must flush all modified data to disk before returning from the call.

- For example, on a write request, not only the data block, but also any modified indirect blocks and the block containing the inode must be flushed if they have been modified.

- Another modification to UNIX necessary for our server implementation is the addition of a generation number in the inode, and a file system id in the superblock.

- These extra numbers make it possible for the server to use the inode number, inode generation number, and file system id together as the fhandle for a file.

- The inode generation number is necessary because the server may hand out an fhandle with an inode number of a file that is later removed and the inode reused.

- When the original fhandle comes back, the server must be able to tell that this inode number now refers to a different file.

- The generation number has to be incremented every time the inode is freed.

3. Client Side:

- The Sun implementation of the client side provides an interface to NFS which is transparent to applications. To make transparent access to remote files work we had to use a method of locating remote files that does not change the structure of path names.

- Some UNIX based remote file access methods use pathnames like host:pathor /../host/path to name remote files.

- This does not allow real transparent access since existing programs that parse pathnames have to be modified.

- Rather than doing a "late binding" of file address, we decided to do the hostname lookup and file address binding once per file system by allowing the client to attach a remote file system to a directory with the mount command.

- This method has the advantage that the client only has to deal with hostnames once, at mount time. It also allows the server to limit access to file systems by checking client credentials.

- The disadvantage is that remote files are not available to the client until a mount is done.

- Transparent access to different types of file systems mounted on a single machine is provided by a new file system interface in the kernel. Each "file system type" supports two sets of operations: the Virtual File system (VFS) interface defines the procedures that operate on the file system as a whole; and the Virtual Node (vnode) interface defines the procedures that operate on an individual file within that file system type. Fig. 5.5 is a schematic diagram of the file system interface and how NFS uses it.

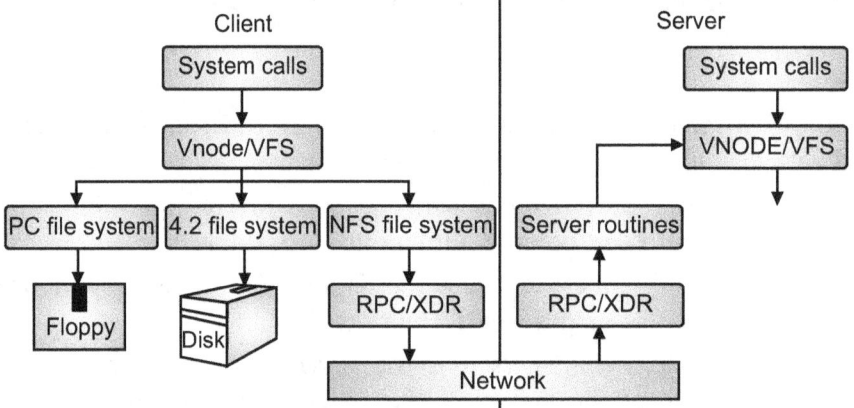

Fig. 5.5: File system interface

The File System Interface:

- The VFS interface is implemented using a structure that contains the operations that can be done on a file system. Likewise, the vnode interface is a structure that contains the operations that can be done on a node (file or directory) within a file system.

- There is one VFS structure per mounted file system in the kernel and one vnode structure for each active node.

- Using this abstract data type implementation allows the kernel to treat all file systems and nodes in the same way without knowing which underlying file system implementation it is using.
- Each vnode contains a pointer to its parent VFS and a pointer to a mounted-on VFS. This means that any node in a file system tree can be a mount point for another file system.
- A root operation is provided in the VFS to return the root vnode of a mounted file system.
- This is used by the pathname traversal routines in the kernel to bridge mount points.
- The root operation is used instead of keeping a pointer so that the root vnode for each mounted file system can be released. The VFS of a mounted file system also contains a pointer back to the vnode on which it is mounted so that pathnames that include ".." can also be traversed across mount points.
- In addition to the VFS and vnode operations, each file system type must provide mountand mount_rootoperations to mount normal and root file systems.
- The operations defined for the file system interface aregiven below. In the arguments and results, vp is a pointer to a vnode, dvp is a pointer to a directory vnodeand devvp is a pointer to a device vnode.

File System Operations	Description
mount(varies)	System call to mountfilesystem
mount_root( )	Mountfilesystem as root
VFS Operations	
unmount(vfs)	Unmountfilesystem
root(vfs)	returns(vnode) Return the vnode of the filesystem
statfs(vfs)	returns(statfsbuf) Return filesystem statistics
sync(vfs)	Flush delayed write blocks
Vnode Operations	**Description**
open(vp, flags)	Mark file open
close(vp, flags)	Mark file closed
rdwr(vp, uio, rwflag, flags)	Read or write a file
ioctl(vp, cmd, data, rwflag)	Do I/O control operation
select(vp, rwflag)	Do select
getattr(vp)	returns(attr) Return file attributes
setattr(vp, attr)	Set file attributes

...Conti.

access(vp, mode)	Check access permission
lookup(dvp, name)	returns(vp) Look up file name in a directory
create(dvp, name, attr, excl, mode)	returns(vp) Create a file
remove(dvp, name)	Remove a file name from a directory
link(vp, todvp, toname)	Link to a file
rename(dvp, name, todvp, toname)	Rename a file
mkdir(dvp, name, attr)	returns(dvp) Create a directory
rmdir(dvp, name)	Remove a directory
readdir(dvp) returns(entries)	Read directory entries
symlink(dvp, name, attr, toname)	Create a symbolic link
readlink(vp) returns(data)	Read the value of a symbolic link
fsync(vp)	Flush dirty blocks of a file
inactive(vp)	Mark vnode inactive and do clean up
bmap(vp, blk)	returns(devp, mappedblk) Map block number
strategy(bp)	Read and write filesystem blocks
bread(vp, blockno)	returns(buf) Read a block
brelse(vp, bp)	Release a block buffer

5.7.1.2 Communication and Processes

- To understand how the Network File System works on the server, you must first understand the communication relationship between a server and various clients. The client/servermodelinvolves a local host (the client) that makes a procedure call that is usually processed on a different, remote network system (the server).

- To the client, the procedure appears to be a local one, even though another system processes the request.

- In some cases, however, a single computer can act as both an NFS client and an NFS server.

- There are various resources on the server that are not available on the client, hence the need for such a communication relationship.

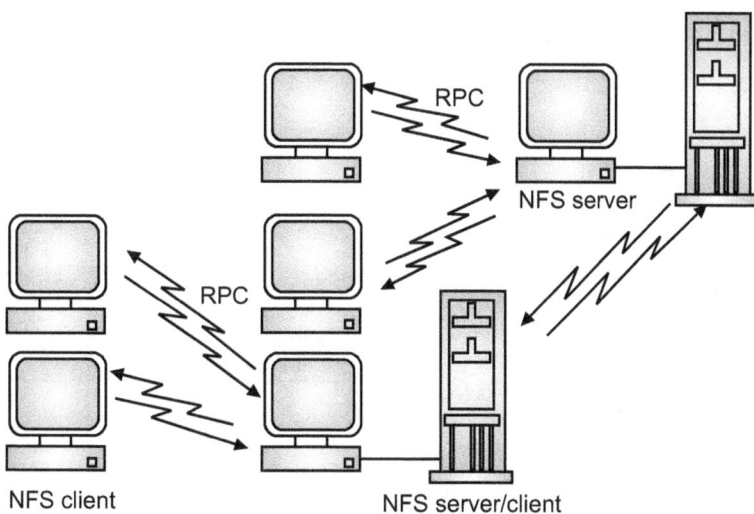

Fig. 5.6 (a) : The NFS client/server model

- The host owning the needed resource acts as a server that communicates to the host, which initiates the original call for the resource, the client. In the case of NFS, this resource is usually a shared file system, a directory, or an object.

- RPC is the mechanism for establishing such a client/server relationship within NFS. RPC bundles up the arguments intended for a procedure call into a packet of data called a network datagram.

- The NFS client creates an RPC session with an NFS server by connecting to the proper server for the job and transmitting the datagram to that server. The arguments are then unpacked and decoded on the server.

- The operation is processed by the server, and a return message (should one exist) is sent back to the client. On the client, this reply is transformed into a return value for NFS. The user's application is re-entered as if the process had taken place on a local level.

Network File System Client/Server Communication Design

- The logical layout of the Network File System on the client and server involves numerous daemons, caches, and the NFS protocol breakdown. An overview of each type of process follows.

- A daemonis a process that performs continuous or system-wide functions, such as network c00ontrol. NFS uses many different types of daemons to complete user requests.

- A cache is a type of high-speed buffer storage that contains frequently accessed instructions and data. Caches are used to reduce the access time for this information. Caching is the act of writing data to a cache.

Network File System Process Layout

- Local processes that are known as daemons are required on both the client and the server. These daemons process both local and remote requests and handle client/server communication. Both the NFS client and server have a set of daemons that carry out user tasks. In addition, the NFS client also has data caches that store specific types of data locally on the on the client.

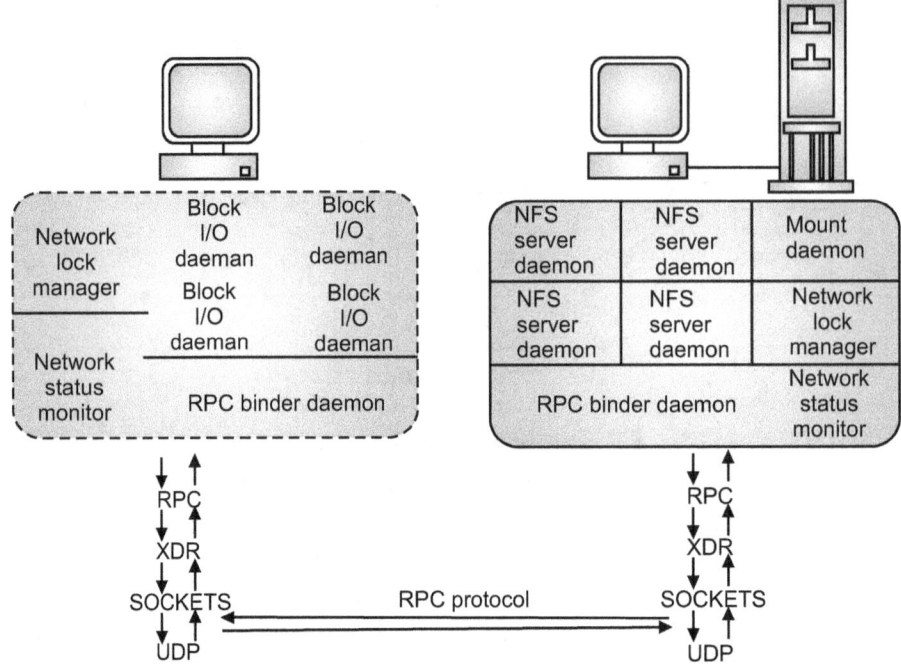

Fig. 5.6 (b) : A breakdown of the NFS client/server protocol

- Simple low-end protocols make up a high-end complex protocol like NFS. For an NFS client command to connect with the server, it must first use the Remote Procedure Call (RPC) protocol. The request is encoded into External Data Representation (XDR) and then sent to the server using a socket.

- The simple User Datagram Packet (UDP) protocol actually communicates between client and server. Some aspects of NFS use the Transmission Control Protocol (TCP) as the base communication protocol.

- The operation of NFS can be seen as a logical client-to-server communications system that specifically supports network applications.

The Typical NFS Flow Includes the Following Steps:

- The server waits for requests from one or more clients.
- The client sends a request to the server and blocks (waits for a response).
- When a request arrives, the server calls a dispatch routine.
- The dispatch routine performs the requested service and returns with the results of the request. The dispatch routine can also call a sub-routine to handle the specific request. Sometimes the sub-routine will return results to the client by itself, and other times it will report back to the dispatch routine.
- The server sends those results back to the client.
- The client then de-blocks.

The overhead of running more than one request at the same time is too heavy for an NFS server, so it is designed to be *single-threaded*. This means that an NFS server can only process one request per session. The requests from the multiple clients that use the NFS server are put into a queue and processed in the order in which they were received. To improve throughput, multiple NFS servers can process requests from the same queue.

5.7.1.3 Naming Structures

- Servers export whole file systems, but clients can mount any sub-directory of a remote file system on top of a local file system, or on top of another remote file system.

- In fact, a remote file system can be mounted more than once, and can even be mounted on another copy of itself!

- This means that clients can have different "names" for file systems by mounting them in different places.

- The NFS paradigm treats workstations as peers, with no fundamental distinction between clients and servers. A workstation may be a server, exporting some of its files. It may also be a client, accessing files on other workstations.

- But it is common practice for installations to be configured so that a small number of nodes run as dedicated servers, while the others run as clients. NFS clients are usually configured so that each sees a UNIX file name space with a private root. Using an extension of the Unix mount mechanism, subtrees exported by NFS servers are individually bound to nodes of the root file system.

- This binding usually occurs when UNIX is initialized, and remains in effect until explicitly modified.

- Since each workstation is free to configure its own name space there is no guarantee that all workstations at an installation have a common view of shared files.

- But collaborating groups of users usually configure their workstations to have the same name space. Location transparency is thus obtained by convention, rather than being a basic architectural feature of NFS.

- Since name-to-site bindings are static, NFS does not require a dynamic file location mechanism. Each client maintains a table mapping remote subtrees to servers.

- The addition of new servers or the movement of files between servers renders the table obsolete. There is no mechanism built into NFS to propagate information about such changes.

5.7.1.4 Caching and Replication

- NFS clients cache individual pages of remote files and directories in their main memory. They also cache the results of pathname to vnode translations. Local disks, even if present, are not used for caching.

- When a client caches any block of a file, it also caches a timestamp indicating when the file was last modified on the server.

- To validate cached blocks of a file, the client compares its cached timestamp with the timestamp on the server.
- If the server timestamp is more recent, the client invalidates all cached blocks of the file and refetches them on demand. A validation check is always performed when a file is opened, and when the server is contacted to satisfy a cache miss. After a check, cached blocks are assumed valid for a finite interval of time, specified by the client when a remote file system is mounted. The first reference to any block of the file after this interval forces a validation check.
- If a cached page is modified, it is marked as dirty and scheduled to be flushed to the server. The actual flushing is performed by an asynchronous kernel activity and will occur after some unspecified delay.
- However, the kernel does provide a guarantee that all dirty pages of a file will be flushed to the server before a close operation on the file completes.
- Directories are cached for reading in a manner similar to files. Modifications to directories, however, are performed directly on the server.
- When a file is opened, a cache validation check is also performed on its parent directory.
- Files and directories can have different revalidation intervals, typical values being 3 seconds for files and 30 seconds for directories.
- NFS performs network data transfers in large block sizes, typically 8 Kbytes, to improve performance. Read-ahead is employed to improve sequential access performance. Files corresponding to executable binaries are fetched in their entirety if they are smaller than a certain threshold.
- As originally specified, NFS did not support data replication. More recent versions of NFS support replication via a mechanism called Automounter.
- Automounter allows remote mount points to be specified using a set of servers rather than a single server. The first time a client traverses such a mount point a request is issued to each server, and the earliest to respond is chosen as the remote mount site.
- All further requests at the client that cross the mount point are directed to this server. Propagation of modifications to replicas has to be done manually. This replication mechanism is intended primarily for frequently-read and rarely-written files such as system binaries.

5.7.1.5 Security

- Network file system basically uses the underlying UNIX file protection mechanism on servers for access checks. Each RPC request from a client conveys the identity of the user on whose behalf the request is being made.
- The server temporarily assumes this identity, and file accesses that occur while servicing the request are checked exactly as if the user had logged in directly to the server. The standard Unix protection mechanism using user, group and world mode bits is used to specify protection policies on individual files and directories.

- In the previous versions of NFS, mutual trust was assumed between all participating machines. The identity of a user was determined by a client machine and accepted without further validation by a server.

- The level of security of an NFS site was effectively that of the least secure system in the environment.

- To reduce vulnerability, requests made on behalf of root (the UNIX superuser) on a workstation were treated by the server as if they had come from a non-existent user, nobody. Root thus received the lowest level of privileges for remote files.

- More recent versions of NFS can be configured to provide a higher level of security. DES-based mutual authentication is used to validate the client and the server on each RPC request.

- Since file data in RPC packets is not encrypted, NFS is still vulnerable to unauthorized release and modification of information if the network is not physically secure.

- The common DES key needed for mutual authentication is obtained from information stored in a publicly readable database. Stored in this database for each user and server is a pair of keys suitable for public key encryption.

- One key of the pair is stored in the clear, while the other is stored encrypted with the login password of the user.

- Any two entities registered in the database can deduce a unique DES key for mutual authentication.

5.8   GLOBAL NAME SERVICE (GNS)

5.8.1 Overview

- A name service maps a name for an entity (an individual, organization, or facility) into a set of labelled properties, each of which is a string.

- The Global Name Service (GNS) accomplishes name services for billions of names distributed throughout the world.

- It addresses the problems of high availability, large size, continuing evolution, fault isolation and lack of global trust.

- A Global Name Service (GNS) is designed and implemented to provide facilities for resource location, mail addressing, and authentication in a distributed computing system.

- GNS can be used in an inter-network to support a naming database that may extend to include the names of millions of computers and eventually email addressed for billions of users.

- GNS also supports that the naming database is likely to have a long lifetime, that it must continue to operate effectively while it grows from small to large scale and while the network on which it is based evolves.

The Design Objectives for GNS are as Following:

- Large size, to handle an essentially arbitrary number of names and serve an arbitrary number of administrative organizations.
- Long life, during which many changes will occur in the organization of the name space and the component that implement the service.
- High availability, because the system can't work when the name service is broken.
- Fault isolation, so that local failures don't cause the entire service to fail.
- Tolerance of mistrust, since a large-scale service won't have any component which is trusted by all the clients.

GNS implies a hierarchical system to accomplish the requirements. Hierarchy is the fundamental method for accommodating growth and isolating faults.

5.8.2 Name Space Architecture

- Global name services can be divided into two levels. At the client level there are hierarchical names and their values, with operations for reading and updating them, and facilities for protection and authentication.
- The naming database which is distributed and replicated is invisible at this level.
- At the administrative level the copies of the database are visible, together with the mechanisms for locating copies and keeping them synchronized.

1. Directory Tree and Value Tree Structure

- Names in GNS have two parts: <directory name, value name>. The first part identifies a directory; the second refers to a value tree, or some portion of a value tree. GNS manages a naming database that is composed of a tree of directories holding names and values.
- Directories are named by multi-part pathnames referred to a root, or relative to a working directory, by which it can be reached from its parent. Each directory is also assigned an integer, which serves as a unique Directory Identifier (DI).
- The arcs of the tree are called Directory References (DRs). A DR is the value of the name; it consists simply of the DI for the child directory. Thus a directory can be named relative to a root by a path name called its full name (FN).
- A directory contains a list of names and references. The values stored at the leaves of the directory tree are organized to into the value trees, so that the attributes associated with names can be structured values.
- An arc of the value tree carries a label (L), which is just a string, written next to the arc in the Fig. 5.7.
- A node carries a Time-Stamp (TS), represented by a number, and a mark which is either present or absent. A path through the tree is defined by a sequence of labels (L*). For the value of the path, there are three cases:

> If the path *P//* ends in a leaf that is an only child, we say that *l* is the value of *P*.
>
> If the path *P//li* ends in a leaf that is not an only child, and its siblings are labeled *l1... ln*, we say that the set {*l1... ln*} is the value of *P*.
>
> If the path *P* does not end in a leaf, we say that the sub-tree rooted in the node where it ends is the value of *P*.

- An update to a directory makes the node at the end of a given path present or absent. The update is time-stamped, and a later time-stamp takes precedence over an earlier one with the same path.

- Iits purpose is to allow the tree to be updated concurrently from a number of places without any prior synchronization.

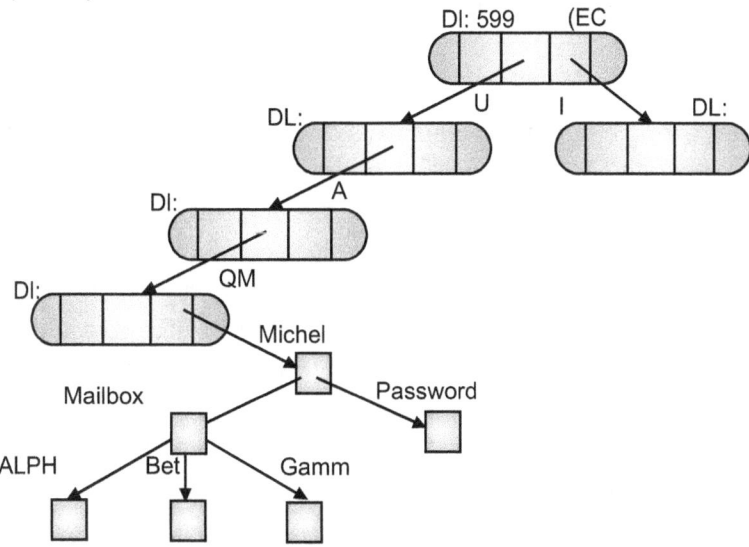

Fig. 5.7 : GNS directory tree and value tree for user Peter.Smith

2. Access Control and Authentication

- Access control is based on the notion of a principal, which is an entity that can be authenticated by its knowledge of some encryption key (which acts as its password). A principal is identified either by a full name or, in case the root of the full name is not trusted, by a relative name, a path through the directory tree starting at the target directory and using '..' to denote the parent.

- Each directory has an access control function which maps a principal and a path into a set of rights drawn from {read, write, test}.

- Each of the operations provided by the name service requires the principal that invokes it to have certain rights to the nodes involved in the operation. For the convenience of the users, the access control function is defined by a set of triples (principal pattern, path pattern, rights).

- Authentication is based on the use of encryption to provide a secure channel between the caller of an operation and its implementor.
- A directory has an authentication function af, which is a mapping from keys to principals; it accepts a message encrypted with key k as coming from principal af(k).
- Each directory has a few values for which afis defined by some external means (such as a courier). In particular, there is a secure channel for each parent-child link; the parent's afmaps this channel's key to the child's name, and the child's afmaps it to.
- The authentication function can be extended by a certificate, a message encrypted with key k' which says, "Key k authenticates the principal whose name is N relative to me." This allows af(k) to be defined as af(k')/N.
- A sequence of certificates can establish a secure channel between any two directories; the relative names to which the directories map the channel will depend on what other directories participated in setting it up.

Administrative Level

- The client sees a single name service and is not concerned with the actual machine on which it is implemented or the replication of the database that makes it reliable.
- The administrator allocates resources to the implementation of the service and reconfigures it to deal with long term failures. Instead of a single directory, she sees a set of Directory Copies (DC), each one stored on a different server (S) machine.
- A Directory Reference (DR) now includes not just the DI of the directory, but also a list of the servers that store its DCs. A lookup can try one or more of the servers to find a copy from which to read.

1. **Replication**

- The directory tree is partitioned and stored in many servers, with each partition replicated in several servers.
- The consistency of the tree is maintained in the face of two or more concurrent updates - for example, two users may simultaneously attempt to create entries with the same name, and only one should succeed.
- Replicated directories present a second consistency problem: this is addressed by an asynchronous update distribution algorithm that ensures eventual consistency, but with no guarantee that all copies are always current.
- This level of consistency is considered satisfactory for the purpose. The copies are kept approximately but not exactly the same. Every directory copy keeps latest updated time stamps called last Sweep time. Each copy also has a next TS value, the next time-stamp it will assign to a new update; this value can only increase. An update originates at one DC, and is initially recorded there.
- The basic method for spreading updates to all the copies is a sweep operation, which visits every DC, collects a complete set of updates, and then writes this set back to every DC. The sweep has a timestamp sweep TS. Before it reads from a DC it increases that

DC's next TS to sweep TS; this ensures that the sweep collects all updates earlier than sweep TS. After it writes back to a DC, it sets that DC's last Sweep to sweep TS. In order to speed up the spreading of updates, any DC may send some updates to any other DC in a message.

- The set of servers in the DR stored in the parent is not suitable, because it is too difficult to ensure that the sweep gets a complete set if the directory's parent or the set of DCs is changing during the sweep.

- To obtain the set of Dcs reliably, all the DCs are linked into a ring, directed by arrows. Each arrow represents the name of the server to which it points. The sweep starts at any DC and follows the arrows; if it eventually reaches the starting point, then it has found a complete set of DCs.

- Of course, this operation need not be done sequentially; given a hint about the contents of the set, say from the parent DR, the sweep can visit all the DCs and read out the ring pointers in parallel. DCs can be added or removed by straightforward splicing of the ring.

- If a server fails permanently, or if the set of servers is partitioned by a network failure that lasts for a long time, the ring must be reformed. In the process, an update will be lost if it originated in a server that is not in the new ring and has not been distributed.

- Reforming the ring is done by starting a new epoch for the directory and building a new ring from scratch, using the DR or information provided by the administrator about which servers should be included.

- An epoch is identified by a time-stamp, and the most recent epoch that has ever had a complete ring is the one that defines the contents of the directory.

- Once the new epoch's ring has been successfully completed, the ring pointers for older epochs can be removed.

- Since starting a new epoch may change the database, it is never done automatically, but must be controlled by an administrator. The servers are themselves named in the database, by Server Names (SN) that are simply full names.

- The value of a SN is a unique Server Identifier (SI) and the network address of the server.

5.8.3 Scalability of GNS

- The structure of the name space may change during the time to reflect changes in organizational structures.

- The service should accommodate changes in the names of the individuals, organizations and groups that it holds; and changes in the naming structure such as those that occur when one company is taken over by another.

- In this section, we shall focus on those features of the design that enable it to accommodate such changes.

- To accommodate the growth and change in the structure of the naming database, GNS adopts merging trees under new root to support the growth and moving directory trees to restructure the name database.

- Although GNS successfully addresses needs for scalability and reconfigurability, the solution adopted for merging and moving results in a requirement for a database (the table of well-known directories) that must be replicated at every node.
- In a largescale network, reconfigurations may occur at any level, and this table could grow to a large size, conflicting with the scalability goal.

5.8.4 Caching

- The potentially large naming database and the scale of the distributed environment make name lookup not likely to be especially cheap.
- Indeed, if the servers that store the name or its parent directories are far away in the network, lookup may be quite expensive. It is very desirable for a client to be able to cache the result of a lookup for a while, rather than repeating it every time the value is needed.
- GNS make use of caching essentially and render it extremely difficult to maintain complete consistency between all copies of a database entry.
- Since it is impractical for the service to keep track of clients that are doing this and notify them when there is a change, the cache consistency strategy relies on the assumption that updates to the database will be infrequent and that slow dissemination of update is acceptable.
- In other words, caching must be paid for either by enforcing a slow rate of change on the naming database, or by tolerating some inaccuracy in the cached information which requires no work from the service, since clients can detect and recover from the use of out-of-date naming data.
- The enforcement mechanism is an Expiration Time (TX) on entries in the data base, and in particular on parent-child arcs in the directory tree and on links.
- The rule is: an arc or link may not be changed until its TX has expired, except that an arc may be deleted by a subtree move if it is replaced by a link to the moved sub-tree.
- One important client for caching is the name service itself which will make use of caching directory names from the root to avoid access bottleneck.
- Authentication is another client of caching, since "key authenticates principal" is the result of a name lookup.

5.9   X.500 DIRECTORY SERVICE

5.9.1 Overview

- X.500 is a directory service. It is primarily used to satisfy descriptive queries and to discover the names and attributes of other users or system resources.
- The uses for such a service are directly analogous to the use of telephone directories, such as 'white pages' access to obtain a user's electronic mail address or a 'yellow pages' query aimed at obtaining the names and telephone numbers of garages specializing in

the repair of a particular make of car, to the use of the directory to access personal details such as job roles, dietary habits or even photographic images of the individuals.

- The ITU and ISO standards organizations have defined the X.500 Directory Service as a network service intended to meet these requirements.

- The standard refers to it as a service for access to information about hardware and software services and devices. X.500 is specified as an application level service in the Open System Interconnection set of standards, but its design does not depend to any significant extent on the other OSI standards, and it can be viewed as a design for a general-purpose directory service.

5.9.2 X.500 Service Architecture

1. Objects and Entries

- The data stored in X.500 servers is organized in a tree structure with named nodes in which a wide range of attributes are stored at each node in the tree and access is not just by name but also by searching for entries with any required combination attributes.

- An entry holds information about an object of interest to users of the Directory.

- These objects might typically be associated with, or be some facet of, real world things such as information processing systems or telecommunications equipment or people.

- Directory objects, and hence entries, can have a one-to-one many-to-one or one-to-many relationship with real world things.

- For example, a directory object/entry may be a mailing list containing the names of many real people (one-to-many correspondence).

- Alternatively, a real person may be represented in the directory as both a residential person object/entry and an organizational person object/entry (many-to-one correspondence). In the latter case, the organizational person directory entry would hold information that is relevant to describing the person in their working environment, holding their office room number, internal telephone extension number, electronic mail address, and the department etc., the residential person directory entry would describe the person in their residential capacity, holding their home postal address and home telephone number etc.

2. The Structure of the DIB

- The complete set of all information held in the directory is known as the Directory Information Base (DIB) which consists of entries.

- These entries held in the DIB are structured in a hierarchical manner, using a tree structure, which is similar to a structure chart used by most hierarchical organizations.

- The DIB can therefore be represented as a Directory Information Tree (DIT), in which each node in the tree represents a directory entry.
- There is intended to be single integrated DIB containing information provided by organizations throughout the world with portions of the DIB located in the individual X.500 servers.
- As shown in the Fig. 5.8 (a), the servers are called Directory Service Agents (DSAs). Clients, named formally as Directory User Agents (DUAs), access the directory by visiting any servers and issuing access requests.
- If the data required are not in the segment of the DIB held by the contacted server, it will either invoke other servers or resolve the query or redirect the client to another server.

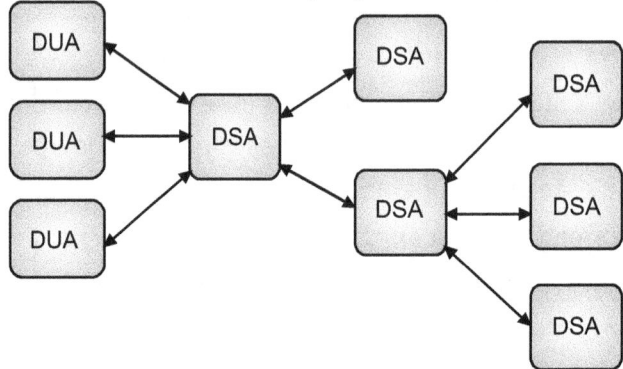

Fig. 5.8 (a) :The Structure of the DIB

3. Naming Entries

- Each object entry known to the directory is distinguished from all other objects by its name. Thus each entry is said to have a distinguished name (DN), the full name of an entry corresponds to a path through the DIT from the root of the tree to the entry.
- In addition to full or absolute names, a DUA can establish a context, which includes a base node, and then use shorter relative names that give the path from the base node to the named entry, which is called Relative Distinguished Name (RDN). An entry's RDN uniquely identifies it from all of its peers. Since each RDN is guaranteed to be unique below any particular non-leaf node, each entry is guaranteed to have a unique DN. Fig. 5.8 (b) shows the portion of the directory information tree that includes the University of Gormenghast, Great Britain. An example of an entry under Pat King is shown here:
- Country = Great Britain@organization = University of Gormenghast@organizationalUnit = Department of Computer Science@organizationalUnit= Departmental Staff@person = Pat King

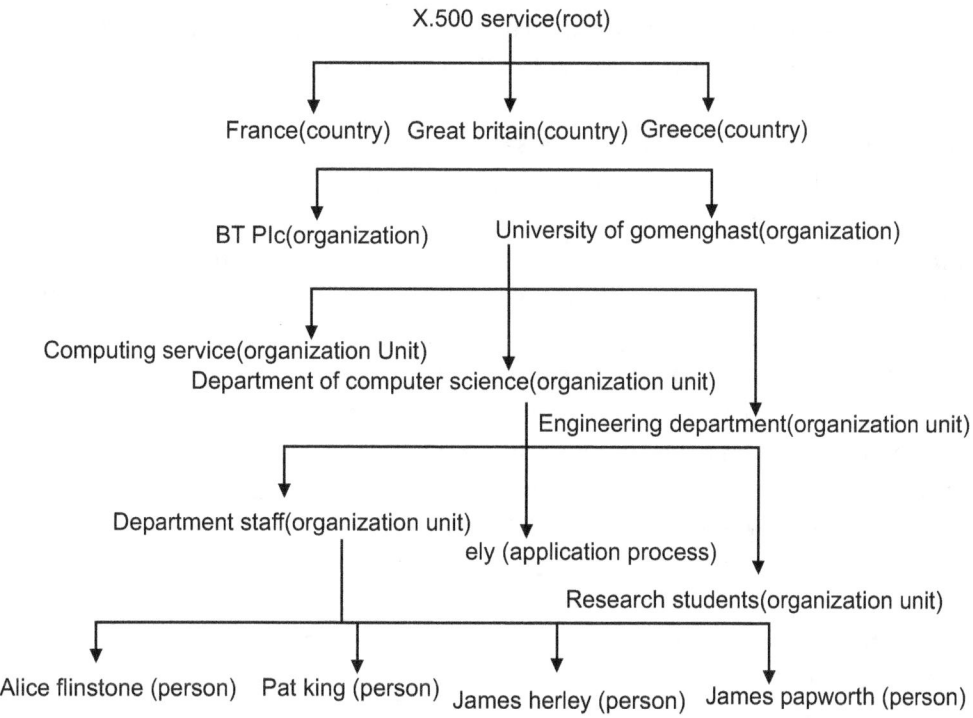

Fig. 5.8(b) : Directory information tree

5.9.3 Access Methods in X.500

1. Read

- An absolute or relative name (a domain name in X.500 terminology) for an entry is given, together with a list of attributes to be read.
- The DSA locates the named entry by navigating in the DIT, passing requests to other DSA servers where it does not hold relevant parts of the tree. It retrieves the required attributes and returns them to the client.

2. Search

- This is an attribute-based access request. A base name and a filter expression are supplied as arguments.
- The base name specifies the node in the DIT from which the search is to commence; the filter expression is a Boolean expression that is to be evaluated for every node below the base node.
- The filter specifies a search criterion: a logical combination of tests on the values of any of the attributes in an entry. The search command returns a list of names for all of the entries below the base node for which the filter evaluates to TRUE.

5.9.4 X.500 and LDAP

1. Introduction

- LDAP (Lightweight Directory Access Protocol) arose from initial experience with deploying X.500 directory services on the Internet in 1989-91.

- The goal of the original LDAP was to give simple lightweight access to an X.500 directory, to facilitate the development of X.500 DUAs and use of X.500 for a wide variety of applications

LDAP is 'simple', relative to X.500, because:

- While the LDAP PDUs are based on those from X.500, elements of the protocol have been modified to produce a protocol that is significantly simpler.
- Names and attributes use text encoding. Names and attributes are pervasive in the protocol. In X.500, these have a complex ASN.1 encoding, whereas in LDAP they are given a simple string encoding. This is particularly helpful for applications that do not need to handle the detailed structure of names or attributes.
- Mapping directly onto TCP/IP. LDAP maps directly onto TCP/IP (the Internet transport layer), and removes the need for a non-trivial amount of OSI protocol.
- LDAP relies on X.500 for the service definition and distributed operations. Because LDAP is defined as an access protocol to X.500 and not as a complete directory service, it is possible to specify LDAP very concisely. The detailed service definitions, while often intuitive from the protocol, are formally specified in X.500. Where the directory service is provided by more than one Directory Server, the procedures for doing this are not defined by LDAP.

2. X.500 and LDAP

The most important thing to understand about X.500 and LDAP is that they have more in common than different. The things that they have in common relate to the information model and standard services, which are absolutely central to both X.500 and LDAP. This section describes the common core:

- **Hierarchical Names:** LDAP and X.500 both define a hierarchical directory with hierarchical names.
- **Typed Name Components:** Name components are typed. This contrasts with other schemes which have typeless names, such as the domain name scheme. It is straightforward to represent typeless names in a typed naming scheme.
- **Typed Objects:** Objects are represented as Entries in an X.500/LDAP directory. These entries are given a type (or types), known as the object class, by use of an Object Class attribute. Typical object classes are People, Organizations, and Computers. X.500 and LDAP share object class definitions.
- **Typed Attributes:** Information within objects is held as a set of typed attributes For example there may be a 'telephone number' attribute with one or more values. Many attributes are encoded as strings. Other attributes have an encoding which is inferred from the attribute type. This can be used for non-string data such as pictures or to handle structured information. X.500 and LDAP share attribute type definitions
- **Directory Operations:** X.500 and LDAP share a common set of operations to access and manage data in the directory. These are: read; compare; search; add; delete; modify entry; modify RDN.

5.10 DISTRIBUTED MULTIMEDIA SYSTEM

5.10.1 Characteristics of Multimedia Data

- Multimedia Streams are Time-Based (or Isochronous)
- Timed data elements in audio and video flow describe the content of the stream. The times at which the values are played or recorded influence the validity of the data.
- Hence systems that support multimedia applications need to preserve the timing when they handle continuous data.
- Multimedia streams are often bulky.

5.10.2 Quality of Service

- When multimedia applications run in networks of personal computers, they fight for resources at the workstations operating the applications (processor cycles, bus cycles, buffer capacity) and in the networks (physical transmission links, switches, gateways).
- Workstations and networks may have to maintain several multimedia and conventional applications. There is fight between the multimedia and conventional applications, between different multimedia applications and even between the media streams within individual applications.
- The key feature of these resources allocation schemes is that they handle increases in demand by spreading the available resources more thinly between the competing tasks. Round-robin and other best-efforts methods for sharing processor cycles and network bandwidth cannot meet the needs of multimedia applications.
- As we have seen, the timely processing and transmission of multimedia streams is crucial for them. Late delivery is valueless.
- In order to achieve timely delivery, applications need guarantees that the necessary resources will be allocated and scheduled at the required times.
- The management and allocation of resources to provide such guarantees is referred to as quality of service management. the most commonly used abstract architecture for multimedia software, in which continuously flowing streams of media data elements (video frames, audio samples) are processed by a collection of processes and transferred between the processes by interprocess connections.
- The processes produce, transform and consume continuous streams of multimedia data. The connections link the processes in a sequence from a source of media elements to a target, at which it is rendered or consumed.
- The connections between the processes may be implemented by networked connections or by in-memory transfers when processes reside on the same machine.
- For the elements of multimedia data to arrive at their target on time, each process must be allocated adequate CPU time, memory capacity and network bandwidth to perform its designated task and must be scheduled to use the resources sufficiently frequently to enable it to deliver the data elements in its stream to the next process on time.

- The QoS manager's two main subtasks: Quality of service negotiation: The application indicates its resource requirements to the QoS manager.

- The QoS manager evaluates the feasibility of meeting the requirements against a database of the available resources and current resource commitments and gives a positive or negative response.

- If it is negative, the application may be reconfigured to use reduced resources, and the process is repeated.

Admission Control: If the result of the resource evaluation is positive, the requested resources are reserved and the application is given a resource contract, stating the resources that have been reserved. The contract includes a time limit. The application is then free to run. If it changes its resource requirements it must notify the QoS manager. If the requirements decrease, the resources released are returned to the database as available resources. If they increase, a new round of negotiation and admission control is initiated.

Three parameters are of interest when it comes to processing and transporting multimedia streams:

Bandwidth: The bandwidth of a multimedia stream or component is the rate at which data flows through it.

Latency: Latency is the time required for an individual data element to move through a stream from the source to the destination. This may vary depending on the volume of other data in the system and other characteristics of the system load. This variation is termed jitter – formally, jitter is the first derivative of the latency.

Loss Rate

QOS manager Tasks

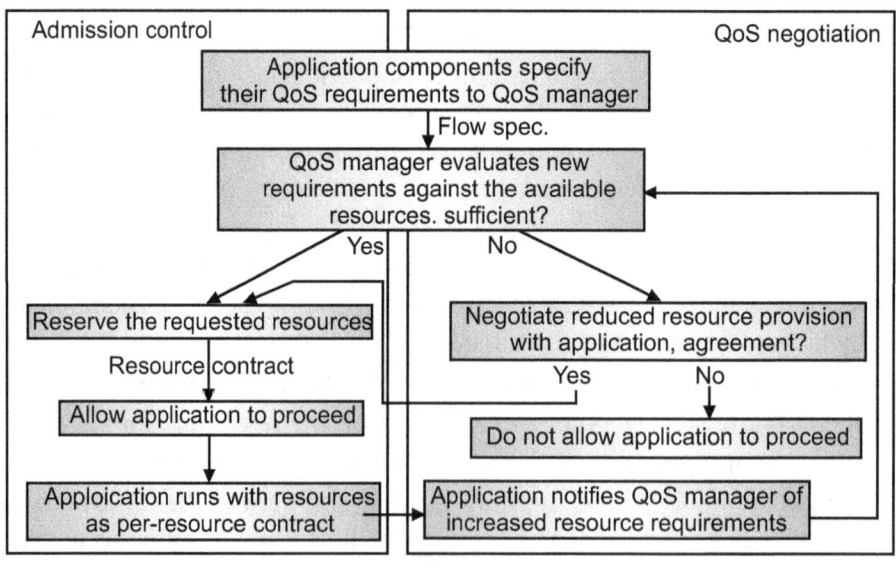

Fig. 5.9

5.10.3 Resource Management

- Processes need to have resources allocated to them according to their precedence. A resource scheduler verify the priority of processes based on certain criteria.

- Traditional CPU schedulers in time-sharing systems often base their priority assignments on receptiveness and fairness: I/O-intensive tasks get high priority to guarantee fast response to user requests, CPU-bound tasks get lower priorities, and overall, processes in the same class are treated equally.

- Both criteria remain valid for multimedia systems, but the existence of deadlines for the delivery of individual multimedia data elements changes the nature of the scheduling problem. Real-time scheduling algorithms can be applied to this problem, as discussed below.

- As multimedia systems have to handle both discrete and continuous media, it becomes a dispute to provide sufficient service to time-dependent streams without causing starvation of discrete-media access and other interactive applications.

- Scheduling methods need to be applied to (and coordinated for) all resources that affect the performance of a multimedia application.

- In a typical scenario, a multimedia stream would be retrieved from disk and then sent through a network to a target station, where it is synchronized with a stream coming from another source and finally displayed.

- The resources required in this example include disk, network and CPU resources as well as memory and bus bandwidth on all systems involved.

- **Fair Scheduling :** If several streams compete for the same resource, it becomes necessary to consider fairness and to prevent ill-behaved streams taking too much bandwidth. A straightforward approach ensuring fairness is to apply round-robin scheduling to all streams in the same class. All basic round-robin schemes assign the same bandwidth to each stream. To take the individual bandwidth of streams into account, the bit-by-bit scheme can be extended so that for certain streams a larger number of bits can be transmitted per cycle. This method is called weighted fair queuing.

- **Real-Time Scheduling :** Several real-time scheduling algorithms have been developed to meet the CPU scheduling needs of applications such as avionics industrial process control. Assuming that the CPU resources have not been overallocated (which is the task of the QoS manager), they assign CPU timeslots to a set of processes in a manner that ensures that they complete their tasks on time.

- Traditional real-time scheduling methods suit the model of regular continuous multimedia streams very well. Earliest-deadline-first (EDF) scheduling has almost become a synonym for these methods.

5.10.4 Stream Adaption

- Whenever a certain QoS cannot be assured or can be assured only with a certain probability, an application needs to adapt to changing QoS levels, adjusting its performance accordingly.

- For continuous-media streams, the adjustment translates into different levels of media presentation quality.

- The simplest form of adjustment is to drop pieces of information. If there is insufficient bandwidth and data is not dropped, the delay of a stream will increase over time.

- For non-interactive applications this may be acceptable, although it can eventually lead to buffer overflows as data is accumulated between the source and sink. For conferencing and other interactive applications, increasing delays are not acceptable, or must exist only for a short period.

- If a stream is behind its assigned playout time, its playout rate should be increased until it gets back on schedule: while a stream is delayed, frames should be output as soon as they are available.

5.10.4.1 Scaling

- If adaptation is performed at the target of a stream, the load on any bottleneck in the system is not decreased and the overload situation persists.

- It is useful to adapt a stream to the bandwidth available in the system before it enters a bottleneck resource in order to resolve contention. This is known as scaling. Scaling is best applied when live streams are sampled. For stored streams, how easy it is to generate a downgraded stream depends on the encoding method.

- Scaling may be too cumbersome if the entire stream has to be decompressed and encoded again just for scaling purposes.

- Scaling algorithms are media-dependent, although the overall scaling approach is the same to subsample a given signal. For audio information, such subsampling can be achieved by reducing the rate of audio sampling.

For video, the following scaling methods are appropriate:

Temporal Scaling: Reduces the resolution of the video stream in the time domain by decreasing the number of video frames transmitted within an interval. Temporal scaling is best suited to video streams in which individual frames are self-contained and can be accessed independently.

Spatial Scaling: Reduces the number of pixels of each image in a video stream. For spatial scaling, hierarchical arrangement is ideal because the compressed video is immediately available in various resolutions. Therefore the video can be transferred over the network using different resolutions without recoding each picture before finally transmitting it. JPEG and MPEG-2 support different spatial resolutions of images and are well suited to this kind of scaling.

Frequency Scaling: Modifies the compression algorithm applied to an image. This results in some loss of quality, but in a typical picture compression can be increased significantly before a reduction of image quality becomes visible.

Amplitudinal Scaling: Reduces the colour depths for each image pixel. This scaling method is in fact used in H.261 encodings to arrive at a constant throughput as image content varies.

Colour-space scaling: Reduces the number of entries in the colour space. One way to realize colour-space scaling is to switch from colour to greyscale presentation.

5.10.4.2 Filtering

- As scaling modifies a stream at the source, it is not always suitable for applications that involve several receivers: when a bottleneck occurs on the route to one target, this target sends a scale-down message to the source and all targets receive the degraded quality, although some would have no problem in handling the original stream.

- Filtering is a method that provides the best possible QoS to each target by applying scaling at each relevant node on the path from the source to the target

5.10.5 Case Study

5.10.5.1 BitTorrent

- BitTorrent [www.bittorrent.com] is a popular peer-to-peer file-sharing application designed particularly for downloading large files (including video files).

- It is not intended for the real-time streaming of content but rather for the initial downloading of files to be played back later.

- The principal design feature in BitTorrent is the splitting of files into fixed-sized chunks and the successive availability of chunks at various sites across the peer-to-peer network.

- Clients can then download a number of chunks in parallel from different sites, reducing the burden on any one particular site to service the download (remembering that BitTorrent relies on the capabilities of ordinary user machines and also that there may be many simultaneous requests for popular files).

- In more detail, the BitTorrent protocol operates as follows. When a file is made available in BitTorrent, a .torrent file is created that holds metadata associated with that file including:

- The name and length of the file;

- The location of a tracker (specified as a URL), which is a centralized server that manages downloads of that particular file;

- A checksum associated with each chunk, generated using the SHA-1 hashing algorithm, that enables content to be verified following download.

- The use of trackers is a compromise against pure peer-to-peer principles, but this allows the system to easily maintain the above information in a centralized manner.

- Trackers are responsible for keeping track of the download status associated with a particular file. To understand the information held by the tracker, it is necessary to stand back and consider the lifecycle of a given file.

- Any peer with a complete version of a file (in terms of all its chunks) is known as a seeder in BitTorrent terminology. For example, the peer that initially creates the filewill provide the initial seed for the file distribution.

- Peers that want to download a file are known as leechers, and a given leecher at any given time will contain a number of chunks associated with that file. Once a leecher downloads all the chunks associated with a file, it can become a seeder for subsequent downloads.

- In this way, files spread virally through the network, with the spread stimulated by demand. Based on this, the tracker maintains information about the current state of downloads of a given file in terms of the associated seeders and leechers.

- The tracker together with the associated seeders and leechers in BitTorrent are referred to as the torrent (or swarm) for that file. When a peer wants to download a file, it first contacts the tracker and is given a partial view of the torrent in terms of a set of peers that can support the download.

- After that, the job of the tracker is done it does not get involved in subsequent scheduling of downloads. This is a matter for the various peers involved and hence this part of the protocol is decentralized.

- Chunks are then requested and transmitted to the requesting peer in any order.

- BitTorrent, along with many peer-to-peer protocols, relies on peers to behave as good citizens, contributing to as well as taking from the system. Crucially, the system has an inbuilt incentive mechanism to reward such cooperation, known as the tit-for-tat mechanism.

- Informally, this approach gives preference to downloading peers who have previously or who are currently uploading to that site. As well as acting as an incentive mechanism, tit-for-tat also encourages patterns of communication where downloading and uploading proceed concurrently, making optimum use of bandwidth.

- In more detail, a given peer supports downloading from n simultaneous peers by unchoking these peers. Decisions of which peers to unchoke are based on rolling calculations of download rates from these peers with this decision revisited every 10seconds. The algorithm also applies optimistic unchoking on a random peer every 30 seconds in order to allow new peers to participate and establish their credentials.

- Note that the incentive scheme has been the subject of significant research, with alternative schemes also proposed for example, see Sirivianos et al.

- BitTorrent couples this with a rarest first policy for scheduling downloads whereby a peer will prioritize the chunk that is rarest amongst its set of connected peers, ensuring that chunks that are not yet readily available will spread rapidly.

REVIEW QUESTIONS

1. How X.500 service implemented ?
2. What is naming service X.500 ?
3. How distributed file system differ from file system used for centralized time sharing system ?
4. Draw and Explain NFS architecture.
5. Global Name Service.
6. Write a short note on :
   (i) DNS (ii) X.500 (iii) NFS (iv) GNS

UNIVERSITY QUESTIONS

May 2012

1. List and explain the forms of transparency which have been partially or wholly addressed by current distributed file systems.   **[5]**
2. Describe basic NFS architecture for Unix system with the help of neat diagram.   **[8]**
3. What is naming service X.500?   **[5]**
4. What are different requirements and pitfalls in the design of distributed file system ? Explain any four requirements.   **[8]**
5. How does mounting of a remote file system take place in NFS ? Describe the functionality of an auto-mounter in NFS.   **[5]**

Oct. 2012

6. What file sharing semantics is used in your network or distributed file system?   **[8]**
7. Compare : Coda and xFS distributed file systems.   **[8]**
8. What is naming service X.500?   **[8]**
9. How does mounting of a remote file system take place in NFS? Describe the functionality of an auto-mounter in NFS.   **[8]**

May 2013

10. How does Distributed File System differ from a file system used for a centralized time sharing system?   **[8]**
11. Describe Sun NFS with its architecture and components for Unix system with the help of neat diagram.   **[8]**
12. How does client side caching is used in NFS? Discuss the role of RPC in NFS.   **[8]**
13. Discuss the issues of improving availability of files in a Distributed File System. **[8]**
    Describe various methods of replica creation in Distributed File System. (You can consider NFS as an example DFS.)

Dec. 2013

14. Discuss different Distributed File System requirements.   **[8]**
15. Explain the architecture of NFS in detail.   **[8]**
16. Discuss automounting and naming of NFS.   **[8]**
17. Write a detailed note on DNS.   **[8]**

May 2014

18. What is automounting? Explain a simple automounter for NFS and how it help to improve the performance and scalability of NFS?   **[8]**
19. Explain in brief basic NFS architecture for UNIX system.   **[8]**

Dec. 2014

20. How communication does takes place in CODA File System? Describe the implementation and resolution of CODA File identifier.   **[9]**
21. Explain file service architecture in detail.   **[8]**
22. What is Distributed File System? Explain different types of services provided by Distributed File System.   **[9]**

May 2015

24. How does the NFS Automounter help to improve the performance and scalability of NFS ?   **[9]**
25. Write a short note on :   **[9]**
    (i) Global name serice
    (ii) X.500 directory service
26. Explain following term with respect to name entities :   **[9]**
    (i)   Names
    (ii) Identifies
    (iii) Addresses
    (iv) Name spaces
27. Explain synchronization and naming in NFS.   **[9]**
28. What are different file sharing semantics used in distributed file system?   **[9]**

✠ ✠ ✠

SECURITY IN DISTRIBUTED SYSTEMS

6.1 INTRODUCTION TO SECURITY

- Security in distributed systems divided into two parts. One part, the communication between users or processes, probably residing on different machines.
- The major method for ensuring secure communication is that of a secure channel.
- The other part concerns authorization, which deals with ensuring that a process gets only those access rights to the resources in a distributed system it is entitled to.

6.2 SECURITY THREATS, POLICIES, AND MECHANISMS

- Security in computer systems is that we attempt to protect the services and data it offers against security threats. There are four types of security threats to consider :

6.2.1 Security Threat : Interception

- The concept of interception refers to the situation that an unauthorized party has gained access to a service or data.
- A typical example of interception is where communication between two parties has been overheard by someone else.
- Interception also happens when data are illegally copied, for example, after breaking into a person's private directory in a file system.

6.2.2 Security Threat : Interruption

- Interruption refers to the situation in which services or data become unavailable, unusable, destroyed.
- Denial of service attacks by which someone maliciously attempts to make a service inaccessible to other parties is a security threat that classifies as interruption.

6.2.3 Security Threat : Modification

- It is unauthorized changing of data or tampering with a service so that it no longer adheres to its original specifications.

6.2.4 Security Threat : Fabrication

- It is the situation in which extra data or activity are generated that would normally not exist. For example, an intruder may attempt to add an entry into a password file or database.

Important security mechanisms are:

6.2.5 Encryption

- Encryption is fundamental to computer security. Encryption transforms data into something an attacker cannot understand. Encryption provides a means to implement data confidentiality. In addition, encryption allows us to check whether data have been modified. It thus also provides support for integrity checks.

6.2.6 Authentication

- Authentication is used to verify the claimed identity of a user, client, server, host, or other entity.
- Typically, users are authenticated by means of passwords, but there are many other ways to authenticate clients.

6.2.7 Authorization

- After a client has been authenticated, it is necessary to check whether that client is authorized to perform the action requested.

6.2.8 Auditing

- Auditing tools are used to trace which clients accessed what, and which way. Although auditing does not really provide any protection against security threats, audit logs can be extremely useful for the analysis of a security breach, and subsequently taking measures against intruders.

6.3 DESIGN ISSUES

6.3.1 Focus of Control

- When seeing the safety of an (possibly distributed) application, here are essentially three different approaches that can be followed.
- The first approach is to concentrate directly on the protection of the data that is associated with the application. For Example, Integrity constraints checked by database
- The second approach is to concentrate on protection by specifying exactly which operations may be invoked, and by whom, when certain data or resources are to be accessed. In this case. the focus of control is strongly related to access control mechanisms.
- A third approach is to focus directly on users by taking measures by which–only specific people have access to the application, irrespective of the operations they want to carry out. Eg denying access to the employees personal record.

6.4 CRYPTOGRAPHY

- Fundamental to security in distributed systems is the use of cryptographic techniques. The basic idea of applying these techniques is simple. Consider as Sender S wanting to transmit message m to a receiver R. To protect the message against security threats, the sender first encrypts it into an unintelligible messagem', and subsequently sends m' to R. R, in turn, must decrypt the received message into its original form m.

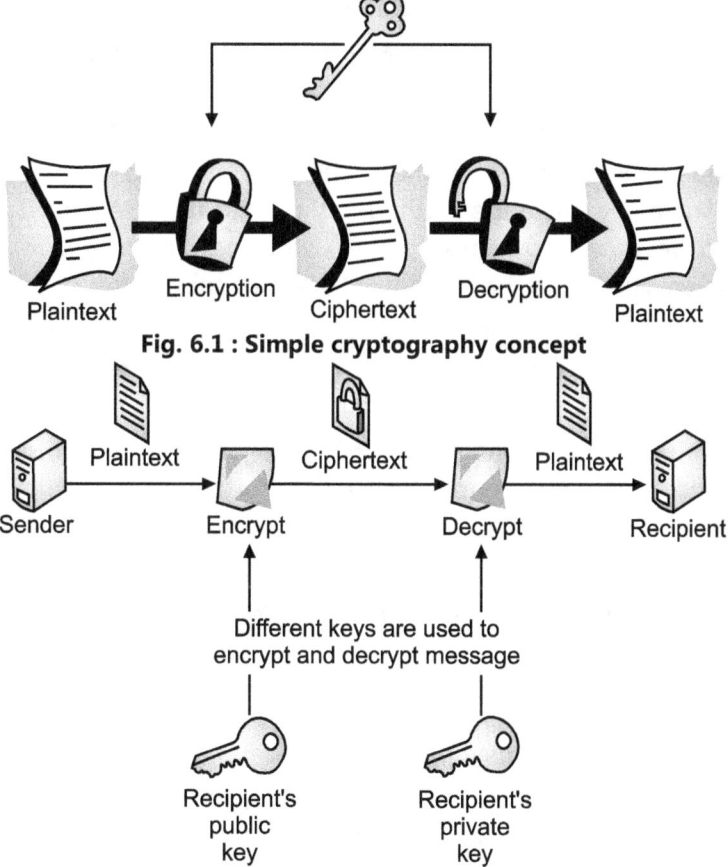

Fig. 6.1 : Simple cryptography concept

Fig. 6.2 : Simple cryptography concept

- As shown in Fig. 6.1 and 6.2, the sender uses the recipient's public key to convert plaintext to cipher text. The cipher text is sent and the recipient uses her private key to recover the plaintext.

- Only the person with the private key corresponding to the public key can decrypt the message, document, etc.

- This works because the two keys, although separate, are mathematically entwined. At a very high level, the RSA model uses prime numbers to create a public/private key set:

- Creation begins by selecting two extremely large prime numbers. They should be chosen at random and of similar length.

(a) The two prime numbers are multiplied together.

(b) The product becomes the public key.

(c) The two factors become the private key.

(d) There is more to asymmetric key creation, but this is close enough for our purposes.

- When someone uses the public key, or the product of the two primes, to encrypt a message, the recipient of the cipher text must know the two prime numbers that created it. If the primes were small, a brute force attack can find them.
- However, use of extremely large primes and today's computing power makes finding the private key through brute force unlikely.
- Consequently, we can use asymmetric keys to share symmetric keys, encrypt email, and various other processes where key sharing is necessary.
- The Diffie–Hellman key exchange method is similar to the RSA model and it was made public first. However, it allows two parties who know nothing about each other to establish a shared key. This is the basis of SSL and TLS security.
- An encrypted session key exchange occurs over an open connection. Once both parties to the session have the session key (also know as a shared secret), they establish a virtual and secure tunnel using symmetric encryption.
- So why not throw out symmetric encryption and use only asymmetric ciphers? First, symmetric ciphers are typically much stronger. Further, asymmetric encryption is far slower.
- So we have settled for symmetric ciphers for data center and other mass storage encryption and asymmetric ciphers for just about everything else.

6.5 SECURE CHANNELS

- We have often used the client–server model as a suitable way to establish a distributed system. In this model, servers may perhaps be distributed and replicated, but also act as clients with respect to other servers.
- When considering security in distributed systems, it is once again beneficial to think in terms of clients and servers.
- In particular, making a distributed system secure essentially boils down to two major issues.
- The first issue is how to make the communication between clients and servers secure. The second issue is that of authorization: once a server has accepted a request from a client, how can it find out whether that client is authorized to have that request carried out?
- The issue of protecting communication between clients and servers, can be thought of in terms of setting up a secure channel between communicating parties.
- A secure channel protects senders and receivers against interception, modification, and fabrication of messages. It does not also necessarily protect against interruption.
- Protecting messages against interceptions done by ensuring confidentiality: the secure channel ensures that its messages cannot be eavesdropped by intruders.
- Protecting against modification and fabrication by intruders is done through protocols for mutual authentication and message integrity

6.5.1 Authentication

6.5.1.1 Authentication Based on a Shared Secret Key

- Let us start by taking a look at an authentication protocol based on a secret key that is already shared between Alice and BobIn the description of the protocol, Alice and Bob are abbreviated by A and B, respectively, and their shared key is denoted as $K_{A,B}$'

- The protocol takes a common approach whereby one party challenges the other to a response that can be correct only if the other knows the shared secret key.

- Such solutions are also known as challenge–response protocols. the protocol proceeds as shown in Fig. 6.3.

- First, alice sends her identity to Bob (message1), indicating that she wants to set up a communication channel between the two.

- Bob subsequently sends a challenge R_B to Alice, shown as message 2. Such a challenge could take the form of a random number. Alice is required to encrypt the challenge with the secret key K– that she shares with Bob, and return the encrypted challenge to Bob. This response is shown as message 3 shown in Fig. 6.3

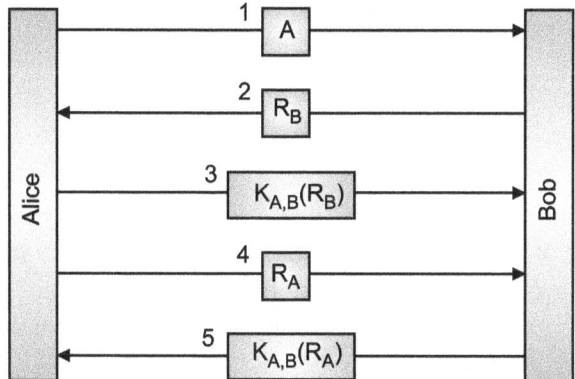

Fig. 6.3 : Authentication based on a shared secret key

- When Bob receives the response $K_{A,B}(R_B)$ to his challenge R_B, he can decrypt the message using the shared key again to see if it contains R_B. If so, he then knows that Alice is on the other side, for who else could have encrypted R_B with $K–t.B$ in the first place? In other words, Bob has now verified that he is indeed talking to Alice.

- However, note that Alice has not yet verified that it is indeed Bob on the other side of the channel. Therefore, she sends a challenge R.tt (message 4),which Bob responds to by returning ~.B(R.tt), shown as message 5. When Alice decrypts it with $K_{A,B}$ and sees her "R.tt, she knows she is talking to Bob.

6.5.1.2 Authentication Using a Key Distribution Center

- One of the problems with using a shared secret key for authentication is scalability.

- If a distributed system contains N hosts, and each host is required to share asecret key with each of the other N – 1 hosts, the system as a whole needs to manage N (N – 1)/2 keys, and each host has to manage N – I keys.

- For large *N*, this will lead to problems. An alternative is to use a centralized approach by means of a Key Distribution Center (KDC). This KDC shares a secret key with each of the hosts, but no pair of hosts is required to have a shared secret key as well. In other words, using a KDC requires that we manage *N* keys instead of *N* (*N* – 1)/2, which is clearly an improvement.

- If Alice wants to set up a secure channel with Bob, she can do so with the help of a (trusted) KDC. The whole idea is that the KDC hands out a key to both Alice and Bob that they can use for communication, shown in Fig. 6.4.

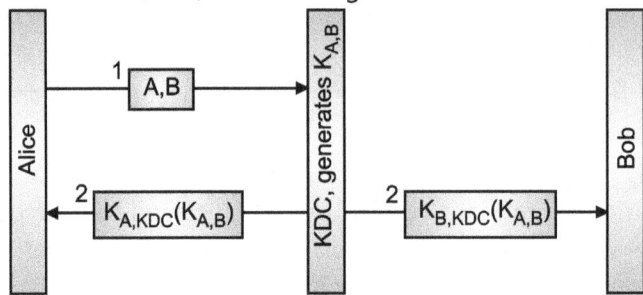

Fig. 6.4 : The principle of using a KDC

- Alice first sends a message to the KDC, telling it that she wants to talk to Bob. The KDC returns a message containing a shared secret key $K_{A,B}$ that she can use.

- The message is encrypted with the secret key $K_{A,KDC}$ that Alice shares with the KDC. In addition, the KDC sends $K_{A,B}$ also to Bob, but now encrypted with the secret key $K_{B, KDC}$ it shares with Bob.

- The main drawback of this approach is that Alice may want to start setting up a secure channel with Bob even before Bob had received the shared key from the KDC. In addition, the KDC is required to get Bob into the loop by passing him the key. These problems can be circumvented if the KDC just passes $K_{B,KDC}$ ($K_{A,B}$) back to Alice, and lets her take care of connecting to Bob. This leads to the protocol shown in Fig. 6.5.

- The message ~,KDC($K_{A,B}$) is also known as a ticket. It is Alice's job to pass this ticket to Bob. Note that Bob is still the only one that can make sensible use of the ticket, as he is the only one besides the KDC who knows how to decrypt the information it contains.

- The protocol shown in Fig. 6.5 is actually a variant of a well–known example of an authentication protocol using a KDC, known as the Needham–Schroeder authentication protocol, named after its inventors (Needham and Schroeder, 1978).

- A different variant of the protocol is being used in the Kerberos system, which we describe later.

- The Needham–Schroeder protocol, shown in Fig. 6.6, is a multiway challenge–response protocol and works as follows.

- When Alice wants to set up a secure channel with Bob, she sends a request to the KDC containing a challenge R_A, along with her identity A and, of course, that f Bob. The KDC responds by giving her the ticket $K_B, KDC(K_{A,B})$, along with the ecret key $K_{A,B}$ that she can subsequently share with Bob.

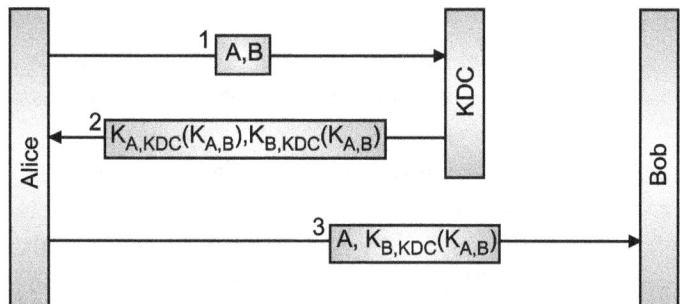

Fig. 6.5 : Using a ticket and letting Alice set up a connection to Bob

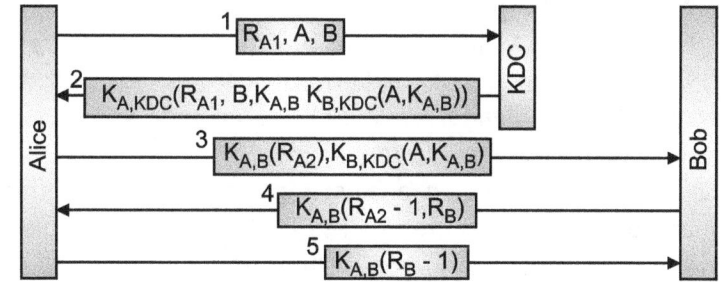

Fig. 6.6 : The Needham–Schroeder authentication protocol

- The challenge R_{A1} that Alice sends to the KDC along with her request to set p a channel to Bob is also known as a nonce. A nonce is a random number that is used only once, such as one chosen from a very large set. The main purpose of a nonce is to uniquely relate two messages to each other, in this case message 1 and message 2. In particular, by including R_{A1} again in message 2, Alice will know for sure that message 2 is sent as a response to message 1, and that it is not, for example, a replay of an older message.

- To understand the problem at hand, assume that we did not use nonces, and that Chuck has stolen one of Bob's old keys, say $K_B{\sim}{\sim}DC'$ In addition, Chuck has intercepted an old response $K_A.K_{DC}C_B, K_{A,B}, KB{\sim}fDC(A, K_{A,B}))$ that the KDC had returned to a previous request from Alice to talk to Bob. Meanwhile, Bob will have negotiated a new shared secret key with the KDC.

- However, Chuck patiently waits until Alice again requests to set up a secure channel with Bob. At that point, he replays the old response, and fools Alice into making her believe she is talking to Bob, because he can decrypt the ticket and prove he knows the shared secret key $K_{.4,B}'$ Clearly this is unacceptable and must be defended against.

- By including a nonce, such an attack is impossible, because replaying an older message will immediately be discovered. In particular, the nonce in the response message will not match the nonce in the original request.

- Message 2 also contains B, the identity of Bob. By including B, the KDC protects Alice against the following attack. Suppose that B was left out of message 2.

- In that case, Chuck could modify message 1 by replacing the identity of Bob with his own identity, say C. The KDC would think Alice wants to set up a secure channel to Chuck, and responds accordingly.

- As soon as Alice wants to contact Bob, Chuck intercepts the message and fools Alice into believing she is talking to Bob. By copying the identity of the other party from message 1 to message 2,

- Alice will immediately detect that her request had been modified.

- After the KDC has passed the ticket to Alice, the secure channel between Alice and Bob can be set up. Alice starts with sending message 3, which contains the ticket to Bob, and a challenge R_{A2} encrypted with the shared key $K_{A,B}$. that the KDC had just generated. Bob then decrypts the ticket to find the shared key, and returns a response $R_{A2} - 1$ along with a challenge R_B for Alice.

- The following remark regarding message 4 is in order. In general, by returning $R_{A2} - 1$ and not just R_{A2}, Bob not only proves he knows the shared secret key, but also that he has actually decrypted the challenge. Again, this ties message 4 to message 3 in the same way that the nonce ~ tied message 2 to message 1.

- The protocol is thus more protected against replays. However, in this special case, it would have been sufficient to just return $K_{A,B}(R_{A2},R_B)$, for the simple reason that this message has not yet been used anywhere in the protocol before. $K_{A,B}(R_{A2}, R_B)$ already proves that Bob has been capable of decrypting the challenge sent in message 3.

6.5.2 Message Integrity and Confidentiality

- Message integrity means that messages are protected against surrepitious modification; confidentiality ensures that messages cannot be intercepted and read by eavesdroppers. Confidentiality is easily established by simply encrypting a message before sending it.

6.5.2.1 Digital Signatures

- The unique association between message and its signature prevents that modifications to the message will go unnoticed. There are several ways to place digital signatures. One popular form is to use a public–key cryptosystem such as RSA, as shown in Fig. 6.7.

- When Alicesends a message m to Bob, she encrypts it with her private key K;., and sends it off to Bob.

- If she also wants to keep the message content a secret, she can use Bob's public key and send K/i(m,KA(m», which combines m and the version signed by Alice. When the message arrives at Bob, he can decrypt it using Alice's public key.

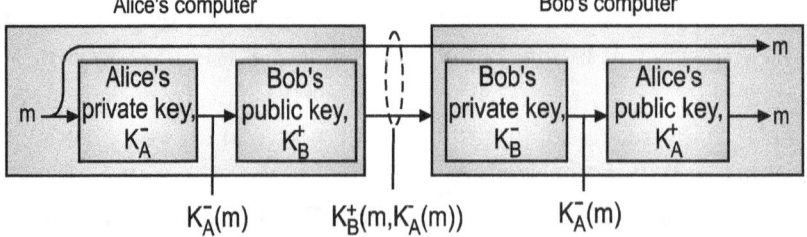

Fig. 6.7 : Digital signing a message using public–key cryptography

- If he can be assured that the public key is indeed owned by Alice, then decrypting the signed version of m and successfully comparing it to 111 can mean only that it came from Alice.
- Alice is protected against any malicious modifications to m by Bob, because Bob will always have to prove that the modified version of m was also signed by Alice.
- In other words, the decrypted message alone essentially never counts as proof.
- It is also in Bob's own interest to keep the signed version of m to protect himself against repudiation by Alice.
- There are a number of problems with this scheme, although the protocol in itself is correct. First, the validity of Alice's signature holds only as long as Alice's private key remains a secret. If Alice wants to bail out of the deal even after sending Bob her confirmation, she could claim. That her private key was stolen before the message was sent.
- Another problem occurs when Alice decides to change her private key. Doing so may in itself be not such a bad idea, as changing keys from time to time generally helps against intrusion. However, once Alice has changed her key, her statement sent to Bob becomes worthless. What may be needed in such cases is a central authority that keeps track of when keys are changed, in addition to using timestamps when signing messages.
- Another problem with this scheme is that Alice encrypts the entire message with her private key. Such an encryption may be costly in terms of processing requirements (or even mathematically infeasible as we assume that the message interpreted as a binary number is bounded by a predefined maximum), and is actually unnecessary. Recall that we need to uniquely associate a signature with a only specific message. A cheaper and arguably more elegant scheme is to use a message digest.
- As we explained, a message digest is a fixed–length bit string h that has been computed from an arbitrary–length message 111 by means of a cryptographic hash function H.
- If m is changed to m', its hash H (111') will be different from h = H (m) so that it can easily be detected that a modification has taken place.
- To digitally sign a message, Alice can first compute a message digest and subsequently encrypt the digest with her private keyNote that the message itself is sent as plaintext: everyone is allowed to read it. If confidentiality is required, then the message should also be encrypted with Bob's public key.

6.5.3 Secure Group Communication

- First, consider the problem of protecting communication between a group of N users against eavesdropping.
- To ensure confidentiality, a simple scheme is to let all group members share the same secret key, which is used to encrypt and decrypt all messages transmitted between group members.

- Because the secret key in this scheme is shared by all members, it is necessary that all members are trusted to indeed keep the key a secret.
- This prerequisite alone makes the use of a single shared secret key for confidential group communication more vulnerable to attacks compared to two–party secure channels.
- An alternative solution is to use a separate shared secret key between each pair of group members.
- As soon as one member turns out to be leaking information, the others can simply stop sending messages to that member, but still use the keys they were using to communicate with each other.
- However, instead of having to maintain one key, it is now necessary to maintain $N(N-1)/2$ keys, which may be a difficult problem by itself.
- Using a public–key cryptosystem can improve matters. In that case, each member has its own (public key, private key) pair, in which the public key can be used by all members for sending confidential messages. In this case, a total of N key pairs are needed.
- If one member ceases to be trustworthy, it is simply removed from the group without having been able to compromise the other keys.

6.6 CASE STUDY : KERBEROS

- Kerberos is an authentication service developed at MIT (Massachusetts Institute of Technology), that uses symmetric key encryption techniques and a key distribution centre; it is an add–system that can be used with existing network.
- Kerberos provides a means of verifying the identities of principals on an open (unprotected) network.
- This is accomplished without relying on authentication by the host operating system, without basing trust on host address, without requiring physical security of all the hosts on the network, and under the assumption that packets travelling along the network can be read, modified, and inserted at will.
- Kerberos performs authentication under these conditions as a trusted third party authentication service by using conventional cryptography.
- It trusted in the sense that each of its clients believes Kerberos's judgement as to the identity of each of its other clients to be accurate.
- The problem that Kerberos addresses is this: a distributed system in which users at workstations wish to access services on servers distributed throughout the network.
- We would like for servers to be able to restricted access to authorized users and to be able to authenticate requests for service.
- In this system the following three threats exist:
- A user may gain access to a particular workstation and pretend to be another user operating from that workstation.

- A user may alter the network address of a workstation so that the requests sent from the altered workstation appear to come from the impersonated workstation.
- A user may eavesdrop on exchanges and use a reply attack to gain entrance to a server or to disrupt operations.
- In any of these cases, an unauthorized user may be able to gain access to services and data that he or she is not authorized to access. Kerberos provides a centralized authentication server whose function is to authenticate users to servers and servers to users.

Kerberos Provides the Following Requirements:

- **Secure:** A network eavesdropper should not be able to obtain the necessary information to impersonate a user.
- **Reliable:** Kerberos should be highly reliable and should employ a distributed server architecture, with one system able to back up another.
- **Transparent:** The user should not be aware that the authentication is taking place, beyond the requirement to enter a password.
- **Scalable:** The system should be capable of supporting large numbers of clients and servers.
- **Kerberos :** Version 5 authentication dialogue.
- A full–service Kerberos environment, consisting of a Kerberos server, a number of clients and a number of application servers, requires that the Kerberos server must have the user ID (UID) and hashed passwords of all participating users in its database.
- All users are registered with the Kerberos server. Such an environment is referred as a realm. Moreover, the Kerberos server must share a secret key with each server and every server is registered with the Kerberos server.
- A simple authentication procedure must involve three steps:
- The client C requests the user password and then send a message to the AS of the Kerberos system that includes the user's ID, the server's ID and the user's password.
- The AS check its database to see if the user has supplied the proper password for this user ID and whether this user is permitted access to the server V.
- If both tests are passed, the AS accept the user as authentic and must now convince the server that this user is authentic.
- Thus the AS creates and sends back to C a ticket that contains the user's ID and network address and the server's ID. Then it is encrypted with the secret key shared by the AS and the server V.
- C can now apply to V for the service. It sends a message to V containing C's ID and the ticket. V decrypts the ticket and verifies that the user ID in the ticket is the same of the one which came with the ticket. If these two match, the server grants the requested service to the client.

- This scheme is correct, but this is not enough in a distributed environment: it has some leaks related to security and requires that the user introduce the password every time he needs to access to a service.
- Indeed, the client sends its password unencrypted to the AS; an eavesdropper could capture the password and use any services accessible to the victim.
- Moreover, it is better to minimize the number of times that the user has to enter a password.
- To solve these additional problems, we introduce a scheme for avoiding plaintext passwords and a new server, known as the Ticket–Granting Server (TGS).
- The new service issues tickets to users who have been authenticated to AS. Each time the user require access to a new service, the client applies to the TGS using the ticket supplied by the AS to authenticate itself.
- The TGS then grants a ticket to the particular service and the client saves this ticket for future use.

The new scenario (Fig. 6.8) is as follow:

- The client request a ticket–granting ticket on behalf of the user by sending its user's ID to the AS, together with the TGS ID, indicating a request to use the TGS service.
- The AS responds with a message, encrypted with a key derived from the user's password that contains the ticket for the TGS. The encrypted message also contains a copy of the session key used by C and the TGS.
- In this way, only the user's client can read it. The same session key is included in the ticket, which can be read only by the TGS. Now C and the TGS share a common key.
- Armed with the ticket and the session key, C is ready to approach the TGS. C sends the TGS a message that includes the ticket plus the ID of the requested service.
- In addition, C transmits an authenticator, which includes the ID and address of C's user and a timestamp; it is encrypted with the session key known only by C and TGS.
- Unlike the ticket, which is reusable, the authenticator is intended to use only once and has a very shot lifetime.
- The TGS can decrypt the ticket with the key that it shares with the AS. This ticket indicates that the user C has been provided with the session key Kc.
- Thus the TGS decrypt the authenticator with Kc gained from the ticket and check the name and the address from the authenticator with that of the ticket and with the network address of the incoming message.
- If all match, then the TGS is assured that the sender of the ticket is indeed the ticket's real owner.
- Then the TGS replies to the client, sending a message encrypted with the common key that they share. It includes a new session key to be used with the server V that must provide the service, the ID of V, the ticket valid for a specific service and the timestamp of the ticket.

- The ticket itself includes the new session key.
- C now has a reusable service–granting ticket for V. When C presents this ticket, it also sends an authenticator.
- The server can decrypt the ticket, recover the session key and decrypt the authenticator.

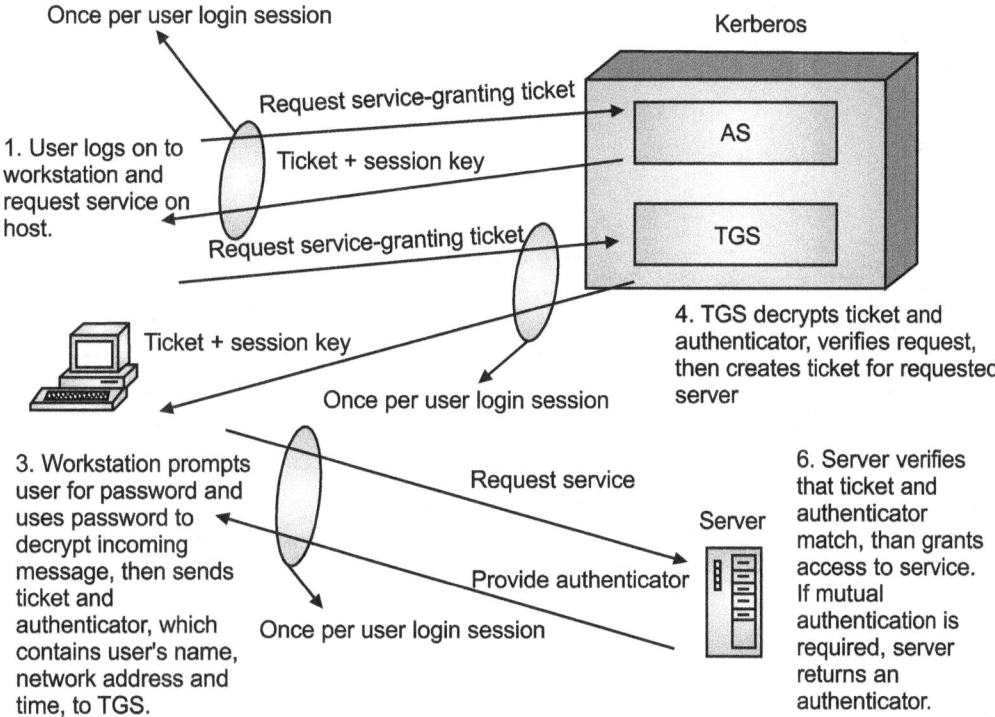

Fig. 6.8 : Kerberos authentication dialogue

- Finally, at the conclusion of this process, the client and the server share a secret key. This key can be used to encrypt future messages between the two or to exchange a new session key for that purpose.
- The Kerberos system is also able to manage more complicated situations which involve more than one realm. Usually, networks of clients and servers under different administrative organizations constitute different realms.
- Sometimes, user in one realm may need access to server in other realms and they need to be authenticated before to use services provided by those servers. Kerberos has a mechanism for supporting such inter–realm authentication.
- The only requirement requested is that the Kerberos server in each interoperating realm shares a secret key with the server in the second realm. The two Kerberos server are registered with each other.

- The communication mechanism between a client and a server in two different realms is the following:
- The client C in the α realm needs a ticket in order to communicate with the server in the β realm. Thus, the user's client follows the usual procedures to gain access to the local TGS and then request a ticket–granting ticket for the remote TGS in realm β.
- The client can then apply to the remote TGS for a service–granting ticket valid for the desired server in that different realm.

The client can now use the ticket obtained from the remote TGS with the server V in the other realm.

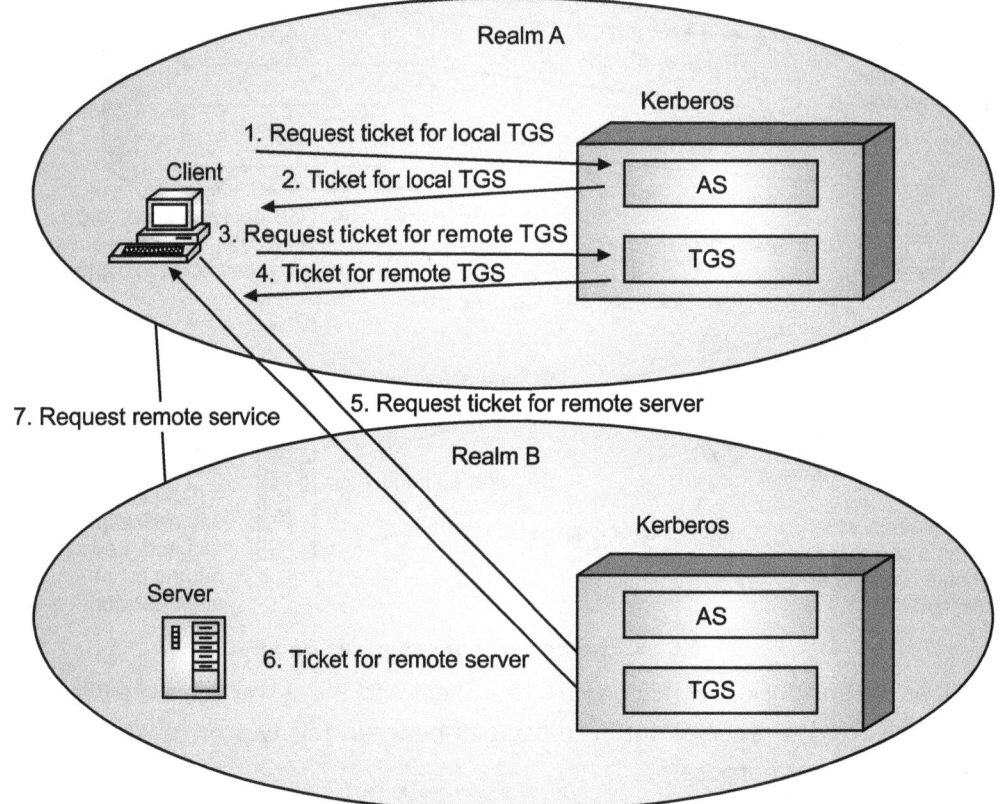

Fig. 6.9 : Inter realm communication

6.6.1 Kerberos Limitations

- Since Kerberos has many strengths, it has a number of limitations and some weakness in its protocol which have made Kerberos is not as extended as it should be.
- One of the main problems of Kerberos (which is not relative to security of the protocol) is that any application which wants to use the Kerberos protocol, have to be modified in the code in order to establish a secure communication.
- This means high costs in terms of time and money, and is not reliable for all applications nor enterprises.

- The timestamps are used to establish secure communication. Therefore, servers have to be synchronized within no more than a few minutes, and for instance, times servers are required to synchronized often their clocks.
- But then, "if a host can be misled about the correct time, a state authenticator can be replayed without any trouble at all".
- A solution to this problem could be performed by "adding challenge/response as alternative to time–based authentication".
- Another problem relative to security relies on the high dependency on the Kerberos server. If this server goes down, then the whole network goes down as well.
- This is something very expensive and not desirable in a distributed system. In addition to this, all security relies on the server, so if someone can access the Kerberos server, then all network connection could be hacked.
- There is another potential problem which is that someone could steal from the network the message from the
- AS to the client, this message, as we have seen above, is encrypted by the client key which is derivated from the client password.
- Therefore, someone could try to guess this key and then he would be able to identify himself as the original client. "Kerberos is not effective against password guessing attacks; if a user chooses a poor password, then an attacker guessing that password can impersonate the user".
- A solution proposed is the using of "exponential key exchange to provide an additional layer of encryption [...] it involves the two parties exchanging numbers that each can use to compute a secret key. An outsider, not knowing how the numbers were calculated, cannot easily derive the key".
- Kerberos by itself cannot guarantee that the password will not travel along the net. It can happen that "the user enters a password to a program that has already been modified by an attacker (a Trojan horse), or if the path between the user and the initial authentication program can be monitored, then an attacker may obtain sufficient information to impersonate the user." Kerberos must be combined with other techniques to address these limitations.
- Kerberos is designed to authenticate clients which are users, but "Kerberos is not a host–to–host protocol". Eventhougth, in last version 5, it has been extended to user–to–user authentication.
- These limitations have made Kerberos became a protocol not as extended nor used as it should be. Most of the networks only need an encrypted communication protocol to establish a minimum security, therefore sometimes Kerberos is replace by programs as simple and transparent as SSH.

6.7 ACCESS CONTROL

- Once a client and a server have set up a secure channel, the client can issue requests that are to be carried out by the server. Requests involve carrying out operations on resources that are controlled by the server.

- A general situation is that of an object server that has a number of objects under its control.

- A request from a client generally involves invoking a method of a specific object. Such a request can be carried out only if the client has sufficient access rights for that invocation. Formally, verifying access rights is referred to as access control, whereas authorization is about granting access rights.

- The two terms are strongly related to each other and are often used in an interchangeable way.

- There are many ways to achieve access control. We start with discussing some of the general issues, concentrating on different models for handling access control.

- One important way of actually controlling access to resources is to build a firewall that protects applications or even an entire network. Firewalls are discussed separately. With the advent of code mobility, access control could no longer be done using only the traditional methods. Instead, new techniques had to be devised, which are also discussed in this section.

6.7.1 General Issues in Access Control

- In order to understand the various issues involved in access control, the simple model shown in Fig. 6.10. It consists of subjects that issue a request to access an object. An object can be thought of as encapsulating its own state and implementing the operations on that state.

- The operations of an object that subjects can request to be carried out are made available through interfaces.

- Subjects can be thought of as being processes acting on behalf of users, but can also be objects that need the services of other objects in order to carry out their work. Controlling the access to an object is all about protecting the object against invocations by subjects that are not allowed to have specific (or even any) of the methods carried out.

- Also, protection may include object management issues, such as creating, renaming, or deleting objects.

- Protection is often enforced by a program called a reference monitor. A reference monitor records which subject may do what, and decides whether a subject is allowed to have a specific operation carried out.

- This monitor is called (e.g., by the underlying trusted operating system) each time an object is invoked.

- Consequently, it is extremely important that the reference monitor is itself tamperproof: an attacker must not be able to fool around with it.

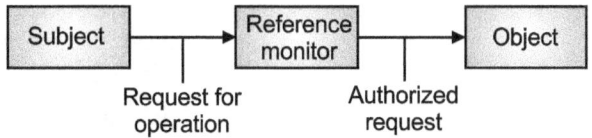

Fig. 6.10 : General model of controlling access to objects

6.7.2 Firewalls

- Firewalls can be an effective means of protecting a local system or network of systems from network–based security threats while at the same time affording access to the out–side world via wide area networks and the Internet.

6.7.2.1 The Need For Firewalls

Information systems in corporations, government agencies, and other organizations have undergone a steady evolution. The following are notable developments:

- Centralized data processing system, with a central mainframe supporting a number of directly connected terminals

- Local Area Networks (LANs) interconnecting PCs and terminals to each other and the mainframe

- Premises network, consisting of a number of LANs, interconnecting PCs, servers, and perhaps a mainframe or two

- **Enterprise Wide Network :** consisting of multiple, geographically distributed premises networks interconnected by a private wide area network (WAN)

- Internet Connectivity : In which the various premises networks all hook into the Internet and may or may not also be connected by a private WAN our general techniques that firewalls use to control access and enforce the site's security policy. Originally, firewalls focused primarily on service control, but they have since evolved to provide all four

- **Service Control:** Determines the types of Internet services that can be accessed, inbound or outbound. The firewall may filter traffic on the basis of IP address, protocol, or port number; may provide proxy software that receives and interprets each service request before passing it on; or may host the server software itself, such as a Web or mail service.

- **Direction Control:** Determines the direction in which particular service requests may be initiated and allowed to flow through the firewall.

- **User Control:** Controls access to a service according to which user is attempting to access it. This feature is typically applied to users inside the firewall perimeter (local users). It may also be applied to incoming traffic from external users; the latter requires some form of secure authentication technology, such as is provided in IPsec

- **Behavior Control:** Controls how particular services are used. For example, the firewall may filter e–mail to eliminate spam, or it may enable external access to only a portion of the information on a local Web server.

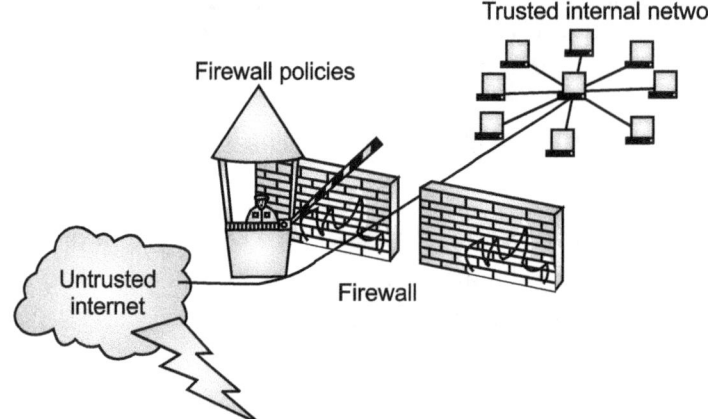

Fig. 6.11 : General model of firewall

To protect private networks and individual machines from the dangers of the greater Internet, a firewall can be employed to filter incoming or outgoing traffic based on a predefined set of rules called firewall policies.

Policy Actions

- Packets flowing through a firewall can have one of three outcomes:
- **Accepted:** Permitted through the firewall
- **Dropped:** Not allowed through with no indication of failure
- **Rejected:** Not allowed through, accompanied by an attempt to inform the source that the packet was rejected
- Policies used by the firewall to handle packets are based on several properties of the packets being inspected, including the protocol used, such as:
- TCP or UDP.
- The source and destination IP addresses.
- The source and destination ports.
- The application–level payload of the packet (e.g., whether it contains a virus).

6.7.3 Secure Mobile Code

- An important development in modem distributed systems is the ability to migrate code between hosts instead of just migrating passive data. However, mobile code introduces a number of serious security threats.
- For one thing, when sending an agent across the Internet, its owner will want to protect it against malicious hosts that try to steal or modify information carried by the agent.
- Another issue is that hosts need to be protected against malicious agents. Most users of distributed systems will not be experts in systems technology and have no way of telling whether the program they are fetching from another host can be trusted not to corrupt their computer.

- In many cases it may be difficult even for an expert to detect that a program is actually being downloaded at all.
- Unless security measures are taken, once a malicious program has settled itself in a computer, it can easily corrupt its host.
- We are faced with an access control problem: the program should not be allowed unauthorized access to the host's resources. As we shall see. protecting a host against downloaded malicious programs is not always easy.
- The problem is not so much as to avoid downloading of programs. Instead, what we are looking for is supporting mobile code that we can allow access to local resources in a flexible, yet fully controlled manner.

6.7.3.1 Protecting an Agent

- Before we take a look at protecting a computer system against downloaded malicious code, let us first take a look at the opposite situation. Consider a mobile agent that is roaming a distributed system on behalf of a user.
- Such an agent may be searching for the cheapest airplane ticket from Nairobi to Malindi, and has been authorized by its owner to make a reservation as soon as it found a flight.
- For this purpose, the agent may carry an electronic credit card. Obviously, we need protection here. Whenever the agent moves to a host, that host should not be allowed to steal the agent's credit card information.
- Also, theagent should be protected against modifications that make the owner pay much more than actually is needed. For example, if Chuck's Cheaper Charters can see that the agent has not yet visited its cheaper competitor Alice Airlines, Chuck should be prevented from changing the agent so that it will not visit Alice Airlines' host. Other examples that require protection of an agent against attacks from a hostile host include maliciously destroying an agent, or tampering with an agent such that it will attack or steal from its owner when it returns.
- To allow an agent to collect information while moving between hosts, Ajanta provides secure append–only logs.
- These logs are characterized by the fact that data can only be appended to the log; there is no way that data can be removed or modified without the owner being able to detect this.

6.7.3.2 Protecting the Target

- Although protecting mobile code against a malicious host is important, more attention has been paid to protecting hosts against malicious mobile code.
- If sending an agent into the outside world is considered too dangerous, a user will generally have alternatives to get the job done for which the agent was intended. However, there are often no alternatives to letting an agent into your system, other than locking it out completely.

- Therefore, if it is once decided that the agent can come in, the user needs full control over what the agent can do.

- As we just discussed, although protecting an agent from modification may be impossible, at least it is possible for the agent's owner to detect that modifications have been made. At worst, the owner will have to discard the agent when it returns, but otherwise no harm will have been done.

- However, when dealing with malicious incoming agents, simply detecting that your resources have been harassed is too late. Instead, it is essential to protect all resources against unauthorized access by downloaded code.

- One approach to protection is to construct a sandbox. A sandbox is a technique by which a downloaded program is executed in such a way that each of its instructions can be fully controlled.

- If an attempt is made to execute an instruction that has been forbidden by the host, execution of the program will be stopped.

- Likewise, execution is halted when an instruction accesses certain registers or areas in memory that the host has not allowed. One approach is to check the executable code when it is downloaded, and to insert additional instructions for situations that can be checked only at runtime. Fortunately. Matters become much simpler when dealing with interpreted code such as JAVA. Each Java program consists of a number of classes from which objects are created. There are no global variables and functions; everything has to be declared as part of a class.

- Program execution starts at a method called main.

- A Java program is compiled to a set of instructions that are interpreted by what is called the Java Virtual Machine (JVM).

- For a client to download and execute a compiled Java program, it is therefore necessary that the client process is running the JVM. The JVM will subsequently handle the actual execution of the downloaded program by interpreting each of its instructions, starting at the instructions that comprise main.

6.7.4 Denial of Service

- Access control is generally about carefully ensuring that resources are accessed only by authorized processes. A particularly annoying type of attack that is related to access control is maliciously preventing authorized processes from accessing resources. Defenses against such Denial–of–Service (DoS) attacks are becoming increasingly important as distributed systems are opened up through the Internet. Where DoS attacks that come from one or a few sources can often be handled quite effectively, matters become much more difficult when having to deal with Distributed Denial of Service (DDoS).

- In DDoS attacks, a huge collection of processes jointly attempt to bring down a networked service. In these cases, we often see that the attackers have succeeded in hijacking a large group of machines which unknowingly participate in the attack.

- Bandwidth depletion can be accomplished by simply sending many messages to a single machine. The effect is that normal messages will hardly be able to reach the receiver.

- Resource depletion attacks concentrate on letting the receiver use up resources on otherwise useless messages. A well–known resource–depletion attack is TCP SYN–flooding. In this case, the attacker attempts to initiate a huge amount of connections (i.e., send SYN packets as part of the three–way handshake), but will otherwise never respond to acknowledgments from the receiver.

- There is no single method to protect against DDoS attacks. One problem is that attackers make use of innocent victims by secretly installing software on their machines.

- In these cases, the only solution is to have machines continuously monitor their state by checking files for pollution.

- Considering the ease by which a virus can spread over the Internet, relying only on this countermeasure is not feasible.

- Much better is to continuously monitor network traffic, for example, starting at the egress routers where packets leave an organization's network.

- Experience shows that by dropping packets whose source address does not belong to the organization's network we can prevent a lot of havoc. In general, the more packets can be filtered close to the sources, the better.

- Alternatively, it is also possible to concentrate on ingress routers, that is, where traffic flows into an organization's network.

- The problem is that detecting an attack at an ingress router is too late as the network will probably already be unreachable for regular traffic. Better is to have routers further in the Internet, such as in the networks of ISPs, start dropping packets when they suspect that an attack is going on.

6.8 GRID COMPUTING

- In grid computing infrastructure resources belong to and come from physically scattered administrative domains to collectively provide various are sources (data, computing, and network) to the users.

- In a grid computing nodes might not be placed at common physical location but can be independently operated from different locations. Each computer on the grid is a distinct computer. Collection of servers clustered together to work out a common problem forms a grid. The computers joined to form a grid may even have different hardware and operating systems.

- Grid consists of a layered architecture model providing protocols and service at five different layers represented Fig. 6.12

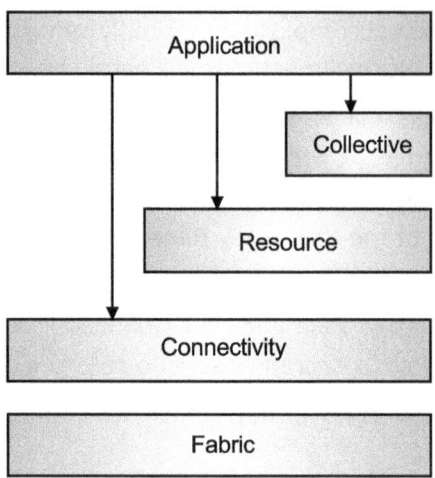

Fig. 6.12 : Grid Architecture

Fabric Layer:

- Fabric layer sits at the bottom of this layered architecture; it provides share able are sources such as network bandwidth, CPU time, memories, scientific instruments like sensors, telescope, etc.
- Data received by sensors at this layer can be transmitted directly to other computational nodes or can be stored in the database over grid. Standard grid protocols are responsible for resource control. Accomplishment of sophisticated sharing operation is the measure for quality of this layer.
- Operating system, queuing systems and processing kernels also form the part of this layer.

Connectivity Layer:

- This layer specifies the protocols for secure and easy access. Protocols related to communication and authentication required for transactions are placed in this layer. These communication protocols permit the exchange of data between resource layer and fabric layer.
- Authentication protocols are meant to provide secure cryptographic mechanisms for identification of users and resources. E.g. GSI Grid Security Infrastructure (built around existing TLS protocols).

Resource Layer:

- This layer specifies the protocols for operating with shared resources. Resource layer build on the connectivity layer's communication and authentication protocols to define Application Program Interfaces (API) and Software Development Kit (SDK) for secure negotiation, accounting, initiation, control, monitoring and payment of sharing resources.
- E.g. GRIP (Grid resource Information Protocol; based on LDAP), GRAM(Grid Resource Access and Management) for allocation and monitoring of resources.

Collective Layer:
- This layer consists of general purpose utilities. Any collaborative operations in the shared resources are placed in this layer and it coordinates sharing of resources like directory services, co–allocation, scheduling, brokering services, monitoring and diagnostic services, data replication services.

Application Layer:
- At the top of the grid layered architecture sits the application layer. This layer consists of application which the user will implement.
- Moreover, this layer provides interface to the users and administrators to interact with the grid.

6.9 SOA (SERVICE ORIENTED ARCHITECTURE)

- A service–oriented architecture is essentially a collection of services. These services communicate with each other.
- The communication can involve either simple data passing or it could involve two or more services coordinating some activity. Some means of connecting services to each other is needed.
- Service–oriented architectures are not a new thing. The first service–oriented architecture for many people in the past was with the use DCOM or Object Request Brokers (ORBs) based on the CORBA specification. For more on DCOM and CORBA, see Prior Service–Oriented Architectures.

Services
- If a service–oriented architecture is to be effective, we need a clear understanding of the term service. A service is a function that is well–defined, self–contained, and does not depend on the context or state of other services.

Connections
- The technology of Web Services is the most likely connection technology of service–oriented architectures. The following Fig. 6.13 illustrates a basic service–oriented architecture. It shows a service consumer at the right sending a service request message to a service provider at the left. The service provider returns a response message to the service consumer. The request and subsequent response connections are defined in some way that is understandable to both the service consumer and service provider.
- How those connections are defined is explained in Web Services Explained.
- A service provider can also be a service consumer.

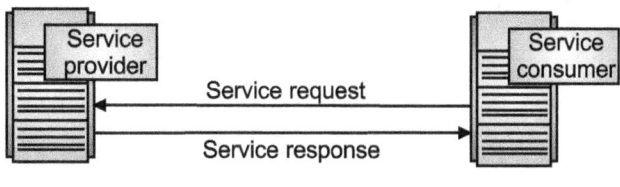

Fig. 6.13

6.10 CLOUD COMPUTING

- Cloud computing is defined as a type of computing that relies on sharing computing resources rather than having local servers or personal devices to handle applications. Cloud computing is comparable to grid computing, a type of computing where unused processing cycles of all computers in a network are harnesses to solve problems too intensive for any stand–alone machine.

- In cloud computing, the word cloud (also phrased as "the cloud") is used as a metaphor for "the Internet," so the phrase cloud computing means "a type of Internet–based computing," where different services such as servers, storage and applications are delivered to an organization's computers and devices through the Internet.

How Cloud Computing Works?

- The goal of cloud computing is to apply traditional supercomputing, or high–performance computing power, normally used by military and research facilities, to perform tens of trillions of computations per second, in consumer–oriented applications such as financial portfolios, to deliver personalized information, to provide data storage or to power large, immersive online computer games.

- To do this, cloud computing uses networks of large groups of servers typically running low–cost consumer PC technology with specialized connections to spread data-processing chores across them. This shared IT infrastructure contains large pools of systems that are linked together. Often, virtualization techniques are used to maximize the power of cloud computing.

REVIEW QUESTIONS

1. Write a short note on :
   (i)   Security Threat
   (ii) DoS
   (iii) SOA
   (iv) Cloud Computing
   (v)   Security Management
   (vi) Fire wall

2. What is secure mobile code ? Explain in brief .

3. Common on : Kerberos.

4. What is Secure channel ? Explain in detail.

✠ ✠ ✠

Time: 1 Hour   **Marks: 30**

1. (a) What is the difference between distributed operating system and network operating system? **(2)**

    (b) Explain what transparency in a Distributed System, and give examples of different forms of transparency. **(4)**

    (c) Highlights desirable features of good distributed file system. List the functions of distributed file system. **(4)**

OR

2. (a) List the goals of DS. **(2)**

    (b) Explain different scalability techniques in distributed system. **(4)**

    (c) What is the role of middleware in a distributed system? Also explain different architectural Models in distributed system. **(4)**

3. (a) What is Marshalling? Explain in detail. **(2)**

    (b) State and discuss implementation issues in RPC. **(4)**

    (c) What is socket ? State and explain socket primitives. **(4)**

OR

4. (a) Write a short note on Java RMI. **(4)**

    (b) What is group communication? Explain Different types. **(4)**

    (c) State the advantages of distributed shared memory **(2)**

5. (a) Write a short notes on **(4)**

       (i) Squirrel

       (ii) SOAP

    (b) State and explain applications of web services **(2)**

    (c) What are distributed objects? Explain in brief. **(4)**

OR

6. (a) Write a short note on : **(8)**

       (i) CORBA

       (ii) EJB

    (b) Compare web services and SOA **(2)**

✠ ✠ ✠

Sample Question Paper for
End-Semester Examination (70 Marks)

Time: 2:30 Hours   Marks: 70

1. (a) What is RPC ? Explain the role of Client Server stub procedures in RPC in the context of procedural language. **(4)**
   (b) Write a short note on **(4)**
      (i) Failure Models   (ii) Group Communication
   (c) What is CORBA? Define general organization of CORBA system with the help of diagram. **(6)**
   (d) Define Distributed Systems. State the advantages and disadvantages of the same.**(6) OR**
2. (a) Explain the general architecture of message queuing system along with roles of message broker. **(7)**
   (b) State and explain the design issues of Distributed Systems **(5)**
   (c) What is EJB? State the important roles in EJB. **(4)**
   (d) Write a note on XML Security **(4)**
3. (a) Discuss any two algorithms to implement mutual exclusion in DS. **(8)**
   (b) Why do we need a global clock? Prove with an example. **(4)**
   (c) Write a short note on CODA **(6)**

                              OR

4. (a) What do you understand by logical clocks? What is Lamport's Contribution for it? **(8)**
   (b) Write a short note on: (i) Election Algorithms (ii) NTP **(10)**
5. (a) How X.500 directory service is implemented. **(6)**
   (b) Explain the architecture of NFS in detail **(6)**
   (c) State and explain features of good Distributed file systems **(4) OR**
6. (a) Explain following terms w.r.t. naming entities **(8)**
      (i) Names   (ii) Identifiers
      (iii) Address   (iv) Name Space
   (b) State and discuss issues in designing Distributed File System. **(4)**
   (c) Write a note on Global Name Service. **(4)**
7. (a) List and explain issues in providing security to DS **(4)**
   (b) What do you mean by cryptography? Explain in brief. **(4)**
   (c) Comment on : Kerberos **(8) OR**
8. (a) Write a short notes on : **(8)**
      (l) DoS   (ii) Cloud Computing
      (iii) Firewall   (iv) Secure Channels
   (b) What is access control? List and explain issues in access control. **(4)**
   (c) Discuss the SOA. **(4)**

                              ✠ ✠ ✠

Time : 1 Hour   **Max. Marks : 30**

Instruction to the candidates:

(1) Answer Q.1 or Q.2, Q.3 or Q.4, Q.5 or Q.6.

(2) Neat diagrams must be drawn wherever necessary.

(3) Figures to the right indicate full marks.

(4) Assume suitable data if necessary.

---

1. **(a)** Write a note on Mobile and Ubiquitous computing.   **[4]**

   (b) Explain the Architectural Models of Distributed Systems with suitable diagrams.   **[6]**

OR

2. **(a)** Explain in brief, various types of models based on fundamental properties and the failures they might exhibit.   **[4]**

   (b) What factors affect the performance of an application that accesses shared data managed by a server? Describe remedies that are available and discuss their usefulness.   **[6]**

3. **(a)** What are the characteristics of multicast messages that provide a useful infrastructure for constructing distributed systems.   **[4]**

   (b) A client makes remote procedure calls to a server. The client takes 5 milliseconds to compute the arguments for each request, and the server takes 10 milliseconds to process each request. The local operating system processing time for each send or receive operation is 0.5 milliseconds and the network time to transmit each request or reply message is 3 milliseconds. Marshalling or unmarshalling takes 0.5 milliseconds per message.   **[6]**

   Calculate the time taken by the client to generate and return from two requests:

   (i)   If it is single-threaded, and

   (ii) If it has two threads that can make requests concurrently on a single processor.

   You can ignore context-switching times. Is there a need for asynchronous RPC if client and server processes are threaded?

OR

---

4. (a) What is Marshaling? List out the different approaches of external data representation and discuss each approach in detail. **[4]**

(b) Explain the RPC exchange protocols used for implementing various types of RPC. **[6]**

5. (a) State and explain different types of data structures with respect to UDDI. **[4]**

(b) List the two design issues for RMI. Explain different methods of RMI invocation semantics. **[6]**

OR

6. (a) Specify the roles played by the objects that participate in distributed event-based systems with the help of architecture for distributed event notification. **[4]**

(b) Write a brief note on: **[6]**

   (i)   XML Security Requirements

   (ii) XML Signature

   (iii) Security Assertion Markup Language

END SEM. EXAM. MAY 2016

Time : 2 ½ Hours   **Max. Marks : 70**

Instruction to the candidates:

  (1) Answer Q.1 or Q.2, Q.3 or Q.4, Q.5 or Q.6, Q.7 or Q.8, Q.9 or Q.10.

  (2) Figures to the right indicate full marks.

  (3) Neat diagrams must be drawn wherever necessary.

  (4) Assume suitable data if necessary.

1. (a) Distinguish between: **[6]**

   (i)   Buffering and Caching

   (ii) RMI and RPC

(b) Consider two communication services for use in asynchronous distributed system. In services A, messages may be lost, duplicated or delayed and checksums apply only to headers. In services B, messages may be lost. Delayed or delivered too fast for the recipient to handle them, but those that are delivered arrive order and with the correct contents. **[4]**

(i)   Describe the classes of failure exhibited by service A and service B. Classify their failures according to their effect on the properties of validity and integrity. Can service B be described as a reliable communication service?

(ii) Consider a pair of processes X and Y that use the communication service B from above to communicate with one another. Suppose that X is a client and Y a server and that an invocation consists of a request message from X to Y (that caries out the request) followed by a replay message from Y to X. Describe the classes of failure that may be exhibited by an invocation.

OR

2. **(a)** Explain Distributed Object Model with respect to: **[6]**

   (i)   Actions and

   (ii) Garbage collection

   (iii) Exceptions

   (b) Explain in nutshell, the different techniques for failure handling in a Distributed system.   **[4]**

3. **(a)** Explain Remote object reference and Remote interface in Distributed Object Model with suitable example.   **[5]**

   (b) What is marshaling? How marshaling and serialization is used in communication between a client and a server?   **[5]**

OR

4. **(a)** Explain three communication primitives of Request–reply protocol along with message structure used in information transmission.   **[4]**

   (b) Describe general organization of CORBA system with the help of suitable diagram. Why there is no explicit data–typing in COBRA CDR?   **[6]**

5. **(a)** What are the Network Time Protocol's aims and feature? Explain the modes through which NTP servers synchronize with one another.   **[8]**

   (b) Explain following points related to fault tolerance issues in Distributed Systems: **[8]**

   (i)   Availability

   (ii) Reliability

   (iii) Failure Models

   (iv) Tripple modular redundancy

OR

6. (a) A client attempts to synchronize with a time server. It records the round–trip times and timestamps returned by the server in the table below.   **[8]**

Round–trip (ms)	Time (hr : min : sec)
22	10:54:23:674
25	10:54:25:450
20	10:54:28:342

Which of these times should it use to set its clock? To what time should it set it? Estimate the accuracy of the setting with respect to the server's clock. If it is known that the time between sending and receiving a message in the system concerned is at least 8 ms, do your answers change?

(b) Describe implementation of ordered multicast in as non-overlapping group.   **[8]**

7. (a) Explain the objectives and architecture of Hadoop Distributed File System in details.**[8]**

(b) How is the X.500 directory service implemented?   **[8]**

OR

8. (a) List the different Distributed File System Requirements? Explain the abstract File Services architectural model with neat diagram.   **[8]**

(b) Write a detailed note on Domain Name System.   **[8]**

9. (a) Write short note on the following (Any 2):   **[10]**

    (i)   Cloud Computing

    (ii) Secure Channel

    (iii) Cryptographic Algorithms.

(b) State and explain various security mechanisms for achieving security in distributed systems.   **[8]**

OR

10. (a) Write short note on the following: **[10]**

    (i)   Applications of cryptography and political obstacles.

    (ii) Symmetric and Asymmetric Algorithms.

(b) Explain the Secure Mobile Code in brief with reference to JAVA sandbox.   **[8]**

END SEM. EXAM. NOVEMBER 2016

Time : 2 ½ Hours   **Max. Marks : 70**

Instructions to the candidates :

(1) Answer Q.1 or Q.2, Q.3 or Q.4, Q.5 or Q.6, Q.7 or Q.8, Q.9 or Q.10.

(2) Figures to the right side indicate full marks.

(3) Neat diagrams must be drawn wherever necessary.

(4) Assume suitable data, if necessary.

1. **(a)** Explain the concept of Heterogeneity in Distributed System in detail. How it deals with Heterogeneity? **[6]**

   (b) List the various challenges during the construction of Distributed systems. Describe the challenges while designing of scalable distributed system. **[4]**

OR

2. **(a)** What are Sockets? Specify Socket primitives. Draw a diagram specifying TCP stream communication. **[6]**

   (b) What are various forms of Transparency in Distributed System? Illustrate Network Transparency with an example. **[4]**

3. **(a)** What are web services? Explain SOAP and REST based Web Services in a nutshell. **[6]**

   (b) Explain two main characteristics of distributed event-based systems. **[4]**

OR

4. **(a)** What is Publish-Subscribe system of communication? **[4]**

   (b) Explain RMI software with respect to: **[6]**

      (i) Proxy

      (ii) Dispatcher

      (iii) Skeleton

5. **(a)** What are NTP's chief design aims and features? An NTP server B receives server A's message at 16:34:23.480 bearing a timestamp 16:34:13.430 and replies to it. A receives the message at 16:34:15.725, bearing B' is timestamp 16:34:25.7. Estimate the offset between B and A and the accuracy of the estimate. **[9]**

(b) Explain the Chandy-Lamport 'snapshot' algorithm for determining global states of distributed systems. **[7]**

OR

6. (a) Describe implementation of ordered multicast in a non-overlapping group. **[8]**

(b) What do you understand by logical time and logical clocks? Explain Lamport's contribution for it. **[8]**

7. (a) With a neat labeled diagram of architecture explain communication in NFS. **[8]**

(b) Write note on: Global Name Service. **[8]**

OR

8. (a) Explain following terms with respect to naming entities: **[8]**

    (i) Names

    (ii) Identifiers

    (iii) Addresses

    (iv) Name Spaces

(b) How does the client side caching is used in NFS? Discuss the role of RPC in NFS. **[8]**

9. (a) Explain process architecture of KERBEROS with security objects namely tickets, authentication and Session key. **[9]**

(b) How is a host protected from mobile code using Java sandbox? **[9]**

OR

10. (a) What do you meant by public-key Cryptography? Explain Digital Signatures with public keys. **[6]**

(b) Write short notes on the following (Any 2) : **[12]**

    (i) Applications of Cryptography and political obstacles

    (ii) Peer-to-peer middleware systems

    (iii) Protection and Access Control in Distributed System applications.

◈ ◈ ◈